SCARE ME

"When did you last google yourself?"

When wealthy businessman Will Frost gets woken in the middle of the night by an anonymous caller asking him exactly this, he has to find out more. What he finds online will threaten his life, and everything he holds dear.

There's a website in his name, showing photographs taken inside his home. And there are six more houses, places he's never seen before. In the first of those strange houses, a gruesome murder has taken place. The threat to his family is plain. To keep them safe, Will must discover where these houses are and find out what has happened... and who is doing this to him.

Seven houses.
> Seven gruesome homicides.
>> Seven chances to keep his own family safe.

ALSO BY RICHARD PARKER

Stop Me
(Writing as Richard Jay Parker)

RICHARD PARKER

SCARE ME

EXHIBIT A
An Angry Robot imprint
and a member of the Osprey Group

Lace Market House	43-01 24th St, Suite 220B
54-56 High Pavement	Long Island City,
Nottingham NG1 1HW	NY 11101
UK	USA

www.exhibitabooks.com
A is for awesome!

An Exhibit A paperback original 2013

Cover photo Getty Images; design by Argh! Oxford
Typeset in Meridien and Franklin Gothic by EPubServices

Distributed in the United States by Random House, Inc., New York.

ISBN: 978 1 90922 301 1
Ebook ISBN: 978 1 90922 302 8

Printed in the United States of America

9 8 7 6 5 4 3 2 1

To Mum and Dad –
who know all my dark places
are imaginary.

CHAPTER ONE

Poppy applied some cherry ChapStick and rolled her lips into her mouth, but the only flavour she could taste was anticipation. It needled her cheeks and burnt at her earlobes.

Brett wanted to go all the way tonight.

She'd positioned herself in front of a blank wall and adjusted the webcam so her head and shoulders were centre of frame on her laptop. Beside her the washing machine grumbled and heaved around a family load.

Brett waited patiently for Poppy to log on and sipped his cranberry and vodka. He was seated at a desk looking at his own image. He swiped his straw hair a few times.

He had a surprise for Poppy.

Poppy logged in. Brett was waiting for her online. She clicked on his name and his live image filled the screen of her laptop.

"Hi, Pop. Need some company?" He smiled, like he knew exactly how much his boyish grin poleaxed the girls.

Brett shifted in his swivel chair. He liked the way the deep chestnut of Poppy's eyes and long tresses of dark hair accentuated her pale, willowy features. He'd quickly noted she was wearing a white towelling robe with the collar pulled tight around her. He wondered how much longer it would remain there.

"So what does Poppy want to do to pass the time?"

"Cool jacket."

Brett was too busy looking at her pronounced bottom lip. He

liked the way it hung away from her teeth as she looked into his world. There were a few moments of silence. "Excuse me?"

"Hanging behind you."

Brett knew it was there, but turned to look at the hooded Japanese street wear on the hook of his bedroom door. A lot of girls did this, played for time before they got down to it. "Yeah. Picked it up in Sawgrass Mills." He kept the impatience out of his voice.

"Can I see it?"

"Maybe after." When she didn't reply, only nodded contritely, Brett knew she wanted him to instigate. This was his third session with Poppy. The adult chat room promised fun and friendship, but everyone who paid up and logged on was after the same thing. The third session was usually when both parties were happy to admit it.

"Let me see some more of your room. Your lair." She swallowed and smiled lopsidedly.

"OK." He panned his camera. The curtains were drawn and only his desk lamp was on, so he knew she wouldn't be able to see too much. He scrutinised her face when she leaned closer to her screen. She wasn't squeaky sugary, more handsome than cute. Her features were elegant bordering on anorexic. She was older than Brett as well. Mid-twenties, he liked that.

"Want to see where I hang out?" She leaned back again.

Brett fought the reflex to say no, but she was already moving, lifting her laptop so the camera could take in her surroundings. She was still delaying.

She held the laptop steady. It appeared she was in a utility room. A lot of girls used anonymous ute rooms for their online quickies. They gave nothing away while they laid everything else bare.

"Need to see more?" her voice said from the other side of the camera.

Brett watched his fake interest wane on the screen as she

opened the ute room door and walked into the space beyond. But his expression rapidly altered to incomprehension as his attention locked on the kitchen. It was the kitchen at the bottom of his stairs.

Poppy moved the laptop past the buttermilk tiles and familiar see-through tubs of cereal on the breakfast bar, produced a key and unlocked the back lounge. When she pushed the door he could see his mother, father and sister in there.

Even though they were sitting up in a row on the couch with their hands covering their eyes he knew they were dead. It was their stillness that made it undeniable before he registered the blood crusting in their laps. Black tape stuck their fingers to their faces.

Poppy wondered if he'd lock himself in his bedroom, but she had the key to that as well. It looked like blind panic had won out, however. She met Brett when she was a third of the way up the stairs. He was naked from the waist down.

She jabbed a Taser into the centre of his chest and he dropped like he'd been filleted. He juddered down the rest of the staircase on his spine and his tee shirt rode up his back. She followed his body to the bottom. Then she took the same broad-bladed sushi knife she'd used on the rest of the family out of the pocket of her robe.

Poppy pushed it into his stomach and his spasms halted. He turned to face her with incredulity. She gripped the handle firmly and dragged it towards her. She felt it hot on the heel of her hand, but Poppy didn't see the blood, had perfected the art of creating blind spots where she needed them. Like biting down on her lip and not feeling it.

She seated herself on the bottom stair and studied the tips of his shuddering toes scraping the Turkish hallway rug. She listened to Brett cry, his voice at an almost inaudible pitch in the back of his throat as oxygen escaped his body.

She wanted to use the pool now, needed to cool off. The blue water had looked so inviting from the window of the ute room while she'd waited for Brett to get back from his day trip. Poppy had figured she and Mom to be a similar costume size.

Brett tried to form some words, but the blood in his windpipe coated then engulfed them. When his lips stopped whispering and clicking, Poppy stepped over his ruined body. She squelched from the hallway, through the kitchen and into the cool breeze skimming the patio. She slipped out of Mom's white robe and kicked off her flip-flops. She only vaguely registered the footprints of blood she left before diving into the pool.

She didn't have to worry about leaving fingerprints or hair strands. Poppy didn't exist.

CHAPTER TWO

Friday cooked the London traffic on a slow heat and road rage bubbled up. The weekend lay tantalisingly out of reach. Feeling his shirt starting to stick at his back, Will turned up the air con and leaned back. He was still learning how to leave the office in the office.

Nineteen years ago he'd just been helming water supply contracts in the UK. Now he was CEO of Ingram International. Surely he could afford a guilt-free anniversary weekend with Carla. He envied his wife and his daughter, Libby. They both knew how to disconnect, Libby maybe too much.

His presence wasn't indispensable at Ingram anymore, but in the past he wouldn't have been able to stay away from HQ at such a critical stage. Every stage to him used to be critical and the Remada project was one he found it difficult to relinquish. But even though he'd also spent the day coordinating secondary phase pipeline ops in Aden and Eastern Navajo, his most rigorous task was still to be completed.

Nineteen years as man and wife,
And still so many years ahead,

It was the first two lines he'd scribbled into Carla's anniversary card in the six minutes he'd classed as lunch. He'd assumed the rest would come as easily. Nothing had. No matter how many times he'd run them in his head. He was committed to those first lines, though, had written them in the card in ink.

Will pulled back on the stick and watched the traffic shrink below. The helicopter used to be his regular mode of transport, but now his licence only granted him these occasional indulgences away from the boardroom. He levelled out and looked down at the metallic congestion glinting like mercury that had trickled into the gaps of the city. The building tops canted to the right as he swung west from the South Bank, their windows winking white sunshine as he climbed.

Carla said the helicopter was the perfect vehicle for him because it was impossible to coast in. It demanded constant application. She also said he wasn't a control freak, just pathologically hands-on. He didn't know what the difference was.

He'd removed himself from frontline project management and still struggled with the frustration of coordinating pipe ops from UK HQ. It was particularly difficult to be hands-off with the contracts he'd doggedly pursued during the years he'd evolved the company, but after the events of the previous year he'd rapidly reappraised the priorities in his life.

Will swung and righted the Longranger. He settled into the current and held it steady, observing the secret roof life spread out under the heat. He navigated his route home by the parks. Hurlingham was first before he crossed the expanse of Richmond.

At forty-two he was hamstrung by his own success. Even though his angular, weatherworn features were more suited to the outdoors, his astute business instincts had sentenced him to a constricting, corporate lifestyle. He hated wearing a collar and, as protest, covered it with his ash brown, shoulder length hair.

After last summer he'd been resolute. Pilot from the back seat and enjoy more home life. He was still coming to terms with it.

He should be sitting in the back now enjoying the view. Ingram's pilot had wanted to fly him home, but Will would have ended up hijacking the controls. He'd always preferred flying clients to site more than socialising with them. Was even happier alone in the air. Seeing everything spread out rather than stacked up always helped his perspective.

He knew he was almost home when he saw the golf courses of Strawberry Hill and Fulwell. He'd never been to either. Didn't like golf. Wasn't comfortable with the private clubs and hierarchical membership. But what would he and Carla do with their time when Libby left home?

She was almost gone. Was her month in Thailand a trial for permanently living with Luke? Will knew the girl he hugged when she came back would be different to the one he'd waved off at departures. He looked across the simmering smog haze of the horizon and thought of her thousands of miles away, three months pregnant and out of reach.

His work had necessitated him spending plenty of time in Southeast Asia. He'd enjoyed the life there and it was probably his accounts that had turned Libby on to the idea of her own pilgrimage. He'd worried about her being so far from his protection. It was no place for the naïve and had plenty of dark pockets to swallow backpackers.

Will had looked forward to having time alone with Carla while Libby was away, but the fact was he missed her more than he'd anticipated. From the half-eaten breakfast apple she always left on the kitchen counter to the smell of her eczema cream around the house. It had taken him a few days to remember only to set two places at the table and it had struck him that it was something he'd have to get used to. She would be back tomorrow, though, for a few days at least. He and Carla were picking them up from the airport.

His plan was then to steal Libby from Luke for the rest of the weekend so they could be a family again. That way he could speak to Libby without Luke answering for her. Find out what she really thought about their plans to move in together and if any of them were hers. He had reservations at Cawley Manor, his wife and daughter's favourite spa and hotel. Anniversary treat. Not very romantic, but he knew Carla would be just as eager to have Libby along after her month away from them. Would Libby be as keen though?

He knew she'd outgrown them and wanted to get on with her own life. She wasn't theirs anymore and had proved it when she'd come home with the lotus blossom tattoo at the base of her spine. Will had been shocked. Not just that she hadn't consulted them, but that she'd scarred the flesh he thought so precious and acquired such an obvious distinguishing feature. He wondered if every parent had the same reaction – would he ever need to mention it as a means of identification?

Will quickly shook off the thought as he flew over the edge of the golf course and the rolling fields took on a familiar significance. He focussed on positioning himself for his descent. Three copses were hurdled and then he dipped into Hanworth. Easton Grey squatted in an elliptical ring of yew trees within walled grounds.

The house had originally been built as a hunting lodge in the sixteenth century but, following a fire in 1797, had been completely rebuilt as a country home. Will loved its history, particularly the period it had been used as a military hospital in the Second World War. He'd bought and renovated the grade two listed building before it could collapse from neglect.

He gripped the collective lever as he started his approach to the orange helipad at the rear. The trees exploded crows as he sank towards it. Nudging the cyclic stick to dip the nose, Will used the pedals to keep the aircraft directed. He'd made hundreds of landings before, but knew he could never get complacent.

The Longranger veered slightly, but he used the cyclic to keep the rotor flat. There was hardly any impact as he felt himself re-engage with the ground. He waited, the weakening vibrations allowing his muscles to gradually relax. He held the controls level and waited for the rotor to stop.

Carla wended her way from the two men she was conversing with at the rear of the house. Three of her rescue dogs bounced on the grass beside her. The only giveaway that she'd recently been working in the office was that her blaze of red hair was piled and clipped to her head. Her pale midriff was visible between her olive tee shirt and wraparound saffron skirt. Nothing about her elegant stride was about show. It was purposeful and it was good to see it back.

As she approached, a call came through on her phone. She answered and bit the fingers of the gardening glove of her free hand. She shook it off and dropped it. Bruce, the chocolate brown lab, dutifully picked it up and circled her. She continued her conversation as she stopped at the periphery of the draught from the rotor blades. It plastered her clothes to her tall, slim frame, but she looked as if she'd been fixed there like a peg. She flicked her shades up into her hair and he could see the vibrancy of her green eyes as she blinked them against the rushing air.

Nineteen years as man and wife,

And still so many years ahead,

It seemed inconceivable that he'd almost lost her.

"You're early," she said with mock surprise, folding her phone shut as he reached her.

He kissed her lips. Her scented perspiration smelt much better than his. "I thought they were running final tests this morning." Will nodded towards the two men staring up at the newly fitted vandal-proof dome camera over the back entrance.

"There were some glitches with the Ethernet connection, but I've just been assured it's all on track." She sounded dubious. "I told you this would be more trouble than it's worth."

"I know you think this is overkill, but just indulge me."

Easton Grey had always had adequate security systems in place, but Carla had acquiesced to the cameras after the unsettling incident in June. Nobody had attempted to break in, but somebody had lit a mini bonfire on the front steps of the house in the early hours of the morning. It could well have been a prank, but Will wanted to be able to identify any trespassers in the future.

"I really don't think it'll happen again." She still sounded dubious.

The reason the episode had left them both feeling uneasy was because of Carla's involvement in a local protest against the redevelopment of neighbouring land. Hanworth's only primary school was threatened with closure to make way for the proposed Motex Radials tyre manufacturing plant. Suspecting payoffs and corruption in local government had led to Carla running for council in order to block the plans.

Motex was a powerful organisation and her intervention had quickly led to an overt smear campaign that they'd first found out about when a neighbour had given them one of the green fliers being posted around the village. Accusations of hypocrisy were being levelled at Carla because of her connection with Ingram and its own industrial pipeline ops.

She'd elected to carry on, organising an open day at the house to rally support. Will suspected the bonfire had been set afterwards as a further intimidation tactic. Carla was already preparing a case against David Wardour. He was the friendly media face of Motex. Will had never had any dealings with him, but it was common knowledge his empire had been built on myriad unscrupulous shortcuts that had secured other sites in Asia and Europe as well as the UK.

There was no way of proving that any of the duplicity was down to Motex. It could easily have originated in Hanworth. Carla hadn't made many friends by muscling into council affairs. Privately Will hoped the fire had been started by vandals paid by disgruntled farmers eager for fallow land to be taken off their hands. It seemed inconceivable that David Wardour didn't know exactly who he was taking on.

They briefly observed a minor fracas between the two men in rolled shirtsleeves as they ran another test with a laptop. A thought occurred to Will that just beat his smile. "Libby's going to freak when she gets back to find the place under surveillance."

Carla nodded and raised one eyebrow. "She'll soon find the blind spots."

"We should have got one fitted in the summer house." Will knew Libby had taken boys, alcohol and marijuana there. "Maybe that's one lot of footage I don't want to show the police though."

Carla gently gripped the front of his shirt. "Come on, before they want us to watch another demo."

Will allowed himself to be led away. He knew where she was taking him. Tomorrow Libby would be home and they'd be a family unit again. Tonight they still had to themselves.

Brett was heavier than Poppy'd anticipated, but she had managed to squeeze him onto the couch with the rest of his family. She squirted some cream from a plastic tube and dabbed the avocado and pomegranate body butter around the insides of her nostrils. Cooped up like this in the Florida heat, the Ambersons wouldn't smell so good in a few hours.

She looked at Mom, Dad and Gemma shielding their faces from what she'd done to them and then at Brett's eyes.

Poppy thought about how the family's murder would be received on the news. How shocked everyone would be. It was inevitable that any wrongs these people had executed would immediately be forgotten because she'd pushed a piece of metal inside them.

Did they love each other as a family? Or, like all human behaviour, was that simply the word they used to describe their survival instinct? Safety in numbers, children clinging to parents until they had to face the same truth; that every human action was to service bodily needs – thirst, hunger, reproduction. Enzymes, hormones and urges drove people to every outwardly romantic or altruistic decision.

She could so easily divorce herself from conditioned emotions.

Could filter out the lighter blood drying in perfect bars in the sunlight coming through the slats of the blinds. '

The movement and sound of Gemma's iPhone on the coffee table startled her. Its ring tone was an excerpt of a pop song Poppy recognised from the radio. She watched it vibrate within its rainbow cover on the coffee table. It was probably one of Gemma's girlfriends waiting for her to pick up.

She set her canary yellow clutch purse next to it. There was also a half empty bag of clipped up tortilla chips and a bowl containing a tangle of Gemma's colourful hair bands on the table. The roll of black duct tape Poppy had put there. She would use it to fix Brett's hands to his eyes like she had the others.

She wasn't done with him yet though.

CHAPTER THREE

Seated by the dark green water, Will leaned against his palms and tried to enjoy the moment. It was always a challenge for him. His hyperactivity was difficult to contain, but Carla was able to harness his energy as well as her own. She lived and breathed organisation and the drive she'd had before the miscarriage was steadily returning.

She'd led Will to the pond in the grounds of Easton Grey. The earthy scent there mingled with jasmine and cut grass. Neither of them really liked champagne, but Carla's sense of occasion continually surprised him. Recreating the day they'd shared a bottle of fizz as registry office newlyweds was the sort of touch that reduced Will's romantic gestures to matchwood by comparison.

She knelt and leaned into the pond to check the temperature of the bottle chilling there. Will examined her determined profile and the freckles the sun had spritzed on the tops of her white shoulders. The pale C-section scar on her midriff was also getting rare exposure.

She was the most resilient person he'd ever met. The miscarriage was less than a year ago and he recalled how, waking from the ordeal, she'd gripped his hand and asked him if he was OK. She'd squeezed his fingers so hard he'd felt the bones grind against each other. After the amount of blood she'd lost he couldn't believe how much strength she'd still had.

She'd been a senior corporate lawyer at Ingram for fourteen years, but hadn't been back there since. The one consolation about their daughter's surprise pregnancy was that it had become a catalyst for Carla's recovery. She was talking about returning in the autumn. She'd always worked voluntarily with the Water Aid Alliance. Her role operated in tandem with his, ensuring Ingram's resources were applied in areas of critical need. Carla had kept herself busy coordinating their overseas projects from home as well as the protest against the Motex plant.

She'd got involved in the demonstrations before the miscarriage. If Jessie had survived she would have attended Hanworth Primary. Will knew Carla was still channelling her energies there to compensate for the loss.

"Libby knows her own mind." She plucked the bottle out of the water. "You have to let her do things her own way." She twisted off the wire and pursed her lips as she unsuccessfully attempted to uncork it.

"She's eighteen." Will gestured for the bottle to be handed over, but knew it wouldn't be.

"Exactly." She grimaced, rotated the bottle and the cork shot out and landed in the pond. "That's why the decision's hers." She shifted herself back up the grass bank so just her bare feet were in the water. The fizz foamed and she took an unrefined gulp from the neck.

Carla had prepared a picnic, just like the one they'd had nineteen years ago. Except then they'd been renting a one bedroom flat. They'd also been sat at the edge of the Serpentine rather than their own lake, and they hadn't had a pregnant daughter to discuss.

He persisted when he knew he shouldn't. "So, are we suddenly trusting Libby to make the right choice because she's passed the adult mark by a couple of months…"

Carla suddenly folded the spread of her saffron skirt over her legs.

Will knew his recalcitrance could prevent the evening turning out the way it was meant to. "I mean, how much do we really know about Luke's history?" He sounded exactly like the Dad he didn't want to be. He actually thought Luke was a good kid, but recognised too many elements of himself in him. It was good to be ambitious, but now he had to put Libby first.

"She's been with him for nearly two years and she's carrying his child. What more do we need to know?" Carla looked past him to the plumes of green weed in the bottom of the pond.

Nineteen years as man and wife,

And still so many years ahead,

He still hadn't found the words. "So you're just going to let her and Luke live together?"

Carla handed him the bottle and he poured champagne into the glasses.

"No. We're both going to let her and Luke live together. If that's what they choose to do." She took one from him and they automatically clinked them.

"Can we not just lock her away and keep her to ourselves?"

Carla smiled ruefully. "The escape is already underway."

"I was thinking maybe we could go camping for a few days. D'you think she'd go for it?"

Carla checked a look of bemusement when she saw he was serious. She knew why he was suggesting it. When Libby had been thirteen they'd had a disastrous weekend in the New Forest. A collapsed tent, cremated hot dogs and all of them had been eaten alive by insects. But it was the best three days the family had spent together and they still talked about it. "I think we've established I'm no girl scout," she deflected. "And I don't think Libby can survive more than thirty seconds without tweeting." She was letting him down gently.

Will hardened his lips. He knew the idea was wishful thinking.

"I think the trip was the best possible idea for them. They can talk; see how they are with each other. And they can make a decision without anyone's interference."

Will swigged and nodded, but only because a reaction seemed appropriate. He hadn't got his head around the idea of Libby leaving home yet. Much as he loved her, he thought she was completely unrehearsed for real life. She hadn't even finished college. Where did she think the money for a family would come from? Luke certainly wasn't qualified to provide for her.

He'd offered to take him on as a trainee at Ingram, but he'd diplomatically refused. Luke's online enterprises were far from paying off. He was sharp enough, but so were thousands of other kids in IT.

"Who knows what they'll decide. We'll support them whatever it is, though."

He nodded emptily again and took a gulp.

Carla put her fingers in her mouth and summoned the dogs with a whistle. Three contrasting heads looked up from nuzzling the opposite edge of the pond and then the lab, cocker and collie bounded round the perimeter to join them. She fed them with snacks and sent them back to the house.

"Now, how about us at least trying to mimic relaxation..."

She brushed at a smudge on his forehead and he kissed the heel of her hand and tasted her skin moisturiser. Her fingertips came to rest underneath the overhang of hair at the nape of his neck.

At eighteen he'd fully intended to lose his virginity to Eva Lockwood, a half-Dutch anthropology student, or Jenny Sturgess, a trainee lab technician. He'd been happy to submit to Carla's gentle dissuasion though. His faithfulness had been implicit since. She was the only person he didn't have to prove anything to. He'd met her at Brunel University and when they'd first been introduced she'd regarded him as if she'd been waiting to resume a conversation they'd already started.

Will had been an only child of low-income, academic parents and their significant investment in his education meant he'd heaped more expectation on himself than they had. His mother and father had Will in later life, and never got to witness his accomplishments. Had he only recently learnt that family was more important than approval?

Libby had her own plans and quality time with her frequently absent, workaholic father probably wasn't one of them. She was as obstinate as he was. Throughout his life he'd made decisions and stuck to them. Now, he was uncertain. Libby didn't have a clue about motherhood or what lay in store for her.

He followed Carla's gaze to the bobbing cork in the pond. Evening pink reflected in the dark water. "Is it our fault? Should we have been stricter?" He knew it wasn't the first time he'd said it to Carla and certainly not to himself. "If I'd been here more..."

"And what were we doing when we were in our late teens?",

"But we were sensible. We knew about consequences."

"How can we possibly lecture Libby about consequences?"

She was right. Jessie had been completely unplanned.

They'd both quickly got used to the idea of having another baby in the house, even though Libby was almost an adult. She'd been as excited as they had. They were still trying to fill the void of a joy that never came home.

"So...." She cocked her wrist. "It's 7.22pm on our last night alone. How much longer are you going to leave me in these clothes?" She raised her chin slightly as she waited for him to answer.

Will tried to keep himself in shape. Morning runs along the South Bank and the nervous energy he expended during office hours saw to that. When was the last time he'd been alfresco naked though?

Carla watched his mild panic with amusement. "Libby's not back until early tomorrow morning." Mischief glinted in the green pigment of her eyes. She took the glass out of his hand. "Summer house if you're bashful."

She got up and started towards the hexagonal structure they'd constructed at the edge of the pond five summers ago. They'd sat outside it on many a warm, family barbecue evening. Libby had appropriated it as her teen hideaway for the past couple of years. She'd hung so many chimes and mobiles of coloured glass from the ceiling you could scarcely stand up in there. For all Will knew, it was where she'd conceived. It was theirs again for tonight and he knew Carla had recently stashed her obsolete CD collection in there. She unclipped her hair as she mounted the steps, her red locks dropping to her shoulders.

Will scraped up a stone and aimed it at the cork. It missed, but shivered the pink clouds on the water. He knew he'd get melancholy if he stared into the pond for too long. When was the last time the three of them had been together? A dull throb at his abdomen interrupted the thought. Another ulcer?

Scott Walker's voice oozed from the open double doors of the summer house. *No Regrets*. She'd found the CDs. It was Carla's favourite Walker Brothers album. He got to his feet unsteadily. Not even a whole glass down and he was already lightheaded. He was such a cheap date. Will followed the sound, to where Carla was waiting.

The crab scrabbled its broken claws against the rusted sides of the empty paint pot, its remaining legs fighting for purchase as it circled its prison. Will looked down at its fractured, dark blue shell and the pinkish white flesh exposed through the cracks.

It wouldn't escape. The pot was too deep. But its pincers scraped off peelings of the coating of white paint that clung to the walls as it frantically tried to scratch its way out. Rain fell hard on Will's scalp, but he was transfixed by its energy.

He often saw the crab between sleep and waking, felt the droplets pummelling his head as he watched it.

The scraping continued even as he opened his eyes. He looked at the digital display of the clock beside the bed, but the numbers were blurred. The mobile phone beside it vibrated brusquely and filed at the bedside table. He snatched it up.

"When did you last google yourself, Mr Frost?" A female asked the question and the timbre of her voice had the forced cordiality of a wake up call.

"Libby?" The pall of sleep was slowly tugged from Will's brain.

"Kiss, kiss, kiss," she added and then hung up.

He looked at the bedside clock again. He panicked that he'd overslept and that she and Luke were waiting at the airport. But as the numbers defined themselves he could see it was only 3.17am.

He was aware of Carla turning to him while he stared at his mobile. He waited for his recent memories to collate themselves and make sense of what he'd just heard. She sensed his anxiety and didn't ask the obvious as he punched up the caller ID. He wasn't surprised to find the number had been withheld. He felt her sit up and wait.

The room and its position in time fell into place. He knew he hadn't been mistaken about what had been said. His heart dropped a gear, but was still battering the base of his throat.

"Might have been a wrong number." But the caller's question and sign off still reverberated.

Carla was as convinced as he was. "What did they say?"

"Something about going online." Not something about going online. Something about precisely what he'd find there, about him. There was no doubt the caller was baiting him.

"Online?" Carla sounded incredulous and relieved. Her daughter was in the air and it wasn't the early morning call she'd dreaded.

Will couldn't release the same sigh of relief. The voice had been economical with its message, lingering briefly before hanging up as if to make sure he'd heard.

Carla took refuge under the duvet again.

Exhaustion was usually the only thing that persuaded them both to sleep. But last night they'd made love twice and been asleep for a good six hours. He wanted to slide back into bed as well, to make love again even though they soon had to get up to be at the airport.

His inflating unease told him he wouldn't be allowed to.

CHAPTER FOUR

After dumping the phone in the bedside drawer Will decided he didn't want to panic Carla. He waited for five long minutes before getting up. It sounded like a prank call and part of him just wanted to dismiss it, but one thing was force-feeding his anxiety, whoever it was had reached him on his private mobile. He owned two, but the one they'd called him on was the phone he used exclusively to keep in touch with Carla and Libby.

"Thirsty?"

Carla's hair hissed briefly as she shook her head against the pillow.

His excuse established, he extracted the pair of shorts Carla had left tubed inside his trousers as she'd tugged them down his legs hours before. He slid them on and padded from the room.

Downstairs he deactivated the alarm and made his way to the office. Despite the time of year the room was still cold and he shivered while he waited for the computer to boot up. He quickly stabbed his name into a search before he could have second thoughts.

William Frost

The results cascaded and he recognised a row of three photographs of himself. He was smiling with a delegation from the US utilities board in the first, stood at the obligatory podium

in the second and shaking hands with the president of United
HydroPower in the third. He looked uncomfortable in all of
them. He'd never been very good at freezing an expression for
posterity. He didn't look as uncomfortable as he felt now though.

Libby was a Facebook addict, was forever uploading photos and
clips to YouTube. Every moment of her life was shared with her
legion of online friends. He dreaded to think how many images
of him they'd been party to. She'd told him about a piece of
software that would allow him to commit cyber suicide, remove
every trace of him from the net. He'd been sorely tempted.

His eyes descended the page. What could he possibly be
targeted for? His family and position precluded him from any
indiscretions, financial or otherwise. But he knew he was
going to find something here. He hoped it was a prank or an
industry journalist trying to probe into his home life. It had been
attempted once, unsuccessfully, in the past.

But he was sure the mock civility of the woman's voice
concealed something ugly. He clicked through the pages of results
and one of them immediately drew his eye as he remembered
what she'd said before hanging up. *Kiss, kiss, kiss.*

williamfrostxxx.net/

Three kisses – triple X? There was no other information below
the listing. Surely it couldn't be a porn site. He clicked on it.

The page quickly configured itself. A deep purple background
loaded up with images of his home. Photos of room interiors
he knew were recent because they'd only been redecorated in
the past few months. They were exactly the kind that Will had
fought to keep out of the public domain. Now his family privacy
was available for anyone in the world to scrutinise. He scrolled
down them, quickly acknowledging that something united all
the pictures.

Briefly he considered that they might have been stolen from

Carla's online archive. She used a community image storage facility to share snaps and décor progress reports with family and friends. A quick scan of the stills of the front lounge, kitchen and hallway confirmed they'd been taken from outside the house. The photographer had stood at each window and furtively captured the interiors.

Cool tingles travelled from his shoulders down the backs of his arms. What was this, the beginnings of a concerted intimidation campaign? Motex Radials glided back into his thoughts like a note thrust under a door. He moved the slider down the side of the screen and revealed photos of the other rooms in the house with their sleek lifestyle appliances – the Blu-Ray home cinema in the TV room, micro-media centre in the lounge and the electronic incline trainer in the gym. The minimalist furnishings made the rooms look more like glossy showrooms than spaces in a family home.

Somebody had trespassed to secure them and he realised the stills had been taken at leisure while Carla had been in. In the dingy light of the one taken of the office he was standing in he could see her working at her desk on the opposite side of the room. They'd been feet away from her.

A car could easily be concealed in the copses of trees around the perimeter and a ladder was all that was needed to gain entry. Would Motex really go to these lengths? If this had nothing to do with the protest then blackmail was the obvious incentive. But did whoever it was think this scare tactic sufficient enough to extract money?

His brain attempted a speedy audit of his past. Was there an industry rival who might bear him a grudge? Or had organised crime decided it was his turn?

In the photo taken of the kitchen he could see through to the window at the other side and the shaded parking area beyond. He recognised the potted sequoia tree that Carla had recently positioned there. How long since she'd been presented it as a gift at the Water Aid Alliance dinner? No more than six weeks ago. Below the last image it said:

CHECK YOUR EMAIL AND GO HOME

Will heard a movement upstairs. Carla was up. He often snuck into the office on weekends and she saw it as her duty to extract him. He'd been gone too long from bed and soon she would be standing in the doorway demanding his withdrawal.

He quickly logged into his Ingram email account and scanned the contents of the inbox. Nothing jumped out at him. A lot of internal memos and holiday snaps from Libby. There were also the usual chasers from people who wanted his presence at industry conventions plus updates from the Water and Health Bureau. He checked his spam for anything that had been filtered out, but found only junk.

Why wouldn't the creators of the website expect him to immediately pick up the phone to the police? He felt a jolt of fear. He returned to his inbox and opened Libby's last email. His eyes had barely grazed the header because he'd received so many of them on an almost daily basis.

Last Snaps

He opened the shots that had been sent using their picture sharing account. He was relieved to find harmless multiple images of his daughter and her boyfriend. She clasped her baseball cap to her head against a strong wind as she leaned on Luke's wiry, brown body in front of Penang Bridge.

Their beaming complexions looked more burnt than tanned. Libby was squinting through her mother's freckles and looked fuller in the face than some of the previous updates. They'd obviously benefited from the emergency money he'd wired them.

Her dark hair, usually in a bob, hung messily around the fringe of the hat, but he registered how happy they seemed together. Luke's head was shaved, but he was experimenting with a moustache. Far from making him appear older, however, he looked like a kid wearing a clip-on from a Christmas cracker.

He scrolled down the multiple photos. Libby and Luke wearing orange lifebelts and seated with a crowd of tourists aboard a sightseeing boat and then several uninspiring shots of the underside of the bridge. The last few were of them perched at a high table outside a bar at night. Rows of orange paper lanterns glowed above their smudged smiles.

"I should've bricked this room up for the weekend."

Will turned and Carla was leaning on the doorjamb in her nightshirt.

"Pictures from Libby," he mitigated, turning back to the screen. He felt Carla standing behind him as he revealed the last image.

The question of whether he should protect her from whoever had targeted their family home was now academic. The last image was of Libby and Luke tied to a rusty strut of what looked like a livestock shed.

Metallic cages were visible in the limited expanse of the flash. It illuminated Libby's dirty tears and the filthy piece of rag that had been stuffed into her mouth. Her eyes bulged in terror and blue plastic flex bound them back-to-back. A piece of card on a string had been hung around her neck. On it was scrawled a mobile number.

CHAPTER FIVE

Carla took one pace back as if proximity to the photo made it undeniable. She burst the numbed silence, gulping in air as if she'd broken the surface of water.

Will felt as if the room were tilting as his eyes roved every detail. Cold dread mushroomed. Was there some giveaway that would dismiss it as a sick joke? But the digital still was saturated with such raw distress that he could almost hear their screams through the gags. "Call her," he said flatly.

Carla snatched up her mobile and shakily punched Libby's number blinking rapidly as she waited, not looking at Will.

How long had the image been awaiting discovery? Will glanced at the time the email had arrived – 19.33 the evening before. How many hours had they been tied together like that? They'd been trapped and imprisoned and he and Carla had been making love.

She cut the call. "Just her answering service." Hysteria warped her voice and tears welled.

"I'll try the number." He nodded at the scribbled digits in the photo.

"I'll do it." Carla moved back to the screen.

Will held up his hand. "No. They called me. I don't want you to speak to them."

"Read out the number." She brandished the phone.

"Carla, let me do this."

Carla blinked once as if his outburst had barely registered. They both took a breath as he picked up his desk phone. It took all his concentration to punch the digits in. He held the receiver to his ear and heard a number of damp clicks before it connected to a speeded up ring tone.

While it rang he prayed Libby would pick up and that he'd soon be chiding her for playing such a twisted prank, but it wasn't her or Luke's style. The phone continued to ring. He felt a bump as Carla leaned against the back of his chair.

He looked at the bunched wrinkles of Libby's face around the rag plugging her mouth. The picture was defined enough for him to make out all the minute details – the raised white bump of her BCG injection at the top of her bare shoulder, the piercing of her ears which had got badly infected when she'd had them done for her ninth birthday and the tiny crater at the side of her left eye. It looked like a chickenpox scar, but was actually the result of her going over the handlebars of her bike after a Halloween party. During all those childhood ordeals he and Carla had been there to comfort her. They weren't there for her now.

Somebody picked up.

"Hello?" It seemed a ridiculous word to say in the circumstances, but Will repeated it when there was no response.

There was a sound though. In the background he could hear an unsettling bed of disharmony, like a room full of screaming children. Then the line went dead.

Will hit redial and waited.

"What happened?" He heard Carla brush her tongue across the front of her dry gums.

"They hung up." He got the same muted click and then an engaged tone. He listened for a while, paralysed by the image of his daughter's anguish and the barrier of sound at his ear. The phone he was trying to connect to could be in the same room as her and Luke.

The background noise he'd heard the first time still resonated on his eardrums. Not children; animals, lots of them in unison – panicked birds.

They both dialled the number repeatedly, but couldn't get through.

"Why are they not answering?"

"They know we've seen the number. Perhaps that's all they want for now." He dragged the slider and examined the other pictures. Libby and Luke beaming at whoever had taken the photo in the bar.

He clicked back to the website where the snaps of Easton Grey were posted.

CHECK YOUR EMAIL AND GO HOME

Carla absorbed them in sickened silence. "What is this, Will?" Suspicion trickled into the question.

"I found this site just now – after that call this morning."

"Don't hide anything from me." She said it as if she expected him to have an even worse revelation.

"I know as much as you." A word in the top left corner of the screen caught his eye.

HOME

He clicked on it and the screen changed to a street, a row of houses extending across the bottom portion of the image. Above it, against a cobalt blue sky, was a message.

IF YOU LIFT THE PHONE TO THE POLICE –
THEY'RE DEAD
IF YOU TELL ANYONE ELSE – THEY'RE DEAD
MR FROST MUST TAKE FIRST AVAILABLE
FLIGHT TO ORLANDO INTERNATIONAL
TAKE LAPTOP AND AWAIT FURTHER

INSTRUCTIONS VIA THIS SITE.
IF YOU DON'T – THEY'RE DEAD

"Why do they want you to go to Florida?" Carla's frown dug deep into her face.

Bar a holiday they'd had there, years previously, Will couldn't see the significance of the destination either. No mention of a ransom. Why was he being personally lured away from where they were holding Libby and Luke?

"Who have you been dealing with in the States recently?" Her eyes darted in time with her thoughts.

"Plenty of people. The contract with Ledwidge has just got underway, but the whole operation's in Colorado."

"What about Ingram's ops in Thailand?"

"We completed over four years ago."

"Perhaps somebody found out Libby was entering the country."

"Maybe." It was clear the kidnappers knew exactly whose daughter Libby was. "Wherever these people are from, they've taken intimate photos of our home. They know we're good for a ransom."

"Who else knew about Libby and Luke going to Penang?" She clenched her eyes shut, trying to exclude panic and zero in on likely candidates.

It was a significant point. Somebody knew exactly where they'd be. "I've hardly mentioned it to anyone..." But he wasn't so sure.

"Hardly?"

Another disturbing thought muscled in. Was the house bugged? It seemed absurd, but then the photo of Libby and Luke as hostages was just as inconceivable. "It's pointless trying to work out how they took them. What's important is getting them back as quickly as possible."

Carla momentarily tightened her mouth as if sealing her emotions in. She nodded rapidly and traded a glance with him, confirming they both knew how real the situation was. "What about the police?"

Will studied the message on the screen. "They've been pretty explicit about that. If they can see into our home..."

She glanced at the telephone, her own paranoia gaining on Will's. "I'll pack our bags."

"I'm going alone," he said before she could turn.

"Don't be ridiculous. I'm not staying here."

"Carla, the instructions stipulate me going–"

"We don't have time to argue this."

"Listen, we don't want to involve the police...yet. But if we do, you'll need to coordinate things from here. We could both end up on a wild goose chase otherwise." He nodded at the screen. "Which is exactly what this looks like."

Carla bit her lip.

"But I don't want you in the house." He looked through the window and into the garden where their watcher had probably stood.

"I'll use your office..." She nodded, her eyes fixing the floor as she imagined herself there. Then she turned and went to her desk, grabbing some hair clips she'd attached to the flex of her lamp. She started rapidly piling and pinning her red tresses, a ritual to ward off the terrible possibilities of the situation.

Will tried to filter the panic out of his voice. "Stay in a hotel. Don't tell anybody where."

"This can't be connected to the Motex protest?" Carla needed immediate assurance that it wasn't her actions that had brought about Libby's kidnap.

"Of course not." The second's delay before his response spoke of his own fears. "Of course not," he said with more conviction. It was ludicrous; scare tactics, doorstep bonfires... but abduction?

Carla's eyes locked with Will's again.

Nineteen years as man and wife,

And still so many years ahead,

CHAPTER SIX

Even though it was Saturday, Will flew Carla to Ingram in the Longranger to leapfrog any traffic. Neither of them spoke for the entire journey. Once they'd touched down at the heliport they strode swiftly along the South Bank. It was 4.58am and the sun was flaring orange on the grey murk of the Thames. They walked through the revolving door of the air-conditioned reception in silence. There would only be a skeleton staff manning the Remada op room on the eleventh floor.

The security guard, Taylor, emerged from the chair behind his station. He was new, a man in his thirties with pockmarked features. "Mr Frost…"

"Car to Heathrow as quickly as possible."

Taylor nodded and snatched up a phone.

Will turned to Carla, handing her his swipe card. "You know the password to the computer."

She nodded, but he could see she was steeling herself for their goodbye. "Get her back. I want all of you home." Her resolve wavered. "Is Nissa here today?"

Will felt emotion choke his throat. He held her face in his palms and kissed her lips. They tasted bitter. "Yes, tell her to give you anything you want. Use her, but don't give anything away."

"One on its way, sir." Taylor tried to imbue his voice with the sound of efficiency.

Will shivered. It wasn't from the cool morning air, but he

swung on the leather jacket he'd been carrying anyway. "Try to think of anyone who knew where Libby and Luke were going." The trip had been planned for so long. How many people had his daughter told? How many times had he and Carla dropped it into conversations? "I'll call you as soon as I've landed."

"I can follow your phone by GPS. Like we did with Libby's. But keep me informed every step of the way."

It was Will's turn to nod. There was nothing more to say, but he realised Carla was gripping his arm like she was on a roller coaster.

She released him and walked to the lifts. She pressed the button and turned to him with tightened lips. Only then did Will register she was wearing the same olive top and saffron skirt from the night before. The doors parted and she stepped inside.

He strode outside to wait, knowing she would turn again to watch him leave as they closed. He didn't want to meet her eyes again.

"Not everyone wants to smile at you, Lib."

It was what he'd said to his daughter the first day he'd taken her out in the pram on his own. He'd been nervous about Carla not being with him, but had soon grown accustomed to showing Libby off to the other parents in the park. They'd stopped at a café garden for a rest and she'd tried to engage the attention of a guy in jogging gear seated at the opposite picnic table. He'd glared unkindly at Libby and looked away. He remembered his daughter turning to him from the rebuttal. She was still smiling, but her young eyes were full of confusion.

His own disappointment that the stranger didn't share the enthusiasm everyone else had displayed for his daughter had punctured his mood for the rest of the day. He'd felt so protective of her then and the notion of how many hard lessons she had ahead of her had blindsided him. He'd taken her home and while Carla had unstrapped her he'd gone upstairs and sat on the bed.

He'd desperately wanted to be a father, but knew his workload would exclude him from much of Libby's early childhood. It was then it had really caught up with him, the enormity of his responsibility. He felt contaminated by the thought of how Libby's innocence would gradually be eroded, that it was his obligation to remove it so she could be conditioned for what life would throw at her.

The sensation surged through him now, concentrated, like a toxin heavy in his veins. That piece of rag stuffed into her mouth, those ropes binding her in that filthy place. What had they done to her? He desperately hoped she'd told them she was pregnant. Would they even care? He thought of her nervously lifting her tee shirt to show him her lotus tattoo. A definitive means of identification.

He felt a sudden heaving in his chest and a sob forcing its way out. He had to bite down hard on his lip to halt it. Lose it now and he would lose her, he knew it. To stand any chance of getting her back, he had to stay strong.

Carla called him while he was in the car to give him the details of the flight she'd booked from his office. There was nothing else to their exchange. They both knew their feelings had to take a back seat while they focussed on getting Libby back. A minute later he had a permission request for GPS tracking on his phone. They'd had to do the same with Libby. In the UK it was illegal to track a mobile's SIM card without it. He granted it and knew as soon as he did Carla would be able to follow his progress on a website map.

At the airport, Will changed up the money in his wallet and checked into the business lounge. And while he was helplessly pacing its plush, lemon-scented interior, what at that precise moment was happening to Libby? He knew she'd be protective of her baby. It was still early days, but she already had her life planned out with Luke and her child. And what of Luke? He must be just as terrified. He was only three years older than her and his parents were completely oblivious to his predicament. But the instructions had been absolute.

He glanced at the handful of execs in the business lounge, rustling papers and absorbed by their iPads. Most of them were probably using their air miles for pleasure trips, heading off to condos and golf weekends. His phone buzzed in his jacket, but it wasn't the family mobile. It was the office one he'd been ignoring since they'd left the house. Several missed messages from the Remada op site construction manager. He switched it off and pocketed it again.

They must have been so easy to abduct, a couple of kids. Libby would probably have put up more resistance than Luke. She had her mother's fire in her belly. Luke was more an observer, an analyser. He told himself his level head was probably just what Libby needed. Would they remain incarcerated together? He still couldn't believe the questions he was asking himself.

He looked at his watch as he felt anger bubble up from the sediment of dread in his stomach. Anger at whoever had put their hands on his daughter, at Luke for wanting to take her away, but mostly at himself for allowing it to happen. If he hadn't filled her head with stories about Southeast Asia she would never have wanted to go. Had his past association with the country put her life at risk? If so, why had he been ordered to the States?

Carla had been back to Will's office since the miscarriage, but as she waited in its silence it seemed alien to her. She felt like an intruder in someone else's reality. There'd been emotional upheavals in both their pasts, but nothing that was so determinately the product of malice. The idea that another human would want to snatch Libby and use her terror as a weapon jarred with everything she'd ever experienced. She thought of whoever had Libby formulating their plan while they were oblivious, prowling the fringes of their lives in preparation for this morning.

It had to be money. Please let it be money. They were wealthy; they could pay. She told herself that this happening was maybe even inevitable. If they'd been determined to take Libby there would always have been an opportunity for them to do so, however close by she and Will had kept her.

What if they'd had the cameras fitted earlier? Will had suggested it a couple of years before, but she'd been against it. She'd firmly believed they didn't need them; that by having them would draw unwanted attention. He'd only just managed to persuade her after the bonfire incident. Nobody would have been able to get onto their property and take photographs through the windows if they'd had the surveillance in place. But would that have stopped them kidnapping Libby when she was away from their protection?

Her thoughts returned to her conversation about consequences with Will the night before. She'd told him Libby could make her own decisions; that she had to set her own life on course. She hadn't told him she'd been just as afraid for her as he was.

Ever since she'd met Will at university they'd never compromised their trust. Had she done that by concealing her reservations? Was this her punishment?

She delicately seated herself in Will's cool swivel chair. The plush calm of her surroundings accentuated the feeling that she was in exactly the wrong place. She looked through the smoked glass windows at Will's impressive vista of the South Bank. It was this success that had imprisoned their daughter. But why no ransom? Was this retribution for something Ingram had done? Did Will know what it was and was withholding from her? She doubted it. But hundreds of decisions were made every day on his behalf. Had a contravention by the company been the trigger? Libby had been taken in territory it had a significant attachment to.

Carla considered the private struggle she'd initiated on behalf of the residents of Hanworth. She knew why she'd taken it on and with even more resolve after losing the baby. Did her heightened sense of injustice mean she'd now lose her only other child because of it?

Outside the window the temperature was rising, but Carla shivered and rubbed the backs of her arms.

Will only seated himself when the steward told him they were rolling out onto the runway. He'd brought his laptop and an overnight bag. If he needed anything else he could buy it in Florida. How long was he expected to be there?

He felt utterly useless, like his body had no physical means to express the turmoil inside him. He needed to shout, injure his fist against a wall and release the build up of negative energy.

He had to centre himself and remember Libby needed him collected. But he couldn't prise away the image of her gagged. Why had he let Libby talk him into agreeing to the trip? She was barely eighteen. He could still vividly recall his emotions when Carla had first presented her in school uniform. She looked like she was playing dressing up, not ready to leave the protection of home.

Whatever they wanted from him, however much it was, he'd pay. Yesterday evening he'd been anticipating hugging his daughter tight, just to have her back from her travels. Now it was something he'd exchange his life for.

That morning he had no choice but to fly away from her. He just had to hope that whatever reasons were behind the journey could lead him to her return, the only conclusion he could consider. He belted himself in for take-off and, as the wheels broke contact with the runway, he briefly wondered when or if he would be coming back.

Her first conscious thought was that her eyes were on fire. She tried to open them, but something pinned her eyelids down. She heaved them apart, but everything was black. She heard her own exclamation of panic inside her head, tasted white spirit on her tongue and the ache of her facial muscles around whatever plugged her mouth. She bit down, heard fibres squeak against her teeth. Fear could only tense her constrained body. She couldn't move her arms or legs and when she turned her head the motion seemed delayed.

Drugged. She remembered the needle in her arm and waited for the events that preceded it to re-present themselves. Nothing came but an echo, the reverberation of something horrible she didn't want to remember.

Her name was Libby Frost. Where had she been before here? Where was she now? All around her a frenzied screeching amplified her hysteria.

Whatever was burning her eyes permeated her nostrils as well, raw and cold inside them, burning its way through the skin there. Was it petrol she could smell? Was that what was soaked into the material in her mouth? She tried to expel the bulk weighing down her tongue, but it met resistance at her lips. Something was tightly covering her whole face. She could feel a weight against her throat, the tension of some binding that made it hurt to swallow. Under the acidic aroma she could detect the vague scent of her coconut sun block.

She cried out and the familiarity of her own voice brought more of herself streaming back. Pregnant. She was pregnant and she'd been drugged and tied up.

Her arms were secured behind her and she couldn't move her fingers, didn't have any sensation that her hands were still at the ends of her wrists. She couldn't get a sense of which way her head was swinging. Her erratic breaths heated the mask of sweat clinging to her face and her lungs ached as they tried to draw in oxygen.

"I can't breathe! Untie me! I'm suffocating!"

The words formed in her brain, but were incoherent as they struggled to escape her obstructed mouth. They vibrated in her skull and through the burn in her nostrils. She could feel warm tears flowing constantly down her face.

But the sensation she experienced more vividly than anything else was at the nape of her neck, a warm buzz telling her somebody nearby was watching her.

Once in the air, Will told the steward he didn't want any meals, only black coffee. Then he plugged the laptop into the power point. He opened the website. There was no new message on the page, but as his eyes roved the area at the bottom of the screen, he realised he could move along the row of houses with the cursor. The buildings weren't figurative, but photo images of real properties cut out and pasted next to each other. There was no consistency in size; they'd been assembled like cuttings from a scrapbook.

The row moved left to right and when he reached the far end of it, he recognised Easton Grey. The picture of his home was spliced next to two more unassuming houses. A red outline appeared around the image when he rested the cursor on it. He clicked it and found himself back on the page of furtive snaps taken of the interior he'd seen earlier. He hit HOME, returned to the row and tried to click on the house that preceded his. No red outline appeared so he tried the one before it. Same again.

He worked his way back through the row to the opposite end, but none of them were active. What purpose did it have? Why not make demands via phone or text?

If this turned out to be some diversion, if he didn't receive any instructions within an hour of disembarking, he was getting the first flight back. But looking at the website, he suspected Libby's kidnappers were dropping him into the middle of a sadistic piece of amusement that was only just getting under way.

CHAPTER SEVEN

Tam had nearly finished deliveries for the day and leaned against the back of the stationary tuk-tuk to finish his cigarette. The motor of the three-wheel taxi had been switched off so he knew he was safe from the sudden belches of oily smoke it occasionally emitted from its exhaust. He sucked the last harsh lungful through the filter and crushed the cigarette under his sandal.

He'd climbed out of the sidecar because his buttocks had gone to sleep for the fourth time that afternoon. He jogged on the spot a few times to get the blood flowing back into them and then rubbed his palm over the sheen of sweat on his shaved scalp. He'd spent Saturday as he usually did, straddling the unsecured wooden bench in the cage welded to the bike. It slid about as they took every corner.

In the morning the cage was full of cooking oil drums, but he'd just helped roll the last one into the corrugated kitchen of one of the many street vendors they delivered to in time for the Sungai Dua night market. Tam looked down the length of the baking main road. It was still deserted, but by 7pm in the evening both sides of it would be full of stalls selling DVDs, handbags and food to a centipede of the rich and hungry.

He examined the black index fingernail of his right hand. A barrel of oil had rolled backwards from a ramp and crushed it last week and although he'd already pricked the pus out of it the nail still refused to fall off. He sucked on it in an attempt to get the blood flowing there as well.

Then he heard the girl scream. Tam slid his finger from his mouth and leaned round the tuk-tuk to see if there was any commotion further down the street. The market area was empty. There was an older white couple, tall and wide, walking arm in arm. No other tourists here yet.

Tam returned to his position between the two vehicles parked outside the Eastern Wish. He gripped the bars of the sidecar and leaned against it, tensing his numb buttocks tight in his shorts. It wasn't a long journey home, but long enough.

The scream came again and this time Tam froze to listen. It hadn't come from the street. He looked to the cafe where they'd just delivered. Beads still swung in the doorway where his father had entered and he could hear the sound of a low conversation. He was positive it hadn't come from through there though. The girl's voice had seemed small, like the echo of someone far away.

His eyes rose to the storeys above. The noise of duelling TVs emerged from open windows. Was that what he'd heard? His gaze descended to pavement level. There was a grille set into the bottom of the chipped, mushroom-coloured wall. He held his breath and listened.

"Tam!"

He turned to find his father already cocking his leg over the bike. He immediately jumped back into the sidecar and seated himself on the bench. He knew better than to delay him. Grasping the bars of the cage he braced himself for the ride home to their estate on the edge of Taman Lip Sin. At least in the morning the oil drums stopped him from being thrown around. He was about to get gut ache from straining to stay upright. He looked back at the grill in the wall, but the sound of the bike's engine being stamped to life would have drowned out any further sounds that came from it, if that's where they'd come from.

He thought about telling his father about what he'd heard. But Tam had already been scolded for his imagination. His nightmares woke his parents on a regular basis. Why would anyone believe the word of a six-year-old? The bike pulled away and then turned in the middle of the street. Tam's eyes followed the grille until it disappeared behind the stationary taxi.

Will kept the laptop switched on and started to fill up on black coffee. Adrenaline had briefly waned and his body felt suddenly exhausted. Anxiety buffeted his empty stomach. He got up from his seat, walked around, sat back down and repeated the cycle.

It was when he refreshed the page for the umpteenth time that a photo appeared.

Above the row of houses was an image of Libby naked. A graphic representation of what was happening to her while he was thousands of feet in the air. She wasn't bound, but was obviously drugged. She was lying across a dirty blue mattress, utterly insensible, her eyes rolled back in her head and her lips sticky with soured spittle.

He gripped the laptop screen by its corners; like it was a steering wheel and everything would crash if he didn't hold it steady. There were words below the picture. Even as he tried to read them his brain echoed the detail of what was just above his line of sight – Libby's modesty dismissed and her physical self callously displayed. It was worse than the photo of her bound.

INVITATION

**A CELEBRATION OF LIFE
BUT YOUR DAUGHTER WILL ONLY MAKE IT IF
YOU CAN FIND THE PERFECT PARTY OUTFIT
TO DRESS HER
YOU CAN COLLECT ONE PIECE OF IT IN EACH
HOME
GO TO THE FIRST**

Will moved his cursor to the left of the screen and the row moved until he was looking at the first cut out. It was the facade of a grandiose, mock colonial property with arched fanlights above the windows and doors. The front entrance was a mosaic of glass. Above it was another message.

THIS NEIGHBOURHOOD ISN'T REAL BUT THE HOMES AND PEOPLE WHO INHABIT THEM ARE CAN YOU GUESS WHAT THEY ALL HAVE IN COMMON?
CLICK ON NUMBER ONE
IT'S TOO LATE FOR THEM BUT YOU'LL STILL NEED TO FIND YOUR DAUGHTER'S BEADED BRACELET
DAD HAS IT
GO THERE BEFORE THE COPS
WEAR GLOVES – IT'S A CRIME SCENE
MAYBE YOU'LL GET TO THE NEXT HOUSE BEFORE I DO

Will briefly hovered the cursor over the second house, but no red outline appeared. He put it over the first again. Not only did it light up red, but a white box appeared with an address inside it.

1815 North Vine Street,
Highway 193,
Kissimmee,
Florida,
347610

He clicked on the activated house and another page of snapshots opened like the ones that had been taken in Easton Grey. There were interior pictures of its downstairs living areas, fitness room, covered lanai and vast island kitchen. But there was one repellent difference; in the middle photo of the lounge the family were seated along a couch. Mother, father, sister and brother; Will couldn't see their faces. The palms of their hands had been attached to them by black tape.

They looked like a grotesque parody of the wise monkeys. Dried blood darkened their skin and their intestines hung jagged from their bellies, flesh hacked and splayed open. He registered coloured beads at the father's wrist.

As caffeine and bile pumped up his throat, a removed voice told him he should prepare never to see Libby again.

Nissa walked into Will's office with the deadpan features of someone who believed they were quite alone. "Jesus!"

Carla rose from her position in front of the computer. "I'm sorry." Carla had felt so isolated since she'd got to the eighth floor, but now having to present an exterior of normality for someone else was the last thing she wanted to do. "I didn't mean to startle you." She didn't elaborate further and realised it made her look as if she didn't have any business there. She'd been away for so long it was probably odd finding her at Will's desk, particularly so early in the morning. She hovered between standing up and sitting down.

Nissa studied Carla through her slim, rimless glasses, the edge of a concerned frown dipping into the magnification. "Is everything all right?" Her Northern Irish inflection made it sound as if she wouldn't believe her even if she said it was.

Carla opened her mouth to reassure her, but the words stalled. Momentum built behind them, the anxiety inside about to burst from her. She had to confide in someone. "Fine."

Nissa cocked her head to one side; her jagged fringe of wheat blonde hair covering one half of her face. "I thought you and Will were off to..." She stopped herself suddenly.

Had Will planned a surprise anniversary getaway for the three of them? If he had, Nissa would have made all the arrangements. "Change of plan; I need to work. Water Aid Alliance has officially annexed my love life." She surprised herself with the speed of the lie.

It briefly disarmed Nissa, however, and a smirk broke through the bewilderment on her face. She was Will's long term PA and was meant to know his itinerary inside out. Will had told Carla she was manning the telephones for the Remada op while he was away, but Carla knew her unexpected presence would be an affront to her. Will's office was Nissa's domain.

Nissa was five foot eight, but still wore precipitous heels that necessitated her ducking through most doorways. She was slim, intense and almost anaemically pale. She was also a decade younger than Carla. Her only concession to cosmetics was the carmine lipstick she wore which drained the last of the colour from her complexion. She'd worked for Will at home and abroad.

"Thought I'd get an early start. We're having security cameras fitted at home and it's a nightmare trying to work there."

"So Will is..."

"At home, supervising. He got the short straw."

Nissa nodded uncertainly, but picked up on Carla's desire to have the conversation over with. "Fresh coffee?"

"No thanks." Although caffeine sounded like a good idea she hadn't been able to swallow one mouthful of the cup she'd made herself earlier.

"Just give me a shout if you need anything, Mrs Frost." Nissa made for the door.

Carla had given up on trying to get Nissa to address her by her first name like she did Will. She assumed it was Nissa's way of distinguishing their different roles. "Wait." A thought occurred to her. "I may need you to pull some files for me."

"Sure."

Another thought. "And can you arrange to have the dogs picked up from the house and taken to the kennels in Hounslow."

Nissa frowned.

"I'll give you the number."

"I have that...But can't Will..."

Of course, she'd just said that Will was at home. "No. Will has to make a trip. He'll be leaving soon." Carla watched Nissa trying to slot the misinformation together in her head. She'd also told her that Will was supervising the installation of the security cameras.

"Sorry, Mrs Frost... I don't mean to ruin any surprises, but is Will not taking you and Libby to Cawley Manor?"

So, a surprise trip had been planned. "No. He has had to make an alternative business trip."

Nissa seemed mortified to have been left out of the loop. "Business?"

"Urgent family business."

Tam couldn't sleep. He listened to the circulation in his ear scratching at the pillow. Across the narrow passage between his room and the kitchen he could hear his mother and father at the sink and the muffled impacts of plates and cutlery as they put them away.

Nine storeys below nighttime kick-started like his father's bike. Taxi motors buzzed, horns beeped and he could hear the low murmur of adults and occasional words he recognised bubbling up like his mother talking in her sleep. There were yells and screams, but none of them sounded anything like what he'd heard today at the grille. These were mixed with laughter and chatter – voices that were supposed to be heard.

If he didn't get to sleep in the next hour he knew he'd be lying awake listening for Songsuda. He hadn't seen his older sister since his fifth birthday. It had been almost a year ago. His mother and father had told him she'd gone to live with his aunt and uncle in Kampung Keladi. He'd seen her once after when he was making deliveries with his father. Tam had pointed her out to him. She'd stood under an umbrella with a man he didn't recognise, but he knew it was his sister. His father had scarcely glanced in her direction, told Tam he was mistaken and ridden on.

On the night of his fifth birthday she'd come to visit with a present for him. She'd looked strange, suddenly older. His father had dragged her out of the block and he'd heard her screaming to be let back in. She'd returned the following evening, but he hadn't even been allowed to go to the window to see her. He remembered how they'd all sat in the kitchen like statues and the way his mother blinked every time Songsuda screamed up at the window. That night his father had said she'd been given enough chances, told Tam she was lazy and didn't want to work honestly.

Tam remembered when she'd worked at their father's hotplate in the night market in Batu Ferringhi. He used to sit at her feet, watching her painted toenails, while she chatted and served the customers with his mother and father. Yum pla dook foo and moo satay for 25 baht each. He made himself sick on Catfish, red pork and dragon hair sweets.

He missed being at the market. He hoped if his father decided to let Songsuda in they could go back to the way it used to be. He knew it wouldn't happen. He dreamt of her out there and had as many nightmares about what had happened to her. His father had pointed out the bad, nighttime men as they drove round. Those were the men that cast a net over Songsuda when he closed his eyes.

His father had explained it to him, but it still didn't make any sense. Why couldn't they let her back in? He often woke because he thought he'd heard her down in the street.

If he heard her again he'd let her back in whatever his father told him.

He listened to the rhythm of the inside of his body and sank his head deeper into the pillow to try and dampen the throbbing in his ear. Tam thought about what had happened to him that afternoon as he'd stood by the grille. He knew what he'd heard. Would he be a statue again?

"I've landed." Will clasped the mobile to his ear as he walked unsteadily along the familiar, polished concourse of Orlando International. The air smelt overpoweringly of sun lotion. He'd cleared passport control and been fingerprinted. In a golf store he'd quickly purchased a pair of black and white chequered leather gloves. Jetlag lurked beneath the sickening prospect of what lay ahead. He remembered being in the same airport under happier circumstances. How old had Libby been on that holiday?

"Have you seen the site?" The tremor in Carla's voice told him she already had.

"Yes." All around him families and vacationers in pastel colours excitedly made a beeline for car hire.

"Those people in the house..." He could discern her lips parting to articulate a reaction. "As if the first photograph of Libby wasn't enough." Her eventual response was inflected with contempt.

"They're giving us a clear message so we don't go to the police."

"Try to get hold of a firearm."

"This is obviously a sick game for whoever has Libby. They're not going to harm me." Yet.

"You need to be able to protect yourself."

"I don't have time." He looked down at his feet against the shiny, champagne floor. "I have to get there before the police."

"What if this is all a trap?"

It had already occurred to Will. But if it was, why be so intricate? "If they can photograph our home they could certainly have saved themselves a lot of trouble."

"Then why are they making you do this?"

"I don't know, but we've no choice but to follow their

instructions." He didn't want to debate the inevitability of what he had to do any longer. "What's the situation there?"

"Nissa knows something's up. I've got her pulling files on the Eastern Seaboard ops. There's a lot of Ingram territory to cover in Southeast Asia, a mountain of data to go through. I don't know what I'm looking for, but there may be something here..." Carla sounded suddenly distant. She was obviously still processing the new images on the site.

"I project managed every phase. There was no friction in the territory during the whole op. Their kidnap could be completely unrelated. Just be sure not to let anything slip. And make sure security only allow senior staff up to that level." He felt like he was issuing his own demands now.

"I'm not worried about me, Will," she said. "The address on the site is only about fourteen kilometres from the airport. I've already booked you a car. It'll have Sat Nav." Like him she was trying to concentrate on the logistics of what they were doing and not why they were doing it.

Will nodded absently.

"If I don't hear from you ten minutes after you've arrived..."

"Do nothing. I'll call you as quickly as I can, but we can't even entertain calling the police until Libby is safe." He thought of the image of her dumped on the mattress. Carla would have it stitched to her mind as well.

"There must be more I can do here." She sounded like the wait would be unendurable.

"Think about everyone who knew Libby and Luke's movements; try to remember anyone suspicious, any strangers who've been in our home in the last couple of months." He knew she desperately needed to be occupied.

"OK. Call me when you get there." Her last word disintegrated as she rang off.

Carla had checked Will in online so he skipped the crowd at the rental booth and picked the nearest blue Volvo S40 from the rows of luxury cars, SUVs and outlanders in the covered lot. The valet sensed his impatience and cut his happy vacation patter short before handing over the keys.

Will slung his bag and laptop into the back seat, punched the zip code into the Sat Nav and took the car out of neutral. He accelerated to the exit, but had to join a long line of vehicles waiting to leave. He regarded the red dot of his destination and felt a current of panic. As he waited, he felt like he was sealed in the vacuum of his worst possible nightmare.

The line shifted slowly.

CHAPTER EIGHT

Will usually relished driving in the States. It always presented a challenge to his usual road reflexes, but now it was the last thing his overtaxed nerves needed. He almost missed the north exit sign and had to swerve suddenly into the middle lane for SR-528. The signs changed from airport brown to the regular green and he settled into the lunchtime pace of the busy freeway into downtown Orlando.

He looked at his watch. It was still on UK time – 5.55pm. The skeleton staff at Ingram would soon be heading for home leaving Carla there alone. He still couldn't help feeling leaving her was a mistake.

Watching the Sat Nav and trying to monitor the lanes distracted him from further speculation. He headed towards International Drive and Interstate 4. The cloudless blue skies and unfiltered sunshine had him squinting his eyes as he attempted to negotiate the traffic.

As he settled into the rhythm of the road, gift malls, miniature golf courses and steak houses started to pop up either side of the freeway. Their neon looked dull in the daylight. It was a place waiting to come alive, waiting to put on its show. His kneecaps trembled as he worked the pedals and took a long sweeping right to the 528 heading west.

He calculated Libby to have been twelve years old the one and only time they'd been to Orlando. They'd done the Disney thing.

He remembered how she'd gone missing from the line for "It's A Small World" and how he and Carla had frantically hunted for her, a dead heat between panic and nausea throughout every long second. That time had felt like hours, but it had been only minutes before they'd found her chatting to a gang of boys.

Boys had a mystique for Libby and she'd always been disproportionately grateful for any attention she got from them. He'd known she was going to be a handful long before her teenage years, dreaded what would happen when she was out of his sight. He wasn't one of those parents who was blinded by the idea of their own child's perfection, hadn't forgotten what he'd been like as a kid.

They'd at least been able to monitor the procession of male playmates that came to the house, but he couldn't remember at which point they became boyfriends. He was away from home so often during that time that he'd been stunned to have Carla show him the condom wrapper she'd found in her wastebasket. She'd been barely fifteen, but Carla hadn't been fazed by it, just relieved that Libby was being sensible.

A chunk of her childhood had whipped by without him registering it. A number of boyfriends followed, of all shapes and sizes, but Will had been waiting for her to get it out of her system before finding the right guy. He still wasn't sure Luke Chandler was. But the pregnancy had suddenly made him more than the occasional visitor to their home the others had been.

Libby had jokingly started to call Will Granddad. He hadn't even considered the implications of that. She was still emotionally immature and it was his fault. He knew he'd indulged her to compensate for his absence.

Libby only believed she was independent; at eight she'd announced she was leaving home to live in the tree house. Before her first night, however, a wild boar had escaped from Joe Sloman's neighbouring farmland and chased her though the grounds. She'd run terrified into the kitchen where they'd been waiting for her and comforted her as they'd comforted her each time things ended disastrously with her boyfriends. It made him feel powerless, like she was always going to be a victim of her own bad choices. He'd allowed her to make her biggest one by saying "Yes" to her trip away with Luke.

He halted at the toll. Tinny radio, body odour and hostility poured out of the window of the booth as he paid with a twenty-dollar bill. The obese male attendant blinked at him as he handed him his change, regarding him as if he had no business there.

Tam looked down into the street, one storey from ground level. He knew how noisy it would be to drop the metal ladder from the end of the fire escape and didn't want anybody behind the shuttered window beside him or in the bottom apartment to hear. He waited for a break in the conveyor belt of people below and then slid through the gap in the handrail. He hung down from it so his feet were as near the ground as possible and then dropped onto the paving.

His light frame easily withstood the impact. Tam rose from his crouching position and a large group of tourists obliviously swept past him, reeking of the perfume and aftershave they sold in the market.

He'd been on the streets at nighttime before, but he'd never walked around this late without his father. His mother had tucked him in and he'd pretended to be asleep. He prayed nobody else would come into his room until morning.

Tam didn't know the name of the street where the grille was, but knew his way to the night market and from there he was sure he'd be able to find it using the landmarks he'd memorised from his father's delivery round. Everything looked so different at night, though. Everything felt different. It was exciting, but at the same time he knew it was dangerous.

He left the commotion of the main street and took the short cut through the narrow passageway he used to get to the school van stop. It was pitch black and somebody passed him coming the other way. He turned to watch them take shape as they emerged into the orange glare of the street – a broad man in a silk shirt. He paused to light a cigarette and looked back down the passage in Tam's direction.

Tam turned and trotted quietly towards the other end, his shoulder scraping the wall as he kept to one side in the hope that he'd slip by anyone else he ran into. He needed a cigarette now; he wanted to suck on the filter of one of his father's discarded smokes and watch the glow die as he took the last vapours into his lungs.

Suddenly he was tempted to go back, climb up the fire escape and into the warmth of his bed. But in front of him was a needle of light and, as his scurrying feet widened it, he wondered if Songsuda might be somewhere beyond.

He told himself she couldn't be the girl behind the grille, that the scream he'd heard could have been anyone, but as he reached the end of the passage and let go of the breath he'd held clenched in his lungs, a larger part of him hoped she was there waiting patiently for him to rescue her.

Taxi horns jabbed their warnings at him as he zigzagged through the slowly rolling traffic and joined the throng of people on foot.

1815 North Street was off Highway 193. A restaurant that had a giant lobster on its roof squatted like a sinister landmark, the extended claw pointing in the direction the Sat Nav told Will to go. The road narrowed as he left the traffic. He passed tall, yellow hedges that revealed brief glimpses of the palatial properties behind them as he rolled by their closed, electric gates. He slowed at mailbox 1801 and then crawled, counting the gates, but finding 1815 much sooner than he anticipated.

The vacation villa lay at the end of a curved pathway demarcated by potted, spherical bay trees. He switched off the engine and got out of the car, noticing the dry heat for the first time. He stood at the gates, peering through the ornate leaves of black metal, but not wanting to touch them. His feet settled on the coarse gravel and the only sound was the buzz of an aeroplane overhead. Everything beyond the gates was still.

Will could still recall the starched feel of his dead father's sepia skin, as he lay motionless on top of the bed in the hospice. He'd fleetingly touched the back of his hand before the orderlies had taken him away on the trolley. It was the only time he'd witnessed death. Never death like this though. He knew the repugnance of the images hadn't even begun to prepare him for seeing it in reality.

He pulled his mobile out of his pocket; grateful he could speak to Carla. "I'm here. I'm outside," he said emotionlessly as soon as she picked up. He knew she'd be tracking him on the GPS and would be expecting his call. "Although I don't know how I'm going to get in."

"Ten minutes. Ten minutes and then I'm calling the police." She was nervous.

"I might need longer."

"Ten minutes."

CHAPTER NINE

The gate was set into an arch in the hedge. The hedge had been recently trimmed, leaving a small gap above the top prongs. Bar trying to scale or hack through the shrubbery, there was no other way in to the front. He wondered if there was a road or lane running behind the property, but it already felt like he'd been deliberating too long. He squinted at both ends of the street – no traffic or pedestrians. Will pulled on the chequered gloves.

The image of Libby on the website launched him at the gates and he found himself clinging below the prongs. He knew if he fell back he wouldn't be able to achieve the same take-off so curled his fingers painfully tighter as they took the weight of his body. The muscles in his sides fluttered from the exertion. He tautened his wrists, bent his elbows and dragged himself higher.

His frame shuddered as he took all of the weight into the crook of his arm and got his foot across the top of the gate. The prongs had gold-tipped leaves that were higher in the middle so he swung his leg over the lower end and shifted across to follow it. The points scraped his stomach as he dragged himself over to the other side.

He was just about to let himself drop to the pathway when something above him caught his eye. The aeroplane had written the words JESUS LOVES YOU against the blue sky.

A shower of leaves accompanied him as he landed hard on the balls of his feet and the impact reverberated harshly through his gut. Something had been pulled or, worse, ruptured, but he ignored the pain and turned towards the house.

He could hear wind chimes tinkling and the low rumble of traffic. But as he made his way up the path the sound tailed away – the tall hedges virtually soundproofed the pathway. He rounded the corner and the house with its mosaic-paned front door, familiar now from the website, came into view.

Will swiftly climbed four dirty, white marble steps and was in front of the door, not knowing whether to ring the brass bell set into the stone panel beside it. He rang it anyway.

He wanted the door to open; wanted whomever it was that had summoned him to greet him, for whatever purpose. But his instructions were implicit and he knew nobody inside would unlock it and release him from his task. After half a minute of waiting he peered through the coloured glass, seeing a red-and-green distortion of the hallway. It was empty, wooden-tiled. Several closed doors led off it, and a low seating area was to its right.

He went back onto the gravel, his feet broadcasting his presence as he made his way across the front of the house and round the side. He could hear the low hum of a generator and smell charcoal smoke. A double garage was at the end of a second driveway, a blue Chevrolet and silver Oldsmobile parked in its shaded interior.

He reached a green, wooden side gate with a heart shape cut out at its centre. He peered through and saw the turquoise water of a swimming pool. He pushed on the gate and its large spring squawked at him. The expansive decked area beyond it presented a conventional image of a vacationing family's occupations. Some fluffy blue towels were stacked on a table alongside an array of lotion bottles and an iPod dock.

Then he saw the blackened food on the barbecue and the muddy footprints leading from the open back door, across the decking and to the white tiles at the edge of the pool. He hesitated at the doorway, muzzling his fear. But as he moved into the house the footprints got darker. He realised they were blood and that they'd been sun-dried brown outside. On the kitchen tiles they still had a dull glisten, some of them smeared by a fainter set coming back into the house.

He moved through the large kitchen to an open door and found himself looking down the hallway. To his right were the set of doors he'd seen from the other side and to his left was a turning to the bottom of the stairs. More bloodied footsteps there. A dark copper slick led from the rug, across the hallway and was cut off by the closed door to his right.

His nostrils discerned something his brain had rarely had to process before, the intensity of which he'd only ever had a suggestion of when he'd visited his father's hospice. It was the aroma every human sense recoils at. His circulation thundered and he put his fingers to the handle and pulled down.

The door mechanism clicked. He put the tips of his gloved fingers against the glazed pine and exerted just enough pressure to swing it inward. He braced himself for what he'd discover the other side, but found himself looking at a framed mural of a cave painting of buffaloes that covered the opposite wall. An ornamental table and chairs were positioned in front of it. He would have to step right inside the room and peer around the door.

Before he moved his body forward he felt the cold presence of the room's occupants brush over him and sting the sweat patch at his back. He gripped the handle again and turned his body to look around the edge of the door.

The family were seated on the couch as they had been in the photograph. A sudden movement made him recoil. For a split second he thought the bodies had made an abrupt motion towards him, but he realised the flies coating their faces had been briefly startled enough to leave their hosts before quickly returning.

Will's senses recoiled against what lay putrefying on the other side of the room. He had to move close to them and tried to focus on the coloured beads around the father's left wrist. As he released the handle and followed the blood path to the couch, the cool neon blue of the pool water glowed beyond the slatted blinds.

He wished he could cover his eyes as they covered their own. They were at least shielded from the spectacle of their own bloodshed. He reached the couch and grabbed quickly for the mulberry coloured beads, grasping a couple against his palm.

The bracelet was tight, pinching into the father's stocky wrist. The beads were connected by wire. The pudgy fingers taped to the dead man's face had to be unstuck before Will could pull it over his hand. He briefly considered getting a knife or scissors from the kitchen to cut the wire, but knew if he left the room he wouldn't return.

He repositioned himself, hearing the blood in the rug crackle under his weight. He moved the beads up to the father's knuckles. Then he grasped the back of his cold hand and yanked it away.

The tape ripped revealing the blackness of a hollow socket where his left eye should have been. Will could see inside the man's skull. The hole looked like it had been burnt into the man's head. He looked down and at the human gristle hanging from his stomach and the caked blood gluing him to his family.

Will gripped the bracelet and pulled it up and over the fingers, all the time the flies landing and taking off from the skin exposed between the gloves and his sleeves. The movement caused the father's other hand to come unstuck. Another carved out hollow where his eyeball should have been. Both crooked elbows remained stiffly in position.

Will had to get out of the room now, not see the twin craters in the man's face anymore. He staggered from the lounge and slammed the door behind him as if he were being pursued.

••••

Tam listened with lips clamped firmly shut. The air coming through the grille was cool, but the putrid smell that accompanied it stung his nostrils. He held his breath and listened.

Nothing. He jammed his index finger in his other ear and flinched; pain from the blackened nail he'd been trying carefully not to touch anything with. He turned from the grille to examine it and took a few deep breaths before returning to his position.

There was a sound, a faint puttering underneath the gush of air through the slats. He pushed the flesh of his ear flush against the concrete, but this blocked it and he heard even less. Tam stood up, his bare legs shaking from crouching.

Whatever the sound, it was nothing like the one he'd heard earlier that day. He looked quickly over his shoulder, expecting to find someone looking down at him. He was in a place he shouldn't be at a time he wasn't meant to be awake. He examined the grille and the metal shuttered window above it. It wasn't connected to the Eastern Wish where they made their deliveries. The dirty, mushroom-coloured building had a set of double doors that had been chained shut. Tam's lips moved as he tried to read the sign pasted inside the dirty glass.

CLOSED PENDING HYGIENE EXAMINATION

There was some other finer print below that, but even when he squinted, Tam couldn't read it through the grubby pane. He walked the length of the wall, away from the breakfast café, and came to a corrugated iron shed next to it. It looked small from the front, but extended the length of the long, junk-strewn alleyway beside the building. Tam could see the lights of fast flowing traffic at the end. As soon as he thought about going down there, a dog barked a warning from one of the tenements on the right. His bladder felt very full.

Ten steps. That's all he'd take. Ten steps and he'd turn back.

He counted them loudly in his head, taking a breath between

each one. Ten became twelve, twelve became fourteen. At sixteen he could see from the weak light shining out of the windows of the tenements that there were no doors or windows for the entire length of the shed. Up ahead of him, however, was a tripwire of thin yellow light, extending across the path about four feet away from him. He moved forward to investigate, pausing when his foot upset a hubcap full of water.

When he reached the light he could see it was escaping from a gap in the corrugated iron. Tam put his eye to it and saw the circular blue neon of a flycatcher inside and the dark shapes of industrial equipment. Two luminous squares glowed feebly beyond. Tam guessed they must be swing doors and, from their position, he could tell they led into the main building. No other lights were on. If Songsuda were inside, now would be the time to rescue her. But the prospect of trying to find his way around in the dark contracted his bladder even further and he suddenly needed to relieve himself.

He urinated against the opposite wall, all the time looking up at the open, second-storey window above him and the ceiling shadow of somebody using an ironing board. The pee kept coming and he looked down at it gathering up fragments of soil and dried moss the rain had washed from the roof above. It snaked and bubbled around his sandals and he stepped out of the pool as he finished and quickly zipped his shorts back up.

Emptied out, he felt less panicky and looked back to the street he'd entered the alleyway from. Less than twenty steps and he would be back out onto the main road. No distance at all.

The gap in the corrugated panel wasn't big enough for him to crawl though, but after briefly checking the lit window again, he gripped its edge. Tam wrenched it and it shuddered loosely, the still-warm metal bending towards him like the upturned corner of a page. Three tugs gave him the aperture he needed. Still nobody was peering down into the alleyway to investigate.

He slipped through the gap, metallic edges scraping his skin as he wriggled through. Every sound he made was suddenly on top of him and he wanted to return to the fresher air. The smell he'd detected earlier was overpowering here, and there was the aroma of sawdust mixed with it as well. He could taste it in his mouth.

He stood motionless for a moment and listened, hearing nothing but his own small breaths. He put his palms out in front of him. They immediately touched something cold and metallic. Realising it was the edge of a worktop; he ran his fingers along it. Tam felt his way to the corner and down the thinner end of it towards the neon flytrap and the swing doors to its left.

His sandals squeaked on tiles and his fingertips butted the door. He pushed and they swung noiselessly open. The area beyond was dimly illuminated. Thick pipes lagged with yellowing fibreglass ran the length of the peeling walls. Dirty, transparent drapes filled a doorway at the far end.

The other direction ended in darkness so Tam turned right and headed for whatever lay beyond the plastic strips. The screeches of his sandals against the polished grey floor echoed loudly, so he removed them and padded down the corridor.

He stopped and peered through the jaundiced and scratched curtain into the gloom. It was a factory floor. More flycatchers glowing blue were fixed up high and extended to tiny pinpricks at the far end. His black nail throbbed. Tam pushed through the drapes.

As soon as he emerged the other side the smell of disinfectant scalded his nostrils and he could hear the sound he'd heard at the grille, only much louder now. Its volume over the buzzing of industrial fans made it easy to identify. It was the rippling sound of many birds; a current of plaints and nervous babble and Tam could see why they sounded so agitated.

Will couldn't remember scaling the gate again. He just sat in the car wiping at the backs of his wrists, still feeling the legs of the flies there. He'd removed the gloves, but his hands felt tacky. He opened his right palm and the coloured beads of the bracelet lay hotly against it.

He'd intended to drive immediately back to the freeway, stop off at a diner and use the bathroom. But the atmosphere of the lounge was still heavily draped over him. He grabbed the mobile from the dash and got out into the fresh air again. He had no idea how long he'd been in the house.

"Will?" Carla waited for him to reply.

Will looked up and down North Vine Street and then walked towards the grass verge on the other side of it. "I've got the bracelet." He could almost feel the air of her exhalation. "Those people..." His own voice sounded muffled as he focussed on the dried yellow leaves of the hedge in front of him.

There was silence from the other end.

"...I don't think I can leave them in there like that."

"You have to." Carla's voice barely registered.

Should he tell her what had been done to their eyes?

"Where are you now?"

Will felt warm air on his neck, but the sound of the passing car only registered when it disappeared onto the freeway end of the street. "Still outside the house, I should get out of here." He looked back at the gates and saw his own faint, bloody footprints leading from the Volvo to where he was standing.

CHAPTER TEN

Carla stared at Will's desk telephone, her body perched on the edge of the swivel seat and her weight resting on the tips of her toes. He'd said he would call when he'd got clear of the house. Her eyes briefly shifted to the computer screen to her right. Her damp palm moved the mouse so the cursor slid to the cut out house next to the one Will had just visited. It hadn't become active yet, no red outline, no address in a box.

She had no doubt the information would appear shortly and that Will would soon be heading there. It looked like whoever was manipulating him had deftly engineered the route.

She glanced at the desk telephone and considered calling the police as she had every other minute she'd waited. The kidnappers' instructions had been categorical, but Carla doubted whoever was capable of the butchery in the family's lounge could ever give Libby and Luke back alive.

She drove the thought away before it could get a foothold. Didn't they have more of a chance of locating them if the authorities were involved? How would she ever forgive herself if she didn't give them that extra chance?

Her hand shot to the receiver and her fingertips rested on the plastic. Luke's parents? The police? The touch became a grip and she heard the click as she lifted it from the cradle. It was lightweight, but felt leaden in her wrist.

"Need me for anything else, Mrs Frost?"

The question was like a rivet shot into in her chest and she almost dropped the handset.

"Sorry." Nissa waited for Carla to share her amusement at having made her jump, but her face blanked when it wasn't reciprocated. "Sorry."

"That's OK. No, that's all. Please... go on home. Spend the evening with your family."

Nissa nodded uncertainly. "OK. The other files you wanted are being sent up. Give me a ring at home if you need anything... at all. I'm there all evening." Her tight red smile was a seal of the promise as she pulled the door shut behind her.

The sound seemed to cut her off her from everything outside of Will's office. Nissa was going home for a routine Saturday evening with her husband and boys. She wondered if she would ever have the luxury of such ordinariness again. Carla looked across the spotless blue carpet to herself smiling with Libby in the photo on the display cabinet. When she considered the photos that had just been posted, the happiness there seemed fictitious. She thought of the new life inside her daughter's drugged body and the metal ropes biting into the skin of her shoulder.

She rose and walked unsteadily to the water cooler. She put both hands on top of it and tried to take some breaths. Carla glanced at the daunting stack of folders on the desk. What did she hope to find within them? Anything but the contemplation of how the situation could end. She couldn't conceive of a world without Libby.

She'd held Jessie for less than a minute, but her absence was still a vacuum within her every time her name was uttered. They hadn't wanted to know the sex when they'd been given the choice. Had decided to name them Jessie whichever way it had gone.

Her lifeless twenty-week-old body had been placed in her arms and the midwife had persuaded them to have a picture taken. There'd been no camera. The midwife had captured it with her phone. It was the only photo that existed of her. A low resolution snap of a low resolution moment, a tiny face like a shrivelled bud that would never open. Carla had bled internally and only emergency surgery had saved her. She'd lost so much blood she'd been delirious as Will had uncertainly leaned into the pillows and circled them both with his arms.

But they'd both been glad the picture had been taken. Knew why the midwife had persuaded them. Jessie's existence in the world, however brief, had been recorded and the image had helped them both reconcile themselves with what happened. Less than a minute later the room and everyone in it had drained away and she felt Jessie's fragile weight lifted from her hands.

Jessie's brief presence still resonated profoundly with both her and Will. How could they ever withstand Libby's removal from their lives? She walked back to the desk, opened another file, but couldn't see the contents. A sense of darkness came at her from all sides and a familiar claustrophobia trickled into the joints of her shoulders.

Even though Will was being manoeuvred on the other side of the Atlantic, he was at least occupied and not imprisoned to envisage what they would have to face. She couldn't allow herself to think that way; even if the fear of it burnt through everything she tried to occupy herself with. If she folded in on herself now, it wasn't going to help Libby one bit.

She told herself she had to focus on what she could control, even if that was virtually non-existent. Every minute was valuable. Analyse the people Ingram had dealt with in Chonburi and Rayong, scrutinise the details of anyone who had recently entered their lives. She tried to perceive a presence – define a face that united outwardly harmless moments of the weeks leading to the abduction.

If Libby hadn't been taken she wondered if Will would have shown her the site displaying the photographs of their home. Would he have concealed it to protect her? And was there

anything else he'd protected her from even if his motives had
been honourable?

She tried to concentrate on the information in front of her.
Libby and Luke had to be imprisoned for a reason. She prayed
a ransom demand would be issued soon but, looking at the
website, it didn't seem like one was imminent. If not, there had
to be a justification, some locatable motive for all this.

In the suffocated blue light coming through the open ceiling
shutters, Tam continued his examination of the machinery. He'd
watched his mother dispatch chickens using a cleaver blade to
the neck, had seen plenty of them escape headless at the market.
But he couldn't begin to imagine how many hundreds of birds
the conveyor of hooks over the metallic troughs in front of him
silenced every day.

When his mother's blade connected with the board it wasn't
the squawk of the animal that unnerved him, it was the moment
it stopped. That was when he held his breath; like a split-second
prayer.

He looked up, hypnotized by the feathers floating in concentric
rings in the currents from the fans, dirty white turning black
against the hazy, teal sky outside. They were everywhere,
circling the floor, brushing his face and sticking to the congealed
blood on the hooks. Tam knew it made no difference how much
further he went. He was far enough away from home now –
beyond the rescue of his mother and father.

Light outlined a large set of double doors at the far end of the
factory floor and he made towards them, his bare feet slapping
the warm tiles.

He put his eye to the crack and, when he was sure there was
nobody else in the cavernous area the other side, pushed the
door slowly open. Tam was in an enclosed loading bay. Two
delivery lorries were parked to his right, the large, red shutter
behind them sealed. To his left, on a raised concrete platform,

were a couple of refrigeration units. Beyond them was a flight of stairs leading down. He scurried along the metal gantry in front of them. The door to the first cold room was closed, but the second was ajar. Inside he glimpsed shelves containing crates of packaged chickens. Then he saw another entrance.

It was a small security cabin tucked at the side and the light and TV within were on. Tam looked around in panic and then heard a door slam. He located the sound. Somebody was emerging from the chemical toilet against the wall behind the parked lorries. He headed for the stairs.

He quickly descended two flights of rough concrete steps, stopping at the first to put his sandals back on. They didn't lead out onto the street though. He found himself in a warm, dark, low-ceilinged area and the sound of the frightened birds was in the air like an electrical charge. Tam worked out he was walking back in the direction he'd just come, underneath the factory floor. The odour here was like an assault and his chest tightened itself against it.

As his eyes became accustomed to the darkness he could see grimy white shapes scuttling quickly out of his path. It felt soft underfoot and smelt like the bottom of his hamster's cage magnified a thousand times. He heard an impact from the level above him and trotted on. Tam thought of his bed at home and the way his parents quietly stacked the dishes away so as not to wake him and his face started to tighten. But terror held his tears inside his head and although his legs kept moving him away from one danger he wasn't sure if there was something worse waiting for him up ahead.

Something struck his face hard and he instinctively put his hands up to knock it away. His fingers closed around something solid. It was a switch on a wire hanging from the ceiling. He held it firmly in his hand and looked back. He couldn't even make out the steps. The door above must have closed. It felt like he had two hearts beating in his chest. Should he turn it on? Maybe for a few seconds, just to see where he was and if there was a way out. He could be wandering around down here forever otherwise.

The switch was stiff and the edge of it cut into the pad of his thumb as he tried to push it. Tam felt dizzy and hoped he wouldn't pass out as he had the couple of times he'd rolled too many oil barrels. Then his father had made him sit on the edge of the road with his head between his knees.

He gripped the thick flex that connected the switch to the ceiling and managed to push in. Nothing happened. Birds brushed past his bare legs as he waited at the end of the wire. Then blinding, circular halogen bulbs clicked on and his eyelids tightened against the sudden, hot light.

He squinted as the living carpet of birds tried to move away from him, their dirty feathers and burnt kneecaps wedging together. Tam saw the door to his left first; a thick metal panel on runners with no obvious lock or handle. He glanced back at the steps and was relieved to see nobody coming down them. Would he have to go back that way if he couldn't open the door from this side?

He returned his attention to the sealed exit and that was when he saw the girl sitting inside the cage.

CHAPTER ELEVEN

Tam held his breath.

It wasn't Songsuda. His sister was slender and slightly built. The girl in the chicken wire cage was slim as well, but her limbs were much more sturdy. Even though she was seated and a handful of prisoner chickens pecked around her, he could also see she was significantly taller as well. She wore a dirty blue nightdress and her tanned calf muscles were locked against the low plastic seat she was squatting on. It looked like a potty. Tam was relieved to see a large padlock on the door of the cage.

She must have heard him moving around. She was as motionless as he was. He bit his mouth shut so she couldn't hear his heart stamping his chest. Could she hear anything at all through the black hood on her head? The thick blue plastic wire that secured it around her neck reminded Tam of his mother's washing line.

He looked at her boobs. Quickly first and then allowed himself a more lingering examination. Songsuda's were only tiny bumps like his mother's. These stretched her nightshirt as her chest heaved for breath.

He quickly surveyed the rest of the chicken house. The halogen bulbs had illuminated a large stack of cages at the far wall, but they were all empty. The girl was alone here.

He remained frozen and tried to estimate how much noise he'd already made. He'd agitated the chickens, but his feet had made hardly any noise on the soft layer of litter and droppings. Had she heard him turn on the light?

Her head suddenly twisted left and she leaned forward on her perch as if trying to listen through the hood. He gritted his teeth and crouched low, but didn't know why. She couldn't see him. Why was she wearing the hood? Was she so ugly that she had to conceal her face? Tam remembered the old lady who used to live in their old complex. Her bottom jaw had been missing. His mother and father had always shown her great respect, as if somehow they couldn't see her hideous appearance.

Maybe this girl had the same problem. Perhaps that's why she was locked away here. He wished the old lady had been. He and Songsuda had dreaded meeting her on the stairs.

The girl swivelled her head the other way and he could hear bubbles rattling in her nostrils and mouth. She spoke, shortly and sharply. Tam couldn't understand what she said. He was sure it was the language of the tourists, but it was muffled, as if she had something in her mouth. From the tone, he knew it was a question though.

She repeated it, but he didn't respond.

The girl locked rigid and the hood suddenly exploded with anger. The words vibrated from her chest, her voice rusting in her dry throat and her body thrashing on the seat. For a moment he thought she had no arms from the elbows down. But as he took a few paces back he could see her wrists were tied behind her spine.

She was dangerous. That was why she was locked up like this. Could she escape? His imagination raced as he envisaged what would happen if she broke out of the flimsy wire cage. This was a place he shouldn't have seen until he was much older. It was time to run.

Tam snatched air into his chest. He realised he'd have to pass in front of the cage to get to the sliding door behind it. The chickens inside and outside her cage babbled louder and flapped up loose feathers, echoing the frenzy in her voice as she screamed at him again. This time the alien words were fractured by sobs. The noise was sure to bring someone down to investigate. They'd probably call the police. How would he ever explain to them or his father what he was doing here in the middle of the night?

Tam made a dash for the door, not even peeping at the cage as he passed it. He could hear her yells burning at his back as he looked for a handle or lock, but the metal in front of him held only a distorted reflection of his terror. He anticipated the hood appearing beside it and feeling her hands at his shoulders.

He looked down and saw the pedal. It was a black and circular and jutted from the bottom of the door. Tam stamped it with his foot and felt its solid impact reverberate in the bone of his leg. But the door didn't shift.

He remembered a similar mechanism in the cold room of one of the restaurants he and his father delivered to and put his toes underneath the pedal. He prised it up, pressure against his bare toes as it refused to give. Then there was a sudden hollow click and bottom of the door was released. Tam got his fingers around the edge of it and yanked it along the runner.

He heard something heavy and metallic rolling in the loading bay above and remembered he'd left the lights on. If the person from the security cabin came down they'd immediately know he'd been there. He turned, spotting the switch swinging on the wire.

He closed his eyes and bolted back to it, his toes connecting with the soft bodies of the chickens. He didn't open them until he'd used both thumbs to push the switch back off and everything was in darkness again. The girl didn't stop screeching as he swerved around the cage and sprinted back to the door.

Tam didn't feel safe until he'd passed through the gap of gloomy light the other side of it and had slammed it back into position. He could still hear the girl, but the depth of the door and the sound of the chickens smothered her. Cool air goosebumped his bare arms and legs. He realised he was outside and at the bottom of a tarmac ramp.

The door juddered back so a small gap let the screams escape again. As he ran Tam didn't pause to consider what was at the top of the road.

Will squeezed himself into a tight cubicle in Burrito Joe's and looked at the plate of food he'd picked at random from the buffet counter. It was ludicrous to try and eat after what he'd just seen. But he knew the light-headedness he was experiencing was because his body was refusing to function on caffeine alone.

He took a bite from a meat-filled pancake, ground it, but couldn't swallow. A rotund and goateed diner sitting in the far cubicle watched his attempts. A waitress refilled the man's cup, but he didn't break eye contact with Will.

"No… thanks," he said, as she came over to Will's table. Hearing his own British accent made him feel even more conspicuous. He pulled his mobile out of his pocket, dialled and used it as an excuse to turn away from his observer.

"I'm clear," he said, as soon as Carla picked up.

The line fizzed. "Are you… OK?" Her tone said she knew what a hopelessly inadequate question it was.

"I can't really talk." How suspicious did that sound?

"Have you called the number?"

"Just about to." He hinged open the lid of his laptop.

"Shall I do it?"

He visualised her sitting alone in his office. "No. I will."

"It was still engaged a couple of minutes ago, but maybe they'll only receive calls from your mobile. Try to reason with them…"

"They haven't spoken to us yet. Look, I really can't talk here."

"I'll keep an eye on the website. Call me if you do make contact with them."

"I will." He couldn't think of anything else to add.

Nor could she. They both hung up at the same time.

He waited for the laptop to boot up and glanced around. He'd scarcely taken in the place as he'd entered. Just beyond his studious observer was a dimly lit Internet café, but the two men having a low conversation there didn't look as if they were surfing. On the radio Tom Petty was "Free Fallin".

His shivered at the thought of his drop from the gate. He took a second mouthful of the pancake and tried to choke it down. The smell of stale fat was suffocating and the hollowed out eyes of the family he'd left behind bored into his memory.

He was just accessing his emails when a hiss announced the presence of someone standing beside him. He turned to find a frown of hostility. The short stack of a man was at eye level and had his remaining straggles of hair pulled into a tight ponytail.

"Sorry, sir, you'll have to use the computers provided." He sucked another breath from his inhaler – the source of the hiss – and nodded to the area at the back of the restaurant.

"It's OK. I'm nearly finished." But Will sensed his transgression had already attracted unwanted attention from the other diners in the restaurant.

"It's ten dollars an hour. You can pay me now."

"There's obviously coverage here. I'm happy to pay, but can I just finish off what I'm doing at this table?"

"This is an eating area. That's the Internet area. Not my rules. I'll take the ten dollars and you can finish in there. You can take a beverage with you, but no food." He hinged the lid of Will's laptop shut like he was grinding an insect flat.

Will sat motionless momentarily and then rose without a word and pulled the money out of his wallet. "Ten dollars."

"Another ten bucks if you need more than an hour."

"I won't."

'Most of the guys here don't. There's no safe browsing here. Knock yourself out." He smiled without using his eyes.

As Will picked up his laptop the two men rose and moved past him. He seated himself in front of the first computer in the row of four. He used the grubby keyboard to sign into his emails via his Ingram account and found the image of Libby.

He entered the digits on the sign round her neck into his mobile so he wouldn't have to look at it each time. But then maybe that's what he needed to see. He dialled.

There was a beeping sound from the cubicle opposite and Will made eye contact with his fellow diner again. He'd pulled his paunch from behind the table and was standing up to reveal the dark blue police uniform he was wearing. The walkie-talkie clipped to the belt of his trousers had been responsible for the noise. He slowly rolled his sleeves down over his tattoos.

Will turned away again pretending to study the computer screen, but saw nothing but the footprints of blood he'd left out of the house, up the driveway and through the gates of the murdered family. He'd wiped his shoes in the dry grass at the roadside, but now he wondered if there were any other droplets on his clothes, any telltale signs that he'd just fled a crime scene. Through the corner of his eye he could see the policeman dump some coins onto the table and take his time cleaning his moustache and goatee with a napkin.

The sound of caged birds poured into his ear again.

"I have the bracelet. Stop this," Will whispered into the mouthpiece.

The policeman paused and Will wondered if he'd overheard. He was trapped between recoiling from his presence and reaching out to him. He could tell him exactly what had happened in North Vine Street. Lead him to the location so the family could be released from their sick tableau.

The sound of panicked birds cut out.

The policeman dabbed at the hairs of his face. Will could hear the bristles against the cheap paper.

No police. And even if he told this officer everything, his tip-off and his obvious presence at the scene would necessitate him being taken into custody immediately. He looked up from the greasy monitor and the officer sauntered away from his cubicle and then angled his waist against the counter while he chatted to the cashier.

Will typed his name into a search engine, his fingers sticking to the keys. He opened up the website. There were six houses in the row besides his, one down and five to go. As soon as the police got into the villa and started to investigate, Will would quickly be implicated in the crime. The longer the family remained undiscovered the better it was for him. All he could do was wait for his next address.

The door slammed shut as the policeman left.

CHAPTER TWELVE

When the plastic pipe came the birds moved. A glow of yellow light seeped into the bottom of Libby's hood as it was untied at the neck and momentarily lifted. The rag was dragged from her mouth and the pipe inserted so its sharp end struck the back of her throat. The liquid in the pipe was lukewarm and the first time it had been placed on her tongue Libby thought she was being poisoned. But it was water. It tasted stagnant and of flower petals and she was only given a few gulps before it was yanked from her teeth.

Perhaps it was drugged. She still felt like her head was gyrating, twisting itself off her body. Then the food came; sickly and full of sugar, warm marzipan-tasting stodge with some sort of nut coating. Fingers pushed a few blocks of it into her mouth; fingers she could taste were sheathed in surgical rubber.

She ground her second ration slowly; knowing that whoever was feeding her was waiting to insert another piece. They appeared to grow impatient and stuffed the rag back into her mouth before she'd finished chewing.

Over hours, the waves of fear had finally subsided. Whoever was holding her liked to watch and no matter what she said to them or how much she screamed they never replied.

She'd decided to choke on the food whatever happened and started pumping her shoulders and retching. There was no reaction from the person standing inches in front of her while she spluttered around the wet bung in her mouth.

After what seemed like minutes, however, she'd seemed to convince them and the hood was swiftly lifted again and the rag removed. She tugged in air and the pipe was thrust back into her throat. She drew a few more droplets before it was extracted. The cloth was rammed back inside her mouth and the hood was secured tighter at the neck.

Did they realise she'd been testing them? Now she knew they couldn't let her die. But for how long? Were they demanding a ransom or was she being fed and watered for another use? She tried not to imagine what else she could be subjected to in this filthy place.

Libby's eyes still stung and she knew it was the ammonia of the chicken droppings she was sitting in. The darkness disoriented her and she tried to repel the surges of dizziness by fixating on an image of where she was by using what she could feel and hear. She was sitting on the seat of what she assumed was a low plastic commode and her knickers had been removed to allow her to urinate.

She knew she was in a cage somewhere damp. The chickens were all around her, their dry claws scratching the tops of her bound bare feet as they walked across them. Their beaks pecked at her shins, but it happened so often she no longer reacted. She could feel the resistance of something on the top of her head. When she tried to straighten, it bit into her neck, but gave slightly against her scalp. She assumed it was the chicken wire roof of the cage, which meant it was about four feet high.

She'd initially thought she was naked. But when she twisted her body she could feel the material of the nightdress she'd been wearing in the hotel as far as her hips. It had been lifted above her waist so she wouldn't soil it.

What else did she know? Not how many people were watching her. It could be one, it could be twenty. She also didn't know what had happened to Luke. She had a vague recollection of leaning against the heat of somebody's back and the flash of a camera before she'd been injected, but the details were as vague as her abduction. She had no memory of being driven or carried here, only of a shape in the dark of their hotel room and a sudden weight on her face. She'd breathed in the fumes coming off whatever had forced her head into the pillow.

Maybe Luke was nearby, imprisoned in a cage like hers. She could hear a reverberation of his voice in her head, his usually calm tone raised in aggression. She was sure there'd been a violent struggle in the hotel room. Libby could feel scratches on her face still burning. Luke's parents didn't have the sort of money that hers did. If it were a ransom he wouldn't be worth taking. Maybe they'd left him in the hotel room and he'd already reported her missing. Or maybe he was already lying dead there – or a few feet away.

Then she heard the sound of her captor's nostrils inhaling at her ear. Then a sudden pain, deep in her shoulder. She'd been bitten. She gritted her teeth, as her attacker moved away and slammed the cage door and locked it.

The wound throbbed and stung. She was alone with a psychopath and nobody knew where she was.

The sand grains stung his bare legs as the wind whipped it underneath his kneeling body. Raindrops pockmarked the beach around him and he was aware of his mother panicking to pack everything away. His prisoner in the rusted paint pot captivated him though, its sideways motion gaining momentum, clockwise circles becoming more frantic. It had been out of the water for a good while and bubbles were frothing at its mouth opening.

He could hear the raindrops inside his head, hard impacts on his skull. He opened his jaw to see if he could change the sound it made like he did when he flicked his cheek and modulated the sound with his puckered lips.

Flesh glistened within the cracks of the crab's shattered shell, but there was no way he would be able to eat the animal. It was too full of life. He could feel its vibration when he rested his fingers on its damp back. But, inside or outside the paint pot, it was helpless.

A shadow fell over the pot. He was stood behind him.

"Refill?"

Will caught his head before it could fall and looked around at the other occupants of the diner. He'd watched the waitress approach a truck driver at the front of the restaurant and she'd just reached him. He hadn't fallen asleep, but his mind had slipped a gear while it was idling.

He looked at his watch. 2.15pm. He needed some fresh air so got to his feet. He was about to sign out, but tried the cursor on the next house one more time.

Ellicott City,
Maryland,
PHONE WHEN YOU GET THERE

His mind blocked out the sounds of the diner. Maryland? The new coordinates made his journey along the entire scrapbook street ineluctable. He seated himself again and, as he nudged the arrow over the red brick townhouse, its outline and address appeared again. He clicked it and found himself looking at a new window displaying images of the interior.

It was an older looking residence with luxurious rugs at the centre of expansive pine floors. There were French windows, transoms over interior doors and a cluttered library lounge.

He dreaded finding the same horrific photo that had been posted of the villa, but nobody was present. He could see family portraits covering one wall of the kitchen, but the picture wasn't high resolution enough to be able to identify distinctive features.

Did this mean the people that occupied it were still alive? Why no address or zip code? He figured it was because he could alert the local police in advance. Even with Libby's life at stake, he still wasn't being trusted. With no accurate details there was no way he could warn them. But what item of clothing was he looking for when he got there?

He opened up a new window and located a map. Maryland bordered Virginia, West Virginia and the District of Columbia. Another quick search told him an average flight took just over two hours from Orlando International. And then he still had to locate the house. If he were to retrieve another item there he would have to be given more specific directions. He guessed they wouldn't be released until he landed.

About eight hundred miles away a family was oblivious to what was about to happen. The only thing Will could do was board a plane and hope he reached them in time.

He signed out, picked up his laptop and headed for the door.

His legs stopped working when he was halfway across the lot. He'd watched the flash of his headlights and heard the warble of the car being unlocked, but stood frozen with the remote clasped in his hand. There was no cramp. It was as if the lower part of his body just shut down, refused to be part of what he had to do. He couldn't take another step forward and suddenly he could feel his guts churning around the morsels of food he'd tried to digest. The laptop weighed heavy in his palm.

Grim images assailed him. The flies, the tattered ends of their insides, the dead sweat of the father's skin as he'd wrenched the bracelet free.

Just a few more paces. But his instincts told him not to get into the car and drive to the airport; told him what he would find when he got to his destination and in all the other houses he still had to visit.

He had to make it home, to believe that Libby would be there, however remote a chance it seemed.

Traffic noise poured into his ears and he found himself moving again, the Volvo shakily magnifying as he focussed on it. He tried not to acknowledge the pumping of his legs in case they stopped again. He opened the door, threw the laptop in the back and slumped into the seat. He placed his feet immediately onto the pedals and sealed himself in.

Faces peered at him from Burrito Joe's and from below the neon sign of the enormous liquor store next to it. He wondered how long he'd been stood motionless in the lot. He swiped Libby's bracelet from the well in the dash and examined the coloured beads. Will imagined her buying it at one of the flea markets she loved browsing. She could never have known the significance it would assume.

She'd probably paid very little for it, but he would put it back in her hand at any cost. He slipped it round his own wrist and turned the key in the ignition.

CHAPTER THIRTEEN

"Enjoy your vacation?" The same bemused valet who'd handed him the car keys took them back from Will less than three hours after he'd taken the car.

Having called Carla while he was stuck in traffic, his flight to Maryland was already booked. He made his way to the lounge to await flight 326. It still felt as if he had a thorn dragging at his gut, but he was glad of the discomfort because it kept him clear of the borders of sleep.

As he paced and waited and was processed into the boarding zone, the same thoughts went round in his head. Was Libby still sedated? If not, was she being fed? Was Luke able to look after her? He had to spotlight the questions concerning her wellbeing and not the cluster of darker ones that surrounded them.

When the plane pulled out onto the runway, he thought of the family he'd left behind in the villa, speculated about who they were and when their bodies would be discovered. Had they been chosen at random? It was unlikely, as he'd been summoned to that specific address. They had to tie in to Libby's abduction and the other houses that led to his front door. He couldn't even begin to make a connection between the murdered family and his own.

Perhaps they were from the UK and had been holidaying in Kissimmee. His memory tried to peer through the blood and flies to identify the father's face, but all he could see were the tunnels in his head.

A wave of self-recrimination washed over him. Would his father have allowed him to travel the distance Libby had when he was eighteen? The lack of money in his family would have precluded it but, if it hadn't been an issue, he seriously doubted he would ever have been given consent for such a trip. They were different times, but maybe the restrictive discipline he'd experienced as an only child was something he'd fought too hard not to replicate.

He'd spent a great deal of his childhood vexed by his parents' curfews and social restraints and a lot of time confined to his room for minor transgressions. His father had enforced all the discipline, but had never lifted his hand to Will. Not even raised his voice. But there was something more insidious in the household – an undeclared but tacit disenchantment.

His father was a botanist, acclaimed in his field, and had published over a hundred papers on photobiology. Will was a slow developer and had shown no aptitude for academia for the majority of his childhood. His mother was a part-time history lecturer and quietly serviced his father's disappointment with Will. By the time he'd stumbled on his aptitude for engineering they'd more or less resigned themselves to an unspectacular son. They'd funded his studies at Brunel, but they'd been in their sixties by then. Both heavy smokers, his father's pipe brought about his death from emphysema in his first year and his mother died of breast cancer in his second. Will felt he'd never vindicated himself.

Had he given Libby too much of the freedom he'd never received? He'd been conscious about spoiling her but, because of Carla's family background, Libby knew she could always ricochet between them to get what she wanted. It was how she ended up with their blessing and the capital for the holiday with Luke.

He studied his new destination again on the laptop. There

was no additional information in the pop-up box but, clicking through to the interior images, he could ascertain it wasn't a holiday home.

In the lounge, sheet music lay open on an upright piano and in the kitchen artwork was taped to the green tile surround of a mantelpiece. He wondered if they were sitting in the room now and if they were being watched via the same window the snapshot had been taken through. As all the photographs looked into the house there was nothing to give away its location.

He navigated round the rest of the site and noticed the picture of Libby on the mattress had been removed. None of the other houses in the row were active and the message above them was unchanged.

• THIS NEIGHBOURHOOD ISN'T REAL BUT THE HOMES AND PEOPLE WHO INHABIT THEM ARE
• CAN YOU GUESS WHAT THEY ALL HAVE IN COMMON?

He clicked through to Easton Grey and the pictures of the rooms seemed like depictions of a life he'd never get back.

He opened a separate window and did a quick search for some stats about Ellicott. It was an historic city with a population of about sixty-one thousand predominantly white people served by the Howard County Police Department. The most dramatic thing to happen there was a tornado in 2001 that killed two people. Only twelve residents were registered sex offenders.

Ingram had never had any business in the district. Will had no connection to the place and knew nobody who lived there.

He spent the remainder of the flight skimming the cursor over the cut-out of the three-storey house and thinking of his young self, pacing the prison of his bedroom.

Looked like there was a Saturday night sleepover planned. From her vantage point, Poppy observed the child being walked to the front door by Mom. How old was she? Nine, ten? She could barely see over the Moxie Girlz sleeping bag she carried. Mother and daughter waited on the doorstep.

A harassed blonde in blue sweat pants and an oversized tee shirt answered the door, too young to be the lady of the house. Poppy had already guessed she was the nanny. There was a brief exchange between her and Mom and then the little girl was handed over – delivered for safekeeping. Mom bent to say something to her, but Poppy could see from the irritation on the child's face that a guarantee of good behaviour had already been promised on the drive over. She was holding her up from joining the others.

Poppy had watched three other girls turn up at the house already. The child turned from Mom and scuttled inside. After the same glibly humorous exchange Poppy had watched the other parents have with the nanny, the front door was sealed. Mom hurried back to the car, the engine still running. What was she doing tonight, something romantic maybe? Whatever it was, she was late. She took off without putting her seatbelt on.

Inside the house it would be popcorn, pizza, DVD then the compulsory exchange of secrets during lights out. She couldn't really conceive of what it was like to be that young again. Have nothing in her head but the innocent apprehension of what lay ahead. Later the girls would be breathlessly discussing the boys at school, then the specific one they could scarcely bring themselves to name.

She recalled only one fantasy she'd salvaged from her childhood. That of the red rose petals she'd dreamt of having scattered at her feet on the day of her wedding. It was like a faint echo of someone else's voice.

Through the front window of the lounge she could see the tops of the girls' heads as they looked up at the wall-mounted TV screen. Some sort of Wii game was underway. The nanny reseated herself at a stool behind the kitchen counter at the rear of the room.

Poppy applied the cherry lip balm to her mouth and considered how soon innocence was over.

Tam lay awake, the bedcovers and the familiarity of his room failing to make him feel as safe as he'd thought they would. He'd made it back, had managed to climb up the fire escape and slip under the sheets without his parents knowing he'd gone. The apartment was quiet, no panicking father or mother in the kitchen talking with a police officer.

Despite the discipline that would have been involved Tam felt disappointed. If an explanation of where he'd been were extracted at least he could tell them about the girl in the cage. It was a secret he didn't want, but he worried that confessing to his break-in at the chicken factory would prompt the sort of punishment Songsuda received. Would he be cast out into the street? After what he'd seen on his solo exploration he knew why his parents had warned him about being alone out there at night.

Maybe the girl in the cage had been disobedient. He knew what he'd done was against the law. Was that how it had begun for her until they had no choice but to lock her away? He wondered if he'd end up in a cage if he refused to listen to what he was told.

He'd learnt his lesson tonight. Now he realised why he had to be an adult to walk around after the sun had gone down. The adults were welcome to what was below his window. The thought of Songsuda being out there all the time she hadn't been at home made him feel like he was suffocating every time he closed his eyes.

He wanted to feel safe again, the way he had before. He got up and made sure the door was tightly shut then positioned one of his pillows along the gap at its bottom before turning on his lamp. If the light shone across the hallway to their bedroom he knew his parents would be in to tell him to switch it off. But he didn't want to be in the darkness with his unwanted companion, didn't want to think of the sounds she'd made as he'd fled over the corrugated gates.

He counted. At four hundred and forty-six he fell asleep, but dreamt about feathers blocking his mouth and trying to flee from someone and not being able to move his legs, like his ankles were fused together.

CHAPTER FOURTEEN

Teddy Boy Pope fought his pants off over his sneakers and threw them to the back of the News 55 OB vehicle like they were a pair of venomous snakes.

"Nice boxers." Weaver appraised them from his perch on the step between the open doors where he was checking his camera and chewing nicotine gum. "Big *Family Guy* fan?"

Pope peered over the overhang of his belly and could just see the edges of them. They were a Christmas present from Lenora depicting some cartoon show he'd never seen "I can feel a draught. Is everything contained?" It was ninety-one and climbing and he only needed to look presentable from the waist up.

Weaver considered his answer and continued to pump up his jaw with the gum. "Like petrified bats in a cave." Weaver was Pope's occasional cameraman. He liked to wisecrack, but left himself open to assault by being barely thirty and having wispy blonde hair that had receded exactly halfway across his scalp. It was an unspoken agreement that everything was fair game except if it was related to either of their follicles.

Pope loosened his tie and turned to the other news reporters limbering up at the crime scene tape like it was the start of a sprint. It was stretched between telegraph poles either side of North Vine Street which kept everyone a significant distance from the gates of the villa.

He didn't know anybody there. Some of the younger police and reporters recognised him though. They treated him like the bachelor uncle at a family gathering, with a mixture of affection and pity. He was fifty-five and they all knew he used black dye on his sideburns as well as his signature quiff.

He'd lost the hunger and aggression, knew his extra pounds and the way the breath caught in his throat made him want to hang back. But he didn't mind that he was fast becoming the last resort of the channel. He'd had his moment of glory in 2008. It seemed like a career ago now. At fifty he'd been considering retirement and then it was all hands on deck when Tropical Storm Fay had made landfall and Bush declared the State of Florida a Federal Disaster Area.

He'd found himself collecting a Society of Professional Journalists Award for specialized reporting. "Your eye at the eye of the storm." He'd come up with that on the spur of the moment. Now it was all he was remembered for. Thirty years of journalism and crime reporting never mentioned. At a small channel weather events were like wartime. When it was over everyone went back to what they were doing before. Perhaps he'd been doing the wrong thing all along.

He was sick of loitering on the margins of people's grief. Hours of tedium and coffee that dried you out while the detectives worked the scene and occasionally came out to stare into the middle distance and tell you what you already knew. He took out his cell and called Lenora.

"How you doing?" She sounded sleepy.

Pope could never keep track of her erratic shifts at the nursing home and wasn't sure if she'd just come in or was about to leave. "Hot and peeved; doesn't look like I'll be home for pot roast." Lenora never cooked. It was their in-joke that only she still found funny. "Sorry to leave you home alone."

"Don't worry. I'll have a few of the girls over."

She tried to sound crestfallen, but actually seemed to brighten at the prospect. Lenora was thirty-three. She hadn't been anywhere or done anything. That had been her choice, but Pope never begrudged her the wine cooler parties she seemed to throw whenever he wasn't in the apartment. Trouble was, those occasions were getting less frequent and he didn't know if she would want him hanging around for anything more than their already dwindling weekend sex.

"Anything juicy going on?" She always asked.

"Family murdered in their vacation villa just off 193 and judging by the police presence – plenty juicy."

No new information had appeared by the time Will landed at Baltimore-Washington International so he dialled the number as soon as he'd stepped off the plane.

He nudged his way through the other passengers in the tight thoroughfare. "I've landed," he said loudly, as soon as he heard the familiar, panicked trill of birds the other end. He waited for the line to go dead, but it didn't. "Can you hear me?" Still the connection wasn't cut. He lowered his voice. "What am I looking for when I get there?" The caged birds babbled alarm. "If you want me to go on with this, I want to speak to Libby." The line clunked and the cacophony ended. "Bastards," he said with enough volume to turn several heads.

He jogged around trolleys and bags oblivious to protests. Will had told Carla not to book a car this time. A taxi would be quicker and who knew how long he'd be in the state. He joined the line outside the exit for the row of different coloured sedan cabs and got into the white Chevrolet that pulled up.

"Ellicott City," he said before he'd pulled the back door shut. He opened his laptop. How much battery power did he have left? He looked up and met the gaze of the driver. He could only see the beanie hat covering the back of his head and his eyes in the mirror. They looked like they'd been peering through smoke for a long time. "Let's get going. I'm just looking up the details. Get me there in quick time and you can double the fare."

The beanie hat nodded and the driver sat up, waggled his buttocks in his seat and pulled out. As they took Route 95 South towards Washington, Will opened the site and put his cursor over the house.

122 Hebron Street,
Ellicott City,
Maryland,
21068

He quickly relayed the details to the driver. Should he call the Howard County PD now? But Will had to get into the house before they did. Once they were on the scene he'd never get access to whatever item of clothing he had to secure. And would they arrive in much more time than he would? A family's lives were at stake though; he had to call the house.

He frantically searched for a local phone directory. The first one he found required a name. Then he found the Ellicott City reverse address search. He entered the address and zip code details:

(0301) 555-1212

He dialled the number and listened to it ring before realising it was an engaged tone. He tried the digits again and got the same result. He telephoned Carla and told her where he was headed and to keep trying the number.

Only then did he register it was getting dark.

The driver adroitly eased the cab through the evening traffic, but even his knowledge of the back roads couldn't prevent them from crawling to a stop as they reached the centre. Will continued to redial and only vaguely registered his surroundings. Ellicott City seemed like a model village after the wide expanses of Florida. Traditional house facades were dwarfed by lofty telegraph poles that lined the sidewalks.

The line remained engaged and Will remembered the burnt food on the barbecue in Kissimmee. He took the gloves out of his jacket pocket and slid them over his fingers. The action made him feel as if he were an assassin himself.

When the cab eventually pulled up at the address he got out and hurriedly fed some bills to the driver, not taking his eyes off the lit windows of the house. Beyond the low fence he thought he caught movement through the bay window. He double-checked the number on the mailbox: 122, it was the right place. The cab sped off, leaving him alone at the open gates.

He jogged up the crazy-paved driveway and then slowed, stopping halfway up it as the light from the lounge illuminated him and he could see inside. His breath stumbled in his chest. It was the last scene he expected to be greeted by. A party of young girls with painted faces were playing a Wii game in front of the enormous TV screen on the wall.

Had he been allowed to arrive in time? He looked back and up and down the street – nobody in sight. Daylight still had a weak grip on the sky, but most of the other homes were glowing from within. It didn't seem possible that anything could disturb the neighbourhood's early evening composure

Was somebody already inside? Or had something gone wrong? Regardless, he still had to attempt to collect an item of Libby's. He pressed the bell and took a step back, pulling his sleeve down to cover his gloved hand holding the laptop and hiding the other in his pocket. He hadn't heard it ring over the squeals from the party, but a shape appeared in the hallway and strode to the door.

"Can I help you?" The blonde girl had her face painted like a tiger.

"I'm here to pick up my daughter." If only it were that easy.

Mystification wrinkled the stripes. "They're all meant to be sleeping over."

"We have an emergency at home."

"Oh, sure." She nodded and removed her hefty frame from the doorway. "Which one is yours?"

"The one you've probably had most trouble with." The line came easily, having picked Libby up from her fair share of parties. He stepped into the hall and it smelt of popcorn and pizza. Will put his laptop on the seat of an ornamental armchair as casually as he could and flitted his eyes to the open rooms. In front of him was a door to the kitchen, to his right the lounge where the girls were and to his left a formal dining area with a long, polished table running the length of it.

"They're just finishing a vital match." The blonde strode ahead of him, pinning her short hair behind her ears. "Hope you didn't try calling the house earlier. We've had problems with the phones all evening."

"OK if I use the bathroom?"

"Sure, up on the right. Who am I summoning from the tournament?"

Will took the stairs before he had to reply. At the top of them he found the doors to darkened bedrooms open, but as he switched the lights on and briefly scanned each one he could hear the nanny ascending. She reached the landing as he was exiting the small guest room.

"What the hell are you doing up here?"

"Sorry, couldn't find the bathroom."

But her tiger face was snarling now and she registered the gloves. "Who did you say you're here to collect?"

Will brushed past her and descended the stairs. "I'm sorry. There's been a misunderstanding."

"You bet there has. You'd better get the fuck out of here." Anger and fear in equal measure.

Will hit the bottom of the stairs and moved past the lounge

where the clamour had ceased. There was no point trying to explain.

"I'm calling the cops," she screeched, higher than the kids.

And that was why. Will turned back to find her standing halfway down the stairs wrestling a mobile from her pocket. He couldn't allow himself to be detained. "I'm leaving now, wrong party. I do apologise." He grabbed his laptop and opened the door, trotting back down the drive. None of the rooms had resembled the ones on the site. What the hell was going on?

From the opposite window Poppy watched Will's exit from the house and smirked before she used her iPhone to change the address on the configuration page of the website. She waited as he moved away from the lights of 122 and then checked his laptop. He turned and looked directly at the property she was standing in.

He crossed the street and glanced up at her unlit window from the driveway. She snapped a photo of him with her iPhone and stepped back into the shadow of the room. Teenage decor and trophies surrounded her. Nineteen-year-old Greg had earned a scholarship to Baltimore University and his absence meant he was now the last surviving family member.

She'd still wanted a connection with him though so she'd slipped on the dark suit she'd found hanging in his wardrobe for a while. He'd probably wear it to the family funeral and she wondered if he'd detect a vague trace of her scent at the graveside. She'd hung it carefully back inside its silver grey PEVA suit cover, but she guessed it would probably end up the property of forensics.

She left the room. Poppy had upgraded 127 Hebron Street from an anonymous family home to an infamous murder scene, but nobody knew it yet. She speculated about the Ambersons in Florida. Did anyone else now know or were the repercussions of that event still being suppressed for Libby's sake?

She hit the bottom stair as the bell rang. Poppy could almost feel the urgent pressure of Will's finger as it jabbed the plastic button, but the oranges and lemons chime wouldn't be hurried. She reached the back door of the kitchen as he rapped the metal knocker. The sound became a light pecking as she crossed the lawn to the back gate.

She placed her fingers lightly on the latch and flicked it, leaving the gate ajar for him. Poppy paused, wondering if he would pick up her scent there as well.

The website had definitely specified 122. A cruel trick to convince him he'd made it in time? But how had they known exactly when to change the details? They had to be observing him. Will squinted at the empty cars in the street and then back at the house he'd just left. If the nanny had dialled 911 then he had to get out of sight as quickly as possible. He looked through the front window of 127 and could see the silhouette of the upright piano against a weak glow from a table lamp. There were no other lights on and he hoped it meant the family were out for the evening.

There was no way he could get inside via the oak panelled door or front window without attracting further attention from the neighbours. He hurried back onto the terrace and along the red-bricked townhouses, looking for a way into the back of the property via an adjacent street. Three gardens along he came to a gravel track between driveways lit by a single lamp that had a cluster of moths pinging against it.

As he strolled down it a young woman was coming the opposite way. As she passed under the lamp he could see she was carrying a canary yellow clutch purse against her chest. He absently thinned his mouth in the automatic gesture of friendly assurance. Her pronounced bottom lip tightened in response, but her dark eyes only darted momentarily to meet his. As she moved by him he turned left into the narrow lane.

Brambles were only just falling back into place after the woman had brushed past them and they tapped his shoulder and snagged the denim of his jeans. The smell of urine pricked his nose. He counted to the third gate and found it off the latch. This lapse of security seemed less foreboding than the lights being off at dusk. Either the occupants were actually out or no one was able to turn them on.

He pushed the gate the rest of the way open and looked up the lush, long lawn to the back of number 127. He could see the back door was open as it had been at the house in Florida. The black aperture seemed to shrink away from him as his instincts tried to restrain him from taking another step forward.

Libby's beads felt heavy around his wrist as light birdsong filled the silence. He strode up the centre of the lawn, his eyes darting to the tall row of conifers either side of him, trying not to contemplate the entrance until he was at the back step.

The sprinklers at the flower borders squirted to life and the rotating plastic and low hiss sounded like a warning from a coiled snake. The kitchen interior delineated itself as he reached the doorway. When he stepped inside he saw Libby.

CHAPTER FIFTEEN

Libby and Luke were positioned where they could immediately be identified as soon as Will switched the light on. A cluster of snaps covered the wall in front of him. A family of five sharing the same fair hair and toothy smiles grouped together across the years the images represented. Libby and Luke's faces were in a matte black frame at their centre.

He placed his laptop quietly on the counter and moved towards it. The photo was screwed into the wall by a bracket in the middle of the top edge. It was a recent shot; both of them smiling, cheeks pressed together and Luke concentrating as he'd held the camera at arm's length and took the picture himself.

He briefly considered they might actually know the people in the house, but the frame's position was too contrived. It was also not big enough to occupy the considerable gap it filled and he could see the outline of the much larger frame that had originally hung in its space. It was clothing he was to collect. Libby and Luke had been fixed in place to remind him who was at stake.

He hurriedly absorbed the rest of the room. There was the grand mantel with teenage fantasy artwork taped to the green tiles. Above it was a professional photographic portrait. The parents had three sons, one of them nearly an adult, the other two he estimated to be early teens. None of them were vaguely familiar.

The chairs were at angles to the table as if the occupants had recently pushed them out to leave. The dishwasher door was open and a half-load of dirty plates had been stacked inside. Two large silver bowls were piled high with dog food and biscuits. Where was the family pet now?

Will listened for signs of movement. The fridge purred, but there was another sound. At first he thought it was the beat of his own heart, but realised there was a muffled knocking coming from beyond the kitchen. He edged into the hallway. The aroma of stale incense was in the air and he looked along the runner carpet to the front door.

The doors to his left were open and the last dregs of evening light struggled through each. There were no windows in the hallway so the neighbours opposite wouldn't be able to see him there. Switches were to his right and he quickly flicked them all down. The bulbs buzzed as they illuminated the closed door beside them. The knocking was coming from behind it.

He pulled on its gold handle and it popped open. He was looking into the interior of a dark utility room. He grazed his glove on a rough cement wall as it sought a switch and found a string to pull. It clicked loudly, strip lights strobing the interior before pinging on. He faced a rack of detergents and fabric conditioners as well as a selection of brightly coloured tennis bats, skittles and a chewed, orange Frisbee.

A motor buzzed and vibrated and the smell of damp and detergent crept cold up his nose as he stepped into the room. It was L-shaped and he turned left, finding two washing machines tucked away at the end, under the recess of the stairs. One was chewing clothes through grey water and something inside it sporadically bumped the cylinder. He could see the dark shape of something nudge through the froth at the glass. As he moved towards it, the drone of the chest freezer to his right suddenly cut out.

He bent his legs in front of the portal and squinted through the dirty foam. Colours flashed and he waited for the knocking sound again. As if on cue, the machine stopped and started draining. He got a glimpse of a blue, rubber sole as it dropped from the top of the drum into the shiny dark clothes below. It was one of a pair of crocs and he assumed the other was buried beneath the rest of the load. He stood as the machine started filling again and turned to leave.

He knew he wouldn't be able to pass the chest freezer. Halted beside it, examining its slightly rusted lid. Cold water rushed through the pipes behind him as he estimated the white unit's depth and what could be fitted inside.

Despite the small fibre of hope he'd entertained, he knew the family hadn't gone out and left the back of the house open.

He gripped the lid handle and heaved it quickly up. Frozen meat greeted his eyes, trays of chops, bags of drumsticks and an enormous turkey all leaking white vapour. He peered down into the mist as the draught from the lid's motion sucked some of it out. Burgers and unidentifiable meat frost bitten and stacked high next to bags of corn and green vegetables; just the staples of a healthy American family. He let the lid drop heavily back into place.

He returned to the hallway. He hadn't seen anyone in the lounge when he'd peered in from the window outside. But he'd been looking across it and the floor had been below his line of vision.

It was one large through-lounge and he'd be able to take in the whole room by stepping through either open door. He stood in the frame of the first he came to and a board cracked as he crossed the threshold.

There was nobody in evidence, not arranged on the quilted throws of the couches at either end or lying on the Moroccan rugs. A clock ticked somewhere, but he couldn't see it. He had already turned to face the stairs.

He started to ascend immediately, his shoes pounding the

mauve carpet runner and the white painted wood sounding like it was splintering with every step. If he stopped he knew he wouldn't climb any higher.

When he reached the top he couldn't believe how dark it had got. A block of solid darkness filled the pane at the end of the landing and he quickly flicked down the switches he found to his left. The light revealed a dark shape lying underneath the window.

It was the dog, a red setter, curled tighter than it should have been if it was sleeping. Carla used to own a similar dog. She'd called him Apollo. He'd been one of the first rescue dogs she'd taken on. He walked towards it, but stopped at the open doorway to his left. It was a tiled wet room. Apart from a few towels piled on the floor, it was pristine.

He moved closer to the coiled pet and peered in the next. A boy's room, monster trucks and glow stars on the wall, duvet tangled at the foot of the bed. He advanced and found another similar – AC/DC and glamour girls as sexual as they were allowed to be by monitoring parents.

The room beyond, on the opposite side of the landing, obviously belonged to the eldest, lots of books and a dusty rowing machine. University pennants also signalled why it looked more like a guest room than a son's daily retreat.

He reached the dog and the final doorway. The red setter's head was crooked into its body and he could see solidified vomit on its fur. Poisoned first to make sure whoever had targeted the family wouldn't be disturbed?

Will didn't need to go into the parents' bedroom. A large mirrored wardrobe reflected the entire interior. The bed had been stripped, the mattress bare and naked pillows piled on the floor. No sign of anybody.

Will looked slowly past the dog under the window to the second flight of stairs. It was a process of elimination, but what about behind those tall, mirrored wardrobe doors? His eyes caught something at the landing pane, a pale shape within the slab of night.

He moved his face closer to the glass so he was peering past the yellow reflection of his surroundings. He was looking into the back garden and there was a light mass at the end of the lawn, not six feet from the wooden gate he'd just entered through. It looked like people crouching against the brick wall there.

They weren't crouching though.

Will quickly descended the stairs. He hadn't looked back as he'd entered the garden. Why would he have when he expected to find the family inside the house? He grabbed his laptop and headed outside where the sprinklers were still hissing.

At first he thought the people kneeling in a circle had been beheaded. But as he moved closer he could discern the two adults and two teenagers were crouching on all fours with their heads entirely buried in the border of earth.

Now he could see the mother's jade summer dress was streaked with dark blood. When he reached them, he could tell how hard the mud had been compacted around their shoulders. They were all buried up to the neck and when he tried to shift the mother back from the circle she didn't budge. The bodies were rooted in the ground, their fingers touching at the centre as if they'd dug themselves in.

Will ditched the laptop and knelt in the dirt with the corpses, felt the impact in his knees as he tried to fix on his reason for being there. He slid his hands into the pockets of the boys' jeans, feeling the pressure of their dead flesh against his gloved fingers. What item of clothing was he looking for? He unbuttoned the back pockets of the father's chinos, but there was nothing concealed within. He looked over the tableau for something that could be removed – no jewellery that he recognised as Libby's.

Then he saw the garden spade leaning against the wall and knew it hadn't been carelessly left there after the family had been positioned. Will got to his feet and grabbed the handle.

He aimed the blade at the centre of the human circle, trying to estimate where their heads would be and lifted one of his legs over the bodies. He slowly exerted pressure on the edge with his foot.

The spade slid slowly into the dry, compacted soil, half an inch at a time. As he waggled it from side to side, he prayed he wouldn't contact bone. The blade creaked, grated and went deeper. He tried to maintain his balance and pushed harder against the metal. It hit the looser earth below and gave to his weight, sinking all the way so the sole of his shoe was almost flush to the ground.

He carefully levered it and, as the ground parted, the bodies slumped sideways and he could see their hair emerge, matted with soil. He tugged them away from the hole by their cold ankles and turned them. The dirt fell inside the hollows in their heads.

There was something protruding from the father's mouth. It looked like a sharpened tongue, but its colour was too bright to be blood red. Will tugged it. It was a piece of material balled there. He yanked the headscarf out and clutched it in his hand.

Retrieving his laptop, Will made his way quickly back through the rear lane. When he emerged onto the terrace, he met the uncomprehending gaze of the tiger-faced nanny and a row of painted children watching him through the front window of 122.

CHAPTER SIXTEEN

While Weaver was out of earshot, Pope made the call. Waiting for a police statement was a good time to use up the free minutes on your cell, but this was one conversation he'd been nervous about since he'd opened his eyes that morning.

"Patrice?" When there was no greeting after she'd picked up, he assumed she still had his name in her phone. "I tried you at home, but I got your voicemail."

"I'm at the mall…" She left the statement trailing as if she might be waiting for specific directions.

They both needed a map for these conversations. Pope gave her the chance to elaborate, but she didn't. "Should I call back later?"

"No," she said a little too quickly. Did she just want it over and done with?

Pope tried to picture Patrice with the phone clasped to her face. It had been three years since they'd seen each other. She'd filled out a little the last time, but it had suited her. She'd let her hair go grey and that had worked too. He wondered if she still had it in a spiky bob. "Just wondered what plans you had for tomorrow."

"Sean's eighteenth, Sean's twenty-first – do you really think it matters if you put in an appearance?" Patrice's voice had the resignation of someone who knew Pope would forever disappoint her, but had given up being angry about it.

He hated to hear that more than anything else. He'd always felt that he'd have time to make amends. But he was fifty-five and nothing had changed since their last meeting. That had coincided with him moving in with Lenora and when he thought his minor celebrity status might have led to better things. Looking back he was sure Patrice might have been looking for friendship if not reconciliation. It had been his last chance to be decent to her and he'd blown it. He'd spent every minute they'd had telling her how good things had been for him when he suspected they hadn't been for her. "I could drop everything tomorrow and head over for the day."

"Drop everything?" For once she wasn't referring to the job that his inability to uncouple himself from had made him a stranger to her and Sean. Patrice was alluding to the fact he had someone else at home now. She wasn't aware his relationship was now based largely on the sharing of an apartment.

"It would be good to see you." Getting older made him mean it more and more. "How are things?" He knew the question was a mistake before he asked it.

"I've got to finish the shopping."

It was like she'd made the conscious decision to shut him out of every part of her life. He sensed she was lonely. "I'm not taking no for an answer, Patrice."

"You might have to," she said tiredly, as if rejecting his demands was the one luxury she'd earned.

Pope resisted the urge to say her name as Weaver returned from the bathroom. He knew she'd hung up so folded his phone and put it on the table top. He looked down at his quesadillas and tried to decide if they were breakfast or dinner. It was dark outside, that ruled out lunch.

"It's ten to." Weaver was still zipping his pants. He sucked the last of his Sprite though the ice in his cup and pointed at Pope's plate. "Don't make a career of those. We've got to get back."

He left Pope to consider how, when he was married, he yearned to be single and now he was virtually single he yearned to be married. He pushed the plate aside and rose unsteadily to his feet.

A waitress approached his table with a pad and pencil.

"I'm good thanks. Just the cheque."

"I was just wondering if I could get your autograph."

Pope took her in a little more. Slim, late forties, dark ringlets and handsome Hispanic features to match her accent. Her eyes were a deep chocolate brown. Flirt with this woman when the cops were about to issue a statement, what was he thinking? "Sure."

"I thought it was you then I saw the news truck parked out front."

"Who am I signing this to?"

"Albertine."

Pope felt her gaze on his exposed legs while he signed the pad and smiled. It was the first time this had happened in a good while.

"Working a story around here?"

"Yeah. I've got to run, but switch on News 55 and you'll see what it's all about."

"It's been quite a happening place today. Glad my shift's over, I can't take any more excitement."

Pope didn't know if there was a proposition there, but smiled again and moved towards the door.

"First the weird guy in the parking lot and now you turning up here."

Pope looked through the window at Weaver pulling the OB vehicle out of its space and waving frantically at him. "Weird guy in the parking lot?" He only repeated it to humour her.

"Came in to use the computers and then stood frozen in the lot on the way back to his car. Didn't move for a couple of minutes. It was freaky."

Although middle age was rounding off Pope's instincts he knew he'd be mad to dismiss any story with such proximity to the homicide in North Vine Street; Pope waved at Weaver to hold on. He turned from the door. "What time was this?"

"Around lunchtime." She rolled her eyes briefly upwards and then nodded to confirm.

Pope moved back into the dining area. "And he used these

computers?" He gestured towards them and walked to the rear of the restaurant. There were four there. Surely a perp wouldn't log into a computer so near a crime scene. "Do you remember which desk he was at?"

"The end one. Where you're stood."

"Any chance I can log in here?"

Albertine looked around. A handful of diners seemed disinterested in their exchange. She joined Pope and quickly tapped in a password. "Don't tell my boss I did this. Facebook is the only way I keep sane in this place."

Pope examined the surfing history for that day. "Has anybody used this computer since then?"

"Maybe. I haven't kept track."

He scrolled through the list. A couple of hotmail accounts had been accessed as well as a selection of employment sites. There was no point looking at those though because he'd need the personal passwords. Google maps had been used prior to them. He clicked on it and a page opened up with a map of Maryland on it. Albertine leaned in to look over his shoulder and he could smell her heavy floral scent.

"I get off my shift now. Just have to get changed and I'm out of here."

She waited for a moment and then he heard her heels clack away from him. "Thanks, Albertine, I won't be long here." Pope said eventually and looked at his watch. He was cutting it fine. There was nothing here. But he still clicked the previous website even though it looked like it was porno:

williamfrostxxx.net/

Momentarily he thought he was looking at some cryptic gaming site, but he recognised the house on North Vine Street before he had time to read the words against the dark blue sky above it. He clicked it and it opened up the page of images taken of the interior.

"Jesus wept."

CHAPTER SEVENTEEN

REST. MORE INSTRUCTIONS TOMORROW MORNING.

Will felt relief partially unlock his muscles.

"Taking it?" The gangly teenager with his tattooed arms folded around him had hung back while Will tested the laptop. Dropping his own hadn't damaged it, but the battery power had run out as soon as he'd booted it up again. There were no electronics stores open and he'd jogged down the main street before making a beeline for "Ellicott Jewelry and Loan". They'd refused to sell him a charger separately.

Will looked at the stack of other battered laptops amongst the jumble of pawned electrical hardware. At least this one worked. "So, you'll throw in a charger for this?"

The teenager raised the metal piercings in his eyebrows, as if keeping open the store had already been trouble enough. But he untied his arms and started hunting through the mess of wires, old mobiles and power packs on the lower shelf. He untangled one and handed it to him.

"Four hundred and seventy-five dollars," he twanged and moved to the register.

Will didn't care if he was being taken for a ride. He needed the laptop and had enough money in his wallet. He followed the boy to the raised counter at the back of the room to pay it into a revolving window. Through the distressed, yellow glass the boy moved his mouth silently, counting every note.

The teenager followed him out afterwards and Will walked briskly away as the shutters clanged down. Gangs had replaced the pedestrians he'd seen earlier. A jacked up Toyota crawled slowly past him, the men inside following him as he walked. He spotted a dirty yellow taxi rank sign on the other side of the street and crossed quickly to it. He held his mobile to his ear and waited for Carla to pick up while he clutched the laptop tighter under his arm.

Pope was ramrod straight in front of the computer monitor in Burrito Joe's, his jacket and tie draped over the back of the chair. He'd dispatched Weaver back to the crime scene and told him to get the statement. They were sure to be releasing the names of the victims. But with any luck the detective would be customarily late and they'd have to hold it over for 55's news at 9. If need be, he could do a hasty pickup and they could stitch it together.

But Pope was already thinking beyond News 55. If what he had in front of him wasn't some sort of bizarre hoax it looked like he'd stumbled on a major story that had barely started rolling.

There was no doubt the cut-out house depicted on the home page of the site was the crime scene they were camped outside. If he'd been in any doubt then there was the exact address in the little box that popped up when he played his cursor over it. He clicked through to the interior photos again and saw exactly what the crime scene team were photographing and fingerprinting while the rest of the TV circus waited outside.

How could this be a hoax when Weaver was probably at that moment jostling with the other cameras in North Vine Street? He'd seen plenty of bodies pulled out of rivers and dumpsters, but the methodical evisceration and arrangement of the family on the blood-soaked couch was unlike anything he'd ever seen. Why had they been made to look like they were covering their eyes like that?

His breaths came unevenly, but he didn't know if that was the prospect of his sudden access to the situation or being privy to such calculated evil. Were the occupants of the other houses on the street to be found disembowelled as well? He considered how the psychopath behind the site would react if Pope's unwanted observation were detected.

Pope had done a search for the man the website was named after and quickly gleaned who he was. He'd confirmed this when he'd found that the person who'd sat in the same chair as he was had logged into a personal Ingram International email account. He had to be the guy the instructions on the site were for. If he were anyone else why would he have used a local Internet café?

When he'd clicked back to the home page the words that had originally been there had been replaced. But he didn't need to read the first again to know the industry millionaire's daughter was being held. It also looked like her release was dependent on Frost visiting the houses and collecting an item of her clothing from each. If it was money being demanded from him, why put the guy through such a horrendous ordeal? It looked like he was being made to play a seriously twisted game.

Only two houses on the row displayed their addresses and interiors – North Vine Street and the one in Ellicott City. No bodies in the photos of the second one. Judging by the Google map that had been opened it looked like Frost was heading there next. He'd been here over seven hours ago.

REST. MORE INSTRUCTIONS TOMORROW MORNING.

They were the new words typed across the dark blue sky of the street. Perhaps he was already done. Pope had already checked the Ellicott local online news for stories, but had found nothing significant. Didn't mean it hadn't happened though.

He saw another waitress taking orders and remembered

Albertine. Looked like she'd gone. He'd been sitting in front of the computer for nearly half an hour.

Every second he kept it to himself he was withholding evidence from the police. Neither victim nor kidnapper or anybody else knew he was in the picture. What the hell was he going to do with this?

When Will had asked his driver to suggest somewhere to stay he'd recommended a place out of town. It had sounded like a good option and he hadn't cared if the cabby was on a retainer.

He got dropped at The Hotel at Turf Valley, which was a converted horse ranch nestling in some hills and surrounded by its own golf course. He checked in to a basic room that smelt of chemical pine, plugged in the laptop and lifted the lid. The aroma of stale nicotine leaked out of it into the air. He positioned it on the nightstand. The cursor was sluggish, but the next house still wasn't active and the instructions hadn't changed. He looked around him. His bed wouldn't be slept in, but he was grateful for some privacy to collect his shredded thoughts.

As he seated himself on the edge of the mattress the silence became unbearable. While he'd been travelling and anticipating the task he'd been set there had been little time to dwell on what he'd seen. Now his perception of events had time to catch up, the nausea he'd been restraining intensified.

He considered the picture of Libby and Luke that had been screwed to the wall in the house. It was a taunt to the police as well as him. Anyone investigating the crime scene wouldn't know who they were, would assume they were just part of the family that lived there. Were the kidnappers getting a perverse thrill out of pushing it right in their faces? It wasn't difficult to guess where they'd obtained it. Libby had uploaded hundreds of photos to her Facebook wall.

He rose and turned on the TV, surfing images aimlessly and then finding purpose. It didn't take him long to locate the news report he was looking for.

"A family of four, whose bodies were discovered at their Florida vacation home earlier this afternoon, have now been identified. St Louis business entrepreneur, Holt Amberson, his wife and two children were found after maintenance workers alerted police. Kissimmee police have cordoned off the property, just off Highway 193, and are appealing for eyewitnesses."

A helicopter's eye view revealed the pool he'd recently stood beside and the curving path of bay trees to the gates. A concentration of white vehicles was clustered where he'd parked the Volvo and, further down North Vine Street, an even larger body of media transports had assembled along the grass verge. If the pilot got any closer, Will could have seen his bloody footprints from the gate.

Holt Amberson. Nothing came to mind even when his lips formed the name.

The voiceover filled in the gaps.

"Mr Amberson, CEO of Consolidated Breweries, made his last public appearance at the Stockwood Alliance Industry Awards only two weeks ago."

His mobile rang. Carla's name was in the display.

"Police say they're treating the case as a homicide investigation."

He could hear the delay of the same news reporter's voice in his office.

"You got a room OK then?" There was a quaver of exasperation in her voice.

Will had spoken to her outside the rank. He'd spared her most of the details of what he'd found and told her that he'd secured the scarf. She'd been silent when he'd described the framed photograph. He'd promised to call her when he'd found a room. "I'm in some golf hotel just outside Ellico–" He grunted as he felt a prong of pain at his abdomen.

"What's wrong?"

"Just stubbed my foot." He hunted for the remote so he could turn up the volume of the news, but the presenter had handed to a reporter at a local flood scene. "You've got CNN there; does the name Amberson mean anything to you?"

"Nothing," she said immediately.

"Something big in the brewing industry…"

"I'm seeing what's online, but I haven't found much."

"Something to do while we wait," he said grimly.

"You have to at least try to sleep. You need to recharge yourself. They expect you to."

Will suddenly felt powerless at the prospect of being manipulated further. "There are another four houses yet…" His voice sounded anaesthetised. He felt anaesthetised. The sightless occupants of the first two addresses were already fused to his memory. "I'm going to demand we speak with Libby before we go any further. I tried when I called the number earlier, but they just hung up."

"I'll try again."

Will heard Carla use his desk telephone to speed dial and then the muted engaged tone over the speaker.

"I'll keep dialling." Despair leaked into her voice.

Will realised how much of an ordeal it had to be for her. Even though he didn't understand the motives, he was at least occupied in responding to the demands being made. Carla had nothing to do but wait and count every second Libby and Luke were being kept prisoner. "The line's only open when they want to hear from us."

"Try to get some sleep while I do some background on Amberson." She tried to sound purposeful.

"Carla, there's no point. I won't be able to." He stretched the skin taut on his forehead with his fingers.

"Just. Rest. Then." She enunciated each word precisely. "I'll call you in a couple of hours. I'll watch the site. It doesn't look as if anything's going to happen until morning there. Even murderers have to sleep." Her voice cooled again.

Murderers. That's who had their daughter. How could he rest when she was drugged and sprawled out in some anonymous cell thousands of miles away? But Carla was right. If tomorrow was anything like today he needed an extra gear. And he wouldn't begin to find that if he didn't shut down for a while.

"OK. Call me in an hour."

Nineteen years as man and wife,

And still so many years ahead,

"I love you." She cut the call before her emotions took over.

Will was suddenly sitting next to her bed in hospital after Jessie had been taken from them, her fingers tightly clutching his. She'd uttered the same words over and over as she'd fought to keep her eyelids open. It had sounded like an apology and it had been months before she'd been able to bring herself to tell him why.

The miscarriage had brought them closer together, but their adjustment to its emotional repercussions still divided them. Carla had mourned the child and gradually released her. They'd kept the picture taken of her in the maternity ward on the mantel in their bedroom, but one day Carla had asked if he minded her putting it away.

For Carla, Jessie would always be a part of her, but the picture represented too painful a memory. Will had felt like it was an act of treachery. When Libby had become pregnant and Carla had gifted her the nursery that had been decorated for Jessie he felt the same again, but had said nothing. He wanted Carla to heal, but her recovery militated against his.

The event had shut him down. He believed he'd accepted what had happened, but knew he still hadn't fully comprehended its finality. Whenever there were photos taken he still couldn't stop himself from imagining another face amongst theirs. How could he consider the absence of Libby from them as well?

He dragged himself up to the head of the bed and didn't take his eyes from the site as he dialled room service and ordered up some coffee and sandwiches. He had to feed his body, fortify it for the next day. He wouldn't sleep, but he could at least allow his limbs to re-energise themselves while he hunted online.

He thought of Carla suffering in isolation. Was she secure while he was so far away? What if Carla were the real target? He recalled the fire that had been lit on the doorstep of Easton Grey. Had they been wrong in assuming that it was the work of Motex or someone connected to Carla's protest? Again he tried to dismiss the notion that he was being kept occupied to conceal a hidden motive. Why send him to these specific locations? What could connect either of them to Amberson and the family in the garden? Water Aid Alliance? Unlikely. A supply contract they'd both been instrumental in implementing?

He racked his brains for any significant events that had occurred when he was in Southeast Asia. A lot had happened in the four years that followed.

He opened up a search engine. It was where he'd found himself listed at the start of his long day. Perhaps Holt Amberson was somewhere there as well.

CHAPTER EIGHTEEN

Holt Amberson has been in the global beer and beverage industry for seventeen years. His expertise in international expansion has introduced Stookey's Lite to several emerging markets including Latin America and Asia.

Previously Chairman of Tandemico, a logistics company jointly owned by the UG Group and Consolidated Breweries, Mr Amberson is also industry chairman of Globas, a US trade organisation promoting responsible alcohol consumption.

He earned his MBA from Olin Business School at Washington University, St Louis.

As well as his corporate bio, the UG Group website also featured a clip of Amberson reciting the brewery's policy on ethical responsibility and environmental stewardship. Stood awkwardly in front of a row of books, a balding and slightly jaundiced Amberson read his assurances off centre so he only engaged the viewer at the beginning and end of his speech.

He was in his late thirties and blinked his weak blue eyes nervously throughout his address. Carla tried not to think of his hands taped over them in the photo posted on the website.

Apart from numerous trade references, there was little other background information online. He had a wife and two children; Carla knew that and felt a hollow of sickness open up when she thought of the family grouped on the couch. There was no evidence of them or his life outside of commerce. He obviously kept his private world as sacred as Will.

She speculated about the family in Ellicott City and if they would be linked by industry. Will and Ingram International had no explicit connection to the UG Group. Perhaps there was some indirect association though. UG was a multi-tentacled organisation.

She'd noted UG's trade connections with Asia, but the Stookey's brewing plant was in Ban Song, which was way outside Ingram's territory. Maybe she was still looking for something that wasn't there. Ingram advocated ethical practices, but vociferous objectors were always waiting on the sidelines as soon as you sunk a spade into the soil. Major and minor lawsuits were constantly pending. Her work for the Water Aid Alliance had been accused of being a smokescreen or, at the very best, penitence for Ingram's worldwide monopoly.

What could Ingram possibly be accused of to justify murdering innocent families? Will had spearheaded the secondary pipe op in Southeast Asia, but they'd never once encountered the mafia presence or the territorial racketeering they'd been prepared for.

She drifted her cursor over the next house, but no address had been inputted. In the left corner of her screen she had the GPS tracking map window. According to the site Libby was still in her hotel; her mobile had obviously been left behind.

With repeater triangulation the app could pinpoint Will's location via his mobile within twenty metres in the USA. But the tiny, isolated red dot signifying his current location made her feel even more redundant.

She played the clip of Amberson again, as if looking into his face and hearing his voice would reveal something more about the man behind the scant data. What had he done to deserve his life and the lives of his wife and children being taken in such a way? What could anybody do to warrant that? Will had said nothing of how he'd found the next victims. She knew he was withholding details from her. Protecting her again.

She searched again for the Ellicott City address, hoping she would find a name. A lot of US properties were rented, however, and she found no details of its occupants. They would know soon enough.

She had to keep refining the small amount of information they had. It was all she could do to stop herself thinking about what Libby was enduring. She was alive, Carla was positive of that – had to be.

She wasn't about to lose her. Life had already taken enough of the people she loved. At thirteen, her parents' death had been unfathomable to her. One severe November night several elements had conspired against them as they'd returned from a rare night out, having left Carla with a babysitter. Their car had skidded on black ice, hit an already weakened barrier and dropped them into the path of traffic on the motorway below. Senseless, but beyond anyone's control. She was still trying to accept that, the randomness of events.

She'd met Will in his second year at university when his mother had just passed away. He'd lost his father the winter before. Their long illnesses and deaths had blighted his life outside of his studies. Justifying their investment in his education had become his only focus. Minor relationships with Eva Lockwood and Jenny Sturgess were short lived, which meant he was still a virgin when they got together. She'd lost hers to a mature student, Chris Wing. Not mature enough to make allowances for her loss though. She'd split with him the same time Will had been dumped.

Nobody else there had a frame of reference for what they'd both experienced. Losing both parents was an exclusive connection neither wanted. As two only children it certainly reinforced their need to establish a safe haven for their own family. Easton Grey was the fortress they'd thought they could be secure inside. And until the previous summer it had felt like they'd been invincible there.

What was happening to them now wasn't random. It was premeditated and they were being led to believe they could still control the outcome. Her career in corporate law had cast her as a facilitator rather than the adversarial figure of her counterparts in trial law. But piecemeal negotiation was a process she spent most of her professional life engaged in.

She couldn't begin to determine why Will was being dispatched to the locations on the site, but until his grim journey was completed they were at least being asked to believe Libby would remain safe. There was always room for manoeuvre, but at that moment the dialogue was one way. They had to engage somehow, demand proof of Libby's wellbeing and find another form of leverage in the meantime.

It was then a name occurred to her. She looked at her watch. It was only forty minutes since she'd put the telephone down on Will so he could rest. She knew he would be doing the same as her though.

"Anything?" He picked up halfway through the first ring.

Carla realised it was pointless remonstrating with him. "Nothing significant. You?"

"I'm peeling away UG's subsidiaries, our paths must have crossed." His voice sounded spent.

"Should I call Anwar?"

"We can't call anyone." But he had paused before replying.

Carla let him take a breath before she continued. "Let me call Anwar this morning. I'll ask him if he has any background info on Amberson. I won't tell him why I need to know. If he's just been found murdered, a lot of people will be asking questions. Looks like his UG Group had interests in Asia. If anyone knows anything about them, Anwar will."

She waited. His room was so far away from her, but its TV, the creak of the mattress and his breathing trickled into her ear. It was excruciating. She could only listen in, not touch him or make him lay down for even a minute.

"OK." He sounded as if OK was the last thing it was. "Any information on the family in Ellicott City?"

"Nothing. We'll just have to wait for the police to find them."

They both let the delayed sound of their TVs fill in the gap while they considered how many hours that could be. How long the dead family would be their secret.

"I could call it in. Anonymously," he said stolidly. "Pretend to be a neighbour. I don't think them being found is important to whoever's holding Libby. But the quicker the police do, the sooner we'll know who they are."

"No." Carla said firmly, even though she could see it made perfect sense. "We can't call in the police, even if we're not telling them about Libby's abduction. They may well have found them by now anyway..."

"Some people watched me leave the house. Perhaps they dialled 911."

Carla could tell he was burnt out. He uttered the words like he was under hypnosis. She would start having blackouts herself soon, but, at that moment, she didn't even want to blink and give exhaustion a chance. "I'll keep searching for information on Amberson and call Anwar."

"You know how to handle him."

"I do. Just close your eyes for a while. Do it for Libby. I'll watch the website and wake you."

"Just thought I'd let you know, you're officially infringing my Internet porn time." Weaver absently squeezed at his blister pack of nicotine gum, but it was empty.

Weaver was the only man Pope knew who referred to porn as a legitimate hobby. He'd said it was the only pleasure his alimony payments hadn't robbed him of. Pope held his hand up while he listened to his own voice chip in on his message at home. Lenora had insisted on him saying his name while she recorded the rest. It finished and he tried to sound as weary and reluctant as possible. "Hi, babes, looks like I'm going to be stuck downtown for the foreseeable, so don't wait up for me. Say 'hi' to the girls." He imagined her and the wine cooler cougars from the block listening to him or making too much noise to hear.

He rang off and regarded Weaver's puffy eyes. "How can you look so tired? You've only been on the clock since lunchtime."

"With you. I had an early start covering the fluoridation protest this morning. I'm dead on my feet."

Pope leaned his body towards the iPad in Weaver's lap. "Any change? I don't want us getting on the wrong flight."

Weaver checked the site again. "Nothing new." He ran his finger along the row of houses. "Fuck…this is some piece of work."

"Any luck tracing the site?" Pope looked at his watch again.

"Finding where a domain is registered is usually easy, but the IP address has been buried amongst a tangle of dead-end email addresses and Liberian servers."

"OK – I understood the bit about it being a piece of work." There was no way Pope could have expected Weaver to be his crew without showing him the site. Plus, Pope's IT knowledge was pretty limited. It was also going to dictate their travel arrangements, so he estimated it would be easier to take him into his confidence. Access to the information they had might enable them to record incidents as they happened rather than having to beg for scraps at the crime scenes. If they got lucky he would worry about constructing a plausible story for their presence after the event.

Maybe there was a substantial connection between the houses, something he could say had prompted them to act on a hunch. Did Frost already know what it was? The website was like a perverse treasure map revealing a little at a time. Was it doing so exclusively to keep the murder locations concealed until Frost reached them or was there a bigger punchline in store for him?

Pope wondered if, as the victims were ID'd, he could figure out what it was, if only to give them a credible story for being adjacent to a homicide. But perhaps this was a personal thing Frost alone could solve. He needed to uncover more about him and Holt Amberson, beyond the fact that they were both powerful men. He knew how he'd be spending the flight and took the iPad from Weaver.

"You positive the channel has cleared this trip, Pope?"

"How could they not?" They hadn't. 55 knew nothing of their destination. "Just remember to keep all your receipts." Pope rose from his seat and arched his aching back. It had been too late to grab a bite in the terminal. Their plane for Maryland left in half an hour.

CHAPTER NINETEEN

Alone for the night in the Ingram building, Carla didn't want to leave Will's desk, didn't want to relinquish her position in front of the computer for a minute. She knew the security guard downstairs was monitoring her dashes to the bathroom and that the staff handling the Remada op would be reconvening early. But, for now, the deserted office floor compounded her sense of isolation.

She kept herself busy, tracking Amberson and his business dealings, but she couldn't pinpoint a tangible connection to Ingram or any of Will's associates. She switched between US news channels, but there were no further details of the murders in Kissimmee or any mention of the family in Ellicott City.

Time dragged and then jumped indiscernibly and Carla knew she fell asleep for brief seconds because she thought she heard Libby's voice in reception.

All the time she used her activity to keep what could be happening to her daughter from the threshold of her thoughts. She only succumbed when she registered the lights of the skyline being extinguished by the morning's citrus glow.

She watched her own pale reflection in the smoked glass brighten as a cloud shifted and sunshine suddenly flooded the room. Usually when it happened, Carla liked to believe it was because something positive had occurred somewhere in the world. She fought the muscles that hardened around her lips. The light wasn't warming, but bathed her with a cruel new reality. She'd been in the office for nearly twenty-four hours. What had happened to Libby in that time?

She recalled Libby's most traumatic episode to date and how petrified she'd been when she'd run into the kitchen having been chased by Farmer Sloman's wild pig. She'd told them the animal had escaped, but Carla was sure her daughter had been trespassing on his neighbouring land. She hadn't voiced her scepticism though; thought that Libby had learnt her lesson.

She never ventured far from home on her own after that and it was an event Libby still couldn't laugh about. Will had fallen out with Sloman over the incident, even though he'd paid him for the escaped pig. If only this could be so quickly remedied. She imagined Libby trembling as she had then, waiting for them to chase her terror away.

The sense of darkness moved in on her, the same darkness that had come at her from all sides when she'd lain on the bed in her auntie and uncle's spare room with the realisation that her parents were gone. They'd turned out the lights and the night had become a solid maze with her at the centre. The room had felt and smelt so strange and she'd known that nothing would be familiar to her again.

It was Carla's unique claustrophobia. She hated enclosed spaces, but this was a sensation that could crush her wherever uncertainty allowed it to. She stood shakily and paced, needing to hear Will's voice again and desperate to call Anwar.

Anwar Imam was Ingram International's cross-cultural management consultant and had been a family friend since before Libby was born. Will had given him the responsibility of briefing company executives and in turn establishing diplomatic foundations for their worldwide pipe ops. Anwar hadn't allowed Will to coax him into the lucrative, full-time position he created for him and preferred to maintain his global consultancy a stone's throw from Ingram HQ.

Today was Sunday. He'd think it unusual to receive a call from her on the weekend let alone so early in the morning. She couldn't let him suspect anything was wrong. Picking his brain would be an invitation, however. Anwar always answered questions with twice as many of his own. Carla knew she'd have to tread carefully. She'd grown accustomed to handling him though and had been deft with his over-familiarity in the past.

She waited as long as she could, but failed to reach him at any of the three numbers she had. She left messages and hoped he hadn't gone away.

Will nudged his cursor over the next house in the row as he had done every minute since he'd entered the hotel room. Still no red outline. The cut-out was of a white and powder blue wood-panelled home. Circular windows punctuated three gables and a triple garage at the front telegraphed the obvious wealth of its owners.

He swung his legs off the bed and stood up, his spine aching, the skewer of abdominal pain reinvigorated with the sudden movement. No new developments about the Amberson family. CNN were running the same footage and summary.

He walked to the bathroom and flicked the light switch. Sprawled around the furniture were the two sightless families, the gaping caverns of their faces unwavering.

The sound of buzzing flies vibrated in his head and he felt their tiny legs on the backs of his wrists again.

A naked and blue figure stood over the sink, shivering and panting. He knew before she turned that it was Libby, could see the lotus tattoo at the base of her spine and her hands taped to her face. She pivoted, breasts grubby and bruised, wrists pumping either side of her head to try and free herself. Behind him he felt a presence, somebody breathing there and waiting for him to look over his shoulder. But he couldn't, he had to see Libby's eyes even though they wouldn't be there. Her palms came away.

Will knew it was a nightmare, but didn't want to wake from it back to his own.

CHAPTER TWENTY

It was Sunday, which meant Tam had only household chores before he was allowed to play on his own in the central courtyard of the complex. Daylight had chased away the uneasy headache that had kept him awake for the remainder of the night and, although he was tired, he felt an increasing sense of exhilaration about surviving the adventure at the chicken factory.

When he'd brushed his teeth that morning the prospect of ever returning to the place he'd fled filled him with horror. But with the normality of a humid and cloying day slowing to boredom he'd already calculated how much time it would take to get there and back again.

His father would remain in bed until they ate dinner. His mother always prepared plenty of salads of pomelo and papaya on a Sunday and while she worked at the chopping board he shelled the crabs she'd bought from the wet market. After helping her tie knots around banana leaf parcels of fermented fish she released him. He had several hours before he had to be back at the table.

He took the steps to the courtyard where some other children were playing and told them he had to run an errand for his mother. Once he'd turned the corner out of their sight he was through the gates and into the bustle of the street. He dispersed a small group of orange-breasted pigeons on the road that normally would have stopped him in his tracks and headed for the narrow passageway on the other side of the block.

The island was experiencing another day of thick haze. The dust particles from nearby forest fires hung in the air so the tops of the taller buildings were almost invisible. But daylight made everything familiar to him now and he felt no trepidation as he entered the slim gap and the echoes of his pelting sandals bounced back at him from its walls. He felt emboldened by the prospect of where he knew he was going and how many hours he had left before it got dark again.

Once out the other side he weaved his way though the tuk-tuks, mopeds and taxis, taking short cuts behind shops he'd avoided the night before. Shutters were up and back alleys were populated now. Children played amongst the dumpsters, and rats stayed out of sight during their noisy activity.

Tam didn't intend to squeeze himself through the corrugated panel at the side of the factory this time. If the sliding door was still open, as he'd left it, he knew he'd be able to access the building from the rear.

For the first time since her capture Libby felt in solid possession of her body. After so many indeterminate hours of tranquillized immobility she started to sense every sinew again. The pain quickly followed. The circulation in her hands had been severed by whatever was binding her wrists behind her aching spine. Her weight on the plastic edge of the commode was numbing the backs of her legs. But the worst sensation was the stinging of the teeth marks. They fizzed and twinged cold, but worse than this was contemplating how she'd sustained the wound that deadened her left shoulder.

Libby's whole frame throbbed with the discomfort of retaining the same posture for so long. Her stomach was folded up and she wondered if her cramped position would have an adverse effect on her baby. She'd considered telling them of her pregnancy the last time they'd removed the gag to give her water and food. They'd been silent to every other question she'd asked, however.

Plus she figured anyone who could subject her to the sort of brutality they already had would only get a sick thrill out of her revelation. She also didn't want to make herself seem any more valuable if they were demanding a ransom.

Were they waiting to hear from her parents all this time or was she being held until she was sold on and imprisoned elsewhere? She had to convince herself that her mother and father had been contacted and that arrangements were already being made for her release. If that weren't the case, though, what did she have to lose by trying to escape?

Again she pushed her head back and felt the resistance of the wire mesh above her. Her legs felt more solid where they were tied about the commode now and her ankles ached where they were bound to the plastic base. She curled her toes against the compacted carpet of droppings and slid herself forward with the seat. She felt the draught from the chickens beating their wings in agitation. Had she been locked in with them so they would act as an alarm?

There was no way of knowing if somebody was already watching her. But now she had some sensation in her limbs she had to act before they used the hypodermic again. Her knees tensed as she re-engaged them and pulled herself further forward until her face was against the front of the cage. She pressed it harder until the wire cut into her nose. But even putting her weight behind it didn't buckle the door above the lock.

The wire above her seemed more flexible so she heaved herself upwards, bracing her body between the commode and the resistance against the top of her skull. She pushed hard, the metal biting through the hood. She hardened her shoulders and the muscles in her stomach as she strained to stand up. She dropped harshly to the seat when the effort sapped her. Libby breathed heavily inside the hood, wanted to stay put, let the pain flow out of her. But she knew this might be her only chance.

••••

"Stop!"

The cab jerked to a halt at the end of Hebron Street and the driver squinted a warning over his shoulder at Pope.

"Sorry, this is as far as we need to go." It was the early hours of the morning, but there was a light show outside a house halfway down the block. "We'll get out here."

Pope paid him and the car reversed quickly away as soon as they closed the doors. They both studied the glimmering panoply of police and media vehicles clogging the end of the street.

"Looks like we're late to the party." Weaver carefully lowered his camera to the sidewalk. He'd tried to take it on the flight as hand luggage, but it had to be stowed. They'd had a long delay as they'd waited for it to appear on the carousel. "Maybe Frost called the cops."

"Unlikely." Pope figured police involvement was the last thing the girl's father would want if he wanted to see his daughter alive again. "Maybe someone found the bodies."

"I can count eight networks here at least."

"Anything new on the site?"

Weaver took the iPad out of his kitbag and checked the row of houses. "No new address..." He clicked inside the residence they were now only yards from. "And no images of dead people."

Pope's strategy wasn't working. The site hadn't given them the edge they needed. A one man crew was ill-equipped to cover this sort of story. Should he take it to a major network? They'd immediately attempt to wrest it from his hands and he didn't want to waste time negotiating. Frost was ahead of them by seven hours.

"He could be anywhere by now." Weaver was having similar thoughts. He looked up and down the neighbourhood as if they might catch sight of him.

"But if the next location hasn't been released to him yet it means he's as much in the dark as we are."

"Perhaps he has another channel of communication with the

kidnappers."

"Then why bother with the website at all? We just have to wait for the next address and be ready to move as quickly as he does."

Weaver nodded and picked up his camera. "We've still got to get the coverage here though, right?"

Pope was reluctant to join the throng at the end of the street, particularly as they were more plugged into the story than anybody there, including the police.

Weaver seemed to pick up on this. "It's our jobs otherwise, right?"

"Yeah, come on. Keep the iPad handy... and concealed." His instincts told him to hang fire. The searches he'd done on the plane had revealed nothing that connected Frost to Amberson, but there were still the other houses in the row left to cover. And they could move the same time as Frost to the next one.

"It did say the next instructions wouldn't come until morning." Weaver hoisted the camera onto his shoulder.

"This is the morning."

Libby tensed her calf muscles and rammed herself against the overhead wire again. A head-sized dome had been left by her repeated efforts. She slipped her head inside it again, shoved her weight into it and bit down on her gag. Her whole skeleton shook with the exertion and the wire sliced into her. She was about to collapse again when something popped. She wasn't sure if she'd dislocated her shoulder, but when she tested the resistance of the cage again it bulged loosely. One of the edges had come loose and, as she slid her head across it, she found the mesh above the door flapping upwards.

There was no way she could climb out still attached to the commode, but there was no time for hesitation. Libby slammed herself against the door, the cage toppling forward and the chickens noisily complaining, as the entrance became the floor.

She felt the cold contents of the bowl pouring around her and the animals scampering panicked over her body. Although she was still secured to it by her feet the commode was only lightweight plastic. She dragged it round her body with her ankles and used it to bash the weakened wire out.

Libby wriggled herself sideways through the hole, the other prisoners scratching at her as they fled. She straightened her legs and used her arms to lever herself up and then stood precariously with her feet still attached to the front of the commode.

She halted, breathing inside darkness, listening for other sounds. But she couldn't hear anything above the screech of the birds and the pulse in her eardrums.

She felt the blood pouring back into her legs. Her hands were still secure behind her back and she could only slide each foot about an inch in front of the other at a time. But she started shuffling forward, her feet sluggishly repelling pecking beaks, and soon ran into a dank wall about eight feet from the cage.

She pushed herself along it, her face and arm scraping off fragments until she could feel cool metal on her skin. She swallowed her nerves and pushed her weight against the solid surface, slithering and squeaking her body and using her shoulder to test it.

Suddenly she was lying on her side, a blow to her temple filling the black hood with orange bubbles. She heard her own hopeless sob and squeezed her eyes against what would happen outside them. She'd been caught and subdued.

But the anticipated restraint didn't come and she realised her skin was bathed in heat. As well as feeling the sun from above and radiating from the ground she was sprawled on, she could also hear loud traffic. She was near a road. Libby had dropped through a doorway to outside, striking her head in the process. She pulled herself upright again and, scuffing forward, followed the sound of engines and horns.

The tarmac felt soft and hot against the soles of her feet. As she edged closer to the noise she could feel the vibrations of the street in her chest. Momentarily she thought she had a concussion and was off balance, but realised she was walking up an incline. Was it a ramp that led straight out onto a main road?

When Libby reached the top of it she hung back. She didn't want to be run over before she was released, but she did want to put as much distance between herself and her prison as possible. She shuffled onwards, hoping somebody might brake for her if she was wandering too near the edge of the road. Then her face collided with hot, corrugated metal. She rolled along its uneven surface.

It was a tall gate that obscured her from the people passing by. She dragged herself to the sides of the space, juddering from brick wall to brick wall. She was in a secure yard that was about six paces square. The only way out was through the gates. She returned to them, jerking and grazing her shoulder along the ribs of metal to find a handle. Nothing. Even if it was just a case of shooting a catch her hands were tied behind her back and unable to lift much higher than her waist. She buffeted them, but they didn't give. They were locked solid, probably by bolts in the ground.

All the time she scrabbled about there Libby attempted to push the bung out of her mouth. But the tight hood wouldn't allow her to expel it and shout for help. She battered herself harder against the gate, but on the fourth attempt her arms were arrested as she tried to move forward. What had she snagged her cuffs on?

It was a finger and it responded to her tugging by yanking the other way, back down the ramp towards the chicken house. Had they been watching her the whole time? Libby's screams flooded her hood, but whoever returned her falteringly to her prison knew they wouldn't be heard.

CHAPTER TWENTY-ONE

At 2.14pm, Anwar Imam walked into Will's office.

"Working on your own?" The question was as genial as his expression, but his dark eyes audited hers.

She looked past him to where Nissa was seated. "I told you I couldn't see anybody."

"Don't blame Nessa." He always got her name wrong. "I barged my way in."

She watched Nissa bite her lip. She'd seemed even more concerned when she'd arrived to find Carla wearing the same clothes as yesterday. They'd both obviously guessed something was wrong.

Anwar closed the door on Nissa's expression with the weight of his tall frame. He was wearing a casual, yellow paisley shirt that perfectly accentuated the dark pigment of his skin.

"Anwar, I didn't expect you to call in."

Anwar nodded his shoulder length black hair and cupped his fingers over his nose as he considered the office and her obvious discomfort at his presence. Egyptian by birth, he was an unrepentant anglophile. He followed Will's lead when it came to property. His own Georgian investment lay only six miles from Easton Grey.

"Where's Will?" He zoned in on the abstract sculpture on Will's desk and frowned at it as if doing so would allow him to continue his casual interrogation.

"Weekend off. I'm still chasing my tail trying to get firm commitments to the trans-African feasibility study." She tried to sound overworked, but realised justifying her presence was suspicious.

"So why do you desperately need to tap my limited knowledge of the late Holt Amberson?" He moved to the desk, picked up the sculpture and pretended to weigh it. His bergamot aftershave wafted over her.

"Will's had some overtures from someone at UG," she lied. "The story piqued his curiosity."

"So much so you tried to reach me at three different numbers on a Sunday morning." He put down the sculpture, a plea for honesty in his gaze.

"Anwar. We've been friends a long time..."

He nodded, blinking his long, dark eyelashes. His expression didn't alter.

Carla knew Anwar wanted to become much more than that. He was as hopeless with alcohol as Will and his customarily diplomatic mouth had got loose from its moorings on more than a few occasions.

She'd told Will about his overtures, but he'd laughed it off, saying it was a huge compliment that an eligible bachelor of Anwar's status was pursuing his wife. She'd never told him everything that Anwar had said, however. Why ruin a friendship when Anwar's designs would remain just that? "We're in the middle of something here." She held his gaze. "If we need help, you know you'll be the first person we come to..."

"You already have." But the harsh line of his eyebrows softened. "You didn't sound your usual self on the telephone. Sorry to intrude, but I had to drive into the office this afternoon anyway and we – I – was concerned."

Carla assumed he'd meant Nissa. Had she told him something was going on?

"Thanks, but this is something we can deal with ourselves."

She nodded quickly to indicate he should do the same.

He didn't. "OK," he said eventually. "If you need me though, you know where to find me." His eyes glinted with the significance of the statement.

"I'll let Will know. He'll be very grateful."

Anwar nodded respectfully. "When will he be back?" He looked around, as if Will had just stepped out.

He obviously hadn't bought her story about him having a weekend off. It was the point at which Carla nearly told him everything. "Soon." She darted her eyes at the website page and Anwar could tell she was eager to return to it.

He scrutinised the back of the screen. "OK. I'll tell you everything I know about Amberson and UG."

Will's mobile rang seconds after the house became active.

Bel Air,
Maryland,
YOU KNOW WHAT TO DO

"I've seen it," he said, as soon as he picked up. He could hear Carla's fingers rippling on the keyboard.

He clicked inside the cut out and found another clandestine gallery. The interior looked brand new – ceramic tiles, maple cabinets and ethnic tapestries on the walls. In the hallway, anoraks were hung on coat hooks in descending size order, one large blue, one slightly smaller red...

One infant's yellow.

"It's about a fifty minute drive according to the online map." Carla had pre-empted Will's search. "Anwar just turned up at the office."

Will knew Anwar preferred face-to-face dialogues, particularly where Carla was concerned. "Did you manage to get rid of him?"

"He seemed suspicious, but he gave me some background on

Amberson. Didn't have anything we don't already know."

"I've already got a cab standing by at reception." The driver had been there since six. It was now 9.34am. He quickly disconnected the laptop and headed for the door.

Weaver jogged up the steps from the lot and waited impatiently for the sliding doors to slowly open. "We've got to move!"

"Can we finish this later?" Pope indicated the pink triplicate forms laid on the desk between him and the car rental guy. They'd opted to hire a vehicle whether they needed it to drive interstate or directly back to the airport. A lot of Ellicott was closed early Sunday so they'd bided their time outside until an old boy had opened the place up.

The septuagenarian looked impassively up from his computer monitor with bloodshot eyes.

Pope's gaze dropped to the desk where the keys lay. He could snatch them up and be out of there before he had time to rise from his chair.

"Bel Air! They're close!" Weaver hovered in the doorway.

But then with the licence plate details and all the info Pope had already given him it wouldn't take long for the police to catch up with them. Maybe before they even got there. Aside from the channel, the cops were the last people he wanted to talk to. By the time they found a cab on a Sunday morning they would probably be done here. Probably. Pope balled his gut and forced a complaisant smile. "Could we please just hurry this along? I'm from TV news."

Nothing registered

"And we're in the middle of an emergency situation."

"Sure." The old boy continued to process Pope's details after taking a long, loud slurp from his coffee mug.

Will seated himself in the back of a battered, red Ford Fusion and relayed the destination to the driver. He'd been anticipating another cab ride to the airport. Now it struck him that if he used a taxi to take him directly to the specific location the police could trace him back to the hotel he was picked up from. He'd used his credit card when he'd checked in.

He also wondered if the detailed coordinates would be given to him as soon as they got there. He didn't want to ask the cabby to drive round in circles or waste time switching taxis. He'd be better off with his own vehicle. He glanced at his watch and calculated how much time he would lose while they drove to a car rental. They were outside town so there was no knowing where the nearest one would be.

"How much money do you earn from fares in a day?"

The brawny, young cab driver raised one faint eyebrow at him in the mirror. His head was shaved so close the small amount of blonde hair growing over the tattoo of tumbling dice there was just a golden sheen. "Three fifty..." he estimated. His voice sounded too small for his physique. Then his eyes narrowed. "Well, I guess between three fifty and six hundred... thereabouts." He could scent an offer.

"Any chance you could call in sick?"

He turned briefly, a smile inflating. "You've already racked up a couple of hundred bucks while I've been waiting, now you want me to drive you round for the day?"

"No. I want to borrow your car."

Both eyebrows raised now.

"And I want you to make a decision about this quickly. The arrangement remains between the two of us. I'll pay you six hundred. I need this car to drive to Bel Air, but I promise I'll leave it there afterwards. You'll have to pick it up."

"How do I know you won't rip me off?"

Will elaborated rapidly. "You don't. Look, I could pay a lot less for a day's car rental, but I need to get to where I'm going right now. Life and death. I've got six hundred in cash and I don't have time to barter. If you want it, pull over. You can give me your cell number and I'll tell you where I've parked it."

Tall willow oaks whipped by for a moment then the driver turned sharply into a truck stop. He started scribbling his number on the back of a cab card. "You'll have to let me have it back by tonight. I sleep in it."

Will left the driver behind as light rain started to settle on the windscreen. The laptop was open and booted up on the passenger seat. He turned off the cab's radio and followed the route to Bel Air that had already been programmed into the Sat Nav. Carla called to say she was following him on the GPS.

The house waited for him less than fifty minutes down I-95.

CHAPTER TWENTY-TWO

The painfully skinny man in the jagged denim shorts rose from his chair and turned in Tam's direction. Tam ducked out of sight. His body was concealed in the gap between the back wall of the chicken house and the stack of empty cages. Three had been dumped bottom side out in the middle of the row and it was these that concealed his position. Several chickens had come to investigate, pecking around his bare legs while he bit his fist and his eyes watered, afraid that even the sound of him blinking would give away his hiding place.

He watched Skinny Man stride casually through the chickens in his sandals, a cackling path opening in front of him until he was near the bottom of the steps. His Malay features were pale and waxy, like he spent all of his time down here. He turned, scratching his navel through his greasy yellow tee shirt as if having second thoughts about something. He then seemed to think better of it and climbed.

Tam heard the door open and close and was grateful Skinny Man hadn't turned off the light. If he hadn't though did that mean he was coming back? He breathed through his mouth again and allowed the muscles at the back of his legs to relax.

Tam didn't know why he'd returned here. Something had bumped the corrugated gates of the yard when he'd been about to scale them. The impacts had sent him scuttling back down the alleyway and he'd circled the building several times before he plucked up the courage to clamber back over. He'd peered into the yard first. There'd been no sign of whatever had pushed at the gates, only a handful of grubby yellow chickens that had climbed the ramp from below.

The sliding door had been half open, but he wasn't sure if it had rolled there after his escape the previous night. As he'd edged into the chicken house, however, he'd registered the light was on and knew for sure he'd switched it off.

He'd panicked when he'd seen the cage overturned and empty and had expected her to pounce. Then he'd seen her lying flat on the bottom of another cage on the far side of the churning floor space. Her ankles had been bound with the same blue washing line wire that secured the hood to her head. The soles of her feet were scraped and bloody and when the chickens that shared her space pecked at them she hadn't reacted.

He'd inched closer to see if she was still alive. Then he'd heard somebody coming down the stairs. The stack of cages had been nearer than the exit so he'd quickly ducked behind them. Skinny Man had appeared carrying a wooden chair in one hand and a bottle in the other. Tam had observed him plant the chair carefully in front of the cage and sit down. The girl had moaned and eventually started to talk. Tam hadn't understood what she'd been saying, but knew she'd been pleading. Skinny Man had just watched, swigged out of the bottle and occasionally checked his phone.

Tam crept from behind the stack and picked up the brown Singha beer bottle. It was empty now, but it would serve as a weapon if Skinny Man reappeared. Having listened to the girl sobbing and choking for the half hour he'd stood with his knees trembling he no longer felt threatened by her. But as he moved closer to the cage and knelt by the door he was still glad to see the large padlock that secured it.

Her back was to him and he could see her shoulders rising and falling with her breath. The hood lifted as if she sensed his presence, but it fell again and she said nothing.

Tam watched her, not speaking, but sure she knew he was there. He didn't know how many minutes passed before he heard Skinny Man on the steps again.

This time he easily covered the distance between the cage and the sliding door and headed back up the ramp.

He launched himself at the corrugated gates, but as he dropped safely down the other side, Tam forgot about the beer bottle he'd left by the cage.

The countryside had opened up, presenting Will with a panorama of cinereal skies. He passed through another toll and took US 1. The information in the pop up box remained unaltered. He knew it would until he got to Bel Air. The pain in his gut fizzed like a dissolving tablet.

As the car rapidly gobbled white lines and moved him steadily closer to the unknown address, he wondered if he should refrain from calling the mobile number until he was at the town centre. At least then he would be able to get to the house quicker. But what if it was on the outskirts?

How close to his arrival had the family been murdered in Ellicott City? Hours before? The website had intimated that he may be able to beat them. Should he dial the number prior to getting to Bel Air? If it was believed he'd got there sooner than anticipated it might cause them to panic. The address would only be released to him when they were good and ready though. Any phoning ahead to warn the occupants of the house would be academic by then.

There was nothing he could do to influence the sequence of events. Still he kept his foot on the accelerator and drove as fast as he felt he could without being pulled over.

Bel Air was a busy, happening retail town in Harford County with spotless malls and restaurants. Will called as soon as he hit Main Street. As his cab crawled to a halt behind a snarl up of traffic, a familiar noise greeted his ear.

"I'm in Bel Air. Will you let me speak to Libby?" He pleaded rather than demanded this time.

Birds shrilled and shrieked.

"I can't go on with this until you've given us some proof she's alive."

There was another sound over the discord, something rubbing against the mouthpiece the other end. They were listening to him.

"Please, put my daughter on."

Another harsh impact.

"Daddy?" a voice whispered.

Will's finger froze on the mouse pad of the laptop.

"Daddy?" it said louder. But it wasn't a word she'd used for a long time. It wasn't Libby. It was a man's voice, raised several octaves to ape a female.

They put down the phone. The information in the box embellished itself.

114 Pepperwood Springs,
Vineyard Oak,
Bel Air,
Maryland,
21015

This time he was ready and opened up the window for the directory that would allow him to locate the house's telephone number with the address. He swiftly dialled the one that appeared in the results and the ring tone seemed ear splitting. Cars behind him beeped their horns as the line in front of him accelerated away.

"Hello?" It was a woman's voice.

Will's mouth opened, but his warning melted on his tongue. If they escaped he wouldn't be able to secure the next item of

Libby's. More horns jabbed at his other ear.

"Hello?"

"Get out of the house." He had to close his eyes to say it.

"Who is this?"

"Just get out of the house. Trust me on this."

"Are you trying to scare me? Not until you tell me who you are." But the tone of her response wasn't right. She sounded like she was mocking him.

"Get everyone out now and call the police."

"So sorry, Mr Frost, I'm in the middle of something," she said politely and hung up.

Will pulled away from the clamour behind him.

He was in no doubt. It was the same voice that had woken him at home. He threw the phone onto the seat as if it were part of her.

He was sure her accent was American, but some other nationality was evident in the accelerated cadence of her voice. Whoever she was, would she be waiting for him when he got there?

He dismissed the idea of calling the police and dispatching them to the address. Even if they took her into custody, Libby would still be at the mercy of the other person holding her.

Every particle of him recoiled from his new destination, but he had to go on. He caught up with the cars in front and reprogrammed the satnav. When the traffic surged, he took his next left and accelerated in the direction of the house where his name had just been uttered. He wondered if anyone else there had heard her say it.

Pepperwood Springs was out of town but only three minutes away. Will followed the satnav directions onto the Bel Air bypass and turned off into a quieter suburb. The houses there were spaced out around the perimeter of a small wood and neatly trimmed lawns fronted each property.

He parked in front of 114 and pulled on the gloves. Despite

the light drizzle in the air, the sudden warmth of the morning accentuated how stone-cold he felt inside. Next door a pensioner, wearing an orange raincoat, was doing circuits on a sit-on lawnmower. He looked up to squint at Will over the top of his spectacles. Will avoided eye contact and walked up the slight incline of the driveway. The old man vanished behind the cover of a cypress tree as he reached the front door.

He knew better than to linger at the front and walked straight down the panelled side of the house and found himself at the back porch. He turned slowly to look down the length of the garden to the fenced off trees at the end, dreading the discovery of another human sculpture. However, a cushioned swing chair, a flattened kids' paddling pool and a leaf covered trampoline were the only things positioned on the lawn.

A sound returned his attention to the porch. A dog's whimper? The screen was closed, but he could see the back door was open wide. He remained rooted at the foot of the four steps leading up to it and listened. The noise came again. No dog. It was like somebody painfully drawing breath. Was she still here? Discovering the bodies was unbearable. Was he now expected to witness their last minutes?

He wanted to run now. Back down the side of the house and across the lawn to the old man. Tell him to call the police and wait until they arrived and went in ahead of him.

But he slid Libby's cheap bracelet up his wrist and held it in his palm like a talisman. Will lifted his right foot and placed it on the step.

The lightweight screen rasped as he swung it towards him. He was looking through the open back door into a kitchen he'd already seen – maple cabinets, dried lavender bunches hanging from the ceiling and corn dollies braided around the cooking alcove. There was a vague smell of baking in the air.

Will heard the sound again. It was indisputably human and female, a grunt through teeth or something covering the mouth.

DINNER'S READY WHEN THE SMOKE ALARM GOES
OFF was the sign on the door leading to the house beyond. He
moved silently across the tiles and stopped in front of it. He slid a
boning knife from the block. Will knew he couldn't use it, even
if he believed he was capable of stabbing another human being.
His task was to collect the items from the houses. He couldn't
interfere with what happened to their occupants.

He cracked the door and peered into the spacious, airy hallway.
Daylight spilled in through the glass front entrance and a skylight
had left the faded squares of its windowpanes in the centre of
the bottle green carpet. The three doors to his left were closed.
He strained his ears and waited for the sound. Something hissed
and he registered the small cloud of vapour that had emerged
from the electronic air freshener on the telephone table.

He moved through the door, but his attention was already fixed
on the group of family photos hanging on the wall. He quickly
scanned them for Libby's face. She wasn't there. But there was
a black-framed picture at odds with the space around it. As he
stepped closer, he confirmed the image had been screwed to the
plaster in the same way it had been in Ellicott City. At first he
thought it was some abstract piece of chalk art, white and blue
configurations on black. He bent to it, discerning numbers in its
top right corner, a date and a name.

It was Libby and Luke's scan. The one they'd had done on
June 29th when she'd been eight weeks. The kidnappers knew
she was pregnant.

A voice, a child's now. Laughter. It was coming through the
front entrance. Kids out in the street. He allowed himself to
swallow. The room nearest to him vibrated with a scream. It was
a woman's, acute agony rupturing her throat.

CHAPTER TWENTY-THREE

The scream tapered and the silence that followed quickly mopped up every other sound and left him in its vacuum. The next scream broke him out of it. He used his body weight on the lounge door and swung it inward.

Inside the darkened room the first thing he saw was the image on the TV. Some slasher film – leather-masked maniac torturing a naked girl tied to a bed. But his relief at finding the source of the sound was short-lived when he turned to find its viewers.

At first he thought their hair was hanging over their faces. The two bodies were sitting in armchairs, their clawed fingers poking through the blood-soaked rope looped around their stomachs.

But although Will could see the cleavage of the woman and the open shirtfront of the man he was looking at the backs of both their heads. They'd been twisted 180 degrees. Tendons had been snapped, muscles wrung and torn, skulls swivelled on their spines to leave them facing the back wall.

His eyes quickly recoiled and darted about the rest of the room; his mind misdirecting itself with one question. Where was their child, the owner of the tiny anorak he'd seen hanging up in the image on the website? The curtains were drawn, but the illumination of the screen allowed him to peer at the carpet around him and the darkly slicked rug the adults' feet rested on.

He moved around them, to the area behind their chairs. It was

the only portion of the room not visible to him. No sign. Had the
child been out when it had happened? Was today a school day?
Now he could see the faces of the adults, the purple deformed
expressions and the tubular stares of their empty eye sockets.

The woman's tongue looked like it had tried to escape her
mouth, extending obscenely over her chin. Both their foreheads
bore the deep indentations of whichever clamp had been used
to rotate them.

Then he saw the dull glint, the clasp of a gold chain. It had
been deposited inside the left cylinder carved into the man's
head, the rest of it coiled in the dark recess. Will heard a low,
hopeless moan, but wasn't sure if it was his or if it came from the
TV. He remembered the knife in his hand.

He placed the tip inside the edge of the opening and pushed
the point carefully against the tiny loop of the clasp. He felt the
scrape of metal against metal and dragged it back, but the loop
didn't budge. It clung to the shiny tissue of the socket.

He exerted more pressure on the blade and drew it back
again. Two inches of fine links dropped from the jagged hole,
shimmering like a gold teardrop.

Then he felt the breath on his cheek. He flinched, a bubble
of revulsion escaping him. He turned to look at the woman's
scooped out face. She couldn't be alive. He examined her
rigid expression and the dead tongue, watched it for signs of
movement.

Air escaping, her body expelling. He tugged the chain clean
from its hiding place with his fingers – pear shaped amethyst
pendant glazed with blood.

He couldn't leave the room until he knew she was dead.
He looked into her, waiting on his knees. Her distended lips
remained motionless.

When he closed the door behind him he breathed in the
normality of the hallway. He could still hear the kids playing
outside and touched his cheek. It felt damp. But it was like he

wasn't really standing there. He was locked away, steering his body from the place he'd retreated into.

He checked the other rooms and then looked up at the mezzanine level above the hallway as if he were looking through two holes; watched his feet climb the stairs like it was a movie. He had to know if the child was there.

He inspected all the bedrooms, but they were empty. He went up to the converted attic space. Nobody. When he was positive there was no one else, he descended the stairs. He headed back out onto the rear porch, round the side of the house and to the car.

The pensioner had finished cutting his lawn and was gone. Will seated himself with the cab door open, one foot still on the road. He twirled the fragile pendant around his finger and uncoiled it the other way, the amethyst almost weightless, blood dripping from it onto his tan shirt. Somewhere beyond him the kids played softball in the street.

Poppy listened to the breath whistling in her nostrils for a few moments longer and then let the daylight into her hiding place. Sliding the fitted wardrobe door open on its runner she stepped back into the attic guest room. She crossed to the circular window and looked down at Will seated in the car. She examined his profile as he stared at the dash.

The sound of police sirens displaced the suburban silence. Poppy stayed at the window to watch.

Will only registered the police car when it had crawled to a stop on the other side of the street. He turned to look at its occupants. Two hat badges flashed as they swivelled in his direction and the engine and sirens shut off. His instinct was to slam the door and reverse away, but Will kept panic confined behind rigid muscles as he looked squarely at the dash.

The red and blue lights played across it and he heard the doors open and close. He managed to hinge his spine forward to ditch the gloves and pendant in the compartment. As he did so, he noticed the blood on the lower part of his shirt. He wiped at it, staining the fingers of his right hand. He balled it into a fist, held it in his lap and waited for the footsteps to reach the car.

"Pardon me, sir." The officer's voice was swollen, like he needed to cough.

Will tried not to consider what was waiting to be discovered less than twenty yards from them both and looked up at the blue-shirted officer's ginger grey nasal hairs.

"We've just received a call about a disturbance in this area. Are you a resident here?"

"No." The sun was peeking round the officer's head and he was relieved he had to squint at his face.

"Could I ask you what business you have here today, sir?"

He remembered the car he was in had the cab number on the side door. "Just dropping off." Will only focussed on the hairs.

"Which house?"

He broke contact with the officer's face and pointed further down the street. "Couple of doors down." The softball kids were coming closer to take a look.

"Where are you from?" The end of his question tailed off.

Will realised the officer had turned back in the direction of the police car. Beyond his ample waist he could see a diminutive young, female officer. She was trotting down the driveway of the residence exactly opposite the one he'd just left.

"Nobody there." She slowed and ambled over to them, pink lipstick and loose trousers flapping.

"Or nobody answering." The first officer turned back and this time Will took in the white cracks around his eyes where the sun couldn't reach. "Report said there's a woman walking round here with a knife. Went into that house over there." He nodded at the opposite property. "You haven't seen anything?"

"I've only been sat here for a couple of minutes, but I certainly haven't seen or heard anything unusual."

"OK. Do you mind waiting here?"

"Sure."

Will watched the two officers stroll back across the street and up the driveway of the house, have a confab in front of the front door and then the female officer make her way round the side.

Will's phone rang. It was lying where he'd left it beside the laptop on the seat. Carla had already left two messages.

She didn't wait for him to speak. "You're at the house?"

"They know Libby's expecting." He glanced back across the street just as the older officer followed her round the side. "Give me a moment..." He started the engine. "I have to drive."

He dumped the phone on the seat. He had to get the blood off his hand. Will looked around the cab for something to use. Nothing. He didn't want to wipe it off on his clothes. He scanned the street. The gaggle of kids had reached the police car, but no one else was in evidence. He reversed all the way back around the bend, keeping his bloodied right hand in a fist and turning the wheel with his left.

"Will?" Carla said from the seat.

Will watched the house slip around the bend, his cheeks burning.

Poppy watched Will's car recede. She'd called 911 as soon as he'd pulled up in front of the house. She'd wanted them waiting in the street for him as soon as he'd retrieved the pendant, but their response had been slow. She'd given them the number of the home opposite and had enjoyed watching his dilemma. But Poppy already knew his compliance was assured.

She couldn't afford to linger long in the house. She had her own schedule to maintain. Poppy would slip out through the back fence when she was done. Her rental car was parked on the other side of the wood behind the estate. A rustle from the wall behind her returned her attention to the task the police had interrupted. Molly, the seven-year-old daughter, had run up the stairs as Poppy had pursued her into the hallway with the Taser.

She'd made it to the guest quarters and had crawled through a miniature door in the wall. Now she was scuttling round the storage space that surrounded the room like a rabbit in a warren. Poppy wondered whether she'd heard the sirens and thought she'd been saved. She felt the handle of the sushi knife sticky in her palm and unbolted the small door again. Beyond was a box full of photograph albums. For the family that lived here, they were now a complete set.

Poppy crouched low and put her face into darkness that smelt of asbestos, looking left and right. "Molly," she whispered. "It's safe now." She tipped her head on one side to listen and heard the child's breath escaping erratically through her nostrils. She probably had her hand clamped over her mouth. The air in the restricted space was tepid with fear. "Molly. It's time to come out now." Sterner now, like her mother would have been.

Poppy pulled her shoulders through the opening so she could pinpoint the sound's location. The crawlspace was wide enough for her to fit. It circled the room. Whichever direction she followed, the child could slither out the other way.

A bottled sob. Sounded like she was wriggling all the way round to the opposite side. Poppy pulled herself out of the doorway and padded to the wardrobe again. She slid the clothes quietly to one side of the hanger bar, crouched down inside and put her ear to the plaster. It was paper-thin. Molly was directly behind it. She could hear the girl's stifled whimper.

CHAPTER TWENTY-FOUR

By the time he'd returned home, Tam was ravenous. His father had risen and shaved and was seated at the table in the kitchen watching a game show on TV. Tam's grandmother had been picked up and ran her dry palm over his shaved head as he came in. She was helping with the preparations even though he knew his mother had tried to do most of them before she arrived so she wouldn't interfere.

He seated himself at the table with his father and looked at the food under the coloured plastic covers. He knew better than to try and sneak a morsel before everyone else sat down.

There was only room for four around the table. Grandmother didn't use to come very often on a Sunday, but he'd been told she'd become very lonely since grandfather had passed away. But grandfather had died over two summers ago and Tam wondered if she'd been invited so the empty chair wouldn't remind them of Songsuda.

From what his father said it was obvious his sister had chosen to become friends with the tourists. They had money so it made sense to Tam that Songsuda had done so because they might share some of it with her. He didn't know why his father had been so angry about it. He used to sell food to them, he was happy to take their notes and coins when they had their hot plate at the market.

His father often spoke about the tourists when he thought

Tam was out of earshot. Tam picked up on things. How could he blame the tourists for what happened to Songsuda when it was him that had shut her out of the house?

He wondered what his father would do if he had one of the tourists locked up in a cage. Would he sit and watch while he sipped his beer like Skinny Man in the chicken factory? He couldn't imagine him being so cruel.

He looked at his father's profile while he watched the TV. His skin looked shiny and smooth after his shave and his hair was wet and combed back. It was the only day of the week he looked so clean. He considered telling him about her then. It wasn't very often his father spoke to him aside from the orders he barked when they were making their deliveries on the bike. This was something important he knew would get his attention.

But Tam liked the idea of knowing something important his father didn't. The girl was his secret. And after that afternoon he wasn't frightened of her, more intrigued. Also Songsuda was gone because she'd made friends with the tourists. Tam was scared his father would banish him if he told him where he'd been going. And he didn't ever want to be locked outside when the sun went down.

Tam wanted to go back, to see more of the girl and find out why she was in the cage. Most of all, he wanted to see under the hood. But he wouldn't ever take anything from her. That had been Songsuda's mistake.

"We're the first team to the scene." Weaver jumped down from the four-wheel's driving seat and opened the passenger door to retrieve the camera.

Pope didn't move. Through the smoked windscreen he studied the two cop cars parked across the house's triple garage. "What's the hurry?"

Weaver looked stunned. "What are you talking about? We've got the jump on everyone else."

"So what? The police will secure the scene and we'll have to wait in line with the rest of the procession. This is worthless." He brandished Weaver's iPad.

"We got delayed. Frost can only have been here minutes ago. Call the channel, see what they want us to do."

"OK, OK." Pope pulled out his phone. "You go get set up."

Weaver hoisted the camera from the back seat and slammed the door.

Pope held the phone to his ear in case he turned back. It wasn't working. Even with foreknowledge they hadn't succeeded in catching up with Frost let alone arriving at the location to capture events as they unfolded. Maybe the occupants of every house were already murdered and it was just Frost's task to retrieve his daughter's items from the bodies. None of the police information about the Amberson family or the corpses in Ellicott City intimated at how long the victims had been dead.

Whatever the case, he needed to get ahead of the story or, at the very least, as inside it as Frost was. But he hadn't established a common thread between any of the victims and Weaver was becoming a liability. He would call the channel if he suspected Pope was acting on his own. It was Weaver's weekend off, but, after today the desk would be in touch with the cameraman's new assignment and then his story would fall apart.

His phone vibrated at his ear. The display told him he'd received a text.

?

At first he thought it was Lenora, but when he checked the number he realised it was Patrice. Shit. Sean's twenty-first. He'd promised to head over there today. He swiftly dialled.

"So you're still going to drop everything for us?"

Pope could hear the washing machine whirring in the background. "Patrice, I had to leave town." He waited for a reaction, but there was none. "Not my choice." Another lie, and he couldn't deny that yesterday's conversation had gone clean from his mind.

"Maybe his thirtieth then." She hung up.

Pope leaned his head against the hand holding the phone. Yesterday she hadn't given him the impression that he was remotely welcome there. Now it was clear she'd been waiting for him to be more insistent. Had waited, given up and called. He should have been round there already, should have just turned up on her doorstep whatever she'd said. Lenora would have understood. Lenora wouldn't even have known he'd gone. Another chance blown. He wished Patrice just got angry with him instead of having to endure her weary stoicism.

He watched an officer moving Weaver away from the perimeter of the house – too late to the scene again.

"Richard Strick." Carla waited with the hot telephone pressed hard to her ear while Will searched his memory for the name. She could hear his lips move as he repeated it. But, after a few moments, she knew it was as familiar to him as it was to her.

"And he's what?"

"Lieutenant Governor of Maryland, he was visiting his ex-wife and their children in Ellicott City." Carla quoted the information from her screen and waited for a further reaction. After the identities of the second family had been reported on CNN, she'd done an online search. "Democrat, lawyer, Roman Catholic, Georgetown University – I've cross-referenced the names, but Strick has no immediate association with Holt Amberson." But Carla was glad she had the new development to distract Will.

Other than Libby's scan photo, he hadn't told her what he'd left behind in Pepperwood Springs. He probably thought the fact their unborn grandchild was being used would be distressing enough. It dragged at her heart. They were truly evil people. Libby had shared the photo online with her Facebook friends.

The kidnappers would only have had to glance at her wall and seen all the messages there to know she was pregnant.

"There must be a local connection..." Will's response was a monotone. Was he really hearing what she said?

There was nothing she could do to mitigate Will's ordeal. She had to keep his mind occupied with the details that had just been made public "Lieutenant Governor of Maryland, Will, the media are all over it. I'll keep searching. Where are you now?"

"Bowling alley car park," he said listlessly. "There's no new information on the site yet."

She could hear him lean away from the phone to check it again, hear the swish of his body against the car seat. Carla maximised the site window and looked at the next house in the row – a stucco-fronted, luxurious apartment block. There were six floors and a crenulated parapet, but it looked like a relatively new structure. The cut out image had been shrunk to fit the others in the scrapbook street. She wondered how Will felt knowing what he would find there. She had to motivate him. Make him think only of Libby. "That's three of the items you have now..."

"It's a woman."

"What?" she said eventually. But she hadn't misheard.

"I tried to call ahead to the house and a woman answered. She was the one who killed them. And the police were looking for a woman with a knife."

Carla's couldn't speak.

"I think she called them. Sent them to a house nearby just to toy with me. I'm going to be arrested soon anyway. There was one definite witness, a pensioner next door. And some kids in the street. I was watched from a window when I left the house in Ellicott City as well."

Carla tried to process how Will could be hunted for the crimes of a woman. "We can explain everything when it's over." *Over.* What did that mean?

The silence from the other end said he was sharing the same thought.

She kept talking, trying to galvanise him. "At this rate you'll be able to stay ahead of the investigation. The site is our edge. We're the only ones who have the window between the murders and the police discovering the bodies." And then it struck her, the reality of what Will was being subjected to. The image on the site of the Ambersons was horrific enough, but seeing death at such close quarters was something she couldn't possibly have faced alone.

"They're all in denial."

Carla said nothing. She knew what he was referring to.

"You saw the Ambersons. The others have been posed like they're refusing to see something. The Strick family's heads were buried in the ground."

Carla clenched her eyes. A detail she'd been spared. She knew Will was thinking out loud. "Let the police work it out. We just have to do what they say."

"The bracelet, the scarf, now the pendant – I've found them all on the bodies of the fathers. I'm taking those things away from the crime scene. They're more or less mocking the police investigation by hanging the pictures. I'm expected to work something out."

"There was no picture you missed at the first house?"

"I don't think so. But then it was a holiday apartment. No family photos to disguise it amongst. Anything alien left there would have stuck out."

At that moment Simon Haste entered Will's office.

"Carla?"

Carla held her hand up to him. "Simon's just barged in," she said loudly enough for her intruder to hear. "I'll call you straight back." She put down the handset.

"Your secretary said you were indisposed..." He his untidy white eyebrows were raised.

Carla was suddenly aware of how much sunlight there was in the office because of the amber halo around Haste's unnaturally dark hairpiece. Haste was in his early seventies, but looked a lot older. Semi-retired and a fifth wheel board member he retained a 23.9 per cent share in Ingram.

"I am indisposed." She said it categorically.

"Another gala dinner in the offing? Hope the venue for this one is better than the last."

The last time she'd spoken to Haste it had been to placate him about the lack of wheelchair access for his wife. She tried to dismiss him. "Can't talk, but give my regards to Mo."

Haste lingered. "She's having another one of her bone scans on Monday. I thought Will was on holiday," he said petulantly.

"He is."

"They've called me in on this emergency strategics committee so if Will *is* around." The words whistled over the acrylic of his dentures.

"He's not," she said with equal economy. Haste was obviously after Will so he could absent himself from the meeting.

"OK," he said with resignation. "Better Sunday here than wrestling with the grandkids, I suppose."

Carla didn't respond to his conspiratorial wink.

"Any idea where the Waterloo Room is?"

"Up one floor, ask Nissa to take you up." She signalled to her.

"Right." Haste looked around the office as if expecting to find Will hiding somewhere.

"He's not here, I promise," she said bluntly.

"Yes. I'm not blind. Hope he's not neglecting you. I wouldn't if I were him." He showed her his false teeth in a smile and left the office.

As he became more fragile it was easy to forget Haste's aggressive corporate past. She watched him leave unsteadily. After Nissa led him away, Carla slammed and locked the door to the office. Nissa turned back with censure in her expression. Was it because Carla had lumbered her with wet nursing Haste or was her suspicion deepening about what was going on?

CHAPTER TWENTY-FIVE

Will pumped the soap dispenser in the Bowling alley's bathroom and kept the laptop clamped tightly between his legs while he scrubbed his face. It was 11.24am and he'd been surprised to find the place open. A few groups of adults had staked out lanes and had turned in his direction when he'd stolen in. He could hear the thud and trickle of balls impacting pins as he dried with a paper towel. Three men wearing the same blue, bowling shirts entered and stood at the stall with their backs to him.

He wasn't sure how far he'd driven from the house. Not far enough, but he had to clean off every trace of blood. This would be remembered though, stranger washing himself in public bathroom. He wondered how long it would be before they found the bodies in Pepperwood Springs. How many of these people would be able to describe him? He kept his head bowed as the men peeled away from the urinals and left without washing their hands.

Holt Amberson, St Louis business entrepreneur, Richard Strick, Lieutenant Governor of Maryland. This was high profile homicide that seemed anything but random.

At first he'd believed the retrieval of Libby's belongings had been a perverse amusement for whoever was holding her. Now he suspected there was a larger significance to what he was being forced to do.

He'd had no dealings with either man, business or otherwise, and while he tried to figure out which extended contacts the three of them might have shared he couldn't dislodge the faces of the new victims from his mind. What had happened to their child?

He rubbed vigorously at his cheek with another towel.

He felt revulsion for himself because Luke hadn't entered his thoughts. He had to be just as terrified. But his mind could barely handle the concept of losing the two people closest to him. Carla would never survive if Libby weren't returned.

His cheek tingled, the dead woman's last breath still on him. That felt like it had happened to someone else, not to the familiar face squinting in the mirror under the strip lights. He was being forced to look while the victims appeared to be punished for refusing to see. Covering their eyes, heads buried in the sand, looking the other way.

His past seemed to stretch back into darkness; as if nothing existed before the task he'd been set. But he was profoundly aware that Libby had been taken long before his first glimpse of the Ambersons. He visualised her, gagged and bound, waiting all the time since he'd left the UK.

He looked away from his reflection to a chunk of emulsion chipped off the wall beside it. He grappled for who he was before Libby's abduction. Recalled a time when paint flakes and all they had come to signify had been his only source of dread.

In his parents house the walls had been constantly stripped. A new colour scarcely had chance to get dirty before a blowtorch bubbled it off the woodwork and a new shade was applied. His mother and father had been pathological about decorating the property. It was how he'd spent many a weekend, holding the ladder for his father or halfway up it putting another coat on the ledges. The family's façade always had to be pristine for the neighbours.

Pipe smoke would constantly drift over him and he'd splutter, his father casting him weary glances before returning to daub whichever wall or guttering needed attention. It baffled Will. They painted everything in rotation, covering each side of the house until they were back where they started. Will found bristles he'd left in his previous handiwork barely set. He could have measured his childhood with a colour chart.

It was the only activity they shared but, far from it connecting them in any way, it merely served to emphasise the gulf between them. His father used the radio as a barrier during those afternoons. Will would try to tune out whichever turgid play was being broadcast and his father would frown intently in an attempt to repel any conversation. He listened to the radio at no other time. Even at such a young age, Will recognised the ramparts his father constructed against showing him any approval or affection.

It seemed like such a dusty and suffocating corner of his past. The breadth of the life he'd made with Carla jarred so severely with it that it seemed like a different age rather than three decades ago. But despite how far he'd come he knew it was the trappings of his new life that had made Libby a target.

He looked at himself again and tried to locate a vestige of courage in the face that stared back. As he'd got older, the resemblance to his father had deepened. They shared the same look of earnest conviction, but he drew his from a different reservoir to his father. He wondered what the depth of his emotions would have been if Will had been taken.

He felt a harsh pinch in his gut. Whatever he'd jolted wanted him to know it needed immediate attention.

"That's quite all right, Mrs Frost. I've got more than enough to catch up on while Will's away. Somebody's got to keep an eye on things."

Although Nissa finished the statement with a tight-lipped smile Carla couldn't work out if she was hiding something behind it. "It's a lovely afternoon outside. Surely you've better things to be doing with Keiron and the children." Carla had unlocked the door as casually as she could to speak to her, but knew that her small concessions to normality wouldn't compensate for the rest of her erratic behaviour.

"He's taken them to his parents in Deal today so they won't be back until this evening. I'd only be at a loose end."

"It's a perfect day to work from home."

"I've got to cover the phones."

"I'll be here."

Nissa opened her mouth to object again.

"I'd rather work here alone." Carla said it more firmly than she intended.

Nissa decided against any further protest. "OK," she articulated as if it categorically wasn't. She removed her specs and fixed Carla. "I'll be finished up here in an hour then."

"I'd like you to leave now...please." Carla didn't move from her position at the door.

"Have you spoken to Will?" Nissa's Northern Irish accent was suddenly heavy and sceptical and she didn't rise from her seat.

"Yes. Just earlier." Why the hell was she justifying herself to this woman? "He's on holiday. Everything will have to wait until he gets back."

"Do we know when that will be? And I thought you said it was family business?"

It didn't matter that lack of sleep had loosened her grip on which lies she'd told. She wasn't about to be grilled by Nissa on top of everything else. "I don't have time for this. Take the rest of the day off and tomorrow I'd like you to report to the Remada ops room. You can take Will's calls there." She turned and strode back into the office slamming the door behind her again. She seated herself at Will's desk and although she didn't look up from the monitor could see Nissa's movement in her peripheral vision. A minute later she was gone.

Carla didn't allow herself any relief. Nissa's presence underlined

just how alone she was and her departure only meant she would
have to interact with anyone else who came into the office.

As if to emphasise this, the phone started ringing in reception.
It looked like Nissa had forgotten to switch it to voicemail. Carla
ignored the phone, but it kept ringing until she began to wonder
who would wait so long for a response. She marched back out of
the office and seized it.

"Hi, it's Lucile in reception."

"This is Mrs Frost. I don't want any more calls to my husband's
office."

"Sorry, Mrs Frost, it's just there's a gentleman who's very
insistent. I think he's a crank. He's been trying to contact you.
Says it's an emergency. I've told him we don't give out private
numbers, but he keeps calling back."

"My husband is unobtainable."

"Actually, it's you he wants to speak to. Keeps asking me to
pass on the same message and says only you'll understand it."

Apprehension slithered across her back. "Me? What was the
message?"

"He keeps saying he wants to help you with your house-to-
house calls."

Carla felt her face drain cold. She hadn't expected them to
speak to her direct. Having repeatedly dialled the number she'd
been convinced they only wanted contact with Will. How could
she converse with the person who'd taken Libby? How was she
supposed to talk with whoever had drugged and stripped and
photographed her and murdered the families Will had found?

"Mrs Frost?"

"Put him on."

"You're sure?"

"Put him on." Her lips barely repeated the words. She waited,
trying to swallow a bolus of apprehension as Lucile patched him
through.

"Mrs Frost?" He had an American accent.

"Speaking."

"Please don't be alarmed. My name is Teddy Pope. I'm a TV reporter with Channel 55."

She didn't register what he'd said.

"I know this is a time of great stress for you, but I believe I can help."

Carla felt her body shrink around the phone. "Who is this?"

"Please don't hang up. I know your daughter has been taken."

Carla shook her head. "No...my daughter has not been taken."

"She has. We both know it. Please spare us both the time neither of us have." His voice was even, reasonable. "She's been abducted and your husband is following the instructions of the kidnappers via a website."

How did she know she wasn't actually talking to one of the kidnappers? Was this a test? How should she react? "If this is a practical joke..." She tried to put some starch in her voice even though she felt instantly debilitated by the notion of someone in the media being privy to what was happening.

"Mrs Frost, at this moment only I'm aware of what your situation is and I know you'll want to do everything in your power to keep it that way. I can help you, but if you refuse to open a dialogue with me now my next call will be to a major network." He waited for her reaction. "At this stage, I know that's something neither of you want. Am I hanging up?"

"Wait." Carla closed her eyes and inhaled. "If what you're saying about my daughter is true..."

He breathed hard his end.

"Why should I trust you?"

"Because you don't have a choice." His impatience softened. "I can't begin to imagine what you're going through at this moment, Mrs Frost. The implications of a human story like this aside, I'm already neglecting my civic duty to report the details I have of multiple homicides to the cops. How I came by the story is immaterial. I just thought I'd contact you first to see if we could come to an arrangement."

"You know who my husband is."

"I do now."

"Then you'll understand that he can better any money you stand to make from this."

"That's not why I made the call."

"Now you're wasting my time. Why else would you be in touch if you weren't going to exploit the situation? If you want to cut to the chase just give me a figure. And be quick, I'm waiting for a call from my husband."

CHAPTER TWENTY-SIX

He'd had myriad similar conversations before, but the mother's obvious distress and desperation to silence him threatened to filter through the barrier Pope erected to keep himself detached. He shifted in his car seat. "This is about exclusivity, Mrs Frost." He tried to remain assertive. "I appreciate I'm an unwanted presence, but that's now academic. The public at large have a right to know about this threat, but I realise that will endanger your daughter's life. As it's a time-sensitive situation we can iron everything else out later." He cleared his throat quickly. "Firstly, believe me, I'd like to see a positive resolution to this as much as you."

"Spare me the bullshit." Her response was solid contempt.

Pope observed Weaver moving to the front of the line in the gas station. He'd given him his credit card and he was liberally hoovering up snacks from the display while he waited his turn. "I'll hold back on informing the cops or anyone else as long as I can."

"That's no guarantee."

"What I mean is that I'll do my utmost to maintain confidentiality, but I obviously can't compromise myself."

"God forbid." She seemed to check herself and reined in her antipathy. "Mr Pope, this is my child's life you're bartering with."

"Mrs Frost, I have a professional duty, but I do want to help."

"You still haven't told me what you want."

"I'd like to cover the story as it develops... at a discreet distance."

"You're going to follow my husband with a TV crew?" Starkly and caustically stated, the proposition sounded ludicrous. "And that will be your guarantee of confidentiality?"

"Either we do or a whole media bandwagon will. Like I say, my involvement is inevitable. But I'd much rather do this exclusively and with your blessing–"

"Blessing? This is pure blackmail. Just give me the figure that'll keep you a hundred miles away from anything to do with this. I can promise you any verbal agreement we have now will be honoured."

"We've already been over that." His eyes followed Weaver's progress as he jogged back from the cashier. "I want to stay in contact with you. We'll be watching the site, but I'd like to be informed of any other developments. I know that your only concern is your daughter's wellbeing at this point, but I'll have questions that could help us both – all pertinent to her safe return, of course. Are the kidnappers talking to you on the phone?"

She exhaled heavily and eventually said: "No."

"Where did they snatch your daughter?"

"She was taken in Penang. We assume she's still in Thailand."

"Do you know the residents of any of the homes on the route Mr Frost is being directed along?"

"Not apart from our own."

"And which is yours?"

"The very last one."

"So why is it part of a virtual street?"

"I genuinely don't know and don't have time to speculate."

"Understood. We can cover everything in later interviews."

He heard a sound, her end, as if she were absently tapping the table while she considered her options.

"I don't want you to have any contact with my husband," she

said, emotion suddenly absent.

Pope knew about her background. It was obvious she'd use all the skills at her disposal to protect her daughter. "Agreed." Pope didn't have to concede to anything, but he knew he should give her the impression he was capitulating. It would ease the way for the negotiations to come.

"I'm to be your only point of contact. Who else but you knows about this?"

"Just me."

Weaver climbed back into the driver's seat and dumped several packs of beef jerky onto the dash. He tore into a fresh stash of nicotine gum.

"Keep it that way and you can have anything you want, exclusive interviews, whatever. If your coverage puts my daughter's life at further risk, Ingram will bury you alive."

He ignored the threat. "Thank you, Mrs Frost, I'll need a direct line to you, of course."

She gave him a number, reluctantly releasing each digit as if it were an intimate secret. Then she jotted down the number he gave her. "I strongly advise you to think about a figure in the meantime. Your credibility here's not going to last very long."

"Please believe me, my prayers are with your daughter."

She rang off.

"She on board?" Weaver clicked his seatbelt into place.

"Of course she is," Pope said dispassionately. Their exchange had brought everything he'd wanted, but he didn't feel satisfied by the outcome. She was a mother terrified for her daughter's safety. Why wouldn't she be?

Weaver gunned the engine and pulled out of the gas station.

Why not just call back and give her the figure? It would be exactly what she wanted to hear. His silence to her was probably worth much more than any network would offer for the story. Plus, if someone else found the website he'd have nothing.

He considered what he could do with the sort of money she'd

pay. The time he had to make good on it was severely limited. But that would mean he'd be one step away from being a kidnapper himself.

Carla stood stock-still in the office, her hand still planted on the replaced receiver. How was it possible to wish for the situation she'd had a couple of minutes ago instead of the one she had now? Libby and her baby's life were now in the hands of the media as well as the kidnappers.

If a TV news reporter on the other side of the Atlantic knew exactly what was going on, how many others did? Her one hope was that his venality would make him call straight back. If she agreed to pay him he'd have to do everything in his power to keep Libby's kidnapping a secret. As the situation was it was inevitable his presence would attract even more unwanted attention and she couldn't allow that to happen.

She wasn't about to tell Will. Not with everything he had to endure already. She would handle Pope. This was something she could take care of. Carla suddenly needed to open a window, but all of the panes in the office were sealed. She turned the air con right up and even though the draught tasted stale the cold blast partially revived her.

While she waited for Will to call she opened up a search and did a quick background check on Teddy Pope.

It was like his blackened finger. Although he knew it would be painful Tam couldn't resist squeezing the nail.

His grandmother had retired early and was sleeping in his room. Tomorrow was a working day so his parents weren't far behind. His bed was the pull out couch that evening. He fed his hamster and waited until he was sure he could identify three different snores. Then Tam climbed onto the fire escape through the window in front of the dining table. It was still dusk when he dropped down onto the street, but he knew he'd have to retrace most of his familiar route in the dark.

He couldn't stop thinking of the girl and Skinny Man who'd observed her from his chair. Did she need to be guarded? Was she really that dangerous? Listening to his father, Tam guessed there was much she needed to be punished for. But when he'd knelt in front of the cage and watched her breathing he hadn't felt scared at all. How much longer would she be there? Maybe if he delayed his next visit she'd be gone.

He'd taken handfuls of what remained of dinner from the refrigerator – the stuffed leaves, cold noodles and salad – and put them in his lunchboxes. The stack of metal canisters secured by a clip and swinging from the handle in his sweaty palm scraped the wall as he thudded through the passage.

He expected it to be easier this time. As he told himself that this would be the last time he'd visit the girl in the cage a sensation sitting heavily on the food in his gut seemed to know it for sure.

He got waves of the same bloated feeling when he saw the mushroom exterior of the factory again and then when he dangled his legs over the corrugated gates. Was he pushing his luck?

Holding his breath he released himself from his perch and, as he waited to hit the tarmac, the empty second was like the silence after his mother's cleaver blade had chopped a broiler chicken's neck.

CHAPTER TWENTY-SEVEN

Chicago,
Illinois,
DON'T TRY TO PHONE THE OCCUPANT

Sitting in the departure lounge, Poppy used her iPhone to type the information into the configuration page for the website. She looked at the Roman numerals on the gold face of her Emile Chouriet watch. Because of the delay in the house in Pepperwood Springs and getting snarled up in traffic, she only had forty minutes to spare before her flight from Baltimore International. She inhaled a few times, shut out the outcome of what she'd just left behind and focussed on the next part of the schedule. He would probably make the flight behind hers, if he hurried. It didn't matter if he missed it though, as long as he made it to his destination by early evening.

Her next appointment was the one everything in her itinerary hinged on and she couldn't afford to miss the one opportunity she had. The others had been in locations that had been easy to choreograph, but at this one timing was crucial.

She'd left her sushi knife behind the cubicle in the ladies. Even though security was lax on domestic flights, she didn't want to risk being delayed. She'd buy another blade when she got to Chicago.

She looked up to see if the gate had opened and snagged the

eye of a middle-aged businessman with tight grey curls. He was pretending to read an ebook through a pair of half-spectacles. His eyes lingered on her for longer than necessary.

Dressed in the navy blue suit and black suede ankle boots she'd changed into on the parking deck she wondered what the man's perception of her was. He probably wouldn't have conceived of how the blood had gotten on the clothes she'd ditched in the trunk of the car. She smiled at him.

He looked down and pretended to arrange his blue silk tie in his lap and then immediately looked up at her again. In that moment she'd risen and walked past him.

Poppy refreshed her mascara in the mirror of the ladies and was just about to push the brush back into the tube when the swing door opening made her look up and at the reflection of the person who'd come halfway through it.

It was the man from the lounge, but his gaze quickly left hers to check for other occupants. When he realised they were alone he returned his attention to her, moved inside the room and leaned his back against the door.

"That's the problem with departure lounges. Nothing in them to help you kill time." He stayed where he was, anticipating a reaction.

She casually applied more mascara that she didn't need and said nothing.

He seemed to take this as a cue and took two steps forward. "I'm an observer. I watch and identify exactly who the people around me are."

Poppy took her time zipping her mascara away in her canary yellow clutch purse, briefly thought about her sushi knife stashed away in the ladies room in the main terminal and then turned to face him. He moved forward another pace and she estimated, even in her heels, that he was a foot taller than her. His figure was starting to exhibit the surplus of middle age, but his frame was solid and stocky and he was using it to block her path to the exit.

"I've watched you longer than I needed to. Know why?"

Poppy knew she didn't need to contribute.

"I can tell you're like me. You take exactly what you want."

Poppy felt no threat from the man, but was interested to see how he would proceed. She registered he'd already taken off and pocketed his half spectacles. She stepped forward to leave and he moved his body slightly, but sufficiently enough to obstruct her. She looked up at his grey blue eyes as he tried to fix her as meaningfully as he could.

"You smelt so good when you passed me." He cocked his head towards the door. "Nothing to do out there but sit and consider time we'll never get back. A cubicle in here, however, that's got potential."

She breathed in through her nostrils as if considering his proposition. He was a tanned, handsome man. Probably had a respectable job, a faithful wife and more than his fair share of wealth and family happiness. What made him and so many like him respond to such a self-destructive compulsion?

"I've put the cleaning sign in front of the door. But we'll have to act quickly." He raised his eyebrows, hard-selling it now.

She wondered how many lackeys he had saying "yes' to him and how long it had taken this man to convince himself that his licence in the boardroom counted for anything in the real, dangerous world. She reached up to his face and put her finger against his lips. He breathed heavily through his nostrils. Under the artificial breath freshener she could detect that he'd been eating spicy meat.

Poppy pushed her finger into the warmth of his mouth. His surprise quickly dissolved and he kept his eyes fixed on her while he greedily sucked it. She felt his hot tongue licking gently under the pad and watched the muscles of his expression relax. Chemicals were already firing inside him, much quicker than normal if public bathrooms were usually where he operated.

She was tempted, but Poppy could ring-fence what was vital.

After a few moments she broke eye contact, pulled her finger from his lips and wiped it deliberately on his lemon shirt. His chest heaved as he waited for her next move. She turned, picked up her clutch purse and made to leave.

"I know you're hiding something." The enticement had left his voice and he moved sideways, his foot intercepting her step so one of her heels was either side of his leg.

Poppy turned and raised an eyebrow.

The man reached inside his jacket and pulled out a police badge. "I'm paid to notice these things. You don't fit in with anybody out there. Am I right?" His tone was suddenly unrefined.

It wasn't what Poppy had expected to hear and she realised she'd betrayed herself with her reaction.

"You're working too hard to appear calm. I've sat opposite a lot of people wearing the same mask as you. It can convince passport control, but if I were to bust you now we both know I wouldn't need to put in too many hours to find something you wouldn't want me to."

Poppy instantly realised the situation would become unsalvageable if they stepped outside the bathroom.

"Now we can deal with this through the appropriate channels or..." He stepped back, leaving her path to the door clear, "...we can pick up from where we were." He pocketed his badge and waited for her response.

Poppy nodded once and it was his turn to use his eyebrows. He flicked them at the row of cubicles. She turned and sauntered along the row, her mind processing possibilities as he followed her. She could suck his cock; let him do whatever he wanted to her. But it would be an admission of guilt and even though there was a good chance he'd leave her alone after he'd emptied his balls it was an option she'd already dismissed.

The cubicles were all open and empty, but she didn't stop until she reached the last one. She stepped inside and turned at the threshold. He was close behind her and filled the doorway.

"We were doing so well before. Sorry about the unpleasantness."

She knew his apology was offered so his own enjoyment wouldn't be marred. She smiled and pushed her clutch purse against the centre of his chest. He instinctively put up both hairy hands to support it. Bemused, he held it in position while she unzipped it, rummaged inside and pulled out her cherry ChapStick. She applied it to her lips and watched his mouth tussling with a grin that threatened to break out over his face. The power was hers again.

She put the ChapStick back in her bag. Then while both his hands were momentarily occupied she grabbed the end of his blue silk tie and stepped further backwards into the cubicle. She slammed the door before he could enter and slid the bolt with her other hand.

He was left the other side of it, but the tie slid loosely through the gap in the door as she tightened her grip. She felt him pull away from her and quickly braced the back of her boot against the bowl before yanking down hard. His head struck the door solidly and she heard him yell.

Poppy allowed the tie to slide almost all the way back through the gap as he tried to stand upright and then tensed again and used her body weight to batter his head against the door for a second and third time. The cries stopped, but he was obviously still on his feet. She gripped the tie further up with her other hand and wound the free end round it before jerking it down again. His skull echoed against the hard door with another tug and she could feel the resistance slacken.

It was just his unconscious weight pulling the tie back through the gap now, but she planted her sole against the door and battered his head repeatedly. The silk slid down the gap and she felt his bulk tip away from her. She released it and heard his impact on the tiles the other side.

Opening the door Poppy quickly checked for other passengers. Nobody else had entered. She looked down at him; the right side of his forehead had split and was smeared with dark blood. It was also pouring thickly from one nostril and his burst lip. She dragged him inside the cubicle by the backs of his shoes and locked herself in while she sat him upright on the seat.

His mouth hissed as she leaned his spine against the wall. Concussion and maybe brain damage would probably mean he wasn't going to move from his position before her flight took off, but she couldn't take any chances. She took a scarf out of her purse and tied his hands behind his back. Then Poppy stuffed the edge of the clutch purse all the way inside his mouth and closed his nostrils with her other fingers.

She used her whole weight to retain her position over his shoulders as he bucked underneath her. He didn't appear to regain consciousness though and the jerking of his stomach muscles weakened until she was able to release his face and watch the last air bubbling red out of his nose and mouth.

She climbed out over the top of the door leaving it locked from inside and then rummaged inside her purse again. She used three cosmetic wipes to remove the blood smudges on the door and then tossed them over the top of it.

Tam was sitting cross-legged in front of the cage, as motionless as the girl.

When he'd arrived he thought she'd been moved. The sliding door had been wide open and a third of the chicken house's feathered occupants had spilled out onto the ramp and the yard above. He thought the door rolled back was a sign that it no longer contained her. But when he'd peered cautiously inside he'd found her in the same position. The chair was where it had been before. Checking that nobody was about, he'd stepped inside. He'd deposited the stack of food canisters on the soft floor and carefully sat down. He'd thought she was dead.

She was on her side and her fellow captives blocked his observation, rooting around the scant stalks of straw that had been scattered over the floor. Only holding his breath and staring unblinkingly through the gloom at her shoulders lightly rising and falling confirmed she was still alive.

He exhaled gradually through his nostrils. He didn't want her to know he was here yet. The cage was still secured by the padlock and the hood still covered her head. He needed to remove that more than anything else. See her face and make up his mind for himself if it should be hidden away.

CHAPTER TWENTY-EIGHT

Since her escape attempt Libby hadn't been given water, food or glimpsed the ration of light she'd seen when her hood had been lifted at the mouth. The darkness had taken on a new consistency now, its bulk blotting out the other colours that had previously thronged her eyes. The tiny space between the hood and her perception of it had closed up and she was losing sense of everything below her neck.

She vaguely acknowledged she was lying on her shoulder. The commode had been removed and she'd been left to relieve herself on the floor. The skin of her thighs stung and the birds pecked and scuttled about her motionless body. There would be no rescue. Ransom paid or not, she doubted she would ever be allowed to go free.

If money had been demanded against her life she again speculated about her worth. How much would be paid to ensure she wouldn't be excised from the lives of others? She was significant to Luke's. He'd asked her to marry him. She hadn't dared tell her parents about their plans though. Dad already thought she was too young to be pregnant.

Now she'd never prove to him what a responsible mother she believed she could be. She remembered how excited they'd all been when Jessie was about to become a belated part of the family. But Libby had been envious as well, thought Dad had only been ecstatic because he needed a daughter he could have a real connection to.

The one thing she vowed her child would have was what her father hadn't given her – his presence. It was why she was determined to marry Luke. She hadn't thought he'd be the one when she'd first met him. Mum had made fun of his single eyebrow, had jokingly said it was a sign he couldn't be trusted. Libby had soon grown tired of shaving out the middle of it with her razor though and Luke had been glad when she'd given up. She considered how it had needled her in the early days and how ridiculous that seemed now.

Was someone here? She lifted her head and strained to listen. Above the sporadic cawing of the chickens she thought she'd heard a metallic sound nearby. Her neck and stomach muscles strained with the exertion and she rested her face against the bottom of the cage again. She waited, grateful that nobody was unlocking the door. Perhaps somebody was watching her all the time. She could taste congealed blood in her throat from calling for help through the gag. She'd given up on yelling Luke's name. If he were a prisoner in the same room he certainly would have answered by now.

Luke had become more of a friend than any of the other guys she'd been with, but she'd still entertained doubts about them lasting longer than her previous relationships. Maybe that was because she'd never passed the four-month mark with anybody, but Luke and it had made her nervous. Becoming pregnant with his child had immediately changed her perception. She wanted to make it work for their baby's sake. That's why she'd come to this place – a trip away to consolidate things before they became a family.

Her parents thought she was just a frightened kid, but Libby was more capable of handling herself than they knew. She'd been to the doctor's for a morning after pill at fifteen when she'd refused to be placated by her then boyfriend's assurances that everything would be OK. Her parents had known nothing of it.

There was much they weren't aware of. From the moment she'd been attacked by Mr Sloman's boar she'd hidden behind their misguided perception of who she was.

At eight, she'd been playing at the perimeter of Mr Sloman's land by one of the collapsed walls and had decided to trespass to pick some sloes from the branches that had seemed so laden in comparison to theirs. They lay only just beyond the wall and she'd climbed through the gap and scuttled down the pile of bricks the other side. She'd stripped the berries from the trees and dropped them into the fold up of her jumper and had amassed quite a haul before the animal appeared.

She'd heard the impacts of its heavy hooves and turned to find the enormous, soot-coloured animal studying her with its tiny, glistening eyes. It had immediately charged her and she'd fled back to the wall, falling against the brick pile and losing her precious cargo. When she'd turned and tried to sit up, the animal had rammed its snout against her belly, the weight of its dense body compressing her against the sharp bricks. Pinned there Libby had cried for help, but the animal refused to release her. She remembered the sound of it snuffling against her, the strings of spittle about its dark features connecting it to her and the stones steadily piercing her spine.

She'd picked up one of the mossy bricks with both hands and slammed it as hard as she could against the boar's skull. The animal didn't make a sound, but its legs had buckled and when she'd struck it again the pig had slumped onto its side. The brick was dark with its blood and her fingers had been red and sticky.

Then she'd buried it under the bricks. She'd been terrified of what she'd done. But even after she'd wiped the blood off her hands in the grass her injuries only necessitated Libby telling her parents part of the truth.

Part of the truth; she supposed every kid was that to their parents. Hers had certainly never guessed she could be so strong when it counted. But having spent these past weeks congratulating herself on being so mature about the trip with Luke she now knew who was to blame for them ending up where they had.

She'd been in the driving seat for every significant stage of their relationship. It had been her decision to sleep with him and she certainly hadn't panicked about a morning after pill on the first occasion they'd had sex without protection. Maybe, despite herself, she'd really wanted this baby with him.

Becoming pregnant made her realise how selfish she'd been when Mum had been expecting Jessie. She now understood even more why it had been so momentous for them. Libby had felt it as soon as she'd seen the result of the test, an instinct to protect. Especially after what had happened to Mum.

Mum had said the best thing she'd ever achieved was being a mother to Libby. Libby always thought it was just something Mum said to her when she was feeling insecure.

She'd only started to comprehend the gravity of becoming a parent and visualised her Mum and Dad thousands of miles away, not knowing where she was and what was happening to her. She wished, more than anything else, she could have had the opportunity to tell them she wasn't in any pain.

Having stepped quietly to the right side of the cage, nearest the hood, Tam had managed to unclip the stack of food canisters. The girl had reacted to the dull click and lifted her head. He'd waited, counting to fifty. Now he carefully stood up and slipped his hand into the back pocket of his shorts. His fingers found the cold metal of the screwdriver he'd smuggled out of his father's toolbox. He clasped it and pulled it out.

He started to painstakingly prise up the staples that held the chicken wire to one edge of the frame.

At Baltimore International Will called the cab driver and left a message telling him he'd left his taxi in long-term parking. It was half the distance he would have had to travel to pick it up from

Bel Air so he figured he'd done him a favour.

He took the bracelet and pendant out of the glove compartment, wrapped them in the scarf and carefully pocketed them. Then he checked in with the new flight to Chicago. He had an hour and thirty-five minutes to wait. He headed to the upper level, trying to ignore the twinges at his midsection. He found a sports bar with a TV, but there was no breaking news about Bel Air.

He considered alcohol to numb the pain, but knew better. In the past it had only led to sleep or blackouts. It was the very last thing he needed, given his physical and emotional condition. He slumped at a corner table. "Anything on the other channels?" Will listened to Carla surf through them as he kept the phone to his ear. He prayed there wouldn't be until he'd at least taken off.

"Nothing. Holt Amberson has been relegated, but Strick is still getting plenty of air time."

"What else?" He opened his laptop.

"A lot of shocked politicians' tributes; he was an environmental and health care reform champion." Carla sounded oddly distracted.

"Has something happened there?"

"Everything's fine," she said defensively. She took a breath and it seemed to focus her. "They're already laying flowers outside Strick's home."

Sleep deprivation and a grim inertia had seized him. It seemed unreal that he'd been there less than twenty-four hours ago, levering the family's dead faces from the dirt. "Have the police department released any other details?"

"Just that it's an official homicide and that the surviving son is a leading light at Baltimore University. There were some minor scandals. Expense claims abuse, but he was cleared after an independent investigation. Another rag accused him of impropriety with his personal secretary, Monro." Her delivery was rapid now, feeding in the new facts to sustain them both. "Anwar's been back to me again, but there's nothing significant in Holt Amberson's background."

"And no connection between them?" Will found the site and clicked on the apartment block with the red outline around it.

"Nothing that's in the public domain."

"Ask Anwar if there's any coincidences between Amberson and Strick's interests."

"Won't that be a little obvious?"

"It's breaking news."

"He already knows we're hiding something."

"You know how to pacify him better than I do."

She didn't respond.

He clicked through to the images taken inside the property. Ultra-modern and masculine. There was a granite kitchen, circular bed, lavish walk-in shower, blue baize pool table and neon-lit bar in the den. It didn't look like someone's permanent residence, more a weekend apartment.

"They haven't posted any more photos of Libby on the website." Her voice was flat with fear.

He was only too aware that it had been nearly twenty-four hours since they'd been presented with any evidence she was still alive.

She muted the TV. "And we have no idea if Luke is still with her."

"I've tried to reason with them, but they only give me seconds on the line."

Her tone hardened. "This time ask for concrete proof she and Luke haven't been harmed and don't take no for an answer."

From their table on the other side of the bar, Pope and Weaver watched Will finish his call and then dial another number and wait for a response.

They'd spotted him ahead of them in the line in the terminal. Pope had followed him up to the sports bar while Weaver checked them in. They were positioned behind him. Pope didn't shift his eyes from the back of his head.

"Looks like we're on the same flight." Weaver gestured to the waitress.

"He must be running on fumes by now."

"I know the feeling. Who do you think he was talking to?"

"Probably his wife."

"You think she's told us everything?"

"Doesn't matter if she hasn't, we're not going to let him out of our sight."

Weaver ordered them a couple of cold beers. While they drank them Pope didn't take his eyes off Frost. He kept the phone against his ear, shifted in his chair, checked his laptop and glanced at his watch. He could almost feel the turmoil emanating from him. With the life of his daughter in the hands of whoever was probably at the other end of the line he couldn't even begin to imagine what was going through his mind.

He used Weaver's iPad to run a check on the new victim, but found nothing obvious to link Strick to Amberson or Frost. His phone buzzed. It was a text from Lenora. He didn't open it.

Nothing from Patrice, his conversation with her seemed like a week ago. Sean's twenty-first was nearly over. Another milestone had passed by without his presence. Should he hit her number? He imagined them ignoring any incoming calls with his name in the ID. He knew they'd done it in the past. But what could he say even if they did pick up?

He promised himself that when he was done with the story he would call to make amends. Over the years Patrice's attitude towards him made it easy for him to disassociate himself. He always thought that was a deliberate ploy because she wanted him out of the picture. But it was Patrice that had sent the message earlier. Was it her way of reminding him why they weren't still together or had she really wanted him to call in as he'd promised?

His dereliction of duty to a life he no longer led didn't make him feel any less guilty. Patrice had never demanded anything from him, emotionally or financially. She'd moved into her mother's old property and had gradually become her full-time carer. His other divorced colleagues, including Weaver, thought that made him the luckiest man to get out alive. But being made to feel so instantly surplus to requirements afflicted him.

Tam freed the last staple. Now it was just a case of bending the wire inwards. That way he could slip his arm through and untie the line around the girl's neck. He planned to pull the hood out and feed the canisters in and estimated that if she saw the food she probably wouldn't scream. He couldn't be certain of this though and had a clear run to the open door. Plus she would still be unable to escape from the cage.

If she allowed him to feed her without noise, he could replace the hood and tie it at the neck again before bending the wire back in place. Nobody would know he'd tampered with it.

A current of excitement passed through his stomach as he put his palm against the loose wire at the edge of the frame. He pushed on it, lightly at first and then more firmly when it didn't give. As he increased the pressure a tiny grunt escaped him. He quickly checked the girl in case she reacted. She remained motionless. The mesh started to curve inwards. If he removed one more staple from the bottom of the frame he would have the corner he needed to reach her.

He bent to his knees again, but as his body crouched it knocked the stack of food canisters sideways. Unclipped, they toppled against the cage, noisily clanging and spilling their contents.

The girl's body stiffened. As Tam stood his eyes rolled upwards. Seconds passed. The girl lifted her head again. The door at the top of the stairs banged.

Feet frantically scuffed down the concrete steps. Tam knew he couldn't make it through the door and over the gates in time. He only just scampered behind the stack of empty cages before the lights buzzed on.

He peered out and saw Skinny Man booting chickens into the air as he made his way to the cage. He stopped only momentarily to absorb the food canisters scattered about it before trotting through the door that led to the ramp.

Tam's relief was only momentary. Maybe Skinny Man would believe he'd fled and scaled the gates in such a short space of time, but chances were he wouldn't. When he came back this way it wouldn't take him long to find him.

He bit his tongue and cautiously picked his way through the chickens towards the steps. He scuttled quickly up both flights and paused at the top to see if anybody was in the loading bay the other side of the door. When he was sure there wasn't, he slipped through.

The same lorry was still parked there. He stole back across the metal gantry towards the main factory floor, swivelling his head to check the security cabin was empty as he passed it. When he reached the door the other side that led back to the slaughterhouse, however, it was locked. He pushed it repeatedly, as if it might miraculously give with a third or fourth attempt.

Tam seated himself on the edge of the gantry and dropped down four feet onto the forecourt. The red shutters were pulled down at the bay and when he reached them he saw they were padlocked into a bracket in the concrete.

He pelted back to the door that led down to the chicken house and opened it to listen. Above his breath he could hear the main door move along its runner and boom shut before a lock was shot. Then he could make out the birds' rising alarm as Skinny Man did a rapid circuit of the room before he started to climb the steps again.

Tam's chest heaved, but he couldn't catch a breath. He was trapped.

CHAPTER TWENTY-NINE

The crab rotated, its increasingly aggressive circuits mesmerising Will as he leaned in to touch it again. He had to stroke its broken body before he let it go.

They had to leave. He could hear the ugly gull wheeling above and the click of his father's teeth on plastic behind him. Will could see his long shadow and the pipe jutting from it, black wisps of smoke across the rain-dappled sand.

He didn't want to abandon his vigil even though there was a bank of grimy clouds rolling in from the sea. The rain trickled down his nine-year-old face and the crab scored the paint pot with its pincers, more flakes of white adhering to its shell. It wouldn't survive back in the water. It was too damaged. There were fragments of its dark carapace scattered around the bottom of the pot and its legs creaked around the slivers that had slipped into its joints. He knew better than to ask if he could take it home. No pets allowed in the house.

"Put it back in the water, Will. Let it crawl under a rock to die," his father said.

A jolt from behind. Will blinked, but as he tried to refocus on the crab, he was looking at a blue pouch with a dog-eared selection of in-flight magazines poking from it.

He'd spent most of the hour's flight boxed in by the surly, teenage children of a drunken couple with New Jersey accents. They were sitting behind him and redirected the aggression from their slurred argument by haranguing the two brothers about how they should behave when they got to Aunt Lauren's. The kids nodded, but listened to their iPods. The couple tried to overcome this by repeatedly thumping the backs of their seats every time they wanted their attention.

Will waggled himself upright and, as he watched the herding of children back and forth to the bathroom, recalled the last time he, Carla and Libby had been on a plane. Libby was sixteen and had reluctantly accompanied them on their final family trip. Capri had been a regular destination for them since she'd been able to walk. It was the first time Will realised he'd lost touch with her.

She'd spent the whole time texting and having muted phone conversations with her friends about why she didn't want to be there. It had been like a stranger had supplanted the daughter who used to love the food and culture and wandering around the bay of the Marina Piccola.

Will had lost his patience. Her behaviour seemed to negate all the years of happiness they'd had there before. He knew there were always chapters to close as a father. Like the time he'd stored all her redundant toys in the empty attic room. Boxed and sealed away, there had been something final about stowing the props of her innocence. But on that holiday he felt as if he'd suddenly become redundant. On the third day he'd wished she'd stayed at home.

Carla had handled their daughter's doleful presence with resigned ease. But it was more than just passively dismissing it as a phase. She'd accepted her moodiness and peer-pressured behaviour because she effortlessly saw past it to the daughter who still needed love and protection.

Libby would always need their protection and Will had felt that unequivocally as soon as she'd announced her pregnancy, but he'd been far too angry with her to offer the implicit support she got from Carla. How much of that anger had been directed at what he perceived to be her carelessness and how much because they were still hurting from losing Jessie?

To Will it had seemed like Libby's announcement couldn't have come at a worse time, but it had a significant effect on Carla and how she was dealing with the loss. It energised her again and even though Will realised that Libby's baby had been entirely an accident, her stepping so quickly into Carla's shoes had been tough to accept. He hadn't put a time limit on his own healing. Suddenly events had necessitated him discarding his feelings for one child in favour of another.

Now his reality had ruptured again and the family-to-be of Libby, Luke and their unborn child – a family he hadn't even yet acknowledged – was in jeopardy. He still felt winded, but fate never waited for anyone to catch up. He knew it was why Carla had put away the picture of Jessie.

He considered his situation and estimated how much time he'd spent speculating about how Jessie could have impacted their lives. During that last holiday with Libby, he'd mourned a daughter he could still see and touch and ignored her presence for the whole week.

The seat was punched again. Will unbuckled himself, stood up and turned on the squat and brawny couple sitting behind him. They both wore the same Somerset Patriots sweatshirts and red-rimmed eyes. Unshaven Dad had a cobweb tattooed on his neck and a lobe-stretcher in both ears.

"One of you want to swap seats with me?" he said, about to lose his temper.

The couple exchanged a slow glance.

"You could even try talking to them then."

"Fuck's it got to do with you anyway?" Dad started undoing his seatbelt.

But his wife placed a hand across his lap. She recognised something in Will's eyes. "We're good here. Swap places, Paul."

••••

Tam gritted his teeth and allowed a nervous belch to disperse itself in his throat. He'd scrambled underneath the lorry and was lying in a pool of pungent oil just behind its cabin. He couldn't see what was going on. His position only afforded him a view to the edge of the loading bay and not what was happening on the gantry above.

Skinny Man was pacing back and forth along it, his feet making the metal tremble. He was talking to someone the other end of a phone. He recognised only a handful of the English words he used from his days in the market with Songsuda and his parents.

The conversation ended and Tam held his breath while the man caught his.

"Puki mak kau!"

Tam flinched from the curse and scrambled further back on his stomach. He heard Skinny Man stride back along the gantry and descend the steps to the cage again.

As soon as he was clear of security at Chicago O'Hare, Will called the number to confirm his arrival. This time they answered. "Don't hang up. Listen to me." He waited. They were silent, but Will was sure he could hear the sound of breath under the clucking and babbling.

He ducked into a bathroom off the concourse. "We want a photo. Something dated." A father and son pushed past him as he stood inside the swing door. He lowered his voice. "Post something on the site and let us know they're unharmed."

"Choose one," a male voice whispered.

CHAPTER THIRTY

The sibilant Asian voice seemed to hang in the air.

"What are you talking about?" Will hissed back. "We want a photo of them both."

"Choose one."

Will could feel the sound of the man's breath moving the hairs in his ear. Now he wanted him to hang up. He shook his head, not willing to concede to what he might be asking. Frantic birds' wings buzzed within the clamour.

"My choice then." The hushed voice was impatient.

"Wait. What are you asking me?"

"Which one you care about the most?"

"I'm her father for God's sake. You don't need to ask me that."

He was amusing himself, relishing his misery. Will tried to visualise himself there, standing by the cages, next to the man with the phone in his hand. He imagined what he'd do if he were there.

As if in response, the sound of metal chair legs scraping ended the conversation.

What had it meant? He wandered to the exit, disturbed by the implication of their exchange. Was he being asked about the subject of the picture he'd demanded? Or had he been forcing him to make a choice between hostages? He'd been using his desperation for entertainment and Will prayed he wasn't abusing Libby and Luke's emotions in the same way.

He joined the lines of people waiting outside for taxis. He'd considered renting a car, but suspected a cab would be quicker for getting into the city. It was a half hour drive from the airport.

The wind cut through him as he opened the laptop against the chrome rail. The pop up hadn't been revised. As the line moved steadily, he slid the casing along it. Soon it was his turn. A car pulled up and a Jamaican woman with a mouthful of tarnished gold was smiling at him.

"You gonna be OK with all that luggage?" She nodded at the laptop.

He climbed into the back of the yellow taxicab and pulled the door shut. It moved off immediately. "Downtown, but we may be detouring on the way." He looked at his watch, 3.33pm.

"First time in the city?" There was a note of peevishness in the question.

He looked up from the laptop, registering it was the second time she'd asked him.

"Sorry," he said absently. "Flown through before."

"Business or pleasure today?"

"Neither."

As he remained riveted to the screen, he could feel hostility from the front seat.

"Well, whatever you're here for, you'll find a truckload of it in Chicago."

The city rocketed upward before them, skyscrapers jostling for position as they folded out across a powder blue horizon. It felt like the cab was shrinking and soon they were dwarfed in the buildings' cool shadows. They jerked through traffic lights and over pedestrian crossings while the driver used one muscular arm to navigate the wheel. Her other hand, fingers tipped by multi-coloured nails, attempted to coax something satisfactory from the radio.

No address was being displayed, but Will's heart was thumping against his ribcage. In one tiny zone of this vast sprawl of civilisation, people were about to die. Or had already been butchered.

"You just tell me where I can let you out," she said above *This Old House*. She was obviously eager for a more talkative fare.

The details could arrive any moment and he didn't want to end up stranded when they came through. But there was no way of knowing how long that would take and he couldn't drive round with her indefinitely.

She dropped him outside The Honky Tonk Barbecue on the corner of 18th Street and Racine Avenue. As he stood on the sidewalk, he felt more alone than any time since he'd left the UK. There was a small coffee house opposite so he dodged the traffic to get to the other side. Cars beeped and he hoped there wasn't an officer nearby to stop him for jaywalking.

When Poppy heard the key in the lock, she knew the rest would be plain sailing. There had been no guarantee he would make the stop off, only a damn good chance.

She was hidden behind the bar, her arms encircling her knees. Her new sushi knife was on the carpet with the Taser next to it, lithium battery fully charged. With so much to do, it was unlikely he would stop for a drink. Maybe he would want to pour himself a stiff one afterward, but it would be too late by then. She listened to his laboured breaths as he entered the apartment and passed the den. Not exhaustion, panic.

She knew where he'd go first and the door opening and slamming confirmed it. The mini fridge in front of her started to hum, the beer bottles inside jingling against each other. Redundant stock now, he'd never put any of them to his lips. She wondered which movie he'd seen last and hoped it was a good one.

She swiped her cherry balm across the smooth tightness of her dry mouth. Patches of heat radiated from her cheekbones and numbed her ears. She listened to the activity in the other room for a while longer and then tensed her legs. Poppy grabbed the knife and Taser and pushed her back up the wall. She slid off her suede boots and padded barefoot down the hallway to where he was.

They met as he left the back room and he had his arms full. Two heavy cardboard boxes, which meant he was unable to defend himself. His eyes were wide before she Tasered him. As he lay shuddering at her feet, Poppy looked down at the middle-age spread hanging over his belt and the grey roots in the dyed black bowl of his hair. Just an oblivious heap of skin and bone now.

This had been the gamble, but he'd behaved in exactly the way she'd envisioned. She was back in charge of the schedule again. Events could unfold at her pace now. She had the rest of the day and nobody to disturb her.

The door to the cage opened and Libby heard the creak of knee joints as someone crouched over her.

Moments later she'd forgotten Luke and Mum and Dad. The place where the needle had been jabbed into her became an indistinct coordinate on a map of what little remained of her. The narcotic in her veins washed away her prison, her predicament, the hands upon her and everything else.

Normally the scent of coffee beans was like a magnet to Will, but the potent wall of arabica he'd walked into had made him feel nauseous. Garish paintings by local artists covered every inch of the walls. He'd squeezed himself behind a table at the rear of the tiny café and hoped nobody would wait on him. They had, so he'd ordered a coffee he didn't want to drink.

He called Carla and told her he'd demanded the photo evidence. He didn't tell her about the choice he'd been asked to make. He was still convincing himself he'd been choosing who was to be photographed. She asked if it had been her he'd spoken to. Will said no – it was a male voice, Asian. He said he'd contact her when he was at the next location.

He opened up the laptop so he could watch the address box. Now he had to sit, wait and speculate.

Even when it did appear, he didn't feel confident about finding the address himself. Interstate driving was all well and good, but he didn't rate his ability to navigate the traffic of such an immense and unfamiliar city. A taxi still looked like his best option.

He clicked through to the photos of the interior again. Thankfully, none of the rooms looked as if children occupied them. He studied the minimalist furnishing of the space with the circular bed in it. He wondered if she was inside, waiting. Or if there was blood already spilt over the oatmeal carpets.

Then it struck him that the images hadn't been taken through the windows. They had to have been photographed by somebody standing inside the rooms. If it was an apartment maybe it wasn't at ground level. Had they broken in to get the snaps?

How could he be seated here when he knew what was about to happen? Every shred of him felt as if he should be moving, feet pumping while he hunted for the place so intimately photographed for him. He knew it was futile. The city was colossal.

Or maybe the location was one block away.

Weaver picked up after one ring. "I'm clear."

"Are you in a cab?" Pope tried to balance his considerable frame on a chrome barstool in the window of the juice bar.

"Just left the pick up zone."

Having sat six rows back from him on the flight Pope had easily tailed Frost from the airport while Weaver recovered the camera from the carousel. "18th and Racine, I'm in the Vita-Shakes bar. Frost is sitting tight in the coffee shop opposite. He got the better deal." Pope looked down at the green wheat grass drink on the plastic orange shelf in front of him. "He could move anytime. Tell your driver he's got a fare for the day."

"Be there soon as I can."

Pope positioned Weaver's iPad on the shelf. He skated his finger over the next house, but no box appeared. Where the hell was the poor bastard being sent next?

CHAPTER THIRTY-ONE

Apt 17,
144 East Went Street,
Chicago,
Illinois,
60510

Relief and panic collided as Will inputted the coordinates into his online map. The apartment was in the Gold Coast area between Cabrini Green and North Lake Shore Drive. It would take him sixteen minutes to get there.

He was just yanking the coffee house door when a hefty guy in a hairnet grabbed him by the arm.

"You haven't paid your check." His fingers pinched bone.

"OK!" Will rapidly pulled out his wallet. "But you're going to have to let go of my arm."

Hairnet Guy unclamped Will's bicep and put a meaty hand against the exit.

His limb freed, Will plucked some single dollar bills from inside and thrust them at him. "Keep the change." He turned to leave, but Hairnet Guy didn't budge.

"This isn't enough. It's for six seventy-five."

He parted his wallet folds, but there was no other money within. Hairnet Guy looked at the ceiling.

Pope was already out in the street looking for a cab when Weaver pulled up. He jogged to the passenger door as his maroon-faced partner swung out.

"Get back in. Frost should be leaving any second." He narrowed his eyes at the coffee shop and wondered why the new coordinates hadn't made him emerge.

Weaver slammed the car door and thrust some dollars into the driver's window. "Keep the change."

The cabby nodded and pulled away.

Pope was momentarily stunned. "Weaver? We've got the new address..."

Weaver shouldered past him into the juice bar and Pope quickly followed. He dumped his camera onto the shelf and unstrung his kitbag from over his head. "Just after I spoke to you I got a text from the channel. I thought it was kinda weird that they'd be sending me an assignment for tomorrow so I called the desk to tell them there'd been a mistake." He widened his eyes, a cue for Pope to explain.

Pope had been preparing for this conversation, but all of the bullshit he'd rehearsed seemed pointless given Weaver's current demeanour.

"So I find out that the Monday assignment is my *actual* assignment and that I've been dragged onto two planes under false pretences by someone who doesn't have a job at 55 anymore."

Will clawed in another pocket and found more change. He counted it out onto the six dollars already in the man's palm. Each coin another second wasted. He just managed to make it up. As soon as the last quarter landed, Hairnet Guy dropped his arm like a release mechanism.

Will shot out into the street and headed for a taxi that was idling in a line for the lights.

••••

"They're firing me?"

"And me along with you unless I'm back at work tomorrow morning."

Pope watched Frost cross the street to the taxi. "We can argue the toss later. He's moving."

Weaver turned briefly and then retrained his hostility on Pope. "You're a son of a bitch. What were you thinking? No contract, no safeguards. Just string Weaver along and risk his livelihood because you think you're a hotshot? The best moment of *your* career was getting caught in the fucking rain."

Pope held up Weaver's iPad. "I can't believe we were on top of this and you're letting it drive away."

"You should have levelled with me."

"If I'd done that you wouldn't have got on the plane."

"Damn right I wouldn't have. This is us concealing evidence, not the channel. I could go to jail for this, Pope. So what was your ultimate plan?"

"I hadn't thought further than staying on top of Frost."

"Bullshit. Who are you taking this to?"

"Taking what to? Every second we stand here it's slipping through our fingers."

"You must have already positioned yourself with one of the big networks. It'll be back to begging for a job at 55 for me though, right?"

"You're right. I should've levelled with you. But we can slug this out later. If we don't move now you would have risked your job for nothing."

"Fuck you." Weaver sat down and folded his arms.

Rush hour meant they could only crawl through the traffic and Will considered getting out to walk, but sporadic surges through the lights moved them across town at a faster pace than if he was on foot. He perched on the rim of the seat and willed the vehicle forward.

He knew getting there faster wouldn't have any impact on the consequences for whoever lived in apartment 17, and his agitation kept tugging the driver's attention in his direction. He had a flat cap and thick lens spectacles that both seemed too big for his head and his magnified gaze was becoming increasingly nervous. Will caught his own waxen features in the mirror.

"You OK?" It sounded like concern for the interior of his cab more than anything else. Will nodded, but the driver wasn't convinced. "You just let me know if you need me to pull over."

"That's the last thing I want you to do."

East Went was like a tree-lined runway to the outer harbour of Lake Michigan with a mishmash of architecture that reminded Will of the street on the website. The apartment building was a relatively new structure slotted between two older buildings. He handed the driver his credit card, got out and stood by the window. He didn't hear his wisecrack as he tossed it back. Will headed up a short flight of steps to the main entrance, sliding his hands inside the chequered gloves.

He found the box and button for 17. It was the last apartment on the top level. He tried the heavy brass handles of the filigreed glass doors, but they were rigid. He trotted back down the steps and looked up at the blank windows, counting the floors. Seventeen. Looked like it was the penthouse. He only had one option so mounted the steps again and pressed the buzzer.

The grille crackled. Will anticipated a woman's voice. Then the door hummed and the front entrance doors unlocked.

The elevator was a capsule of dread. Will had almost taken the stairs. Running up them seemed more appropriate than listening to the kitsch muzak inside the plush, mirrored box delivering him to the top level. He looked at his own reflection as the container rose and shuddered around him. Who had let him in? If it was her, why was she allowing him to get closer?

The elevator lurched to a stop. When the doors eventually opened, a sickly sandalwood scent poured over him. He was standing in a private lobby. The carpets there were the same dark honey colour as in the elevator. There was an occasional table with a bowl of ornamental wicker balls beside the front door, which was ajar.

The elevator started to close behind him. He put his body back in the frame. If he allowed it to descend, there was no quick escape. He grabbed a fire extinguisher from a bracket on the wall and positioned it on the threshold. The doors closed on it, bounced and opened. Closed on it, bounced and opened.

He listened, no sound except for the elevator and his own internal percussion. He could see the glow of daylight on the plain white wall to the left of the cracked door. Somebody was waiting inside.

Will placed his laptop on the occasional table. A set of keys was hanging motionless from the lock. He gripped the leather fob and pushed the door slowly inward. It glided open soundlessly and he was peering down a hallway he'd already seen. It had several doors off it; the one at the far end was the only one left open. Then he recognised what was lying on the bureau beneath the mirror to his right. It was a canary yellow clutch purse like the one he'd seen the girl carrying when he'd passed her at the back of the house in Ellicott City.

He was about to dismiss it as coincidence, but the object's presence prompted him to reconsider the memory for the first time since it happened. There were only a limited number of houses she could have exited from down that overgrown walkway. It also now seemed too coincidental she'd been leaving as he'd arrived. He remembered her face, lit by the streetlamp. He could see her pronounced lip and a hint of the expression there, but all he could recall in any detail was the purse she'd held against herself that matched the one in front of him now.

The lift doors kept chopping at the extinguisher, a sluggish metronome keeping time as he hovered in the hallway.

CHAPTER THIRTY-TWO

Will moved soundlessly to the first closed cherry wood door. He had no choice but to work his way methodically along the rooms. The gold handle felt cool through the glove as he gripped it and pulled it down. The interior was bathed in the cold light of day. It was the den with the pool table and bar. It was much bigger than it looked in the digital image. An old Wurlitzer jukebox was installed against the far wall, unplugged

Will guessed the last open room had been an invitation, but a movement drew his attention to the L-shaped couch in the top left corner. A naked man was lying there, bound on his front but alive. He was middle-aged, his dyed, jet-black hair contrasting with the wiry grey covering his chest, arms and beer belly. Tape bound his hands behind him and to his ankles and his eyes were protruding so much they looked like they were about to eject from his head. His eyes locked on Will. He yelled through the gag.

"Mr Frost," a female voice stated, as if his name was an answer quickly needed.

It came from behind him.

"Mr Frost," she said more imperatively. He turned in its direction.

He walked back out of the room. It had come from the door opposite. He had to put himself between her and the man on the couch.

Will crossed the hallway and pushed into the room. He anticipated assault or to be greeted by the sight of more mutilation. But all he saw was her profile and the whip of her long, dark hair as she left the room via a door at the back. She closed it quickly behind her.

He speedily crossed the room and gripped its handle. It wouldn't open. He tried turning it clockwise and anti. She'd locked it. He looked about, registering the circular bed and hurried back to the door he'd entered by. It slammed before he reached it and he heard the lock snap into place. She'd circled around.

He realised what was about to happen before his shoulder was against the door. "Open this!" he yelled at the panel.

He waited for a response, his face still ringing. She was there. He could sense her presence the other side of the door. "Open the door," Will said levelly. He put his ear to the crack and listened, hearing only the wood brushing his ear. She'd moved away.

He stepped back and held his breath, trying to pick up any footfalls in the apartment. All he could discern was the hum of the air con unit in the ceiling. Had she left? He doubted it.

One note of masculine pain answered the question. One extended, animal-like protest. It vibrated through nostrils as it held its hopeless pitch. A choking followed, as blood drowned the cry.

It was too late to save him. If they arrested her, he'd never see Libby again.

Or would that outcome be the same whatever he did? He was incapable of doing anything except sitting by and allowing it to happen. She knew it as well.

He tugged at the other door again, muscles wrenching against its solidity. He moved to the back window and yanked the nets along the rail. The glass was sealed and it was a sheer drop to a deserted, private parking courtyard below. He returned to the door he'd entered by and repeatedly booted the handle. He didn't know what would happen if it gave. What could he do, even if he escaped? But he only stopped when the scream did.

His exertions evaporated with the sound.

"Mr Frost." She was at the door again, her tone cordial. "If you break the lock, I won't be able to let you out. If I can't let you out, you won't be able to finish the task."

"Am I going to see my daughter again?" There was no sharpened edge to the question. Will waited.

No response.

"Where is she?!"

"Out of sight, out of mind," she whispered.

"Open this door!" His palms were against it, then the edges of his fists.

Will could hear a strangulated vomiting sound coming from the other room. Then it was cut off.

One glimpse of her had confirmed it. She was the woman he'd passed behind the house in Ellicott City. He thought she'd been a neighbour. Hadn't considered she could have been leaving the Stricks' home. But the same pout to her lower lip had been evident when she'd exited the room he was in now.

She was the one who'd baited him on the telephone at home and when he called the family in Bel Air. He thought she might have had an accomplice, but it looked like this woman was mutilating and arranging the bodies herself.

He registered the black-framed photograph above the bed. It wasn't hidden amongst others, but screwed into a central position over the headboard. It was Carla.

Carla couldn't begin to speculate what the motionless red dot on her GPS map meant for Will. How long had it been since he'd reached the address?

She speed-dialled his number and waited. Pope would have the location as well. How far behind was he? She knew she couldn't trust him to maintain the distance he'd promised.

Maybe he'd tried to get too close.

"This is the answering service for William Frost. Please leave a message."

Had Will turned off his phone before he went into the apartment? A minute passed and she dialled again. Answering service. She repeated the process, but still he didn't pick up. She called Pope.

"Mrs Frost?" Pope sounded startled.

Carla could hear the drone of people around him. "What's happening there?"

"There's been a slight complication."

She became angry. "What the hell have you done?"

"Stay calm, nothing that would expose our presence. I just have to iron out a couple of things here."

"Are you at the apartment?"

"No. I promised I'd keep a discreet distance and I am."

"Where are you now?"

"A couple of blocks away."

"Don't lie to me, Pope. If there's anything you can tell me about what's happening right now I need you to tell me." She didn't want to betray her distress to Pope. "He's not answering his phone."

"OK, listen. Keep trying him and, if I have your permission, I'll move in for a closer look."

The only dialogue Carla had wanted with Pope was to negotiate his silence, but with Will not responding he was her only way of finding out what was going on.

"Call me back when you hear from him." Pope hung up and put the phone down on the table between him and Weaver. "Frost's not responding. She's asking us to take a look."

Weaver still sat opposite him in the juice bar, arms folded and implacable. Pope had been working on him and hadn't made any headway. Without a cameraman it was futile continuing.

"Weaver, it's fine if you want to get on a plane home afterwards, but this is a plea for help."

"Which would be very convenient for you."

Pope sifted the conversation he'd just had. "If you want to look at this cynically then at least helping the Frost family will make things easier for us in light of what we've been concealing."

"What you've been concealing." But something registered in Weaver's glare and his jaw began working his nicotine gum again.

Pope took this as a good sign. "If we're withholding from the police at the Frosts' say-so as well as shadowing under her instruction then our motive is purely to protect their daughter."

Weaver eventually nodded then shook his head to signify that he knew Pope had got lucky. "OK, but wherever this story goes I'm in for fifty per cent."

"That's a conversation for later." Pope was already clambering down from his stool.

"Fifty per cent, Pope. Agree now or I split."

Pope nodded. He'd already used up his credit. "Agreed."

Weaver grabbed his kitbag and hefted the camera.

5.10pm. Will estimated he'd been confined to the room for just over fifteen minutes.

Whoever had been on the couch was dead. Slaughtering him while Will had been powerless was part of the design. Why? How were these people significant to him, or to her or to Libby?

Again he examined the colour photograph of Carla. He knew when the image had been captured. It had been in June when they'd had an open day at Easton Grey. She'd invited the village residents to rally them for the protest against David Wardour and his proposed Motex Radials plant. Even though it was only a head and shoulders shot he recognised the suit she'd worn and could see the summer house behind her. She'd addressed the assembly from its platform and in the background were the

SCARE ME

fliers Libby had decorated it with. It would have been so easy for someone to enter with the crowd and slip away to capture the other pictures of the house that had been posted on the site.

There was a scratch at the door beside the window. Will got to his feet and returned to it. He tried the handle. Still locked. He waited there, expecting to hear more whispered instructions. Realisation took him back to the first door. He depressed the handle slowly and it clicked open.

He stepped cautiously into the hallway. She'd misdirected him to the inner door while she unlocked the other. He ran to the lobby, noticing her yellow clutch purse had gone from the bureau. The elevator was descending. He considered the exit to the stairs, but knew he'd never make it down seventeen flights to intercept her in time. And what would he do if he did? He turned back to the apartment.

His own life had been spared, but he felt another part of himself collapse. He still had to collect something from inside.

CHAPTER THIRTY-THREE

Will was standing outside the den, the spotless hallway an anteroom to a grisly slaughterhouse. Whatever she'd done, he had to secure his souvenir with his fingers and his mind. The screams of the man's death now only echoed in his memory. The silence from behind the closed door seemed bloated and ugly. He drew in some scented air through his nostrils and opened it.

When he saw the body of the man who, less than half an hour ago, had been living and breathing and frantically trying to free himself from his bonds, Will immediately recalled the last words the woman had said.

Out of sight, out of mind.

He was seated on the couch, but still bound, the black tape in place over his mouth. Blood circled him like a dark spotlight. His cheeks ran with it and thick streams had escaped from his nostrils and soaked into his moustache. His eyes had been carved out, the deep pits of shadow removing every trace of sentience from the shell of his head. But what made the dead man appear to be nothing more than a husk, a macabre Halloween ornament, was the fact the cap of his skull had been removed.

Will knew where he was to find his prize. The man's head had been emptied out so a substantial object could be concealed in the place where his brain had been.

••••

213

Will put the polythene parcel into his inside jacket pocket and made for the pool room door. He would take the stairs. He didn't want to summon the elevator and breathe the same air as she had.

"Anybody home?" It was a friendly, cautious male drawl of a voice.

Will stopped dead in the doorway. Somebody had walked into the apartment through the open front entrance. He could hear tentative footfalls in the hallway moving closer. There was no way he could close the door and conceal his presence; his shadow had already fallen on the wall opposite. Whoever they were, they knew he was there. He had to seal the room from the other side and conceal the body.

Will thrust his gloved hands into his jacket pockets, stepped forward and was confronted by a man in a tan suede suit with shoulder length, white locks and a solid potbelly poking his check shirt out of his belt. His facial hair was the same colour and wavering between stubble and a beard. Standing next to him was an emaciated, leather-clad teenager who would have been entirely androgynous if not for the pencil line sideburns that slit his gaunt cheeks. They stopped in their tracks just inside the hall.

"Sorry. Who are you?" The man spoke first, bushy eyebrows like shutters of suspicion over his piercing blue eyes.

He seemed strangely familiar, but Will could still see the butchered body out of the corner of his right eye.

"I was under the impression that nobody would be here this weekend." The man gazed past Will's shoulder as if looking for other interlopers.

A neighbour? Will was relieved they'd halted where they had. "Well, I'm sorry...you were misinformed." If he closed the door in the middle of their surprise encounter it would look immediately suspicious, particularly if they saw he was wearing gloves. Should he be reacting more to the fact these people had just walked in unannounced? "Can I help?"

"Jake gave you your own keys?"

Nodding, Will looked from his inquisitor's face to the teenager who looked sleepy, stoned or bored. "Yes." He met the man's gaze again, but resisted asking him who he was. The corpse waited to be introduced. "I'll be gone in a couple of days."

The man looked at the carpet and waved his hand dismissively.

"Do you have a message I can give Jake?" Will used the name he was expected to be familiar with. Did it belong to the victim?

The man closed his eyes and sternly shook his head, like even suggesting it was foolish. "No, no, no – nice to have made your acquaintance, come on." He hurried the teenager back out of the door and closed it behind them.

Will waited, not allowing relief to relax his shoulders. The pair didn't speak as they got into the elevator. As soon as he heard them descend he sealed the doors to the pool room and the apartment, grabbed the laptop and took the stairs.

He felt as hollowed out as the man he'd left behind. His legs attempted to maintain rhythm as he spiralled down the stairwell but, after three flights, his feet became unsynchronised. He almost fell headfirst and had to put one palm against the concrete wall. He wanted to leap down to each level, but had to compose himself and take the steps one at a time.

When he eventually made it through the exit into the foyer, he burst the front doors wide. The keen breeze played over the mask that had set into the muscles of his face. There was no sign of the visitors. The package was in his pocket, violet silk that had been compressed inside the sealed polythene. He peeled off the gloves, took the steps slow and kept walking.

He headed down East Went Street, towards the glow of green water at the end. He didn't know where he was going, he just knew he had to keep moving, not give himself any pause to contemplate. Suddenly police vehicles were pulling up behind him.

He turned, pacing backwards. A white car with blue stripes had already ejected its pair of uniformed occupants. His heel slid off the edge of the sidewalk, but he managed to right himself before he toppled. Somebody was meeting them at the entrance.

Had she called them again or was it the neighbour? The apartment seemed pretty well soundproofed, but if they hadn't picked up the screams they might have registered the impacts when Will tried to kick the door down. He turned and strode faster, almost at the end of the block. The lake expanded before him, grubby malachite water on the shoreline extending to deep blue. As he reached the corner, he looked back again. There was significant distance between them now, but Will could see the blobs of their faces turned in his direction.

Could they see his face? He felt as if testimony was tacked there. He took a few breaths and tried to squint their expressions into focus. One of the officers moved quickly to the car. Will hastily rounded the corner onto the busy street.

He slid himself into the back of an available cab and turned to observe the police car exit the end of East Went and glide past. Distance seemed like the best option so he told the driver to take him to the East Side. The pensioner in the front seat nodded his remaining wisps of silvery hair and peered over the wheel for an opening. They pulled out, overtook and quickly left the police car behind.

As the taxi weaved through the rush hour, Will grazed the cursor on the next house. It was a cut-out of an institutional frontage – tan cinder blocks and a characterless grey door, a window to its right and above. It was not yet active. How could it be? She was only ahead of him by a handful of minutes.

"You want me to take you over the state line?" The driver's acid enquiry seemed to come only moments after they'd set off. But when Will glanced at the meter, he realised how far they'd travelled. The sign said they were about to hit the highway.

"Where's the nearest park?" Will didn't want to incarcerate

himself in another coffee shop or restaurant.

The driver said nothing but hung a right. Soon they were on East Columbus Drive before taking a left at Donut Kingdom. Will spotted a phone shop. He got the driver to drop him outside and paid him off with his credit card. He bought himself a disposable mobile and then walked down to the entrance of Washington Park.

It was bizarre to be suddenly surrounded by such a natural backdrop. The sun prickled his scalp and the sound of birds seemed surreal. Lone readers, sunbathers and small congregations of people had spread themselves over the rich green expanse in front of him. It reminded him of flying the Longranger over the parks in London, looking down at the pockets of civilisation. He wanted to be hovering above this place now, a divorced observer and the activity below only insignificant pinpricks of colour.

The peace of the place should have been welcome, but it only accentuated the hollowed out man's suffocated scream in his memory. He kept putting one foot in front of the other and hoped the grass wouldn't run out.

CHAPTER THIRTY-FOUR

Pope and Weaver got out of the cab in East Went Street to an all too familiar scene.

"Two patrol cars, what do we do? They're not going to let us anywhere near the place." Weaver looked back the way they came as a siren announced another car's arrival.

"We shoot the apartment, find out what we can, cover ourselves here until we know where Frost is headed next." Pope leaned in to the driver. "Can you park up and wait? We might need to leave in a hurry."

The cabby pulled in snug against the sidewalk and switched off his engine.

Weaver slipped the iPad out of his kitbag and checked it. "We're good for now."

Tam shivered under the lorry. He didn't know how long he'd been hiding there, but although there was no natural light in the loading bay he knew not enough time had elapsed for it to be morning. His parents probably didn't know he was missing yet. Even when day came, with the factory closed for hygiene checks, there was no guarantee that anyone would lift the shutter or unlock the door to the main floor.

At the moment his only path out were the steps to the chicken house and Skinny Man was still down there. Plus it sounded like he'd locked the sliding door. He'd heard him striding back and forth along the gantry a few times. Unless he was conducting a search elsewhere it appeared he believed Tam had managed to escape over the gates.

His neck straightened as he heard Skinny Man's muffled phone ringing. A childlike tune he didn't recognise. He heard footfalls on the steps and then the door opening and his progress across the gantry again.

Tam edged backwards as the loading bay went quiet. Keys scraped a lock and the door to the factory was opened. He heard an apology from Skinny Man in his own language and then another male voice speaking quickly. He couldn't understand what he was saying, but recognised it was tourist language and that he was telling Skinny Man off.

The door slammed and the keys rattled before the bay fell silent again. Tam counted to fifty and then crawled slowly forward through the slick of oil. When he peered out from behind the front tyre of the lorry he quickly ducked his head back in. The two men hadn't gone through the door, but were standing silently in front of it surveying the loading bay.

He closed his eyes and counted onwards from fifty in his head, willing everything outside of the numbers to evaporate. At eighty-eight the men moved across the gantry again and went back down the stairs to where the girl was. Tam continued counting.

Will came to a beaux-art statue in Washington Park called Fountain of Time. The oppressed figures of Taft's procession of the doomed cowered from the warm daylight. Across the water, the imposing and hooded Father Time looked down at them from his pedestal. Its static participants reminded Will of the cadavers that had been composed for him. He circled it then seated himself on its low sidewall. He called Carla on the office number with the disposable phone.

"Please don't switch your mobile off again. The GPS says

you're heading back towards the airport...Will?"

He could hear her breathing and leaned into the sound. He closed his eyes and took the weight of his body against the phone.

She spoke before him. "They've found a child alive." It was a development she knew he had to hear.

The statement slowly filtered through. "Where?"

"At the Monro place, their daughter."

"Monro?" His blunted senses started to revive.

"She was found wandering in the street and the police were called."

"Who's Monro?"

"Strick's ex-private secretary, Wesley Monro, the one he'd been accused of having an affair with."

"Monro is a man?"

"Married and living with his family in the house in Bel Air."

"Their girl survived?" He had to make her say it again.

"Molly Monro, she's in police custody, too traumatised to speak. It's on CNN."

Will had left the little girl behind. The implications of that jolted him deeply. But he'd searched all the rooms. Had she fled or been hiding in the house?

"The reports are connecting the two murders because they were committed so close together. And obviously because of Strick and Monro's association."

Will recalled the yellow raincoat hanging in the hallway. She'd escaped.

"They don't expect the girl to make a statement anytime soon, but they're still questioning witnesses."

Will guessed the police officers, the old man next door and the softball kids in the street. He wondered if they'd seen anyone but him enter the address.

"But there's still no description of this woman." Carla sounded frazzled.

"I've seen her."

"At the apartment?"

An elderly lady in sweats and pushing a shopping cart full of flattened beer cans shuffled in front of Will. He got to his feet and turned away from her. "I've seen her once already, leaving the Strick's house, although I didn't realise it at the time. And today in the apartment." He gazed at the constituents of the statue, the lovers, the mounted soldier and the crouched, hooded figures.

"What happened?"

How could he begin to tell her? "I got what we needed. I glimpsed her face." The mobile suddenly felt too small for the conversation. "Slim, long, dark hair; I don't know who she is."

"It's not a lot to go on."

"Doesn't sound like anybody who's ever come to work for us at the house?"

"It's just Regina now, you know that."

"Think harder. I'm out of ideas here." His temper briefly spiked.

Although the sun was starting to burn his head, fat raindrops fell.

She waited for him to collect himself. "I'm doing background checks on everyone who's been in our employ. They still haven't posted any new photos of Libby and Luke."

Will recalled the unsettling conversation he'd had when he'd landed at O'Hare. "We shouldn't expect them to. Listen, I want you to step up security there."

"What's happened?"

"There was another photo…you this time." Now it was his turn to mollify. "It's just a device to terrorise us, but I want you to take every precaution. Speak to security."

"Which photo?" She couldn't disguise her alarm.

"It was taken at the rally."

"So is this a caution from Motex?"

"Seems way too heavy-handed and obvious, even for Wardour. But that open day was an ideal opportunity for someone to gather the images for the site."

"We shouldn't dismiss it as a possibility."

"I'm not dismissing anything, but time's running out and we need to gain some ground. There's a reason you couldn't reach me in the apartment."

"What did you do, Will?" There was immediate condemnation in the question.

"When I arrived there I found a purse I remembered her carrying the night I ran into her in Ellicott City. I opened it. It was full of cosmetics, ordinary things."

"You took something from her?"

"No."

"There would have been some DNA on a comb or a lipstick."

Carla was right, but Will had acted on a more immediate solution to tracing her. "I muted my phone and hid it there."

There was only a buzz from Carla's end.

"Slipped it into one of the makeup pockets and zipped it up." When Carla didn't react he continued. "We'll be able to track her using the GPS."

"That was a stupid risk. What if she finds it?"

"I haven't broken any of her rules. But I'm two houses from home and she's murdered everyone along the route. We need some sort of insurance."

"Molly Monro was spared."

"That could have been an accident, an oversight. What makes you believe she doesn't plan for us to suffer exactly the same fate as everyone else? This whole campaign has been built around us. We're the targets. I didn't think. I just did it."

Carla fell briefly silent. "It's done now." There was reproach in her voice. "We just have to pray it stays hidden."

"Can you see her on the GPS?"

A pause. "So it's her that's en route to the airport. Where are you?"

"Washington Park." Will activated the laptop. "What's your password for that?"

She told him and he opened up the same tracking map. "Another flight ahead." He closed his eyes and exhaled.

"Look, we've got this far... *you've* got this far."

The words were familiar. It was what he'd said to her, or something very much like it, when she'd been pregnant with Jessie.

Carla's initial excitement at being an expectant mother in her forties had swiftly been bulldozed by severe cramps and intense morning sickness. Every step of her pregnancy had been hard won, but he'd blithely offered the same words of encouragement, never believing anything could possibly go wrong.

They both knew the risks of being older parents, but having brought up Libby they'd been looking forward to enjoying the experience with foresight and not as the terrified couple they'd been seventeen years earlier. Even when he'd driven her to the hospital in agony, Will never expected what had happened less than an hour after their arrival.

He remembered Libby standing at the end of the driveway when he'd brought Carla home, the part of them they'd all waited for left behind in the hospital. The complexion of the house that, until then, they'd only enjoyed happy memories in had changed irrevocably. But they'd all shared an unrefined conviction that they'd emerge the other side.

Droplets trickled down the screen as he studied the basic façade of his next destination.

They had to have the same faith, no matter what was waiting behind its door.

CHAPTER THIRTY-FIVE

Tam's eyes were starting to hood, but he squeezed his black nail so the pain kept him awake. The men had been downstairs for a good ten minutes, but he knew the longer he left it to try the factory door again the more likely it was they'd come back while he was in plain sight.

He strained his ears for signs of them on the steps and when he was sure he had at least the time it would take the men to climb them, emerged from his hiding place under the lorry and scurried over to the gantry.

He gripped its edge, using his arms to pull his body up and over the metal lip. Tam listened where he crouched, but hearing nothing padded as quietly as he could to the door leading to the slaughterhouse. He pushed on it, but it had been locked again after the other man arrived.

He tiptoed the other way to the security cabin, but there was no telephone, only a switched off TV on a desk. Beyond it was a row of empty lockers and a dirty, wall-mounted mirror. Catching his own reflection almost frightened a shriek out of him, but he quickly bit down on it. He hesitated only to examine the large black oil stain over his orange tee shirt and his own rigid expression of fear. He opted to go back to the lorry to wait until they returned. Maybe then he could try to slip down to the chicken house and try his luck there.

As he dangled his feet back over the bay he could hear the

men's voices arguing again. Only this time they were yelling louder than before. He coiled his legs back up and edged to the steps. Birds screeched as something landed with a thud and Tam could discern them both grunting. Sounded like a fight. Tam cracked open the door and the sound became distinct and ugly.

He slipped through it and told himself he would only listen at the top of the steps.

Will had given Carla the number for his disposable phone, but had told her he'd call back as soon as he'd found shelter from the rain. Again her tired brain fumbled their conversation. Will's actions in the apartment had been impetuous. Was he right? Did they need to assert some control, however marginal? Was this the leverage they needed? It was impossible to decide between risking Libby's life and trying to instigate something that might protect it.

Like Pope, it was another complication that was academic. She watched the red dot approach O'Hare and felt a pang of revulsion as she considered the person moving thousands of miles from the office she was in. If the woman didn't find the phone in her purse they could now monitor exactly where she was heading. She also wouldn't be able to disappear after whatever endgame she'd planned for them.

But what advantage would it give them during the critical events leading up to it? Carla could call the police now and have her apprehended, but it wouldn't guarantee Libby and Luke's safety in Thailand. It would probably mean the reverse. Their survival was dependent on Will obtaining what he had to from the houses. Would tracking this woman to the locations he would inevitably visit afterwards make any difference?

She tried to imagine how Will had felt when he'd found her image on the wall of the victim's apartment. Did it signify she was in real danger? She suspected Will had been right about one thing: kidnapping the daughter of a local protest group organiser was way too extreme even for Motex.

She called the Ingram security guard and told him an email bomb threat had been received in the Remada ops room from a Tunisian extremist group. She requested he discreetly draft in as many staff as he needed to ensure the reception patrol was on elevated alert, but to report only to her. Then she thought about calling Pope. She couldn't deny she'd actually been glad of his presence minutes before and considered that, perhaps, she might even need him again. She knew he would only try to extract information about Will's whereabouts if she called now though. Carla decided to leave him to his own devices. He was sure to be in touch.

Relaying the news about the child's deliverance to Will had given her a significant sense of release. It was exactly what he needed to hear; the sort of words she wished she could have whispered to him the day they'd stood in the hospital chapel and seen their tiny coffin arrive.

Her counsellor and the hospital chaplain had encouraged them both to attend a special service for the babies that had been miscarried at St Andrew's that week. It was an opportunity to connect to some of the other bereaved parents, but Carla had been too weak to attend. They'd opted for the private ceremony a week later and Libby had laid a single white lily on the lid. It had been vital to Carla. She'd said goodbye even though she knew the loss hadn't begun to sink in. As the coffin had been taken for cremation the ritual had at least allowed her to feel that Jessie's existence had been acknowledged.

Will hadn't cried as she and Libby had. He'd barely recovered from the ordeal, was still numbed by how close he'd been to losing a wife as well as a daughter. He'd gently escorted them to and from the service and busied himself with the coordination of the day. She still caught him with the same removed expression, knew he still thought about how their lives could have been if Jessie had made it.

It was the reason she put away the photo the nurse had taken. They would never forget Jessie, but Carla knew they couldn't allow her absence to overshadow the future. Libby's new baby seemed to be recompense for what the three of them had suffered, but Will remained desensitised to her impending motherhood.

His grown daughter and her new child should have been his focus. She knew he worried, irrationally, about a repetition of events as she did. Carla was sure he would resent their grandchild if he wouldn't submit to what had happened. He refused to talk about it, rejected the idea of professional therapy and Carla felt helpless to remove the spectre of a life unrealised.

In the early days she'd been consumed by guilt she'd concealed from Will. He'd been hurting enough and it was months before she found the courage to betray herself. She feared she'd been responsible for the miscarriage. She'd known the risk of having a baby later in life, knew half of all pregnancies after forty-two ended in miscarriage. She'd gone ahead regardless, believing that fate couldn't possibly remove what they seemed so entitled to.

Will had immediately dismissed her fears and, when he'd realised the private torture she'd been subjecting herself to, had at least partly emerged from his abstraction. He spent the following months presenting her with evidence to the contrary. However many times she analysed it though it appeared that randomness had once more left her in its wreckage.

She'd fought the darkness again and busying herself with preparations for Libby's child had slowly repelled it. The pain and guilt were still there, but she'd allowed the tide of the present to wash around what had happened. Will still hadn't. Even though the funeral had been nearly a year ago and she'd gradually removed every reminder of her. He still couldn't put to rest a daughter he'd never known.

As she waited she prayed for Libby, Luke and their child's sake that it would be the hardest thing she and Will would ever have to do.

The telephone rang and she quickly picked up.

"So you *are* still there?" Anwar sounded as if he was disappointed to have an unpleasant rumour confirmed.

Carla's heart sank. Then she remembered she'd called Anwar after Will had asked her to pump him for more background info. Anwar had poutingly said he couldn't sacrifice more of his time if they were both going to keep him in the dark. She looked at the taskbar and it was just after midnight. She was too exhausted to give an excuse, even if she could think of one. "Is this important? I'm waiting for a call."

"Are you going to tell me what's really going on there, Carla?"

"Anwar..." She used his name as a caution.

"OK," he acquiesced. "Give me one minute; I've been doing some digging on Amberson and Strick. No Asian connection."

She'd almost put the handset back. "But you've found something?"

"It's tenuous."

"What is it?"

"First, you tell me where Will is and why you're in his office at this hour."

"Will's at home, I'm working late," she said, as if she had said it a thousand times already.

"How long did we say we've known each other?" It was Anwar's way of calling her a liar. He'd undoubtedly tried to contact Will at Easton Grey.

"I know you probably believe there's some vital insider loop we're excluding you from, but there really isn't. Believe me." She emphasised the last two words.

Anwar was silent for a moment. "The Business and Human Rights Summit."

"What about it?"

"It's been running in Toronto for eight years now. Ingram always send a delegation."

"Amberson and Strick were there?"

"Only Amberson was an official delegate this year. Strick attended the year before because of his volte-face about bio-energy. The summit was a good place for him to be seen before he was re-elected."

"You know this for sure?"

"I've just sent you a link to an online article about it by Strick. Amberson was on the panel for bilateral investment treaties."

"It's a start..." She blinked as she tried to gauge its relevance. "Although it is pretty tenuous..."

"Have you heard the news about Strick's ex-private secretary?"

"Yes," she replied without elaboration.

Anwar picked up on that, pausing before continuing. "I'll see what else there is available, but I might have to pay for the information." But his petulance had vanished and there was sudden purpose in his voice.

"Invoice us. Thanks, Anwar." Carla rang off.

The Business and Human Rights Summit. If Strick had attended the previous year, it was very probable Monro would have been present as his secretary. It was a major international event though; not surprising that big business and politicians rubbed shoulders there. Was it related in any way? It was all they had.

She stretched open her eyes and sat up straight in her chair. Refine the search. She opened the article that Anwar had emailed and pinpointed the keywords within it. Her fingers pecked them in and she told herself that each time she clicked through to another page, she was inching closer to Libby.

Molly Monro in safe custody. Will clasped the news tightly to himself. He'd returned to the park gates he'd entered by, knowing it would be necessary to hail a cab back to O'Hare. Just as he reached them the rain suddenly became torrential and he took cover under a hickory tree. He watched the remaining players in a baseball diamond gather up their gear as the dusty play area turned a deep brown. A cannonade of thunder made him wonder if he should find alternative shelter. Everyone else hovered where they were, as if expecting it to pass. The fresh scent of wet mud and grass was potent.

Molly was his new talisman. Somebody's daughter had survived. He wondered if it had been deliberate. No, the families of the first two houses had been shown no mercy. She'd killed them all and would have butchered the Monro child as well.

Until he'd planted the phone Will had felt powerless. Clawing them one minor advantage made him feel it was possible to alter the course of events. The girl's escape meant the itinerary was prone to circumstance. The outcome wasn't as predetermined as the website suggested. She'd made a mistake. Surely the child could identify her, if she'd seen her. The notion emboldened him.

The face of the man with shoulder length white hair whom he'd met in the Chicago apartment still bothered him. He was sure he'd seen him somewhere before. What had he been doing there? Was he a visitor or a neighbour keeping an eye on the place for Jake? His mobile rang.

"Anwar thinks he's found the beginnings of a connection. The Business and Human Rights Summit, both Amberson, Strick and, I assume, Monro have attended in the past."

Will waited for more, but felt anticipation deflate. "That's hardly surprising. The summit would be an inevitable destination for men like Amberson and Strick."

"And Ingram."

"OK..." It was the first association, but it seemed pretty flimsy. "Plus several thousand other delegates. Are you saying they were there together last year?"

"Amberson was. Strick the year before."

Will tried to energise himself, but it sounded like a long shot. "Anything else?"

Carla sounded exasperated. "That's all so far."

"Too early for the news to have caught up with what happened here, but the police are already involved. Maybe once they identify the man in the apartment we might have a little more to work with."

Nineteen years as man and wife,

And still so many years ahead,

Will mentally swatted at the echo of the rhyme. "You've heightened security there?"

"I've been assured we're airtight. Don't worry, it's probably unnecessary."

Will felt a little better. "So there's nothing in Ingram US contracts to tie us to either man?"

"We officially haven't had dealings with any of Amberson's UG Group subsidiaries. Jesus…" Her voice was suddenly muffled, as if she'd turned away from the phone.

"What is it?" Will felt the thistle of pain in his stomach.

Her voice was crystal clear again. "You've got your next instructions."

Will traced his cursor over the house. It glowed red and the box appeared.

Serangoon,
Singapore
TRY TO SLEEP IT'S AN 18 HOUR FLIGHT

CHAPTER THIRTY-SIX

"That's an early shower for us then." Weaver showed Pope the iPad as they watched the overspill of press outside the apartment block from the other side of East Went Street.

Pope couldn't conceal his astonishment, but his mouth was already an argument ahead. "Then this is a bigger deal than simple abduction. It could be connected to some major international transgression by Frost's company."

Weaver shook his head. "And in the unlikely event that we can get our passports Fedexed over to us in time to get on a plane with Frost, do you really think either of us are capable of handling something like this? You know why dogs shouldn't chase cars, Pope. They might just catch one."

"Come on, Weaver. You have to see we can't quit this now."

"This is as far as we take it, Pope. It's time to offer this to the majors before this..." He jabbed the iPad. "... is nothing more than the game of the event that just happened."

Pope looked at the screen and the four buildings they'd been shut outside. Only three addresses were left and the next one was several thousand miles away. Much as he hated to admit it, Weaver was right. He had to let it go. Time was running out and soon the website would have as much exclusivity as the multitude of reports being delivered on the opposite sidewalk.

Tam was sitting with his back to the stack of cages, his arms encircling his legs. He kept his eyes fixed on the dirty wall in front of him, glad of the birds that picked at the ground around him, their low griping providing a bed of sound to conceal his shallow breathing.

As he'd inched down the steps and around the chicken house while the two men scuffled with each other, he'd figured he was in the right place. It was an area they'd searched and he felt safer here than in the loading bay where they hadn't.

The fight had finished abruptly and, as he'd reached his hiding place, he'd glimpsed Skinny Man mopping blood from around his right eye socket with a handkerchief. The girl had remained motionless in the cage. The new, taller and wider man had had his back to him and used his phone. He'd left a message, paced and waited.

He dared not peep again, just listened and counted. At three hundred and thirty-one the new man's phone rang.

"Where the fuck have you been?" Pause. "OK, listen, you may have problems, but I've got a bigger one. I'm going to have to move Libby." Pause. "Because it looks like somebody knows she's here." Pause. "I don't know. Manap found some food that had been left for her." Pause. "It's under control. He's got another location we can move her to and has promised to make amends by finding whoever broke in here and slitting their throat himself."

Tam couldn't decipher a word.

Pope and Weaver had decamped to a couple of leather-covered box seats in the minimalist foyer of the Wintershore Hotel that overlooked Lake Michigan.

Pope tried to balance himself, phone at his ear. "Mrs Frost?"

"Don't you have a flight to catch?" She sounded bushed.

"I take it you've contacted your husband. We've been waiting to hear from you."

"If I really am a consideration then you'll know exactly what

I want you to do next."

"That's just it, Mrs Frost. As of now, we're withdrawing."

A moment of sceptical silence. "So you've arrived at a figure. I'm going to have to demand some firm guarantees if you want to be paid promptly."

"That's the problem. We have issues with that."

"I can pay the money straight into an account. There's no issue there."

"Professional issues. I'm a reporter. I'm paid to deliver a story. I can't in all good conscience capitalise on your daughter's abduction."

"In all good conscience?" Her voice sounded too weary to muster any scorn. "Look, I don't care how you square this with yourself I just want you as far away from my husband as possible. Give me a figure."

"I'm just calling out of courtesy. I wanted to let you know we have to hand this over now."

"To whom?"

He could hear her start to pace. "It's becoming a high-profile story. Particularly given the people involved. Now unless you're holding out on me, unless you and your husband know exactly who these homicide victims are but are trying to conceal something Ingram doesn't want out there..." He watched Weaver knot his arms and wriggle impatiently on his leather box.

"Mr Pope, don't you think I wish I knew who had taken Libby? Don't you think I wish I knew why anyone would want to murder innocent people who are total strangers to us?"

Perhaps she was concealing something to protect her daughter, her husband or her husband's industry reputation, but the disconsolation in her response sounded genuine. Pope leaned on his elbows. "Like I said, there's plenty of people who'll want this—"

"Be straight with me, Pope, is this a tactic? Because if you're wasting my time trying to extract information I don't possess or to arrive at a figure you already have in your head..."

"It's not. It's really not. I'm sorry, but we're going to have to make some calls."

"Mr Pope, do you have children?"

He had to keep the barrier up. "I just thought you should know. I hope this ends well for you."

"How can it end well–"

Pope cut her off and clasped the phone in his lap, as if he was trying to smother it.

Weaver's had waited patiently to voice his disapproval. "I told you not to waste time calling." But even he sensed Pope's misgivings about what they were about to do. "It's the best way to go. Let one of the majors assume responsibility. You should never have taken this on. We held off for as long as we could."

"Because of their daughter, right?"

"Right."

Pope wasn't ensuring they were getting their story straight.

"This is way above us, Pope. We need to know somebody's got our backs. We can have a deal negotiated before Frost touches down in Singapore and then it's up to somebody else."

"OK, OK." He shouldn't have called her.

"Where do we start?"

Pope massaged his eyeballs, but his phone rang before he could reply. He glanced at the display. "It's Mrs Frost."

"Ignore it."

Pope answered.

She didn't wait for him to speak. "What if I can give you something bigger than you have already? What if I can give you the killer's exact location?"

CHAPTER THIRTY-SEVEN

In the washroom back at O'Hare, Will could smell his own stale body odour. Removing his leather jacket and taking out the package from the inside pocket, he tore the polythene from the wrinkled silk and put it in the waste bin. He pumped soap into his palms and hastily scrubbed his hands under scalding water. After repeating the process for the third time, he held up Libby's violet garment to examine it.

It was a slip with flimsy shoulder straps that bordered on lingerie. It evoked every heated argument he'd had with her about how she dressed to leave the house since she'd been thirteen. As another passenger entered, he carefully folded and put it back into his pocket with the bracelet, scarf and amethyst pendant. Those and the laptop were his only carry-on baggage.

He was still sucker-punched by the distance he now had to travel, but one significant consolation sprang to mind – he was moving closer to her.

Singapore was an eight hundred and eighty-mile flight south of Bangkok airport. His sudden extraction from the US left him with no inkling as to how the victims were connected, but he got a definite sense he was being moved nearer to an answer.

Ingram had no association with Singapore, but it bridged the territories. There were only two houses left on the website before his own. There was the simple, cinder block structure and grey door of the next. To its right was the frosted entrance of its neighbour, set into crude yellow rendering. Easton Grey finished the row.

Would he really be allowed to return home? It was pointless trying to speculate what pay-off had been devised or even if the cut-out of the last address was anything more than a cruel decoy. Southeast Asia had the potential to swallow a small percentage of the people it welcomed. Was that why he was being lured there?

He withdrew some more funds and got them changed into Singapore dollars. Next he called Carla and got her to extract the contract details from the files she'd pulled on Ingram's Eastern Seaboard ops. Four years earlier they'd laid pipes for raw water supplies to industrial estates and factories in Chonburi and Rayong. Were they tied in? If so, what sort of party would have engaged the services of a woman who butchered innocent families?

When he'd worked in the country he'd learnt of the Thai Mafia's associations with the Yakuza and heard stories of contract killings and territorial protection rackets. It wasn't something Ingram had ever got embroiled in. Anwar would have known about it if they had. If it were the case, how were Amberson, Strick, Monro and the dead man in Chicago relevant?

Carla emailed him the PDFs of the contracts to study during the flight. It was going to be the longest eighteen hours of their lives.

"It's a bluff." Weaver popped in a fresh nicotine gum.

"Are you telling me she concocted the story about the phone being planted in the few seconds she had between calls?"

"So what if it is the truth anyway, means she's probably hiding other information from us. And I thought we'd agreed this was way out of our league."

"It is, but it's going to be worth a hell of a lot more if we can clinch the story ourselves. She'll let us assume credit. We'll not only be reporting the crimes, we'll be leading the police directly to the perp. All she wants is for us to hold fire until they have their daughter."

"Till the whole thing is over, you mean. Even if she does have a lead on the killer, how good are these promises of immunity from prosecution going to be if their daughter shows up dead?"

He remembered what Mrs Frost had said. Weaver didn't have kids. Pope knew that if he did he wouldn't have written off the girl's life so nonchalantly.

"We both know that's how the majority of these things end."

"We haven't come to that yet." Pope's irritated response drew the attention of a nearby family.

Weaver momentarily stopped mashing gum with his jaw. He lowered his voice." This is just another ploy to delay us."

"Of course it is. But we're agreed the website is calling the shots?"

Weaver suspected a trap and stalled his reply. "Yes."

"We know that Strick had only just arrived for a weekend with his estranged family and the other homicides have taken place in populated neighbourhoods. So we can assume the victims aren't murdered until shortly before Frost arrives. Let's say we agree to Mrs Frost's terms and she gives us the GPS information for the phone. If the person being tracked turns up at the location before the specific address appears on the site, we'll know she's telling the truth."

Weaver chewed again, nodding quickly, but almost indiscernibly as he considered it. "And if she's not?"

"There's two addresses left after the next and the story is still ours. She knows that, it's why we've got nothing to lose."

Weaver scratched noisily at the thickening stubble on his chin. "OK, call her. But we're not getting on another plane until we know if this GPS is for real."

Pope dialled, slowly exhaling through his pursed lips. Was he relieved because he didn't have to relinquish their involvement or because he could go back to Mrs Frost and tell her they hadn't sold her daughter's life on? "We'll check in to this hotel and get our passports Fedexed. Regardless of where Frost has to go in the meantime, we certainly want to be there the moment we send the cops in."

Having temporarily secured Pope's silence Carla put the phone down on him and collapsed into Will's seat. Her temples sang. She hunted through the drawers for aspirin, but found none. Her emotions were tapped out, but at least another complication to contend with had kept her from torturing herself about Libby's situation.

She'd bought them some more time, kept them off the media radar for a little while longer, but now she had to hand over the GPS password. She'd neglected her observation of it while she'd negotiated with Pope, but now it looked like less of the bargaining chip she'd sold it as. There was no red dot.

Carla tried not to panic. Coordinates were mapped using land masts so she was sure it was because the woman had boarded a plane. They knew exactly where she was headed. Like them, Pope would have to wait until they'd both reached Singapore.

Darkness had ambushed her again. She walked to the window and observed the tiny lights of aeroplanes winking in the blank void over the skyline. She wobbled on her heels and stepped out of them, releasing the pressure on her toes. It felt good, but she was still unsteady on her feet, almost drunk with the exertions of everything that had happened. She slid her feet back into the shoes and the pain reinvigorated her. Had to keep awake. Carla checked the clock on the taskbar, 1.22am. She went to make some coffee to pour into herself.

During the flight, Will's discomfort was exacerbated by the agony radiating from his stomach. He was sure something was seriously wrong. The pain was intensifying and he was terrified he'd have to be hospitalised as soon as they touched down. On the move he'd been able to ignore its nagging, but now his body was stationary it demanded his full attention. He swallowed the painkillers the air steward administered to no effect. He was told if he needed more he'd have to purchase his own medication when they landed.

The red dot on the GPS site had vanished. The same had happened when Libby had taken off for Bangkok. It would be a good few hours before the woman would materialise again.

He tried to concentrate on the contracts and the territories Ingram's pipes intersected, scanned correspondence relating to objections to the work and the settlements that had been reached. But past the pain his mind could only project what was happening to Libby at that very moment, that very second. No further photo of her or Luke had been posted on the website.

The pain seethed, its every spasm growing more urgent. He needed to be examined soon, but prayed he could remain mobile for as long as he needed to. Sleep only overpowered him for seconds at a time.

Tam had resisted sleep for as long as he could, gripping his black nail and squeezing it to keep his eyelids apart. But when the sliding door slammed open he briefly thought he was curled up in his bed at home.

Morning daylight flushed out the halogen yellow. His parents would know he was gone by now, but why would they ever look for him here? As the chickens stirred and recoiled he switched from sitting to kneeling in the droppings and risked a peek around the side of the cage stack.

Skinny Man was pushing the cage with the immobile girl in it towards the open door. The bottom of it hissed and scraped against the matted floor. The other man was silhouetted by white light.

"She's out of it. Leave the cage here. I'll reverse down and we can lift her in."

The taller man disappeared up the ramp. Tam hadn't understood what he'd said, but it was obvious they were moving her. Would they leave the door unlocked after they'd left or would this be his only chance to make a break for it?

He watched Skinny Man extract a key from his shorts and unlock the cage. He dragged the girl out by her ankles like she was a sack of feed and stood looking over her, touching his tender eye socket while he waited for the other man to return. The woman seemed to have delayed reactions and from her position of lying on her spine tried to lift her shoulders from the floor. Skinny Man leaned down and struck her harshly with the back of his hand. Tam winced as the impact reverberated around the chicken house.

Cold reality poured over Libby like dry ice. She'd been tucked into the recesses of unconsciousness for hours on end and wanted to burrow back inside. Her instinct told her only pain awaited her outside of it, but she knew she couldn't hide there forever. Awareness of a physical self and her location in reality sluggishly returned.

Not at home. Penang. Darkened hotel bedroom with Luke?

Her face buzzed as she took some deeper breaths. The sourness of panic and stale air reminded her of what covered her head. She could still hear the chickens; feel the bite in her shoulder and the chill moisture between her legs. Her body reconstructed itself, nerve endings rushing signals to her brain.

Protect the baby.

She had to get them both away from harm. But having lain bound and motionless for so long her body felt like a rusted and reluctant engine.

Libby imagined herself encircling her child with her arms, every sinew contracting and bracing for the supreme effort needed to move.

••••

The girl didn't make a sound as Tam watched her shoulders rise again. This time Skinny Man knelt over her and clamped the bottom part of her hood so she couldn't breath. His arm trembled with the exertion and her body started to buck. A scant smile scuttled over his face and Skinny Man only glanced briefly away from his enjoyment of her suffocation to check the other man hadn't returned.

Tam felt something jar loose inside him as Skinny Man released her face and struck her again. The blow was even harder and her head twisted to one side.

He remembered his father striking his sister and his mother striking his father to make him stop. It was the night Songsuda had been thrown out of the house, when she'd said all those things to him that hadn't made any sense.

Skinny Man checked the doorway again and then dragged the girl's head up by grabbing hold of the line around her throat. He was going to hit her again and balled his fist in readiness.

Tam was already out of his hiding place, had the handle of the screwdriver clutched tightly in his fingers. He aimed it at Skinny Man's calf and felt the skin resistance burst as it went in. Skinny Man howled and his body rolled away from the girl. Tam bolted for the daylight.

He looked down at his sandaled feet pounding the tarmac. Maybe the other man had opened the gates. Don't look back. Skinny Man's wails shrunk in his ears. Then it felt as if he'd run into an iron bar. He heard the air being thumped out of him and watched the ramp circling his view of the chicken house wall as he rolled back down it.

CHAPTER THIRTY-EIGHT

It was much later in the flight, during one of the moments his head nodding whipped him awake, that Will was hit by the realisation. The thought emerged unbidden from the blank void of his mind's brief shutdown. Was she ahead of him or could she be on the same plane?

Her timetable so far allowed her to release location details after her own arrival. But she'd only left the apartment in Chicago minutes before he had. He'd cabbed it from the park to the airport in under an hour. How many flights had there been prior to his?

At least four different airlines were operating flights out of Chicago so she must have made an earlier departure. The one prior to his had been cancelled, however. He hadn't checked the GPS at the airport because he'd assumed she'd already left and that he wouldn't need to track her until he got to Singapore. He turned on his laptop and opened the map, still no red dot.

The idea dug in and, having taken his place in first class after the rest of the plane had been boarded, he speculated as to who was seated beyond the curtains behind him. He considered how synchronising her arrival at the different homes with the presence of the victims would necessitate knowing exactly when she would find them in. The Ambersons had been the easiest. They were first and had been on vacation. But what about Strick's visit to his ex-wife, Monro's schedule and whoever had been murdered that afternoon in the Chicago apartment? She obviously knew their routines. Her journey hinged on careful timing.

Molly's escape had proved the woman was fallible. Had she not been able to find Monro's daughter or had she run out of time? He weighed the thought for a couple more minutes and then unclipped his seatbelt. He'd drawn it tightly across the pain and felt the ache spread as it was released. He got unsteadily to his feet.

A young, Singaporean air stewardess, wearing a multi-coloured smock, smiled at him through immaculate cosmetics as he made his way past her. He parted the orange curtain and stepped into business class.

The flight wasn't oversubscribed and only twenty or so people populated the short section of black leather seats. Windows were shuttered and lights were dimmed and many of the passengers were under blue blankets or dozing wearing headphones. Will still had a vivid recollection of the slender profile and build of the woman as she'd left the apartment bedroom. He squinted through the dingy light at each occupant.

There was nobody that vaguely corresponded with his mental identikit so he moved into the standard accommodation beyond. The largest seating area was only two thirds full, which made it easier to glimpse down the rows the inhabitants had spread out in. It was the same scenario, post-meal snoozing and only the occasional reading light switched on. The atmosphere was cool and dry.

With most of the reclining passengers asleep it was easier to look directly at them and eliminate faces row by row. A whiskered pensioner looked briefly up from the glow of his iPad. A woman's head twitched in his direction as he passed, but her mascara-rimmed eyes remained closed. Will was soon halfway down the cabin.

"Excuse me," a female voice said behind him.

He turned and then stood aside in an empty row while another stewardess dragged a trolley backwards. She passed him, heading towards the curtained area at the tail end of the plane. She smiled and he nodded, waiting for her to get nearer to her station before following behind.

He continued his examination. A teenager wired up to the in-flight movie ignored him, as did a woman whose stark white hair was the same colour as her knitting. There were only two rows left before he was at the curtain. He got a quizzical look from the stewardess.

"The restrooms are the other way," she advised, while she emptied the trays from the trolley.

Will nodded, but kept on walking towards her, as if he hadn't heard.

The stewardess knew he had and the smile became a deterrent. Will nodded and opened his mouth as if it had suddenly sunk in. He turned. He'd be able to inspect the last rows on his way back. He glanced left then right as he passed the first. Empty. In the second, however, a woman was under a blanket in the seat nearest the window.

She was lying on her side facing him, but the blanket was over her head. He stopped and examined the only parts of her that were visible – the white, ringed fingers of her hand uncoiled in the seat and the tops of her legs clad in black slacks. He could still feel the eyes of the stewardess on him. Without deliberating further he leaned across and gently tugged the blanket.

The face that was revealed was of a sleeping woman with broad cheekbones, her dark curls tucked up under a black velvet headband. She looked to be mid to late forties. He scrutinised her oblivious features for a moment longer and then felt the stewardess behind him. He started back to first class without turning round.

Before he'd made it through the curtains to business, she appeared from the bathroom.

She saw him, but didn't react, merely returned her attention to pulling the door closed. Then she casually turned and gauged his expression. It prompted a faint, lopsided smile. His discovery of her presence didn't faze her at all.

"Pardon me," she said almost imperceptibly, nodded respectfully and then angled her lithe body to move past.

Will's senses stalled, his sudden proximity to her allowing him to absorb the human details of somebody far from human. The intense overhead light made her pale features seem anaemic. Even though she looked tired and fragile there was no denying the bony elegance of her face. It was without blemish, but he could see a small group of dark freckles below her right ear, just peeping from the high-necked collar of her fawn suit. It was like somebody had flicked them there with a brush.

He could smell her scent as she tried to move round him: berries and incense. Her slender fingers clutched the canary yellow clutch purse. Was the phone still inside? Her long, dark mane shone glossily as she moved to his left.

As he remained motionless, her elongated eyelashes flicked up. Something was missing, something humane absent from her demeanour. As their pupils engaged it allowed him to see past her facade to what hid behind it – raw, hostile intelligence appraising him.

She returned her attention to the gap beside him. "Pardon me, please." She spoke slightly louder, but retained a similar politeness to the stewardess. It was the voice from the end of the telephone. American accent.

That the slight, fragrant woman rustling around him was capable of mutilating women and children would have been inconceivable to anyone on the plane. His joints remained jammed.

She addressed his chest. "Ironic that we meet properly on a plane." Her tone was companionable. "Excuse me..." She waited, a muscle slightly twitching below her ear. Will noticed her eyebrows were pencilled on.

She'd acknowledged their association and Will realised he had no choice but to comply. He leaned his body away from her as she stepped past.

"Please, return to your seat now," she said without turning.

He watched her walk to hers. An athletic guy in a Foo Fighters tee shirt was dozing at the end of the row. He got quickly to his feet and bowed slightly as she squeezed past to get to the window.

He realised her presence had no consequence. What could he do? Restrain her; attack her? He would probably end up being pinned down by the other passengers and taken into custody. How could he prove anything? Show them the website? Why would they believe she'd constructed it?

Nothing had changed. Whoever she was, she still had the power of life and death over Libby. Nothing he felt compelled to do could result in his daughter's safe return. The woman may as well have been seated in first class with him.

She leaned forward and plucked a magazine from the back of the seat, opening it casually and tilted her head so her hair hung down one side of her face. She flicked it back. He knew she wouldn't look up until he'd left.

The manner in which she'd casually navigated past him proved she was sticking to the programme, regardless of any unforeseen events.

She licked the edge of her thumb and turned a page.

She didn't care that he'd seen her. That in itself was more frightening than where they were headed.

Her instruction had been genteel but categorical and all he could do was obey. Will staggered back to his seat. The plane was experiencing turbulence and the stewardess asked him to secure his seatbelt. The pain throbbed against it.

He visualised her sitting back from him, leafing through the magazine, considered what those fingers had done.

He maximised the website on his laptop and again examined the images of the Singapore address. Whenever the photos had been furtively snatched the rooms had been in the middle of being decorated. Will could identify a small bathroom and kitchen. Most of the furnishings in the other quarters were covered in dustsheets and slid out of the way of metallic stepladders. For the second time the snaps had been taken standing inside the rooms. Was she showing him how easy it was to intrude?

His flight was about to deliver the murderer of whoever lived there. And soon he would be visiting the real rooms to examine her handiwork.

Ironic that we meet properly on a plane.

What the hell did that mean?

The first of Tam's senses to revive was his smell. He identified an all-too familiar aroma and knew where he was before he opened his eyes. He was inside the cage, a terrifying place that had seemed so far removed from his world even though only thin wire had separated him from it.

The girl was with him. He was lying on his side facing her and through the murk of waking he could just discern the dark material of her hood gently bowing inwards and outwards with her breath.

He tried to sit up, but couldn't. Blood pumped heavily at his wrists and ankles where they were bound and his cheeks ached around the large bung of cloth in his mouth. He instinctively yelled, but doing so vibrated the mucous at the back of his throat and blocked the air supply through his nostrils. He spluttered and punched some holes through the snot to let in oxygen.

The girl didn't react, even when he nudged his shoulder against hers. The beating she'd taken had probably put her out cold. Another pain hit him and his scalp clung tighter to his skull with each pump of his heart. The other man had struck him on the head and the injury had been waiting for him to wake. He remembered rolling down the ramp and wondered how badly the fall had injured the other parts of his body. But his bonds were cutting off all sensation and he could scarcely move anything below his neck.

How long had he been lying here unconscious? He thought of his mother and father looking for him and his eyes immediately boiled over with tears. The sliding door was shut again now and probably locked. The halogen bulbs were out. His lashes chopped the tears across the bridge of his nose and he felt them pool cold under his cheek. Fear released itself in whimpers until it eventually subsided.

Then he remembered the cage wire he'd unstapled. If he could just sit up he could push himself to the back with his feet and slither through the gap. His stomach muscles tensed. Dark shapes swooped over him like birds across a skylight. His body wanted him unconscious again. The floor of the cage capsized as he bit down on his gag and hinged upwards.

He hung there, a furnace of blood in his ears as he tried to lever himself all the way. The birds flocked around him, sensations draining away. He ground his eyes, clenched his stomach hard and counted to eighteen before he was sitting straight.

He let the dizziness ebb. His vision adjusted to the dimness. Through the shadows he could see Skinny Man sitting in his chair in front of the cage.

CHAPTER THIRTY-NINE

Fatigue snatched ever-longer moments from Will. His brain slid into a familiar place and, for a moment, he inhabited the wet body, choked on the bubbles and felt the urgency of the prisoner's revolutions within the paint pot. He opened his eyes, but still heard its claws scoring the sides.

The crab had dropped from the sky. They'd been anticipating rain but, as they'd waited for the grubby gang of clouds to reach the beach, it had landed on an outcrop of rocks at the shoreline. He'd turned to his parents for an explanation. Neither of them had shifted their gaze to his, but their expressions clearly said they didn't have one.

Nothing ever happened in their small, private, Dorset cove a hundred and thirteen steps from the bottom of their garden. It had been predominantly his territory for line fishing and building driftwood fires and his mother and father's presence had been rare. But that afternoon his mother had suggested they all eat together on the beach and had even managed to drag his father from his study for the occasion. They were just about to get a head start on the storm, when the animal had crash-landed a few feet away from where they were seated on a blanket.

The crab had pitched on its back and its legs clawed at the sky until it toppled from the edge of the rock pool and embedded itself on its side in the wet sand. Then the ugly gull had swooped down. It had been huge and had patches of feathers missing and a yellow, misshapen beak. It had flipped the crab onto its back and viciously pecked at its stomach until it had impaled it. It had taken off again, circling and then swooping at the rocks, releasing the crab so the velocity of the fall broke it against the jagged ridges. It had been trying to split it open.

Will's family had watched as the gull relentlessly repeated the process, shards of shell and legs pinging off the crab as its body was battered by each new impact. Will hadn't been consoled by his father's assurances about the food chain and had frantically waved the gull away before rescuing its prey.

He'd emptied out one of the many paint pots that he'd confiscated from the garage to make sandcastles with and had dropped the crab inside it in the hope that it could convalesce there. His father had told him he was wasting his time and that it would have been more use as feed for the gull. He was sure it had been his father's indifference to the animal's fate that had made him want to save it.

As the wind had picked up and the rain started hammering the beach, his mother had packed away their picnic. His father had loitered behind him, puffing on his pipe and peering into the pot. Will hadn't wanted to return its injured body to the sea and had been determined that the ugly gull wouldn't snatch it. The clouds gushed rain and the broken crab had scratched its circuits, froth pouring from its mouth. Will had stood guard.

The pot had filled with rainwater. The bird had kept circling, as had the helpless crab.

He rubbed the image out of his eyes again and thought of the predator biding her time in his present. Will's attention returned to the screen. Clicking back to the home page of the website he found a new message above the houses. She'd made time to send him a warning.

LEAVE THE AIRPORT AS SOON AS WE LAND DON'T LOOK BACK FROM ARRIVALS

Will obeyed the instruction as he left passport control at Changi International and limped through the pristine décor of Terminal Three. He paused for breath under a decorative palm tree and hoped she wouldn't pass him.

If the phone remained in her purse he would know exactly where he was being sent before she told him, but if he wanted Libby back he was still effectively powerless to prevent what would happen there. He felt a desperate need to be out of the airport before her. If he watched her leave, he would feel even more complicit. He inhaled sweet air and felt dizziness swell as he looked up at the shutters in the ceiling. The humid climate made him feel like he was wearing a hot face towel and he hadn't even stepped out of the air-conditioned building.

He'd changed his watch to local time as he'd got off the plane. Even though it was just before three in the morning, when the sliding doors opened, he walked into cloying heat. As he approached the polished, blue taxis under a row of orange lights, he called Carla.

"Will? She's only just appeared on the GPS."

"I know. She was on the same plane as me."

A smart, Chinese driver in his fifties grinned and opened his back door for Will.

He didn't wait for Carla's reaction. "So much for the phone giving us a jump on her, she's right behind me." He dropped onto the leather seat and the impact felt like he'd fallen a hundred feet.

"I should have monitored her closer at the airport, but I was… dealing with an emergency."

"Emergency?"

"Dealt with now so forget it. I've sent a request to start tracking your new phone." A wary pause. "Did she speak to you?"

He gulped the pain down. "Hardly. But then she doesn't need to." Will recalled the moment he'd met her raptorial eye. "She knows we'll be obedient."

The driver slid in front of the wheel and turned the key in the ignition.

"Are you heading straight there?"

"Going to find somewhere to wait." He grimaced as he pulled the door closed.

The driver turned to him, beaming emptily. There was a deep scar across his chin that looked as if it had been carved there with a blade.

"Serangoon, please."

"You want Serangoon Central?"

Will registered it sounded similar to the woman's voice. "How long to get there?" He tried to find a comfortable posture.

"Twenty minutes, but because you're with me – fifteen."

Will nodded and spoke into the phone with a lowered voice again. "I have to check into a hotel. I don't feel so good."

"What's wrong, are you sick?"

"I just need to lie down properly." He let his head loll back on the seat.

"Did you sleep at all?" She didn't sound as if she had.

"It's just been a bad flight."

"I can take you to a hotel in Serangoon. Cheapest rate." The driver assured him as they dropped down a ramp.

As the taxi jolted him, Will grimaced with pain. "OK. Did you catch that? I'll call you when I'm there." He rang off. His eyes swam.

Outside the cab window the sprays of spotlit flowers hiding the ugly new buildings became impressionistic blobs.

"Just enjoy the ride." The driver's smiling mouth was hidden below the edge of his mirror.

Pope and Weaver monitored the red GPS dot on the iPad they'd propped up on a stack of brochures. It was positioned on the low table they were seated around in the lounge area of their Wintershore suite.

"Do we really believe that's her? That could so easily be Frost." Weaver chewed hard, a vein jutting out on his forehead.

"We're about to find out." Pope checked the afternoon daylight at the window, looked at his watch and did a calculation. They were twelve hours ahead so it was early morning there.

They'd been in the hotel room for less than twenty-four hours, but it looked like he'd been holed up with Weaver for a week. Bottles from the mini-bar and empty food trays were dotted around and the whole place smelt of armpits. They'd both slept and taken showers, but neither of them had a change of clothes.

They had NBC on and, just over an hour ago, the police had announced they were making headway in relation to the suspect wanted for the murders of the Ambersons, the Stricks and the Monros. More details were about to be released. Weaver was right, the website was fast becoming a record of the past.

"Surely she should have landed earlier than this. Frost should be there by now." Weaver stretched in his armchair and his spine cracked.

They had the website open as well as a detailed Google map of Serangoon positioned beside the GPS coordinates. They could follow its progress street by street. Pope zoomed the display with his fingers. The dot was halfway along the Pan Island Expressway that led from the airport. Was it Frost?

All the information Mrs Frost had submitted to him when she'd given up the password for the GPS seemed too bizarre to be faked: where Frost had planted the phone, the killer being a woman. He'd asked her if she had anything else that could help him tie Ingram to the victims and she'd answered flatly that she didn't. That seemed extremely suspect but, after eighteen hours ransacking the Internet had yielded nothing, he was beginning to believe she was telling the truth.

The cops certainly hadn't named Frost as a suspect so it looked like his evasion of suspicion so far and the fact they hadn't heard about anyone else discovering the website ruled out any obvious link. Was Mrs Frost lying about anything? If the phone was a ploy to stall them she knew that would run out at the next address.

If the GPS was actually pinpointing the woman's location that also troubled Pope. Why should she be present if the victim had already been murdered? There was only one reason for her to be there. Somebody was very probably about to die and they were going to sit by and allow it to happen from nine thousand miles away.

He'd made a promise in return for the live information they were now in possession of. It was Libby's life if they interfered now.

Serangoon was in the northeast region of Singapore. It was the sort of place that was changing every day, its own redevelopment casting new shadows over its inhabitants as it rapidly grew upward and outward. The streets were spotless and, as they passed under the boxy high-rises, it felt like they were driving through an architect's model.

Will got the driver to call at an all-night pharmacy and bought the strongest painkillers he could obtain without prescription. He chewed a mouthful while they took a straight, tree-lined road to the Ambrosia Hotel. He just needed to get horizontal, however briefly.

The driver pulled them into a car park at the back of an unlit, green tower block that glowed luminously against the smog-choked stars. He pointed to the small entrance.

"Tell them Shoushan sent you. Better room that way."

Will paid him and the taxi purred away. He headed for the door, the noise of traffic and his footsteps muffled by the night's thick heat.

Inside reception the smell of damp caught in his throat. Shoushan's name didn't stir the compressed features of the old woman hunched over the tiny desk. A single lamp angled down at the guest book allowed her to duck out of his scrutiny. He signed and paid in cash and her shadowed head nodded towards the fire exit.

"Floor three. Elevator not working."

He climbed the concrete steps and wondered how long he'd have before he was summoned. As he turned the handle of room 39, the fresh paint sucked at his knuckles. The bedside lamp came on automatically. Will was in a tiny cell with a silver blind closed against the window. He opened the laptop. No update in the box. On the GPS site he could see she was moving through the east quarter of Serangoon. At least he knew she hadn't followed him. Will collapsed on the mattress.

Lying flat didn't alleviate the pain. He closed his eyes and gritted his teeth against it then scrabbled the phone out of his inside pocket. It rang before he could hit Carla's number.

Her voice was an ominous whisper. "The Senator for Illinois has been found murdered."

CHAPTER FORTY

Carla rewound the news and read the crawl again. "His body was discovered in a Gold Coast apartment." She heard bed springs as Will sat upright.

"I don't have a TV, but I'll find it online. Could it be the one in East Went Street?"

"It's the only information they've released. That and the fact he was in Chicago to attend a charity ball for Alper's Research. There's a photo of him on MSN."

She heard Will stabbing the keys on his laptop. There was a long pause.

"Will?"

"It's him," he said, both words empty of emotion.

Carla studied the picture on her own computer and then the one on TV. It was the same publicity still of a moustachioed Franks beaming from the centre of his square jaw. Will had been the last person to see him alive. She knew the image would be an echo of whatever he'd witnessed in the apartment. "You're sure?"

His breathing was his only response.

Carla studied her two triangulation maps. "So, you got a room at the Ambrosia."

He answered eventually. "Looks like she's settled for the rest of the night as well."

The other red dot had stopped moving in the Fortuna Gardens

district. She was in one of two hotels that were next to each other, the Mercure or the Fantasia.

"Senator..." He sounded distant.

Carla knew it was pointless trying to persuade Will to sleep. She opened up another window. "Jacob Franks' bipartisan efforts have secured meaningful legislation for Illinois and the first increase in fuel economy standards for more than a decade." She quickly read it aloud from his official bio. "Franks serves on three Senate Committees providing him with multiple channels to benefit Illinois. He currently serves on the Financial Services and General Government Committee, the Energy, Natural Resources and Infrastructure Committee and the Senate Ethics Committee." Her eyes glided down the details of his working class background. "Graduated Harvard's Kennedy School of Government." She could hear Will's fingers at the keyboard again.

"Let's see if he has any connection to the Business and Human Rights Summit. What's this Alper's Research organisation?"

Carla lodged the handset further into the crook of her neck to free her hands. "He's a patron. Alper's is a neurological disease." She opened another window.

"Is a member of his family a sufferer?" His syllables were slurred.

"There's no mention of a family in his bio." She found the website for the charity and heard Will suck in air through his teeth.

"What happened to you?" She didn't anticipate a straight response.

"No mention of Franks in relation to the summit, let's see what we can both find on him. I'm going to try and stay awake, but call me if we get an address on the site or if she moves from the hotel." He rang off. He obviously didn't want to speculate about where he was headed next.

She glanced at the clock on her taskbar – 8.47pm. Carla had

secured the blinds at the partition window now. She had the whole wing of the floor to herself.

Tam's belly felt like it had started to eat itself. No food had passed his lips since the dinner he'd had with his parents and grandmother. His home seemed like a make-believe place now. He didn't know how long he'd been in the cage with the girl. He tried counting every time he woke, but he couldn't even get past a hundred before he lost track. His aching head made him confused, made him lose his place. Acid rinsed through his gut. He was too dehydrated to wet himself.

The girl had been fed. He'd pretended to still be unconscious as somebody had entered the cage, lifted the hood and pushed food into her mouth, but there had been nothing for him. He'd seen her face and she wasn't hideous. No missing jaw, just a glimpse of a pretty nose.

Who was she? The only thing he was sure of now was that it was the men who were bad and not the girl. He'd been scared of being punished for the secret he'd kept, but saw that what the men were doing was something much worse than his trespass in the factory. What was it they wanted from girls like her and his sister? Was it the same thing Songsuda had allowed them to have that his father had never forgiven her for?

He recalled his father striking his sister, remembered the sound it had made when Skinny Man had used the back of his hand on the girl's face. He felt as if he would never understand cruelty, even if he got to be grown-up. Why would they want to hurt this girl? Had she lied to them like his sister had lied to him?

Every time Tam moved and dared to peer out of the cage he saw Skinny Man sitting in his chair. But he couldn't risk giving away his only escape route through the unstapled wire until he was sure he was gone. He had to stay as still as he could, make them think he was dead.

Maybe they were still deciding what to do with him, or perhaps Skinny Man was just going to watch him die anyway. He remembered the way he'd smiled when he was suffocating the girl.

He tensed his legs in the ropes again, gently moved his ankles in a saw motion, so indiscernibly he was sure Skinny Man couldn't see. It was like his nightmare, being chased but unable to move his feet, but Tam thought that if he kept on gently running he could loosen the ropes.

He heard the cage door unlock and closed his eyes. A weight was on his legs, somebody leaning their whole body on him. He tried not to cry out even as the needle went in his arm and it felt like his head was filling with warm water. He exerted pressure on his nail to repel the drowsiness, but the pain rapidly diminished until it was nothing but a distant beacon in a jet black sea.

Poppy surveyed the nondescript office, examining the diploma on the wall. Bachelor of Medicine degree, Guangzhou Medical University, China; she assumed it had been paid for. Leaning against the portable air con unit was a bag of golf clubs. She pictured Dr Ren wheeling them down the fairway of the Serangoon Hills Country Club.

Her presence meant the police would soon dissect everything in the room. Every physical item and then every background detail of Ren's fifty-three-year history would be scrupulously combed through. There was more than enough for them to work with. The celebrated herbalist's counterfeit qualifications were as good a place to start as any.

No family. No dependants. People like Ren never accumulated others, only fed on them. She examined the photos of him at balls and charity drives, stood grinning with various social luminaries. Was this all it amounted to? Was a one-bed apartment over his surgery and these framed moments of sycophancy all he'd scrambled to the top of the pile for?

She heard footsteps in reception. Poppy strolled to the window and opened it.

Will came violently awake as if he'd just been resuscitated. The lamp was still on, but its yellow light had been neutralised by the day glowing through the blind. He clicked away the laptop's screensaver and was relieved to find he hadn't missed an update. The GPS told him the woman was no longer at the hotel, but somewhere behind Serangoon Stadium.

He checked his mobile. No messages from Carla. He'd asked her to call him when she moved from the hotel. She'd obviously let him sleep. 6.22am. He'd been out solidly for nearly three hours. He couldn't remember losing consciousness, must have blacked out moments after he'd spoken to her. God knows what sort of painkillers he'd taken.

He wondered if her research into Franks had yielded anything. He punched up her number, but had second thoughts about dialling. If there'd been a vital development, she would have called him. If he spoke to her now, they'd do nothing but unnerve each other.

The sensation in his stomach had altered. It wasn't so intense, but the area of dull discomfort had expanded to his diaphragm. He knew that wasn't good and chewed a few more tablets.

He couldn't wait in the room. He had to get away from the cloying smell of damp and paint. Will took the laptop with him.

Once out of the building he waded through the heat and along several quiet lanes towards the sound of cars. He clamped his jaw as he tried to stem the pain. He opened the website and GPS map on the laptop and headed towards the stadium.

Pope had observed the dot of the GPS move across town and then halt.

Weaver came out of the bathroom naked from the waist up, dabbing hotel shaving soap from his face. "Still static?"

"Yeah. In Yio Chu Kang Terrace. Maybe she's stopped for breakfast."

"Or Frost's stopped for breakfast." Weaver draped the towel on the back of his armchair and seated himself next to Pope.

Will made his way along the orange frontage of Serangoon's ultra-modern sports stadium. He weaved around the brand new cars parked at its perimeter and the multi-coloured support struts of its triangular roof. A cooling breeze glanced him as he followed its curve.

He knew his best recourse was to turn back and wait it out at the hotel. What purpose would shortening the gap between them have? Putting himself nearer to her would only present him with a harder choice than he had already. Could he watch while she prepared to kill again? When he considered what had happened at the Chicago apartment he suspected shadowing her gave him little advantage. Even without the GPS she had been allowing him to get steadily closer anyway. When she summoned Will this time would he be forced to witness death instead of just eavesdropping on it from behind a locked door?

He kept marching; working his way clockwise to the east side of the stadium where he suspected someone's life was running out. Would they have any more relevance to him than the others had? His mobile rang.

"Will, what are you doing?" Carla had obviously been monitoring his progress.

"I need to walk. You should have called me when she moved."

"Wait for her to release the location or she'll suspect something." He knew she was right. He had to hang back, no matter what that meant for the person targeted. He guessed that was why she'd let him sleep.

"Will?"

"How can we let it happen again?" His pace hadn't slowed.

"It's them or Libby," she said intractably.

Will kept following the curve of the wall, his view ahead unchanging as if he were on a treadmill.

"Go back to the room and wait."

He didn't want to stop. Couldn't be motionless. Will wanted to circle the stadium, circuit after circuit, keep kicking the pain and the thought of what he was allowing to happen a couple of feet in front of him.

He didn't have to kick it much further.

CHAPTER FORTY-ONE

22 Yio Chu Kang Terrace,
Serangoon,
Singapore,
(545412)

"Jesus wept." Pope picked up the iPad and double-checked the address on the GPS with the one that had just appeared on the site. They corresponded.

"Let me see." Weaver took the iPad out of his hands.

"She's been straight with us." It was official; they were spying on a serial killer. What they had would not only allow them to pre-empt her crimes, but locate her immediately after she'd committed them. It was unprecedented.

Weaver's nodding accelerated, his eyebrows making a break for his hairline. "So if that's her..." He blinked rapidly and removed his gum. "Where's Frost?"

Will memorised the short route he had ahead of him and closed the laptop. "I'll hang up now." But he kept the phone pressed to his ear as he hastily began to skirt the remainder of the stadium wall.

"You're already so close." Carla gulped breath as well. "She can't hurt you. There's still one more address before ours." She was trying to convince herself as much as him.

"I'll call you as soon as I can." He chopped his promise short, sliding his phone into the top pocket of his shirt. Somebody's life was about to be taken and he had to believe there was a slim chance it could be saved.

Will raced towards something he knew would overshadow his discovery of Jacob Franks. He could still hear the empty sound when he'd pulled the polythene package out of his skull.

He thought of Molly Monro safe in the hands of the police and Libby still bound and gagged, alive even though they'd been given no evidence to prove it. It was all he could believe if his feet were to keep propelling him towards the woman who held her. .

He heard another set of footsteps, just out of time with his. Momentarily he thought it was the reverberation changing as he rounded the stadium, but suddenly a figure overtook him. It turned and stopped to block his path.

"Give me the laptop."

Will almost ran into them and dragged his arms behind him to slow his impetus. His chest stopped an inch from the box cutter in the boy's hand. His thumb knuckle glowed white as it clicked the blade out a few more notches for effect.

He was white, skin pasty and face covered in downy teen stubble. When Will looked into his blue eyes he could see they were lacquered blank by his last fix. This he had expected in Ellicott City or Chicago, not here.

The boy nodded at Will's bounty as if he might have forgotten what had been demanded. "Laptop, motherfucker."

Even though he suspected the junkie was capable of cutting him for the money he could get for the laptop, Will didn't feel an ounce of fear. Not after what he'd been put through in the last three days. He saw this registering in the boy's hardening features and knew what would come next.

"Your timing sucks," Will said and simultaneously swiped the boy's face with the front of the laptop. Will heard his nose burst against the hard plastic. His sinewy body arced into the gutter.

He started running again, not even looking back at his mugger. The encounter was already dispensed with and his senses braced themselves for the real confrontation ahead. He left the boundary of the stadium and cut across a vast car park towards a busy main road. He darted between the stationary cars there and then the honking, moving vehicles as he crossed to the neighbourhood on the other side.

He left the main road, heading up Yio Chu Kang Place. The terrace was the first turning off it on his left. It was a short street that appeared to be a mixture of residential blocks and one-storey industrial workshops. He could hear the hum of a vacuum somewhere, but the only visible occupants of the area were two red boiler-suited electricians kneeling by an open manhole. Neither of them looked up from the trunk of coloured wires they were examining. He sprinted to the right side of the street.

He'd spotted a row of four grey doors across the front of the tan, cinder block building he recognised from the website. Squeezing past the cars on the small gravelled forecourt he checked the apartment numbers beside each one. Twenty-two was behind the second door on the sixth floor. Will yanked on the gloves before he jabbed the buzzer.

No response or sound of the lock being released. He quickly opened his laptop and checked the GPS. She hadn't moved. She was definitely inside. He tried again. This time he strained his ears and heard a muffled warble from within the building. It was definitely working so she knew he was there. Maybe she hadn't reckoned on him arriving so quickly.

He stepped away from the door and looked back at the electricians. They were still hunched over their work. Nobody to register his presence, she'd probably walked by them as well. Everyday activity belying what was happening only a few flights of stairs away.

When there was no answer to his third buzz, Will guessed

she'd probably left him another way in. He steered himself around the cars and headed for an alleyway at the side of the building.

Doctor Ren's lips chomped at the black tape over them. The action yanked his features down. He couldn't see her. Didn't know she was still in the surgery. The last Taser shock was just wearing off

Poppy finished applying her cherry ChapStick and looked at the gold face of her watch. She dropped from her perch on the side of Ren's desk. Mr Frost had better hurry. He wouldn't hold on very long. Seconds rather than minutes.

She picked up the sushi knife where she'd left it on top of his in-tray.

Will had followed a creosoted fence down the side of the building and arrived at a small, enclosed courtyard at the back. To his right was some green, plastic garden furniture surrounded by flattened cigarette butts. He'd left the street sounds behind. The only noise he could hear now was water gurgling down the drainpipe beside the metal rear entrance.

He pushed on the dented door and felt the bolt grate across the floor as it gave inwards. He had no doubt it had been left open for him. Before he could step inside, however, he heard a sharp squeal from above.

He looked up and saw a blurred, white object plummeting towards him.

CHAPTER FORTY-TWO

Will realised he couldn't get out of the way in time and waited for the impact of whatever had fallen from above. After a few seconds, however, he opened his eyes and relaxed his shoulders. He examined the flagstones for signs of what he'd seen. There was nothing.

He glanced up again. The object was suspended about twenty feet above his head. He was looking at the benign, alabaster features of a medical bust with Chinese characters on different subdivisions of the cranium. A white cord was tied around its neck. It spun slowly, the face circling him before it suddenly dropped a few inches more. Will quickly sidestepped it, but the bust remained in position. Beyond it was the open window to the room it was dangling from. Will assumed it was 22.

He watched the hovering bust for a few seconds more before a guttural sound escaped the window. He hit the stairs, taking them two at a time. The motion rammed a hot bayonet of pain through his side. He paused only to suck in breath before he took the next flight up the windowless stairwell.

Just before he reached the landing of the fourth floor, he heard an ominous smash. The bust had dropped. He didn't know why, but he was positive its descent signified an end to whatever had been happening in the room. He gripped the handrail and hauled himself up.

When he pushed the door to the sixth floor, he was in an

aseptic, white corridor facing a wall of green, frosted glass. An elevator was further down. Underneath large Chinese characters on the translucent wall it also read:

Zisuzi Treatment Centre
Doctor Zhi Ping Ren CMD

He tried the handles, but the doors didn't give. It was still early in the morning. No patients yet. Then the lock whirred and opened.

He pulled them wide and found himself looking at a small waiting room through a short corridor of floor-to-ceiling fish tanks. Will crossed the dark carpet, illuminated by their blue bulbs. He was standing in the centre of a small space edged by leather-seated chairs. The only sound was bubbles and the low murmur of pumps.

A few prints of botanical species were the only decoration. The reception hatch was closed. He put his laptop on the counter. The patients' entrance to the surgery was shut in front of him.

A man's jagged voice, speaking some kind of Chinese. The curses were stifled, only half their volume escaping. Will opened the door into the room beyond.

The woman was leaning beside the open window, arms folded. She was wearing another high-collared, two-piece suit buttoned tightly to her slim frame, this one coral. Her hair was tied up in a bun. The door opened wider and he took in the rest of the surgery.

A high-backed swivel chair with its occupant facing away from Will was positioned between them. She was looking blankly at whoever was seated in it. The chair trembled and Will could see the ankles of its prisoner bound with metal links. Chain was also looped around him to hold his shoulders in place.

She tilted her gaze up to Will. "You might still be in time," she said, her rapid words overlapping.

She bounced her back from the wall and picked up the canary yellow clutch purse from the desk. "Although I think he's going into shock." Her concern for the man in the chair made it sound as if she hadn't actually been responsible for his condition.

Will stepped into the surgery and moved around the chair. The squat figure seated in it had long, straggly white hair that hung down from a broad, tanned bald patch. Agony was wringing out his Chinese features. In his hand was a bloodied knife. He moved his head in circles, his shuttered eyelids stretching and his tongue pushing against the black tape over his mouth.

"I'd summon assistance right away," she respectfully advised and moved past Will to the door. "Call a real doctor though."

"Wait!"

She turned, analysing him from behind still features. "You should hurry. There's no first aid kit here, but you could try the other office." She nodded towards a second door then turned on her heel.

"Who's paying you? I'll pay you!"

"Everyone does," she barely whispered as she left.

"What are we supposed to have done? I'm not going on with this!" He wanted to mean every word. Will contemplated Dr Ren writhing against the chains. She knew he couldn't follow her.

He knelt in front of the bound man. His eyes hadn't been cut from his head, but Will realised they'd been glued. One lid was sealed; the other was stuck to his eyeball. The skin of the lids stretched taut as they attempted to open. Why not do the same as she'd done to the others? Why take his sight, but allow him to live?

"Try to calm down." He touched Ren's shoulder, but the doctor twisted his head sharply to the side. "I'm here to help you."

He continued to squirm, incoherent words inflating the tape at his lips and erratic breath sucking it in again. His body started to buck.

Will ripped away the tape and Ren screamed. Will darted to the desk. "I'm calling you an ambulance."

Ren coughed violently and dark fluid jetted from the back of his windpipe. Will snatched up the handset and held it to his ear. Where was the blood on the knife and his fingers from? The blade dropped to the floor as his body spasmed.

Ren was choking, but his grip remained tight on something in his other hand. It was the frayed end of his intestine. The medical bust had been suspended from it. Ren had cut himself free before the weight of it could disembowel him.

CHAPTER FORTY-THREE

The operator patched Will through to emergency services. While he relayed the location, he watched in horror as Ren's neck muscles locked. His head pressed into the back of the chair. As soon as a female voice assured him an ambulance had been dispatched, Will dropped the handset and attempted to release him.

The metal was biting tight into the doctor's chest and was secured there by a small padlock. His hands weren't bound, but trembled in his lap where the pressure of the chain held them. His bloodied right fist clenched, the fingers of his left gripped tightly onto the tattered viscera protruding from the slit in his stomach.

"They're on their way." Will picked up the sushi knife from where it had fallen. His gloved fingers slipped on the bloodied handle as he tried to insert the blade between the links and Ren's shuddering rib cage. If he could just prise a gap to give him some room to breathe...

The chain had been wound too tightly to his frame. Ren's bound feet stomped against the carpet and a low growl chased out another geyser of blood.

Will ditched the knife, wrenched open two wall-mounted cabinets, but found only rows of glass vials. He yanked the drawers in the desk and pens rattled against golf balls and tees. Then he recalled what she'd said about the first aid kit.

Crossing the room he entered the reception office, frantically scanning it for an implement he could use to sever the chain.

Will found a familiar face staring at him from the back wall. Not one expression within a black frame, but a whole gallery of them screwed there. There were photographs of him with Carla and Libby, images of him at Ingram events with the company's name and logo emblazoned on pulpits and plaques, and then there were the more recent shots. He'd been captured walking up the driveway of the house in Ellicott City, snapped sitting in the cab he'd commandeered outside the residence in Bel Air and fleeing the apartment in Chicago. She'd waited for him and taken the pictures. This time nothing was to be hidden within the crime scene.

Below the gallery, positioned for his convenience, was a can of petrol with a Zippo lighter lying on top of its metallic screw cap.

Ren gagged in the surgery. Will tore his gaze from the wall and focussed on what he needed to do. He dragged more drawers, tipping out their contents and finding only stationery. He threw the doors wide to a metallic locker. Below the coats was a blue toolbox. He slid it clear and opened it, hinging out the cantilever drawers and discarding the boxes of fuses and tacks in the top section. Underneath he found some flimsy pliers and a larger pair of wire cutters.

When he got back to the surgery the doctor was still alive, but his lips were tugged back from his gums and there was no sound coming from his mouth.

"Hold on…"

He knelt beside Ren again, jamming his fingers under the chain so he could draw breath. Ren briefly turned his distorted expression towards him. His sealed eyelids strained against the tension and the interior of his mouth glowed bright red.

The padlock was too substantial to tackle so Will clamped the wire cutters round a link of the chain. His wrists and the heels of his hands ached as he increased pressure on the metal. He could feel the handles bending as his body shook. He ground his teeth, the plastic grip biting into the muscles of his hand. The cutters weren't even scratching its surface.

He kept trying, swapping hands and his body going rigid about the titanium shackles even when he knew Ren's movements were only because of his.

Will dropped from him, stumbling back into the desk. His wrists throbbed angrily. The doctor's chin was fixed to his chest, his strands of hair overhanging his dead features.

Only Will's chest struggled for breath now. He was alone in the room.

The entry telephone chirped in reception and the noise seemed absurd. Will moved unsteadily to the far window and looked down at the red and white ambulance. He hadn't even heard a siren.

He had to go. They'd be coming round the back soon. Doctor Ren, whatever significance he had, was the one he'd nearly saved. How could he leave him when the last air was still escaping his body? He thought of Monro's wife and her breath on his face.

The ambulance men tried the entry phone again. Libby couldn't afford for him to wait.

His eyes scoured Ren's slumped corpse. There was a signet ring on his finger. It was inset with an identical amethyst stone to the pendant.

The entry phone went silent.

Will seized Doctor Ren's lifeless and bloodied right fist and pulled the index finger from the ball it was curled into. But the ring only slid halfway up it before it got jammed behind the skin of his knuckle.

Will tugged the metal firmly against it. He heard an impact downstairs. They'd found the stairwell. It hadn't taken him long to climb the stairs to the surgery.

The ring still wouldn't slide off. Ren's knuckle was swollen, pumped up from the tension in his hand. It had to be removed.

The wire cutters.

They still hung from the chain holding Ren. He unhooked them, their handles slipping back into the trench they'd already made across his palm.

Were they on the first floor, second floor by now?

Will slid the end of the cutters against Ren's extended finger. He gripped his manicured nail firmly. Screwing his eyes shut, he squeezed the handles again. His wrist shook and the grips slipped and buckled. There was a loud click as the pincers connected.

He bent the ring where he'd severed it, parting it at the gap and slipped it off Ren's finger.

He returned to the reception office. How long before the surgery was an official crime scene? And how would he ever be able to leave Singapore to make it home if he left what was on the wall intact?

He picked up the Zippo lighter and gripped it between his teeth while he unscrewed the lid of the petrol can. Hefting its full weight he jabbed it towards the wall, clear liquid striking the photos. Will heaved it higher so he soaked every frame. As petrol cascaded off the images he dumped the can and flicked the lid of the lighter, rolled the flint and held the flame to the wall. An orange tapestry unfurled upwards and the heat immediately tightened his face.

Staggering away from the room he looked at the doctor's slumped body as the flames hooked under the top of the doorway. Everything was as she'd planned. But as the temperature shaved the hairs off his neck he knew there was one thing he wouldn't allow her.

The fire alarm activated. Will grabbed the chair Ren was lashed to and rolled it out of the surgery and into reception. The closed hatch there was already bruised black. Choking, he grabbed his laptop and shunted the body through the waiting area, bursting through the glass doors and out into the cool air of the corridor.

He could hear two ascending sets of feet reverberating in the stairwell so left Ren where he was and headed for the opposite end of the corridor. He pressed the button to summon the elevator and then hid in the turning beyond the shaft.

Will watched a pair of black shirted paramedics halt at Ren's body and exchange a glance before shielding their eyes against the smoke being disgorged by the surgery. One of them shouted through the doorway and waited for a response. He made to enter, but his colleague stopped him. A brief but heated exchange terminated with the first paramedic entering and the other reluctantly following.

Will emerged to wait for the elevator doors to open. The arrow and red numeral of the digital display indicated it was on its way up from the second floor. How long before they came out again? It was probably only a matter of seconds.

The numeral still hadn't changed. He wondered if he'd need a swipe card to get out of the building through the main entrance. Plus there'd probably be other members of the emergency services waiting out the front. He trotted back to the fire exit, taking a last glance at Ren before he took the stairs again.

He slipped down the first two floors as quietly as he could, but then the door slammed against the wall above him. As he took longer, heavier strides he heard a panicked exchange of male voices echoing down. Will ignored the agony and leapt the bottom steps of each flight.

Back in the enclosed courtyard he deliberated whether to return the way he'd come. Rapid footfalls hammered behind him. He jumped shakily onto the green plastic garden chair and looked over the creosoted fence to the other side. It was a graveyard of industrial gas ovens and it was at least a ten-foot drop to the yard. He hooked his laptop over the edge and heaved himself over.

He landed hard. Pain took on a whole new dimension. He limped away from the perimeter and through the metallic clutter. Will looked back and saw black smoke boiling from the surgery window, flames spiking from within.

His mobile rang. It would alert them to his hiding place. Will scrabbled for it in his pocket as he slalomed round the rusted hulks. He pulled it from his jacket, muffling it with his hand and darted in the direction of an open pair of warped, aluminium gates.

Nobody spoke when he put it to his ear. He looked about him, half expecting to find Ren's killer observing him from behind the scrap.

"Carla?"

Will jogged through the gates, trying to discern what the sound was on the other end. It had been her name in the display. "Carla?"

There was the sound again. A constricted breath.

He vaguely realised he'd emerged into a residential street. "Speak to me."

Carla was distressed. "They've killed Luke... and posted the picture on the website."

CHAPTER FORTY-FOUR

The image had been posted on the site at 12.33am, Carla's time.

She'd been following Will's progress on the GPS map, but had still kept the row of houses minimised on her screen. She'd seen the top corner of it appear in the partial window and had thought it was going to be another photo of Libby.

Having been exposed to the earlier screenshot of her daughter, her finger had hesitated on the mouse. When she'd blockaded herself against what she'd expected to find, Carla had opened it. Luke's dead face had stared at her through polythene and the rest of the office had disintegrated behind it.

High resolution and vividly illuminated, she could see the droplets of condensation around his face and the dark hairs of his moustache plastered damply to the transparent hood. It was sucked tightly into his nostrils and mouth, his last inhalation holding it in place.

She'd clicked it away, but had remained immobile.

It was only light knocking on the office door that had allowed the hum of the hard drive and murmur of the TV back into her ears. She'd got up robotically to answer it, hadn't considered the hour when she'd released the lock.

"Just thought I'd check in to see if everything's OK." The pockmarked security guard's guard tried to see past her shoulders into the room.

"Everything's fine." She'd briefly met his cold, blue eyes. He was as convinced by her reply as she was. She'd closed the door on him and sat down to call Will. It was hearing his voice from so far away that had elicited the tears. They were the ones she'd been restraining for all the long hours since they'd found out Libby had been taken.

When she told him the news, Carla heard him slump to the concrete as he seated himself on the edge of the road.

"The last time I spoke to them, when I demanded a photo, they asked me to make a choice between Libby and Luke." She heard him swallow. "They made it sound like I was choosing which one they'd photograph..."

"Don't do this, Will. You can't allow them to make you feel responsible." She wound the phone wire around the knuckles of her free hand.

"But I chose."

"They never cared about Luke. They weren't making demands on his life, so why spare it? He was an inconvenience." She was rationalising, trying to make sense of his murder because of what they had to believe for Libby's sake. But amongst the myriad thoughts racing through her mind, one selfish consideration was paramount. Luke's death made the chances of them ever seeing their daughter again slimmer.

"Why take him? Why didn't they just take Libby?" It seemed an insane thing for him to say. Wishing Libby had been captured alone. Captured in the first place.

"Because they always planned to do this, to terrify us into doing what they want." Cool nausea, prompted by the image trickled through the heat in her face.

"His parents don't even know he's missing." A motorbike passed him, its vulgar engine buzzing like an insect.

"He's the father of Libby's child." She barely breathed the words. *Was* the father.

"Maybe we should call the police in now." He didn't sound sure.

It was what Carla had been tempted to do from the start. As more people had been butchered and the TV news highlighted how far from establishing a motive the police investigation was, the authorities' capacity to intervene seemed pointless. Carla was now petrified by the notion. "Why now? Because Luke's dead?"

"Yes." Anger coloured his response. "The other people – we don't know who they were or what they did. Luke was just a kid..."

"Women and children, Will..."

Had he become desensitised to the abhorrence of that? "There has to be a reason behind the deaths of these families." But he knew there could be no possible justification. "I've just left a doctor disembowelled in his office. I have to believe he wasn't innocent."

The concept of another lifeless face, another brutalised human, was too much for Carla to contemplate. Luke's death had momentarily dislocated those of the scrapbook street. Will must have looked directly into the doctor's eyes. Not through a computer screen.

"When I pulled Libby's ring from his finger, I still had to believe I'd understand everything at the end of this. How can I continue now?"

She knew he couldn't say it, didn't want him to say it; that Luke's death was an intimation of what would surely happen to Libby. "This is all about Libby and what you've been instructed to do. What they want from us." Whatever he'd just endured, Carla had to convince him to persevere.

"And what is that?"

"Everything else to them is irrelevant. Maybe we could have this woman arrested at the next address, but if she were in police custody it would only take one phone call, or her being out of touch with whoever's at the end of that mobile number. How can we put that much faith into the hands of people who know nothing about the situation?"

He exhaled sharply.

It boomed in her ear. "There's only one door left before ours. She's close." Carla wished she felt the conviction of her words.

"No police then." His voice was composed but squeezed of all emotion. "But how can we not tell Luke's parents?"

It was a loathsome reality. There was nothing they could do for Luke now and there was never any right time for parents to grieve their child. "We still can't endanger Libby by telling anyone else. But we will, the moment this is over."

There was that word again: *over.* She'd reluctantly begun to understand what it meant.

Before they hung up on each other Will told Carla about the nature of the photographs he'd had to burn up and the details he'd memorised from the door of Ren's surgery. Another name that meant nothing to either of them. The darkness started to close in on her. She knew she wouldn't be able to push it back. Luke was dead and there was scant hope for Libby and the baby. She couldn't halt the panic and allowed it to soak through her.

Voices that had been murmuring for a long time intensified. Voices Carla had ignored over the years she'd been too busy juggling and coordinating the multiple elements of her life. She should have kept Libby closer, but had compensated for her career by giving her daughter everything she wanted. She'd granted Libby freedoms she'd asked for even though she wasn't actually ready for them.

She'd got distracted by trying to orchestrate the perfect family environment and filling it with the accessories of happiness. There should have been the same tough love for Libby as her parents had shown her. How could she have expected her daughter to learn hard lessons when Carla always chose the most convenient options for showing affection?

Randomness? Her own actions had surely influenced what was happening now. She thumbed the moisture from her eyes, blinking it away as she checked the GPS. The woman was almost back at the hotel. Would she immediately pack for another flight?

She did a search for Dr Zhi Ping Ren CMD and found a rudimentary website for his Traditional Chinese Herbal and Qigong Surgery. There was a low-resolution image of the Doctor peering impassively from his health manifesto page. The site offered nothing more beyond some suspect testimonials and his hours of business.

She located a few other photographs of him at a charity ball for the Horizon Children's Hospice. They'd been taken at the Capella Hotel on Sentosa Island. A spruced-up Dr Ren with shorter hair and sunglasses grinned beatifically between two statuesque women in silk gowns.

There seemed to be very little else and Carla was about to try a different engine when she realised she'd almost missed one of the links. It was immediately below his website, but her eyes had skimmed it because it was a video result.

The capture image was just a blank, white square. But there was "Doctor Zhi Ping Ren CMD", as the title of a YouTube clip with a URL below it. She clicked on it and was taken to the site. Maybe the Doctor had shot and uploaded some instructional or promotional clips. She played it and the dot clock appeared on the black screen as it was cued up.

The one-minute excerpt started and the shaky first shot was focussed on a red car outside a grey door. A short, balding Chinese man came out of the building carrying a leather case in his hand. He strode purposefully past the car and down the street, oblivious to the fact he was being recorded. It was definitely the man from the images she'd just seen online. The camera zoomed back and it was clear its operator was stood some distance away.

The clip cut to a market, the microphone not close enough to discern the conversation Ren was having with an old man at a raised counter. Next the camera was panning around some fish tanks and coming to rest on a closed door beside them. Again the microphone couldn't pick up the low murmur beyond.

The screen became white, but whatever subject was being shot was outside because Carla could identify the sound of birds. The lens shook, and as darker contours within the white came into focus Carla realised the camera was slowly zooming out from a black and white photograph.

It was of Dr Ren, more hair in evidence, but still the same impassive expression. Even when his entire head and shoulders were framed, the photo continued to shake. Carla could see why as she glimpsed the top of a thumb holding it in position. The photo was released and it dropped onto three polythene sacks of shredded paper below the camera. They were positioned next to each other on a stone step.

The camera jolted a few times and a jet of liquid came into frame soaking the image and the bags. Was the operator urinating on the picture? She heard the scrape of a lighter and a hand entered shot and played a flame over the saturated photograph. It went up quickly and the camera recoiled as the fire momentarily bleached the lens.

When the shot steadied the camera had retreated and was recording the growing bonfire from a safer distance. Carla recognised where it had been set. It was at the front doors of Easton Grey.

The lens quickly panned over the house just so she wouldn't be left in any doubt. Then its operator fled in the direction of the east wall. She could hear them breathe over the familiar sound of crows cawing in the nearby copse.

CHAPTER FORTY-FIVE

Will anxiously watched two fire engines and three police cars part the traffic before he crossed the road from the stadium and headed back towards the Ambrosia Hotel. The humidity was stifling and his hands and arms pounded just out of sync with the low-key sensation in his torso. The pain had spread around to his kidneys and the muscles behind them were becoming numb.

Since receiving Carla's call his emotions felt even more gridlocked and he wondered if the accumulation of events would break him before his body gave out. He couldn't allow himself to think that what he'd said on the phone had condemned Luke to death.

He had to believe Carla was right, that his cold-blooded murder had always been part of their plan. The bodies in the houses were an irrefutable demonstration of their capacity to see their threats through. They knew for sure that murdering Luke ensured Will's obedience for whatever awaited him at the end of the row.

He didn't know what time of day it was. Hadn't even the strength to check the laptop, never mind look at the repugnant image that had been posted there. He gripped his abdomen as he hacked some more smoke out of his lungs.

He kept repeating the name he'd memorised on the doctor's door to dislocate the spectre of his shackled body and the implications of Luke's death. Would Ren be the significant connection to the other names? As Will's journey took him further down the cut-out street he was no closer to realising why they all shared the same cobbled-together neighbourhood.

He and Carla were defenceless. Up until then a small potentiality had lived and breathed. There'd been a tiny hope that the authorities would eventually catch up, step in and absolve Will of having to see the ordeal through to Easton Grey. Now it was undeniable. They were alone to the end. Libby being returned alive seemed less likely to be part of the outcome, but he and Carla obeying her captors was her only chance. However slim it was.

Just as he got back to the hotel Carla called again. She told him about the YouTube clip. As he spoke to her he realised he was still wearing the gloves. The heat had dried droplets of Ren's blood on their fingers and over the digits of the phone.

Will hurried through reception, the woman at the desk quietly monitoring him from the shadows behind the lamp as he carefully climbed the stairs.

Pope put the phone down on Mrs Frost and relayed her information to Weaver. "She said it's the victim her husband just found."

They stared in silence at the image on the iPad. None of the houses since the Ambersons' home had depicted the bodies, so the photo of the dead man's smothered features had been doubly shocking.

Weaver didn't move his eyes from the bag sucked into the man's face. "Do they know him?"

"No. At least that's what she said. She seemed very upset though. I think she's still concealing something."

Weaver nodded. "So we now know for sure the phone is planted on the perp..." He left the statement hanging.

"And?"

"Just means Mrs Frost doesn't have anything left to barter

with. If she's holding out on us we can go wherever we want with this now." Weaver didn't shift his gaze from the iPad.

Pope had been anticipating Weaver's arrival at that conclusion and was surprised he'd taken so long. "We made a deal with her."

Weaver turned to Pope, petulance gathering his eyebrows in. "So we're going to sit here and watch it all play out? Even though we don't need the GPS to know exactly where this is going to end?"

"I didn't say that."

Will watched the YouTube clip in his hotel room. The video had been uploaded only a day before his arrival in Singapore. It was an explanation of the fire that had been set on their doorstep in June and another illustration of how long planned the kidnappers' actions had been.

It was an intimidation device, planted in the knowledge that it would be found. They knew they'd be searching for Ren online as soon as Will had set the blaze. As he watched the man he'd left dead in the surgery for a third time he knew he was delaying.

Will didn't want to see the image of Luke, but had to go to the site and the penultimate house. The photo was suspended above it and it seemed to eclipse everything he'd witnessed. Was it because he knew Luke? He'd eaten at their table, laid on the couch with them in front of the TV and Will had carefully monitored him hanging around the summer house with Libby. He tried to remember his voice, any exchanges they'd had. He was quietly spoken, but had an explosive laugh that had raised his and Carla's eyebrows the first time they'd heard it.

He couldn't deny he'd perceived him as an interloper. But he'd regarded all of Libby's boyfriends in the same way because he hadn't believed her ready for an adult relationship. Luke had been a part of their lives for nearly two years and the idea of his last breath being wrung from him so callously was sickening.

His life had ended because he'd been with Libby. Had they both been taken because of something Will had been party to? He thought of Luke's parents and how oblivious they were to his death, recalled the evening he and Carla had invited them to the house. Will had been on autopilot, believed it was time wasted because the boy wouldn't be around long.

His behaviour then revolted him now. Everyone had been in on the pregnancy that night except Will. Carla had known how he'd react and had saved the news for when they were alone. He'd been dumbstruck, had quickly realised why Luke had been grinning so nervously for the entire evening. Then he'd been furious. He hadn't concealed the depth of his anger from Libby either.

He thought of Luke tied up with the bag being held around his neck, but it was Libby's face he saw breathing in the polythene. He tried to remember the last thing he'd said to her. It was probably a response to a text or an email.

He minimised Luke's fogged expression and searched for Ren. He found the photos of him at the ball. What was the charity Carla had said Franks had been a patron of? He opened another tab to go to the Senator's bio, but decided to visit CNN online first. Maybe there were more details released about Franks and what he'd been doing at the Gold Coast apartment.

When he ran his cursor along the breaking news clips, there was a face there that, this time, couldn't be burnt away.

CHAPTER FORTY-SIX

"An all-out, state-wide manhunt has been launched by the FBI for the murderers of Richard Strick, Lieutenant Governor of Maryland, and his family who were found dead in their home in Ellicott City last weekend. The murderers are also wanted in connection with multiple homicides committed at the Bel Air home of Strick's ex- private secretary, Wesley Monro, and the Florida holiday apartment of Consolidated Breweries CEO, Holt Amberson.

"FBI spokeswoman, Trisha Thorn, says there is 'compelling evidence' to suggest they may be seeking the same individuals, a man and a woman, in connection with the murder of Jacob Franks, US Senator for Illinois. Senator Franks' body was discovered in a Chicago apartment on Sunday. Eyewitness reports and CCTV footage have enabled authorities to release a sketch of one of the suspects. The public is advised not to personally confront them, but to report any sightings immediately."

A sketch of Will stared blankly from an image superimposed beside the anchorman. Carla's call came seconds after. He froze the news clip on his laptop.

"Have you seen it?" Her tone suggested she already understood what the release of the picture signified.

"I'm being hunted," he said darkly. He studied the artist's impression. The hair length was shorter than his, the composition of the features slightly disproportionate, but it was a pretty accurate likeness. Where had the CCTV cameras captured him? "They obviously haven't managed to get a statement from Monro's daughter yet."

"She's probably still too traumatised. But you're still ahead of them." Her words were leaden. She knew it did little to better the situation.

"Even if they can't identify me from prints, every airport will have security footage. They only have to check the flight manifests to see who flew between the specific crime scenes and they'll have an answer."

"They still obviously believe you're in the US."

He knew she was trying to bolster him, looking for hope in every dirty crevice. "They'll soon know where I've gone, though."

"What about any evidence she's left behind?"

Carla's words prompted him to consider something he hadn't before. She hadn't worn gloves in the doctor's surgery. Had she been wearing them in the Chicago apartment? What about hair, fibres from her clothes and the bloodied footprints she'd left by the pool in Kissimmee? Will knew nothing about forensics, but why hadn't she made any attempts to conceal her presence? "OK, they have to be closing in on her, but it's my face on TV."

Carla was silent. Both of them knew they would soon catch up to him, maybe before he could make it to the next address.

"I've paid for cabs, checked into hotels, used the credit card every time. I didn't exactly cover my tracks. If we don't get the next location soon there are probably a hundred different ways of them finding me."

It was an undeniable fact, the very people who should have been able to help them could now remove the one slender chance they had of ever seeing Libby alive.

"And who knows when I'll get the address – a couple of hours from now? A day?"

"She's still at the hotel. She's got to be monitoring the news as well. She wants you to finish this."

The last time they'd spoken, they'd discussed police intervention. Now they would have begged to be led to the end of the street without them. "But maybe amusing herself further isn't worth the risk. Perhaps now they'll tell us what they want."

"There's an agenda, Will. She'll make sure you see it through. Killing Luke was the ultimate example of that."

Silence; both their minds reluctantly recalled the depiction of Luke's final moment.

"She wants to terrify you."

It *was* Will. He felt like he and Carla had faced everything together, but it had been his name explicitly in the instructions. He'd been told to fly to Florida. In the absence of a ransom demand, the campaign had to be aimed at him. What could Carla have done, even indirectly, to have this inflicted? Again he speculated whether it was something way back; an oblique involvement in an episode he was being held to account for. He looked down at the laptop and the soulless eyes of his figurative countenance staring out at him.

"But we know nothing more than when we started." He wanted to curl up against the pain now. "The people she's killed are strangers. There's no connection between them or me. Dr Ren seems even more far removed."

"Apart from the website for the practice and the odd charity photo he's managed to avoid making any real digital footprint. You'd expect there to be more out there. Maybe that's significant. Perhaps he's hiding something behind all the respectability." She didn't sound convinced.

"They know we'll be looking for him online. Perhaps there isn't anything to find." He stood and walked the pain off. Didn't want his body to shut down.

"What about money? Have you got enough so you don't have to use an ATM?"

"For the moment, but I suspect I'm going to have to get on another plane soon. I'm going to need some the other end."

He was right, but the destination he received, just over an hour later, wasn't the one he'd anticipated.

Tam woke with jolt. There were lots of noises around him and as they perforated his oblivion he became aware of how cold he felt. His teeth chattered and he curled his body into himself as much as his bonds would allow.

The halogen lights had been turned on and their glare steadily invaded his senses. Through slits he could see nothing but hot yellow and waited for his sight to accustom itself to the light. But then the bulbs were extinguished and darkness fell.

He heard slow, dragging footfalls ascending the concrete steps and opened his eyes wider to see shapes amongst the shadows. But there was one he couldn't see that had been there before. He rolled sideways, anticipating his soft impact against the girl. Until then her presence had been blocking the draught across the floor. Tam shivered. She was gone.

The instructions obliterated Will's last hope of a reunion with Libby. He stared unblinkingly at them and knew Carla would be doing the same.

Dundee,
UK

Eight hundred miles was the closest he'd got to his daughter. Now he would be flying six thousand miles away from her. The location drained his final reserves of nervous energy and he contemplated what his return to the UK meant.

Another flight of thirteen hours and at the end of it...? When he'd left the UK, he hadn't expected to return. Walking off the plane without her and having to look into Carla's eyes would be the worst thing he'd faced.

There was only one door left before his. Libby wasn't going to be there. What would they have him believe? That they'd fly her back as a prisoner?

Ingram had no pipelines in the territory. He'd never been there. Did someone they'd done business with in the past operate in the district? How could it possibly be connected to the locations he'd already visited? He was sick of stacking questions. The blow of the coming return allowed fatigue to intervene.

He massaged his face and clicked on the cracked, yellow rendered front of the house. He went through the images. It was the most basic of all the addresses that had been photographed. The downstairs walls were a grubby mint green. The only furniture in the living area was a double couch, TV and glass cabinet of ceramic figurines. The bedrooms upstairs had the curtains drawn. In the larger one, the yellowing, coverless duvet on the king size divan was in disarray. When Will examined it closer he could see it wasn't just unmade, but that there was actually somebody twisted up in it.

It was an adult, but in the dinginess it was impossible to identify if it was a man or woman. The body was concealed and the head sunk into the dirty pillow. The most terrifying aspect of the image was that the photographer must have stood in the doorway and taken it while they slept. Her intrusion on the homes seemed to be becoming bolder with each address. Easton Grey was next.

It was probable whoever lived at the property in Dundee had as much time left to live as it took Will to reach them. He'd nearly been able to save Ren. Would she allow him to rescue anyone here? He doubted it.

Luke's pointless death proved they were inhuman. They obviously wanted to draw out Will's torment. It didn't matter that he wasn't imprisoned; this was slow asphyxiation.

How could he not go? Even though they'd given him every reason to believe Libby was already dead, they knew he'd finish.

Carla called, neither of them vocalising the thoughts they

shared about his return. They'd made the choice to see it through. It was all they could do. But now the concrete futility of it removed any speculation from their exchange. Their dialogue was truncated by bleak resignation.

Carla would make the arrangements. She would use the new location as a starting point and cross-reference Ingram's client base to see if they had any network there. It was what they'd both been doing since Libby had been abducted and it had led nowhere. The Ambersons, the Stricks, the Monros, Jacob Franks and Dr Ren. All dead within the time it had taken him to navigate the street.

When he hung up he did something he hadn't told Carla he'd do. He rang the kidnappers' mobile number. He would plead with them, promise anything if they only agreed to let him speak to Libby.

It was still engaged.

The GPS told him that the killer had been at the airport an hour already. He hoped it meant she would be taking off soon. He couldn't be on the same plane as her. He snapped the laptop shut, choked down some more pills and dragged himself to the stairs.

Carla had spent another long night alone in the office. As she'd visited the bathroom she'd encountered a few staff members returning to their desks to check emails before returning to the Remada ops room. Will's phone had been silent since Nissa had been fielding his calls from there and Carla had kept the blinds closed against the empty reception.

With everything that had happened she was glad of the isolation. While she looked for answers that weren't there she could only contemplate the conversation she would have with Luke's family and wait for Will to return without Libby.

Somebody tapped the door so lightly that, at first, Carla thought she'd imagined it. She looked up from her position in front of the screen and waited. It came again.

"Yes?" She didn't disguise her agitation.

The door opened and Nissa gingerly slipped her tall frame in, quietly closing it behind her as if something might escape the room.

"What are you still doing here?" She realised the comment only highlighted her own continued presence.

"It's just that things are hotting up out there and a lot of people need to speak to Will..."

"Of course. I'll pass that on when I speak to him later." Carla felt a tug in her chest when Nissa made no move to leave.

"I hope you don't mind, but in light of our last conversation I got the impression you didn't want to be disturbed here." Her accent couldn't make it sound anything other than an understatement. "So I tried contacting Will on his mobile and at home...and on his private mobile." She pressed her spectacles into the middle of her nose, a microscope to study Carla's reaction.

"I told you he was in Sussex on family business."

"Yes. See I just tried him there and they all seemed very confused by your story." She raised her eyebrows as she emphasised the last word and cocked her head to one side.

Carla opened her mouth, but her mind went blank, all the sleepless hours voiding any fabrications she should have had in reserve.   .

"So I just thought I'd let you know, I've called the police," she said, her lips tightening.

CHAPTER FORTY-SEVEN

The cab ejected Will at Changi International in a dosed-up stupor. As the passengers buffeted him in the terminal he wondered how much damage the fire had caused and if the police had unchained Ren's body from the chair. It was 10.32am and his flight left just before midday. He sluggishly estimated it would be around ten at night when he got back to the UK. He picked up his tickets from the machine and joined the line for check-in.

Anxiety overrode pain and he darted his head at every female in the vicinity. He couldn't share a flight cabin with her again. After what had been done to Luke, he doubted he could restrain himself. He quickly scrutinised the GPS map. Her dot had vanished again. She was definitely in the air. He told himself insomnia and the medication were making him paranoid.

There was a police presence in the terminal. Blue uniforms and red berets mingling with the passengers. He counted three armed with rifles. Was this standard procedure or had there been an incident? Could it be a response to Ren's murder?

Carla had conceded she'd lied about Will's whereabouts but with good reason. It wasn't sufficient for Nissa, however, who was still standing cross-armed, refusing to take the receiver from her.

"Please, call the police back. Tell them it's been a mistake."

"First, where's Will? Or should I ask Anwar?"

"Nissa, I don't have time for this, what are you talking about?"

"I booked the Cawley Manor trip that you, Will and Libby were meant to be taking the weekend. What happened on Friday to make you turn up here for the first time in eight months having panicky telephone conversations and booking rapid travel arrangements?"

Carla wondered which events she could pick out of the last handful of days that would satisfy Nissa, but wouldn't sabotage everything. She couldn't risk having a conversation about any of it with the police.

"What makes you not want to go home for the night even though you tell me Will's there? Before you changed that story, of course."

"Will was with me here early Saturday morning. You can ask security." But it seemed like such a long time ago she almost doubted it herself. "I've told you I can explain everything, but you have to trust me and call the police back now."

"Then you have me pulling files to keep me out of the way before Anwar turns up."

"So, that's what this is. You think Anwar and I...?"

Nissa raised her eyebrow. "It's no secret he's smitten with you. Will told me about the night they both got drunk. He might have brushed it off, but I know exactly how persuasive Anwar can be." The intimation in her eyes was unmistakable.

"You and Anwar are an item?"

"Were, a long time ago, the Thailand trip. So over now."

Carla doubted that. "But he always gets your name wrong."

"No. You always get my name wrong."

"Your name is Nessa?"

"Don't insult my intelligence. I know you do it to bait me."

"No, I've always called you Nissa because I thought that was your name. Why has Will never corrected me?"

"It was our in-joke. It amused him, but I know you do it because you've always resented our professional relationship."

Carla knew she had to discard every triviality she was hearing.

If she allowed this to continue several minor misunderstandings were about to expose everything she'd protected for the last four days. She slammed her palm flat on the desk. "Please listen, I haven't disposed of Will. I'm certainly not having an affair with Anwar, but I do need you to call the police and stop them coming here. If I told you somebody's life actually depended on it would you please do it for me now?"

The line moved quickly until Will was listening in on an animated conversation between the young, male Chinese check-in attendant and the pregnant girl in front. She moved away and the smile emptied out of the attendant's face. He hitched his sand blazer up his shoulders, shot the cuffs and dubiously accepted Will's ticket and passport. Will guessed he must look a pretty ragged spectacle by now.

The attendant's wispy black moustache undulated while he mouthed the details of Will's passport and checked them on his screen. He nodded uncertainly and the smile slightly returned. Will's phone rang.

"Carla?"

"Will?"

Momentarily he struggled to identify the voice. "Nessa, how did you get this number?"

"Mrs Frost just gave it to me. Where are you?"

Speaking to Nessa here disoriented him. Carla couldn't possibly have let her in on the situation. "Look, I'm in the middle of something...what has Mrs Frost said?"

"Nothing, but she's allowing me to ask you if you're OK. You are OK?"

"Of course." He could already feel his body shrugging off the painkillers. "Everything's fine."

Nessa hung up and Will examined the phone with bemusement.

••••

Nessa put the phone back on the cradle.

"Now you need to make another call." Carla lifted it again.

"I don't. It's OK, I didn't call the police."

Carla closed her eyes briefly.

"I wanted to see how you'd react. I'm sorry." She examined Carla's dishevelled appearance. "I don't understand what's happening here, but something's badly wrong. Is there anything I can do?"

"Yes. Go home and don't say a word to anyone, not even Keiron."

"Checking any bags, Mr Frost?"

Will shook his head and gripped the laptop tighter.

"If you'd like to make your way to the lounge."

Somebody was at the boy's ear. An older, taller Chinese man who only seemed to say one word to him. He was dressed in a blue shirt, but there was no ID badge clipped to his breast pocket like the others. The check-in attendant nodded quickly and looked past Will to smile at the next passenger while the new man gestured Will aside.

The man briefly examined his face, contemplatively chewing gum as if Will were the flavour. "Would you come this way?" It was polite, but it wasn't a request. He scraped up Will's passport and ticket and nodded towards a door behind the desk.

"What's the problem?"

"Would you come this way?" He didn't alter his intonation and looked at Will's throat while he waited.

Will followed him behind the counter and the man led him through the exit to a cement corridor that jarred with the modern gloss of the terminal. A row of red doors stretched along the right side of the passage. The man opened the first one they came to and gestured for him to step inside.

CHAPTER FORTY-EIGHT

Will was in a large room that smelt of fly spray. There was only a low table with two empty noodle cartons on it flanked by two stuffed, green chairs. He tried to remain calm. Was it standard practise to detain passengers at random? His appearance was probably pretty alarming.

The man quickly patted him down, said nothing else and left with Will's passport and ticket, closing the door behind him.

He couldn't dismiss the sight of the armed officers in the terminal and the possible reason they were there. His face was on the World Wide Web. How long since he'd left Chicago? He calculated just over twenty-four hours.

Will listened for the sound of the door being locked. He only heard the man's receding footsteps.

An older Chinese man wearing the same clothes as the last entered. He was paunchy, had white hair and winged eyebrows. He said nothing, but gestured to Will's laptop. Will placed it on the table.

"My flight leaves soon. Can you tell me what this is about?"

Winged Eyebrows nodded, snatched up the computer and left the room. Will felt panic throbbing through the vein at his temple. One of the last sites he'd hit was Ren's. He'd been searching for his name immediately after he'd been murdered.

He waited, checking his watch every few seconds. Over ten minutes had passed since he'd been taken out of the check-in

line. He would miss his flight if he were held up any longer. His
back ached, but he couldn't sit down.

Winged Eyebrows re-entered the room minus the laptop.
"This way, please."

Will followed him back into the corridor and they turned
left, heading away from the door that led to check-in. Two girls
standing in one of the doorways were chatting in low voices that
lowered further as they passed. Will's legs felt like they were
wading through a snowdrift.

Winged Eyebrows opened another door and gestured him
through.

He found himself the other side of the metal detectors that led
into the business lounge. His laptop was just emerging from the
x-ray machine. Winged Eyebrows handed it back to him with
his passport.

"Thank you, Mr Frost."

Will didn't feel secure until they'd boarded. The plane's take off
was delayed, the doors remaining open while Will entertained
every conceivable reason for them sitting on the runway. Had
they halted their departure while they hunted for a murder
suspect?

But when they were finally sealed in and rolling back he felt
the last dregs of hope dwindle. He was about to be launched
away from Libby, the gap between them growing ever wider.

The wheels lost contact with the runway and it felt as if he'd
cut her loose.

Pope and Weaver had slept for the majority of the flight and
wandered blearily through London Heathrow while their
faculties slowly re-engaged.

Pope checked his phone. Two missed messages from Mrs
Frost; he didn't want to speak to her just now. She'd want to
know exactly where they were. "Let's ask at information about

renting some wheels."

Weaver dragged his camera bag like it was a corpse. "I still think we should be getting on a connecting flight."

"We've been over this. It's futile following them to Dundee. We won't know what we'll be walking into until after the address is posted."

"And you're sure this isn't just misplaced sympathy with the Frosts?"

"How close could we get without putting everything at risk? What we do know for sure is where the last house is. At least, we know from Carla Frost's online campaigning that she's fighting a local battle in Hanworth. How big could an English village be? We'll rent a car, drive out there, ask round and get an idea of the terrain. We'll have to know every possible escape route their unwanted visitor could take before she arrives."

Weaver didn't respond.

"Then we'll check into the nearest hotel and wait there for the GPS to tell us exactly when she does."

"*If* she does, we don't know if she's definitely heading there."

"It's the last house on the site."

"Yeah, but who's her target?"

It was a good question. "We know Frost will have to return there. Who knows what she'll have waiting for him."

"Somehow, I don't think it's going to be his daughter."

As soon as they were in the air, Will opened the laptop, but knew there'd be no further instructions until he'd landed in Dundee. Carla was booking his connecting flight from Gatwick. It was approximately six hours, which meant he would be arriving there around five in the morning.

He tried to focus on the screen as he cross-referenced the other victims' names with his new location, but the painkillers and his own exhaustion were eager to catch up with him. As the sound of the aeroplane cut out and his mind wandered, a face slipped into his thoughts. It was the man with shoulder length white hair he'd encountered as he'd fled the Chicago apartment, but in a different context.

It was an album cover. He looked like Jimmy Farina Jr, the 70s lounge crooner that Carla listened to. She had a couple of his old CDs in the summer house. That was why he'd looked so familiar. The surreal solution to a minor enigma amongst so many larger ones was his last semi-rational thought before he lost consciousness.

He awoke sporadically, glancing around the cabin expecting to find the woman's anorexic figure sitting nearby. She shared shifts with the crab, its disintegrating body going faster round the bottom of the pot.

He'd stayed alone on the beach watching over it, even after it had stopped circling. Its motionless dark blue body had been mottled with the flakes of paint it had scratched from the sides of its cell. The ugly gull had continued to hover, but he'd buried it deep enough so the bird couldn't dig it up. He'd pulled the sand over it, wet clothes clinging tight to his body while the wind had blasted rain into his skin.

He never usually wanted to ascend the hundred and thirteen steps back up to the house after his visits to the little cove. That afternoon he'd realised it was nothing to do with the climb.

Before they'd left him on the beach, he'd turned and found his father still standing there. His mother was already heading away with the picnic things and the billowing blanket, her back to him as she hurried for the steps. But it was his father's contemplation of the captive in the pot he remembered more vividly than anything else.

His mouth was clamped to his pipe and he'd studied the animal with resigned antipathy. Will realised it was exactly the same way his father studied him.

He felt then like he'd dropped unwanted into his father's life, as helpless as the animal he'd buried on the beach. From that moment to the day Will had seen his body lying on top of the bed in the hospice, his father never gave him any reason to doubt it.

When his fingers had made contact with the back of his hand he hadn't recoiled.

His father had left too early. Will had wanted to show him how he could do things his own way.

"Put it back in the water, Will. Let it crawl under a rock to die."

Tam gently flexed his legs in the ropes again. He'd been doing it every time he woke before exhaustion overcame him once more. There was some give around his ankles now. Maybe he had enough strength to crawl to the unstapled wire and squeeze out of the cage. He shifted his body a quarter turn so he could squint through the shadows

Skinny Man was still sitting there, watching.

Whatever they'd done to the girl he was sure they'd want to do it to him. His father had warned him about the night-time people, just like he'd warned his sister. But they'd both ignored him. Something had happened to Songsuda after she'd been with them. She was never the same when she came back.

He didn't like to think about how frightened Songsuda had made him when she'd seized him and whispered those words, those strange lies he could sometimes convince himself had been part of a bad dream. Songsuda had told Tam his mother had deceived him and that she was his real mother. She'd held his face in her hands, creamy spittle at the sides of her mouth and looked deep into him when she'd said it. Then his father had struck her hard. His mother had beaten his father with her tiny fists and everybody had cried before Songsuda had been dragged out.

Nobody had spoken of what had been said since. Only when he went through the boxes of Songsuda's things and touched and smelled her old school clothes did that afternoon seem like it had actually happened. Tam could never imagine a time when he could make what was happening now seem quite so unreal.

CHAPTER FORTY-NINE

Although it was August, Will felt the colder climate of the UK bite at him as he descended from the plane. As he walked through baggage retrieval the shivering intensified and he realised it was a symptom of something else other than the change in temperature. During the flight he'd found that sleeping with his knees raised had eased the ache in his back. But after thirteen hours in one position his sudden mobility was sending his system into shock. He just made it to the bathroom in time to vomit. It felt like the pain had outgrown him.

His mobile rang.

"You depart at 10.40am. You should just make it. She registered on the GPS for an hour before her flight, but now she's in the air again." Carla relayed the information.

Will leaned a shoulder on the cubicle wall, his body still quivering but his face burning hot. "Which terminal?"

"A."

Neither of them wanted to acknowledge the fact he was back in the UK.

He emptied the last of the painkillers into his mouth, his jaws grinding four tablets as he snapped upright. "Another six hours..." He considered what he was flying to and what was to come afterwards. "The reception's hopeless here. I'll have to hang up."

Will rang off, feeling poisoned, desperate for sleep.

••••

Seven hours later he was standing in the driving rain outside Dundee's modest airport. The sign told him it was gateway to the home of golf. It was 5.18am and the ash coloured clouds hurriedly plastered up each crack of white daylight as soon as one emerged. The droplets bounced off the pavement as he waited under an empty shelter. He leaned one hand against the fibreglass and the wind dented the leather jacket he'd zipped tight around himself. No sign of a taxi.

"I'm here, but it's over," he said, registering that he couldn't hear the imprisoned birds when the call was answered.

Water ran off the back of the shelter and splattered noisily behind him.

"I'm sick and need to get to a hospital. I don't believe Libby's alive anymore. What you did to that boy..." He inhaled and his breath wavered with anger. "You can go on with this, but I won't. Not until I know she's alive. You know this number. Call me back with proof."

"Speak." A male voice, the word was almost indiscernible.

"Say again." Will thought he'd misheard and jammed the mobile closer to his ear. He blocked the other with his finger and squinted his eyes as he tried to zone out the rain.

"Who's this?" The female voice was stoned and emotionless.

"Lib?"

"Dad?" Her voice sounded like it was passing through several filters, but its familiarity immediately blurred his vision with tears.

"Lib. Are you OK?" He anticipated the call being terminated.

No reply. Then he realised she was crying and the choked sobs were struggling to register. "Speak to me, Lib. Have they hurt you?" A warm tear dropped from his eye onto the wet pavement.

Noise ruptured the call, feeding back on itself.

"Lib?" He crouched low, flattening his ear to the mobile. "Keep talking."

He halted everything, breath, circulation, pain; he suspended it so he could decipher what clear words bubbled up.

"...treating me OK. They haven't hurt me."

These were the only decipherable words to emerge from the churning static.

"Try to speak louder," he pleaded.

The last sound was a long, metallic squeak and an impact, like a hinge straining and a door slamming shut.

The call ended and rainfall rushed back into his ears. He realised his knees were against the wet pavement, another waterfall from the shelter splashed noisily beside him. A taxi pulled up to him, headlights burning through his closed eyelids.

The rag was crammed back into Libby's mouth and the hood tugged down. Two hot palms shoved against her shoulders so she was lying on her back again. Had her Dad's voice been a hallucination?

She didn't know how long she'd been subdued and had only recently started to wake in a different place. Even through the hood she could smell the rug she was lying on. It had an overpowering aroma of creosote. She also realised the door to her prison was metal because she'd heard it squeal as it slammed shut. She could vaguely discern faint traffic, but knew she didn't have the strength to yell loud enough through the gag.

There were no birds and the air and the floor beneath her felt warm. Her thoughts were in disarray and she didn't know if her eyes were open or closed. Her limbs felt like they needed to stretch, as if she'd been asleep for a long time. Libby registered her hands were bound in front of her now, her ankles tied firmly together.

She'd wanted to tell Dad about what had happened to her. But she knew how helpless it would have made him feel. Libby refused to let her captor have the satisfaction of that, to use the pain they'd inflicted on her to secure what they wanted.

Had she really spoken to him?

The weight of her thoughts exhausted her, but she heard laboured breathing other than her own. Libby had thought whoever had slammed the door was outside it. Now she felt them touching her. They were locked inside. She clenched up again and screwed her eyes tightly as their rubber fingers traced the bite mark on her shoulder.

She remembered the wet snout of the boar as it had compressed her against the toppled bricks, recalled the sound it had made when she'd caved its head in. She knew it could be her last chance to defend herself. Libby thrust herself upright, her face connecting hard with a chin or elbow. She heard a grunt through nostrils and sprang from her sitting position so she was crawling forward on her knees. Aim for the doors. She knew they were somewhere ahead of her.`

She held up her bound hands, shins grazing metal as she took short steps with them and dragged her trussed ankles behind. Her body hit the doors and they bowed, but didn't open. Her nails scratched steel as her tied hands scrabbled for a lock. She slammed herself into them harder, her already injured shoulder mashing with the impact. This time one hinged outward.

Fingers were around her waist, but she jabbed backwards harshly with her elbow and felt it connect. The hands released her and she fell headfirst through the doors. Her temple hit concrete and her right eardrum went dead, but she kept scrambling forward.

But, as she put more and more distance between herself and her captor, Libby realised why they didn't pursue her. It was unnecessary. They were in no hurry.

Flashes of white at her chin, the hood was loose. As she crawled, she shook her head violently from side to side. The hood slipped off. Cool air and light swamped her senses. She squinted around the room and looked back the way she'd crawled. A figure strode casually towards her. His hand held a black nightstick.

Before her eyes could open she heard a sound like cotton wool squeaking on her teeth and then warmth trickling down her face.

CHAPTER FIFTY

"I've spoken to Libby." Will was slouched against the back seat of the cab.

There was no audible response from Carla, but Will waited a few moments.

"It was only brief, but it was definitely her."

"What did she say?"

The taxi's wipers noisily cut semicircles out of the rain.

"The line was pretty bad. She recognised me though. It sounds like she's being held in a different place."

"You're sure it was her?"

Through a clamour of renewed energy Will felt a tiny surge of doubt. No. He couldn't have been mistaken. "It was definitely her." He slid the cursor over the image on the wet laptop screen. No specifics, but he could see the red dot had appeared on the GPS map of Dundee.

"This confirms what I was saying. They'll do anything to make you finish this."

Libby was alive. At that moment, it was everything they could have hoped for.

"I'm being driven into town." Will sat up and peered through the rain hosing down the side window. He could see the dark green of the golf courses against the skyline.

"She's stopped near the university."

Will got dropped on the edge of the pedestrianised high street of the city. He paid with the crumpled British currency he had tucked behind the Singapore dollars and put his hand on the door. The driver had already stepped nimbly out and opened it for him. He'd barely registered him as he'd got in the back, but as he stood up he took in his furrowed features for the first time.

"Will you be needing any help?" His enquiry was deliberately measured, his accent soft. The man's silver moustache met his neat beard so no trace of his mouth was visible. His pale blue eyes searched Will's.

Will knew he wasn't referring to the laptop in his hand. "I'll be fine."

"You're sure? Sounds like you're in a heap of trouble. Do you want me to call somebody?"

"No." He considered what the driver had overheard from his conversation with Carla. "Please don't."

The man nodded slightly. "You take care then." He held Will's eye briefly, then got back in his taxi.

Still alive.

Carla filled her chest with air for what seemed like the first time in days. Then sobs of relief squeezed it out. She fought to restrain them. The ordeal was far from over, but her fear that they were obeying the kidnappers' instructions, even though Libby had suffered the same fate as Luke, had briefly been suspended.

She repeatedly speed-dialled the kidnappers' number, getting an engaged tone every time. She had to speak to her. Tell Libby they were doing everything they could to free her.

Two more addresses were left, including their own. The revelation of the reason for the torture they'd been subjected to suddenly seemed imminent. She looked up at the TV. There'd been no new developments in the US manhunt. All the channels were still running the same story and artist's impression.

••••

Will stood at the glass doors of the Overgate shopping centre in the high street, but they were locked shut. It didn't open until nine. The rain slanted at him in the doorway and he zipped the laptop under his jacket before making a dash for cover.

He dodged around the revolving circular brushes of a street cleaner, its driver hunched over the controls in a DayGlo jacket, and turned right into West Marketgait. He hoped to find somewhere he could boost himself with caffeine. The street was a mixture of old properties and newer five-storey buildings, but everywhere was still closed. He had to escape the downpour by sheltering in the doorway of a modern, concrete Methodist church.

Hearing Libby's voice had given his body the shot in the arm it needed. He put his back to the rain and, as he lifted the laptop to open it, noticed a dent and a dark smudge on one side. He'd almost forgotten his confrontation with the mugger in Singapore. He leaned the edge of it against the wall, booted it up and then the screen wavered and cut out.

Not now. Could it have run out of power? There was no way of knowing if the second-hand piece of equipment had been pawned for a good reason. It looked like it had fallen apart before he did. He shook it a few times. Everywhere was closed. Where would he get Internet access? He shook it again.

The screen flickered and glowed. He didn't pause to register relief. He quickly opened a window to the site and put the cursor on the Dundee house.

18 Stirling Crescent,
Dundee,
DD1 3HT

He opened the GPS map and confirmed she was there.

••••

Carla sensed a movement outside the office, vibrations through the floor. She turned down the TV with the remote and listened.

It was nearly six in the morning. Most of the Remada staff would have gone home to grab some sleep before returning in an hour. The cleaners came in on Fridays only. A security guard?

Carla picked up the telephone and dialled the security desk. A shadow fell across the blinds that were slatted against reception. Somebody was stood outside. She watched the door handle to her office pulled down from the other side. She'd kept it locked. Security picked up.

"Who's come up to my floor?" As she spoke into it, she gripped the handset tighter.

"It's OK, Mrs Frost. It's the breakfast you ordered." The security guard reassured her cheerfully.

"I didn't order any and I told you no unauthorised personnel were allowed up to my level."

"I understood that," he said, his voice hardening. "But as he has a staff pass..."

"Who?"

"Mr Iman."

"It's Mr Iman?"

"Yes. He said you were expecting him."

Anwar was obviously still suspicious about what they were hiding and was going out of his way to find out.

"OK... apologies." Carla replaced the receiver and walked to the door.

She'd send him on his way. There was no way she would jeopardise everything at the last moment. But however briefly it took her to repel him, she was glad she'd see a friendly face.

She opened the door and there he was, in an immaculate, olive wool suit and clutching two paper bags.

CHAPTER FIFTY-ONE

Will turned off West Marketgait into Candle Lane and had already given up on finding a cab. Stirling Crescent was tucked behind the university and his shoes squelched and slapped the wet pavement as he jogged the route he'd memorised from the laptop.

His clothes were saturated and the rain blurred his vision as it gathered in his eyebrows and ran off his face. The painkillers were rapidly wearing off, failing to cushion his injury from the pounding of his feet.

The bumper of a car chopped his shins as he gambled with the lights at the crossroads. He halted, waiting for the agony. He could feel the sting of the impact, but his legs still supported his weight. Will turned and briefly registered the shock of the woman who'd barely braked in time. He headed into South Ward Road, vehicles blasting their horns as he weaved through them.

He hoped nobody thought he was a thief fleeing with a stolen laptop and tried to restrain him. He felt safer when he'd rounded the corner into Barrack Street. The buildings dampened the sound of the cars and he could see the red sandstone of the university at the end of it.

Stirling Crescent was a street in disaccord with its surrounding area. The small run of debilitated council houses seemed to double as a permit-free car park for four-wheel drives. Will squeezed past the vehicles obstructing the pavement until he'd found 18.

Only ripped bin liners occupied the crazy-paved area at the front of the dirty, yellow property. Eggshells and unidentifiable packets faded blue by the sun had blown under the window. A grubby net curtain hung off a rail along the top. It was in significant contrast to the other addresses he'd visited. Did anyone really live here?

He knew better than to linger at the front door. The gloves slid easily on now as he made his way down the narrow passageway at the side of the house. The space between 18 and its neighbour was waterlogged, beer cans and cigarette ends bobbing away as his shoes became submerged up to the ankles.

The small back garden was stacked high with more bin liners, as if they'd just been slung from the back door. Movement amongst the bags confirmed the presence of rodents. A rusted rotary washing line lay out of reach beyond them like a forgotten idol. Will squinted through the open, chipped wood door to the tiny kitchen. Rain poured down a green patch on the back wall from a broken gutter above. The water splashed onto the dirty lino inside.

Will's quickened breath reverberated inside his head. His body quivered against the cold and wet. The noise of the drumming rain changed as he moved inside and shook the water from his hair.

The kitchen didn't appear to have been used for its legitimate purpose for a very long time. There was a spoon with burnt sediment in its bowl beside the sink. Looked like the home of an addict. He could hear water leaking inside the room and moved past the filth-caked oven to the hallway.

A thick, sulphurous aroma pervaded the downstairs. The rooms off the hall looked more grimy and dingy than they had in the stark flash of the pictures on the site. In the front lounge was the cabinet of figurines. No sign of the occupants.

He climbed the small flight of stairs and stood at the top

looking at the three partially stripped doors closed to him. "I'm here," he said combatively, his words filling the confined space.

He booted the first door. It opened into a compact, turquoise tiled bathroom and juddered against the wall. There was nothing but a ladder of different tidemarks up the side of the bath. He kicked the next and it revealed the empty spare room, curtains drawn.

He turned to the last and noticed the piece of paper jammed in the doorframe halfway down. He yanked it out and unfolded it. The words were hand written.

sorry I couldn't wait
have to be somewhere else
nobody could have saved this one
you know where to go now

Will pushed the door wide.

He didn't know if it was a trick. Wasn't sure if she would be concealed somewhere in the room. But as the door swung inwards he quickly realised the spectacle that greeted him was one she wanted him to absorb alone.

There was no immediate cause of death visible. No traces of blood on the emaciated figure lying on her back in the dirty blue nightdress. Her right arm was draped over her eyes as if the bulb in the heavy shade over the divan was too bright. It illuminated her pale, white body through the diaphanous material. The other arm hung over the far side of the bed and the soles of her feet were black with dirt.

Rain sizzled behind the closed curtains. Will quickly scanned the shadowy bedroom for someone else. The only other piece of furniture was a dressing table at the window. There was nowhere for anybody to conceal themselves. Was she here?

He stepped further into the room, the cold air heavy with the aroma of the woman's demise. A shiver reactivated the chattering of his jaw. Will put his hand over his mouth and nose and moved to the foot of the bed to examine the corpse. Which item was to be collected? Her body had no adornments.

Then he saw the thin, purple leather strap of the watch on the wrist across her eyes. If she was a junkie, it seemed an odd thing for her to wear. He moved round to the other side of the bed, knowing he'd have to lift her arm away from her face to retrieve it.

Will angled his body to sidle along the gap between the mattress and the dressing table. He was halfway to the head of the bed when he saw her opened wrist. Her left hand was glued to the floor. She'd bled out through her arm and Will was standing in the pints of blood the carpet held.

He remembered the Ambersons and the noise the rug had made when he'd stood before them. Footprints of blood, he'd followed them and left them in his wake. He looked down at the liquid pooled around the leather of his shoes, its darkness up to the stitching of his soles.

Closer up he could see track marks on both arms, a mottled rash of multiple pinpricks amongst the purple bruising.

He heard the blood squelch as he leaned forward to the silvery, pale limb hiding her face. Will reached out and lifted it away. It was almost weightless.

Her eyes hadn't been removed, glued or mutilated; they were open. They fixed him, lustreless pupils slightly rolled upward so she appeared to be glaring at him.

Above her on the wall was a small, black-framed photograph. Clarity and simplicity was the key in this his most squalid destination. Its isolation meant there was no possibility he'd misunderstand. It was a group shot that contained Will.

The body's eyes had been left intact for a reason. It was so he could recognise her. And now, despite her cadaverous features, he did.

CHAPTER FIFTY-TWO

Carla had seen the new address posted on the site and had reached standoff point with Anwar. After deflecting his breakfast ploy she'd told him he had to leave. But he'd repeatedly attempted to re-engage her so he could remain in the office.

She picked up the telephone and kept her voice as level as she could. "Anwar, I've told you to go. Do you really want me to have you removed by security?"

He frowned theatrically. "Carla…" He aimed his dark eyes at her and relaxed his shoulders as if his body language would do the same to her.

"Why do you think you have a share in everyone you meet?" She surprised herself with the statement.

His humour briefly evaporated. A nervous smile appeared, unsure if she was joking.

"You don't own us, Anwar." She had no time to spare his feelings. She just wanted him gone.

He stiffened. "You and Will are my friends…"

"Or is it because you want what Will has?"

He held her gaze, confirming she referred to what he thought she did. "If you mean what I said to you last summer, I know it was…indiscreet."

It had been during her early convalescence after the miscarriage. Anwar had visited Easton Grey and got drunk with Will. She'd thought it was exactly what Will needed, but in the small hours Will had been calling him a cab and he'd chosen his moment. Anwar had set out his stall, promised her a better life with him. She'd dismissed it as nonsense, told him he needed to sober up. But he'd held her arm and repeated the offer until she had to prise away his fingers. "I love Will." She said it again as she had said it then. "I'm always going to be with him." Carla declared it as emotional policy. Something Anwar would understand. "If you have any respect for me, you'll leave now."

He clasped his palms to his chest. "You can't possibly hold things together here without him."

She was about to screw her eyes shut and yell at him, but at that point the artist's impression of Will appeared on the TV beside Anwar. It accompanied the same news report that was being televised on a loop.

Her eyes darted to the screen and back to him. "What are you talking about?"

"His absence from the office, him not answering my calls, you pumping me for the sort of inside track he normally does. Where has he gone?" He took a step towards her. "Are you telling me he hasn't walked out on you?" And another step, hands extending.

Carla felt her buckled patience snap and pressed the number.

"Mrs Frost?" The security guard's bored tone failed to defuse her anger.

"I need someone removed from my office." She didn't take her eyes from Anwar. He halted and she watched his face shift through a spectrum of mortification.

"Removed?" The security guard seemed equally surprised.

"Now." She slammed down the receiver.

Anwar's palms were turned outwards now. "OK. I'll leave. I can see you're becoming upset."

"Go!"

The harshness of the word registered like a physical strike. His fingers scrabbled behind him for the handle.

Carla watched him leave before the door clicked shut behind

him. She dialled reception and told the security guard to stay where he was, but to take Anwar's pass and make sure he left the building. When she dumped the handset back on the cradle it rang immediately.

She drew in breath to repeat the instructions, but it was Will.

"The body." She could hear rain rattling around him. "It was Eva. Eva Lockwood."

Will stared at Eva's body. He couldn't look away.

"Wait, the GPS says she's still in the house," Carla said.

"We can forget tracking her." Will recovered his phone from where it had been left for him on the dressing table. "She's ditched it here." "She found it?" Carla's dismay was palpable. "That was our insurance against Pope."

"Who?"

A pause, then Carla said, "A US TV reporter found the website and knows about the kidnap. He's promised to keep a lid on the story in return for the GPS coordinates."

Will absorbed the revelation. "Why didn't you tell me?"

"It was the last thing you needed to deal with. He's told me he'll suppress it until we get Libby back. But now we've got nothing to trade off. He knows our home is the last on the row."

"So he's been tracking her as well as us?"

"Was. But as soon as he finds out she's dumped the phone we'll probably have the international media descending on the house."

"But he doesn't know yet?"

"He hasn't contacted me or responded to my calls for hours. I don't know where he is."

"Don't engage with him again. As far as he's concerned, she still has the phone. I'm following the same route so he'll think I'm her."

Carla digested what he'd said. "For how long though?"

Will's mind assimilated the new obstacle.

"Why Eva Lockwood, Will?" The question was almost accusatory.

"I can't even begin to fathom why she would be part of this."

"Did she suffer?"

Will looked at her skeletal body. "Long before today."

Pope and Weaver read the new message as soon as it appeared on the website in their creaky room in The Man In The Moon.

Easton Grey
MR AND MRS FROST COME ALONE
BRING YOUR MOBILES

Pope and Weaver had checked into the inn just outside Hanworth village and had already done a thorough recce of the immediate area. They'd located Easton Grey after a few enquiries at the bar. Pope had done some pieces to camera outside the gates. It was the first time he'd ever pre-empted a crime scene.

On the GPS map Pope could see she was heading back to the airport. "Just a matter of hours now. We give the Frosts the time they need before we move in." He did another search for breaking new stories in Serangoon. He'd found one report of a fire in the specific vicinity, but no details had been released.

Weaver was checking his lens. "We can't risk this slipping through our fingers. I want us to be in close. And we've got to be prepared for the situation to change."

"We give the Frosts the time they need before we move in," he reiterated. "Then we'll tail her from Easton Grey and lead the cops straight to wherever she heads afterwards. I've got the networks on speed dial. When we tell them who we've run down we'll get ourselves in position and they can scramble us an aerial crew for the live arrest."

Will assumed there wouldn't be any further need for the website.

His last destination was all-too familiar, but he'd kept the laptop on for the duration of the flight. He'd focussed on the photos taken inside his home and dreaded the addition of any new ones. The Amberson family tableau vividly re-presented itself every time his eyes lingered on the familiar couch in his TV lounge.

They landed bumpily and his mobile rang as soon as he exited the cabin.

"Carla, stay exactly where you are."

"But we have to do what they say."

"We know this is going to be a trap..."

The certainty of that hung between them and the chasm separating him from his wife suddenly seemed wider than when he'd been on the other side of the Atlantic.

"We've done everything they've asked. If they've requested both of us, I have to go." It sounded like Carla was already getting up to leave.

"This is where we get to call the shots. Whatever's waiting at home is an end to this. They have to finish it there and will have to accept it'll just be me."

"It's *our* home, Will," she countered, anger distorting her voice.

"I'm being made to pay for something I did. Eva Lockwood was part of my past."

As he'd left the house in Stirling Crescent, Will had told Carla the scant details he remembered about his brief acquaintance with Eva in college. Her death proved the campaign had to be directed at him.

"If I can exchange myself for Libby..." A shoulder bumped his as he slowed in a bottleneck of passengers in the concourse entrance.

"This isn't your decision to make. Do you really expect me to let you do this on your own?"

"We can't waste time arguing this."

"I'm driving back to Hanworth." He heard his drawer open and the clatter of keys.

"No. Don't go anywhere… yet. Let me think for a minute." He looked at his watch. It was 3.16pm. With no specific directions to wait for, was it assumed they'd go straight to Easton Grey?

An incoherent passenger announcement barked metallically. Their dialogue suspended, Will closed his eyes. He shut out the ache and noise and again imagined himself hovering above, looking down at his insignificance. What was his clearest path?

The announcement ended.

"Will?"

"Did you get that?"

"What's going on?"

"Bomb scare, looks like I'm going to be delayed getting out of the terminal." He heard her exhale and closed his eyes. "I'll call you as soon as I'm clear. We'll arrange a place to meet between here and the house. Sit tight until then, OK?"

"OK," she said reluctantly.

He cut the call before he could say anything else. Will guessed it was the last time he'd speak to her. An intense pain overrode the one in his gut, pricking the back of his throat. He fought it as he strode to the exit.

CHAPTER FIFTY-THREE

It was just over fifteen minutes later that Carla realised what he'd done. She'd prepared herself to leave, checking the news sites for signs of a bomb scare story. But she assumed that what invariably turned out to be hoaxes weren't worthy of coverage.

She'd tried his mobile, but it went to his answering service.

Carla maximised the GPS map. The dot told her Will was already outside the airport. He'd never deceived her in all the years they'd been married. It made the realisation doubly devastating.

She immediately grabbed her mobile and handbag and left the office, her prison door bumping wide as she hurried to the lift. As she headed down to ground level, anger at his betrayal burnt through her.

She couldn't summon the police. Not after having obeyed the kidnappers' instructions until now. They'd done everything they'd been told. Her presence had been demanded. They both had to be there.

In the downstairs car park, Will's blue Audi Q7 was parked in its space. She deactivated the alarm and had the door open before she noticed the front tyre was flat.

The back one was deflated as well. Carla moved round to the passenger side and found the same situation there. How could it have been vandalised when the car park was so secure?

A pair of hands slid around her waist.

• • • •

"She's almost on top of us." Weaver shifted in the driver's seat and looked up from the iPad across the tarmac to the main gates of Easton Grey. Their Lexus was parked twenty yards away from them on the opposite side of the road under an overhang of trees. Pope had wanted them to position themselves further back, but Weaver wanted to be as tight in as possible.

The red dot shifted. It was heading north of their location.

Weaver started the engine. "Looks like she's going to come in through the back."

Having surveyed the boundary it was evident that access could easily be gained to the grounds from most points using only a ladder. The north wall bordered secluded farmland, however, and had collapsed in several places making entry even easier.

Pope put his hand on the wheel. "She can't know we're following her."

Weaver chewed faster, nodded dismissively and accelerated hard.

Minutes later, Will stepped out of a black taxi in front of the same gates. The first cabby he'd found at the airport had been bemused by his request to drive without a passenger. Will had handed him the first GPS phone and said he had to deliver it to Sloman's farm. He was to wait outside until somebody came to collect it from him. His second ride had brought him to Easton Grey.

How many cabs had he used in the last four days? He looked up the length of the empty lawns flanking the gravelled driveway that led to the house. The cloudless blue sky of a drowsy afternoon allowed the sun to bathe the sandstone bricks and glint off the mullioned windows.

"Thinking of breaking in?" The driver remained stationary with his engine puttering while Will stood at the towering electric gates.

He knew how it looked to him. Had he really only been away four days? But it wasn't just absence and the state of his clothes that made him feel like an intruder to his own home. He sensed a deviation in the normal atmosphere.

She was waiting for him.

He paid and fished out his keys. His jacket was still saturated from his visit to the house in Stirling Crescent, but every item he'd collected was safe within the inside pocket.

Crows squawked in the nearby copse. The cab driver lingered to watch him activate the gates with his fob and then pulled away. Will strode up the gravel, lobbing the laptop to the side of the drive.

Carla twisted onto her back and slammed both heels of her hands repeatedly against the ceiling of her prison. She'd almost escaped her attacker, but had been forced into the boot of the car beside Will's. She should have recognised it. Should have questioned its presence.

"Let me out!" Every fibre pumped the scream from her, her temples buzzing with the exertion. She continued hammering the lined metal, not caring if she broke her wrists. She thought of Will surrendering himself. "Help!"

Somebody had to hear. It was late afternoon, but too early for people to be leaving the building.

She tried to focus in the dark, but couldn't even see the backs of her hands above her. She'd dropped her bag. Her mobile had been inside. She started kicking with both feet, driving the pointed toes of her high heels into the lid. She tested with her fingers above her head and then down the sides of her body, searching for any object that might have been left in there. Was there something she could use to bash her way out? Her fingertips only brushed the carpet lining the bottom. She kicked harder, pounded harder, screamed harder.

Then she listened. Nothing. But the car hadn't moved yet. She had to attract someone's attention before she was driven away. She felt her own laboured breath bounce back hot and acrid on her face.

Somebody had once told her if you were locked in a boot you should try to poke your hand through the rear light. She angled her body so she could make a space to manoeuvre her arm and clawed in the corner above her. Her nails rasped against metal. Was the light unit sealed in?

She started kicking again, shouting at the lid and battering it with her fists.

There was no mistaking who had locked her in.

Will bypassed the front door and entered the house through the back, but was puzzled when he had to deactivate the alarm inside the kitchen. No way in left open for him? Perhaps she thought it unnecessary. But how could she elude the movement detectors?

He couldn't have beaten her back here. He wandered cautiously around the rooms, the office a suspended moment in time reminding him of the life he had lost. The swivel chair was still in the middle of the floor, pushed back after they'd hurriedly left on the morning he'd found the site.

Nothing downstairs was out of place.

He headed upstairs. Their bed was still unmade. He entered Libby's room, something he hadn't done for some time as she'd insisted on privacy for her and Luke. Photos of her nuzzling him were arranged in a clutch of frames on the dresser. He was relieved that no black-framed pictures were present. The last image he'd seen of Luke popped into his memory.

An oil-effect shot of Will, Carla and Libby at her eighteenth birthday party was mounted on the wall over the bed. He remembered Luke taking it. It had been a distraction while Will had been trying to install their new gas-fired deck barbecue.

He went back downstairs again, opening each door and taking in the emptiness of the rooms. Spaces embellished with every conceivable lifestyle appliance. He recalled how his home had looked like a showroom when he'd seen it broken down into flat images on the site.

Although he'd spent his life in disavowal of the figure that had stood over him on the beach, Will recognised he'd been replicating him in every way. He'd applied the cosmetics of a happy family life here just as his father had incessantly painted the outside of the house and neglected what was at the heart of it. And, like him, he'd been unable to hide his disapproval from his only child, had shut them out for not becoming the person he'd envisaged.

He didn't know anything about Libby's world even though she'd existed so close by. He'd ignored everything that jarred with his own perception of her. All of his positive recollections of her were from the time she'd been a child. It was his own expectations at fault, his projections of who he wanted her to be. Her life had always been there for him to participate in, but he'd been in denial of the woman she was becoming.

Even though he'd been so happy when Jessie had been about to join the family, he disapproved of Libby's pregnancy. He hadn't kept that a secret from her and he wondered if she'd been waiting for him to forgive her.

Consequences. That's the word he'd used. Had he been so secure in his own immunity from them?

He padded onto the landing and listened to the stillness of the house. Nobody was here. Had this been a diversion? He thought about Carla and how he'd tricked her into being excluded.

He suddenly remembered the new security installation and went to the utility room where they'd set up the monitor. He switched it on and a black and white mosaic display of different camera angles allowed him to survey the interior and exterior of the house. No sign of her. But as his eyes skimmed over the summer house he recalled the picture of Carla there that had been hung in the Chicago apartment. They were drawn back to it again. Candles flickered in its window.

CHAPTER FIFTY-FOUR

As he made his way down the incline of the lawn, a cool breeze played against his ears. The wind rippled in the ring of yew trees beyond, but he knew the serenity of the scene belied what was hiding within it.

His mind returned again to the one victim he knew: Eva Lockwood. He'd rarely thought about Eva let alone uttered her name in such a long time, but at eighteen she'd briefly been the epicentre of his universe.

He'd first caught glimpses of her on campus at Brunel in his first year. She was tall and pale and nobody else seemed to notice her. Will had been drawn to her; she was quiet, demure. She'd worn her tight brunette curls in a selection of colourful headscarves and seemed to be a willing outsider.

His own background had made him feel like an impostor at Brunel, so he'd felt an immediate affinity towards her. Soon after he'd been more familiar with her timetable than she was. Having discovered that her anthropology and his engineering curricula were never likely to unite them inside the same building, he took to attending parties at human sciences.

He managed to engage her at the department's Christmas Punch Ball. She was half-Dutch with wealthy parents and had been sombre and indifferent about her education. She'd wanted to travel, but her family had tethered her until she'd completed her studies. Will had been besotted and had rationalised her apathy. To him her aloofness had been enigmatic. He'd thought about nothing but her during the intervening holidays.

When he met her again, the following term, she had no recollection of him or their previous conversation. He'd been devastated, and it was Eva's detachment that precipitated events a few months later.

By then he was casually involved with Jenny Sturgess. He'd already heard Eva had personal problems; that she was dropping out. But after an all-night campus party ended with his new girlfriend dumping him, it was Eva that persuaded him to allow her back to his room.

He'd already convinced himself that the two of them were never destined to be together, but her abrupt interest allowed events to develop at a speed he'd never envisaged. There had been some impromptu, drunken passion, but when he'd woken up she'd been clothed and asleep on the couch. He'd assumed they'd both been too drunk to perform, that his virginity was still maddeningly intact.

Alcohol ensured he remembered little of the night they spent together, and Eva repeated her talent for selective amnesia afterwards. He'd played down the fact to himself that he'd barely registered on her radar by discovering that nobody else had either. Will found out why she'd been such a willing pariah. She was addicted to amphetamines.

He still looked for her on campus, but one day realised she was no longer attending. He'd met and fallen in love with Carla soon after and Eva had dissolved into his past. Carla knew of her, but had never encountered her during her own time at Brunel.

Did everything end at a woman he'd briefly known over twenty years ago? Or did it begin there and he'd been working his way back along the website's street towards her?

Twenty-five years ago. There was one possibility, one he'd been desperately trying to dismiss, that had been terrifying him since he'd walked out of the rundown house in Stirling Crescent.

As the distance between him and the hexagonal wooden building diminished, he could hear the sound of Libby's glass wind chimes gently striking each other.

He knew no lights had been left on the night he'd been in there with Carla. They'd blown out the candles and lanterns before they'd returned to the house, they'd have burned out by now in any case. The double doors at the front hadn't been left open either.

He stopped at the threshold, as he had at the other addresses, squinting through the doorway into the gloomy interior. He could see flames newly lit and their light bouncing from the reflective, coloured glass hanging from the ceiling.

He opened his mouth to speak, but decided against it. She knew he was here. She had Libby. He had no leverage. He was at her disposal now.

He took the three steps into the summer house and, for a moment, his eyes had to readjust from the glare of the sun outside. The inside had its familiar aroma – cut grass and citronella – but there was a different scent here. One he'd first encountered on the plane.

As the details of the room defined themselves, he saw her. She was standing to his right, glinting mirror shards obscuring her expression. For a split second he was walking in as he had four days ago. Carla had been waiting for him then, naked as this woman was now.

She padded forward on her bare feet. This was no seduction. Her pallid, bony body exhibited scars like constellations, raised blisters and circular black blemishes scattered from her shoulders, between the gap in her tight breasts and down to the tops of her legs.

She darted through the winking glass and Will felt a punch to his sternum. It was hard, but not enough to force him backwards, but the sensation that chased it fastened the muscles across his chest and dropped him onto his side.

Will could hear his body spasm and knock the wooden floor with the heel of his shoe. He saw the Taser in her hand as she bent to examine his convulsions.

Her pencilled eyebrows rose. "No stepmother?" she enquired amicably.

Carla felt the muscles in her shoulders throb with the exertion of her screams. She kept knocking and kicking, not daring to stop in case someone was passing by.

Her toes tingled painfully, bruised. Her caustic breath gripped her face and, as her own situation elbowed speculations about Will's aside, delayed panic rapidly inflated.

She was a child again, curled up on the bed when she knew her parents would never return to pick her up. Strange space, strange smells, no chance of her waking up to find it was a nightmare.

Carla squeezed her eyes shut against the blackness, coloured patterns swirling in them as she tried to inhale slowly. She wondered if it was airtight in here and how much oxygen she had left. Her fear of suffocating threatened to quickly devour the scant supply around her.

Skinny Man wasn't breathing. As time had passed and he still hadn't risen from his position in the chair, Tam had become bolder with the glances he'd snatched at the figure seated in the shadows beyond the cage.

He hadn't shifted in all the time he'd been there. The other man was gone with the girl. Was it him that had injected him? Had Skinny Man been dead all this time?

Tam decided the only way to find out was to attempt to escape through the gap he'd left in the wire. He snaked his body to the corner of the cage and looked back. Skinny Man's silhouette didn't budge. He pushed his bound wrists against the corner and it gave. He hadn't had time to remove the staple from the bottom, however, so the gap that opened was very small. Could he push it out far enough to crawl through?

He looked back at Skinny Man again, expecting him to be crouching and smiling at the front of the cage. He still hadn't moved. Tam crawled as close as he could to the opening and started pushing his body against the wire.

Libby struck metal. When the space around her had lurched, she thought the needle had been pushed back into her vein, but she quickly realised she was lying inside the van again. The gears ground and the engine snarled and rattled as it rapidly accelerated. She could hear the axle turning under the warm floor as they sped over uneven terrain. Her teeth vibrated, head bounced and body rolled as they took each sharp turn.

The motion shook away some of her stupor. Her eyebrow pulsated where she'd been hit. Where were they going? She howled through the gag in case anyone could hear her as they passed. The radio came on. Loud, pneumatic rock engulfed her feeble cries.

She weakly lashed out with her feet, trying to strike the doors of the van, but they failed to connect. The vehicle rounded another corner and turned her again. The bridge of Libby's nose struck a sharp edge and her vision flared white.

Her body was too weak to react to the motion. She couldn't escape, couldn't defend herself against whatever awaited at their destination. Unconsciousness returned, like black bricks rebuilding themselves into a wall that shut out the world.

Pope and Weaver waited at the entrance to Sloman's farm. A mud track led through the open gates and wound out of sight beyond the forest.

"Fuck this. We should drive in there." Weaver's hand was on

the ignition.

"No. We hang fire."

"But what is she doing in here?"

Pope shook his head and studied her stable position on the GPS. "We wait. But reverse further back. She might return this way."

Poppy jabbed Will with the Taser again, two hundred and fifty thousand volts to his central nervous system. His body bucked, his brain's attempt to send signals to his muscles shorting out a second time. She quickly bound his hands behind his back with chain and left him lying on his side.

It wouldn't take long for him to recover. Then they had the whole afternoon together.

She patted his jacket and then reached into the inside pocket. Her fingers clasped the contents and pulled out the silk he'd wrapped the other items in.

There was a wicker table by the sound system. She swiped the stack of CDs there to the floor and unfolded the violet material across its top, revealing the jewellery and scarf.

Carla heard a voice outside the car. She slid her ear to the metal and listened to a low exchange of male dialogue.

"I'm locked in here!" The words tore the last volume from her throat and she tasted blood.

She waited. The conversation stopped.

Light gushed in and Carla felt a current of air cool her skin. She looked up to see the security guard peering down with his cold blue eyes.

CHAPTER FIFTY-FIVE

Carla opened her mouth, but the words couldn't form. She sat upright.

"Mrs Frost?"

She propelled herself out of the boot, rooting her legs to the car park for fear of being shut in again. Her leg skated out to one side and the security guard supported her.

"I was just coming off my shift and heard you."

She coughed and tasted the blood in her mouth again. "Anwar locked me in," she croaked.

The security guard nodded uncertainly.

"I have to go, but call the police immediately and let them know what happened. Anwar Iman," she repeated for his benefit. She'd recognised the sleeves of his olive suit and his tanned hands. It was his car she'd been locked inside.

"But Mr Iman is here." The security guard nodded behind her.

She turned from the security guard to where Anwar was leaning apprehensively against a concrete pillar clutching her handbag.

"I'm sorry, Carla." His palms were out again, like he was anticipating aggression.

Carla yanked her arm from the security guard's grasp. "Anwar?"

"I was acting under Will's instructions." Her incomprehension prompted him further. "He called me. Told me to stop you from leaving. After you'd thrown me out. You'd taken my pass so I had to wait for you here. He knew you'd try to use his car."

Will had known she'd make her own decision and had tried to intercept her using Anwar. She didn't have the energy to be angry with him. "You know what's happening?" she whispered through vocal cords that felt frayed.

Anwar shook his head once. "Just that it was a matter of life and death and that I had to do everything in my power to keep you here. Please... tell me what this is all about."

There was no time for further exchange. Even though his actions had been misguided, he'd been protecting her for Will. She made for the exit, but Anwar blocked her path.

"Carla, I can't let you go."

"Anwar, step aside," she said, meeting his eye.

The summer house was hot and stuffy and Poppy had been relieved to be free of her clothes. But having waited for Will to recover, she dropped the flimsy dress over her head again, arranging the thin straps on her shoulders and pulling down at the waist-high hem to straighten out the wrinkles. She slipped on her beaded bracelet, her amethyst pendant and ring. Then she re-attached her Emile Chouriet watch, the one she'd left on her mother's body.

Poppy knotted the red scarf retrieved from Strick's mouth around her neck, covering the rope burn at the base of her throat. There was no mirror, but she could see herself in multiple mobile reflections gently swaying in the draught through the door.

Will watched her from his position on the floor. She had her back to him and he could see a mottled burn mark on her right hip and blackened welts down her spine and across her buttocks.

As her figure shifted in the violet dress it evoked the purple background colour of the website. The amethyst pendant, ring and other accessories belonged to her. She hadn't lied. He'd collected them and his daughter had made it to the party.

Beyond her, on the summer house wall, was a chain of black-framed photographs. The one of Libby and Luke he'd found in Ellicott City, the baby scan from Bel Air, Carla's image from Chicago, a copy of one of the snaps of Will he'd burnt in Serangoon, the university group shot of him with Eva Lockwood that had been fixed over her bed in Dundee and, to finish the row, a pensive portrait of her. She hadn't just been taunting Will and the police with the pictures; she'd been assembling her family.

It couldn't be the truth. But the hours of the blackout he'd suffered the night he'd spent with Eva Lockwood were irretrievable. Had his first intimacy not been with Carla as he'd thought? This obscene possibility revolved in his brain.

He felt the cool metal chain cutting into his wrists and remembered Dr Ren.

She didn't turn. "As you weren't there, I thought I'd show you how I was when I came into the world." Her voice was sedate and composed. "And the medals I've earned since." She angled her body to display the brands and disfigurements.

Will rolled onto his back, crushing his hands. Then he painfully levered himself so he was sitting up.

She turned, biting her pronounced bottom lip. Not as if she was internally debating what to do with him, but when to do it.

"You're Eva's daughter." He couldn't implicate himself.

Her facial reaction was almost imperceptible. "I only really got to know her these past few months. Looking after her. Taking her what she needed...."

Will recalled the drug paraphernalia in the kitchen. "She abandoned you?"

She ran her fingers round the scarf about her neck. "Who would have thought a junkie's womb would be so fertile."

"You think I'm the father."

She flushed then, pinpricks of red radiating at her pale cheekbones.

Your father. Will couldn't bring himself to say it, couldn't accept he could be bonded by blood to the death he'd witnessed. He looked into her collected, barren expression, terrified of seeing a glimpse of himself there.

CHAPTER FIFTY-SIX

"Eva had no one else," she continued with the same hollow tenderness. "She slept only with you at Brunel. Said too much drink meant you weren't really present at my conception. Remembered your name though. You were easy to find."

"Eva never told me. She just disappeared." The stunned defence was as much for his ears as hers.

"Eva decided to deal with me on her own." She left the magnitude of what that had meant for her suspended between them for a moment. "Her recreational habits ended her studies. She'd already started training as an air stewardess when she moved up to Class A drugs."

Will remembered what she'd said about the irony of meeting on a plane.

"She met Dr Ren during her stop-offs in Singapore. Ren wasn't as respectable then, more a back street practitioner. No surgery, but plenty of demand for his prescriptions. They had a relationship. He was only too eager to dispose of me for her." She ran her fingers down the edge of her bare arm and touched the watch on her wrist.

Will looked round for her knife. He couldn't see it, but located the Taser on the wicker table.

"I was a premature, junkie baby born in Ren's kitchen. My mother had eclampsia and had severe seizures throughout the birth. The toxins in her system nearly killed her." She paused, as if in respect for the woman she'd bled out on the mattress. "Dr Ren cut my umbilical with a fish knife. Then, while he helped my mother shoot up, he left me too near the stove and my blanket caught fire.

Her words evoked Ren's suffocated curses and what she'd done to him in the surgery. "Ren didn't burn like you wanted him to. I pushed him out of the fire."

Her dark brown eyes didn't flicker, but restrained his. "Eva said I looked like something that had fallen from a burning nest." She showed her teeth as if in affection for the description. "By the time she'd recuperated, Ren had sold me."

Will watched her lips move, her head dipping with the words and their connotations. He sensed nothing, but the mechanism of her speech. There was no bitterness to the account. None of the words were imbued with anything more than civility.

"He sold me to a man named Li Shanchi. Shanchi used child labour in the textile factories he operated in Geylang. He called me his Poppy. I had no shortage of father figures." She gently tapped one of the pieces of coloured glass with her fingertip so it spun on its wire. "When I was twelve I was put to work in the brothels. I watched Shanchi cave a man's head in. Soon after he helped me dispose of a customer I had to deal with myself." She showed him the watch, offering it like a hand to kiss. "This was a birthday gift. I don't know my real birth date, but Jake decided on today."

"Jake?"

"Jacob Franks. He was a regular visitor to Geylang. I was a profitable commodity at fourteen. I even got to leave the district when Shanchi drove me to the exclusive hotels in his car. I was blessed."

Will's regard shifted from hers to the red scarf at her neck, he didn't want to see the memory in her eyes or the scars of her ordeal.

"Shanchi sold me to Jake. I didn't know then how much

influence he had. Jake gave me a birthday and a passport. I never saw Shanchi again. I would have arranged for you to meet him too, but he died of bowel cancer in 2008." She briefly closed her eyes as if in quiet reverence.

"Would you have murdered his family as well?"

Her features didn't fluctuate. "I lived in the Chicago apartment Jake bought me. He didn't need to imprison me there. I knew how fortunate I was. I was safe. Then I began to understand who he was. How powerful. The people he was connected to." She paused and something guileful glimmered in her eyes. "His mistake was allowing me to educate myself. He wanted me to learn. Sometimes Jake said he thought of me as his daughter. Like he would have choked his own daughter while he sodomised her."

Will realised he couldn't allow the revulsion of her testament to restrain him. He had to remain as removed as she was.

"For nearly a decade he showered me with what he thought I wanted. I used his money to enable myself. He even helped me locate my mother through Shanchi and Doctor Ren. But I was his currency. There was a VIP club in Chicago called the Lupus Rooms, an exclusive drop in for high-profile clientele. It was how Jake met Holt Amberson and Richard Strick. A lot of men came to visit me at the apartment. Faces without names; I learnt how to block out a new sort of pain there."

If she was his daughter how could Will have prevented what had happened? How could he have when he didn't know she existed?

"Amberson and Strick were regulars. Always called when they were in town. Amberson used to stub cigarettes out on my spine. Strick liked to watch Monro slowly fracture my arms with a G-clamp." She offhandedly itemised the abuse, a treadmill that had become the everyday. "I left one of the recordings at Monro's place for you." She worded it as an enquiry, as if soliciting approval for its contents.

The footage the two bodies had been sat in front of in the lounge – Monro had been behind the mask. It was her screams of agony that had led him into the room.

"I ran out on Jake five months ago. He'd given me insight. I'd extracted as much as I could from his intellect. I didn't need him any more."

Will could still hear the sound of his empty skull as he'd pulled out the polythene package of silk she now wore on her body.

"He panicked when I killed Amberson and Strick. He was in town for the Alper's Benefit so I knew he would try to dispose of the rest of the discs. There were hundreds of them. They sat on the shelves right next to all the books he bought for me about political science and philosophy."

Will understood now that every spark of who she was had been systematically ground out. But there was no doubt in his mind. What she'd forced the people she believed wronged her to endure was the work of a calculating monster. "And their abuse justifies the deaths of innocent women and children," he said. He thought of Eva and all the blood leading back to a night he couldn't remember.

"How could men like that live at the bosom of their families and never be suspected? They were all in denial. They didn't think twice about sacrificing my innocence."

How could she be so contained? Will guessed it was the only way she'd survived, hiding within the abused vessel of herself. He was back in the Monro house, controlling his limbs from a place removed from the horror he witnessed, moving his legs up the stairs.

"I met Amberson's son online. Tried to see past the father that had visited me in the apartment. But there was the same predator. That's when I decided they all had to be rubbed out. Every trace. They were inhuman."

"No human being could possibly take lives in the way you have." He met her eye now, found his own brown irises there.

"Those men did. All principled members of society, but they needed somebody like me. The civilised can't function without having their real nature serviced. I was bred for it. A cheap fuck, it's what I started out as and what I was made to aspire to."

Will had no answer. Her words, as carefully constructed as everything else had been, obviously led to an ultimate act of penance.

She picked up the Taser.

"So how are you going to butcher me? Do I get extra irony with my death?" He staggered upright, confronting her, a creature so far removed from him because of what had happened to her. But there was nothing in her story he could discount, nothing that allowed him to deny who she was.

"Relax." Cordiality suffused her voice again. "Make yourself comfortable for a moment." She was mimicking what she'd been her whole life. "Have a think about what you'd like me to do." She held out the Taser and smiled, but her lips hardened white.

Will stepped back and dropped onto the couch. Once he was seated, she jabbed his chest. His body stiffened into painful paralysis again.

"Choose a woman you'd like," she said attentively. "Mother or daughter?"

CHAPTER FIFTY- SEVEN

Will trembled as he watched Poppy wander out of the summer house and sit with her back to him on the step. The breeze picked up her hair and she wiped one side of it behind her ear.

"I'll let you decide. Summon Carla or I'll give the word for Libby to die like her boyfriend," she proposed matter-of-factly.

He couldn't speak; his jaw was still locked against the convulsions.

"You can make the call to your wife or not. Your choice." The fringe of her hair lifted as she blew breath into her face to cool herself down. She stood and moved out of sight and into the garden.

Will remained immobile. The pieces of mirror and coloured glass jangled in the breeze.

The tremors in his body gradually subsided and he flexed his arms against the chain. If he could get upright he could run at her when she came back through the door. But what would that achieve? He still had to do exactly as she asked.

How could he bring Carla here? He wondered if Anwar had got to her in time. He prayed she wouldn't pick up when he called. Maybe he could play for time that way.

Then he heard a familiar sound, the soft boom and cleaving of the Longranger's rotor blades. The noise intensified. He got to his feet and walked to the doorway to watch it land. Birds dispersed as it disappeared behind the ring of yews and then took quickly off again.

He waited. The crows returned noisily to their branches and it reminded him of the flies that had swarmed around the bodies of the Ambersons. Moments later, Carla emerged from the perimeter of the trees striding purposefully. She'd sent the pilot back. They were alone.

"I'll welcome her." Poppy was stood beside him, watching her at the same time.

The wire scored the skin on Tam's scalp and then tightened around his throat as he slid his head clean through the gap and it flapped into place. He quickly turned back to check Skinny Man's position. He was still motionless. But now Tam was trapped. His shoulders were too wide to fit and he couldn't pull his head back inside.

Chicken claws scratched around his face and he blew dust and droppings away from his mouth. Grunting, he pushed his body against the opening, ramming his bound hands under his chin and attempting to pull his shoulder blades together to squeeze them through. Panic pounded at him, taking his last reserve of energy. All the time his feet struggled in their bonds, the coils gradually loosening at his ankles.

He was too big. He couldn't move either way now.

"No." The word was dry in Carla's mouth as she contemplated the length of chain in Poppy's hands.

From his position seated back on the summer house couch, Will saw Poppy's fingers tighten on the Taser. "Do as she says."

Carla didn't move; her face balefully analysed Poppy's.

"My father, I've shown respect for." She nodded at Will. "I'd like to do the same for you." Her hand lifted toward Carla.

"Do as she says!" Will yelled.

Poppy's arm halted an inch away, the blue electric charge flickering between the contacts.

Carla slowly held her hands out, wrists against each other.

Poppy bound them tight with chain. Carla gasped as the link tightened.

"You're cutting off her circulation." He was still angry that Carla had endangered herself. Anwar had promised to do everything in his power to hold her. Poppy indicated the couch and Carla perched on the edge of the cushion. Poppy held the Taser to her chest and gestured for her to sit back.

Carla complied. "Father? What the hell is she talking about?" Her voice was spent and hoarse. She continued to glare at Poppy. When Will didn't reply she turned slowly to meet his gaze.

He didn't need to utter a word. He saw the realisation register. Horror swept her face, disabling the aggression there. "Eva?"

He nodded once.

Poppy waited for her gaze to return to hers. "Yes, a real daughter." She bent low to fix Will's eyes. "Help me understand. My life is thrown away and then you adopt Libby. How can you care for a child who's not even your own flesh and blood?"

Poppy reached into Carla's handbag and pulled out her mobile. Her thumb flitted over the keypad and she sent a text. Then she positioned the wicker table between them and placed the telephone on top.

CHAPTER FIFTY-EIGHT

Weaver staggered back down the muddy track to the car. "We've been fucked over!"

"What are you talking about?"

"There's a cabby parked up there. Frost sent him here with the phone."

Pope closed his eyes and smiled resignedly. At what point had the phone been returned to Frost? It didn't matter. The decoy had served its purpose.

Weaver slammed the door and started the engine. "We've got to get back to the house."

"Weaver..."

"That son-of-a-bitch."

"He's protecting his family."

"We can still salvage this."

"I told you, we're not going in there."

Weaver turned the car to head back the way they came. "Get on the phone."

"Stop the car, Weaver."

"Are you nuts?"

"Stop the car."

Weaver accelerated.

Pope slugged Weaver once. A lucky shot. It was enough to put him out. The car coasted across the road and Pope yanked the wheel to stop them hitting the barrier.

Pope's fist buzzed. "You're right, Weaver. Dogs shouldn't chase cars."

The revelation flooded Carla. Will already had a child. All those years of failed IVF and adoption screening before they'd brought Libby home at fourteen months old. All that time his daughter had been living and growing outside their world.

She'd moved behind them, was stood at their shoulders. They both faced front, not wanting to turn. Would they be found with their hands taped to their faces? Carla could feel the air from Poppy's nostrils caress her neck. She focussed on the mobile. It had been positioned there for a reason. Even if they were to die here soon, the mobile was significant. It gave them valuable seconds.

Will straightened and shifted forward in his seat, his body tensing. "Let them both go. I'm the one who abandoned you." He spoke slowly.

Carla turned to him, but he didn't meet her eye, just kept staring at the mobile on the table. "Will, no."

"Abandoned? No, my mother abandoned me," Poppy said dismissively. "But Eva at least suffered remorse. Your existence continued unbroken. I absorbed all the impact for you while you gave Libby what I should have had."

"I can't even conceive of what you went through." Will closed his eyes.

Carla wondered what Will had been told. Or was he buying time to consider every dead option they had?

"But you don't have to." Her voice sounded slightly louder, as if she was leaning between them.

He opened his eyes again. "But I thought that's what this was all about. Making us feel your pain."

"No. Not you," she said, as if he'd misunderstood the rules of a game.

The mobile buzzed, its vibrations making it move on the table.

She reached past them, plucking it up. It passed Carla's face and she heard it beep. Then she felt its plastic pressed to her ear.

"Mum?"

The word undid her. Libby's hysteria burst at the same time. Sound bounced and echoed. She couldn't decipher the words through the distortion. "Speak slower, darling." What could she say to her? "Speak slower, speak slower," she whispered.

Libby's breath thundered against the mouthpiece. "They locked us in cages. I don't know what's happened to Luke."

Carla screwed her eyes shut and saw his face. "Hush, we're both here, Libby. Dad's here, I'm here."

"They drugged me. Then they tied me up and drove me round." The words pumped out of her in between her sobs.

"Keep talking. Take it slowly. Where are you now?"

"They let me go. Left me outside the police station. But there's still no sign of Luke."

Carla opened her eyes. "Say again?" She could sense the intensity of Will's gaze on the side of her face.

"They just dumped me here. I'm with the police."

Carla gasped. Something burst inside her.

"I want to come home."

She turned to Will. "She's safe. She's with the police." She felt warmth on her face, saw Will's frozen terror blur.

But through their tears they both knew there would only be a short interval between the knowledge of this and realising what part of the design it was.

The phone was taken from her ear.

"Mum?" Carla could just hear Libby's tiny voice stranded in the earpiece before the call was cut.

"She was always going to be released," she reassured them. "Now she'll know what it is to be alone."

Carla saw a metallic flash from the corner of her eye.

CHAPTER FIFTY-NINE

Will rolled quickly away from Poppy to the other side of the couch. He found his feet and when his body turned he could see the sushi knife in her hand. Her fingers tightly gripped Carla's hair. "No!" He launched himself back at the couch, his weight pushing it back and crushing her behind it and the back wall.

Her body pitched forward, but she still maintained a firm grip on Carla, her wrist twisting her neck so it was exposed. Her arm circled to make the fatal cut. Will crawled quickly forward on the couch with his knees and headbutted her in the face.

Her body slammed against the back wall. Blood poured from her nose and over her lips, but she maintained her hold of the knife and jabbed the Taser at Will.

He twisted away from her as the edge of it glanced his shoulder. He anticipated the jolt, but only plastic connected with bone. The movement knocked it from her hand and he saw the Taser drop to the couch. He was teetering on the edge of the seat, his weight dragging him backwards.

He slammed hard against the floor, the impact to the back of his skull and the hands bound at his back winding him and inflaming the pain already there.

He sat up, agony blenching his vision, and found Carla had swivelled around on the couch and was now on her knees with her teeth in Poppy's wrist. Her mouth dragged the knife hand away so her other couldn't reach the Taser. Although Carla's hands were bound in front of her they were blocked by the back of the couch and pinioned there by her body.

Poppy screamed and Carla bucked herself against the couch, shunting it to keep her pressed against the wall. Poppy beat the side of Carla's face with her fist and then stretched away from her, trying to reach the Taser on the cushion. Will crawled forward.

Poppy screamed again as Carla bit deeper into her wrist. Will heard the knife drop from her hand to the wooden floor. His shoulders connected with the front of the couch. Poppy's fingertips could just touch the plastic casing of the Taser as she flexed further to grab it. He could use his face to swipe it out of the way.

With a yelp of exertion, Poppy snatched it up and jabbed it quickly into Carla's neck. Carla dropped sideways off the couch, her body curled up on itself.

Will heard the air leave her body and climbed to his feet. Poppy shoved the couch away from her and rounded it to attack him with the Taser. He put his head down and ran at her, connecting hard with her slight frame. Both of them smashed into the back wall.

Carla lay incapable, every sinew contracting and restraining her from extending her bloodless, bound hands towards the area of floor less than two feet in front of her. Beyond the scattered CD boxes lay the sushi knife, but her muscles wouldn't obey, couldn't unclamp so she could bend her elbows.

Will rammed his shoulder repeatedly against Poppy. With his hands restrained breaking her against the wall was all he could do to save them. He felt the spark in his side and his body seized again. But he was still on top of her, his weight restraining her there. She grunted under him, her fingers trying to find leverage.

He felt himself lift slightly and looked down to see her bloodied face, trembling with exertion. He met her eyes as she gritted her teeth and pushed against him. Her face contorted and, in that brief moment, he imagined it was how her entire life had been.

His body toppled and he fell hard onto his back in front of the doorway, his teeth locking over his tongue.

Carla could feel her limbs starting to respond again. The knife was in reach; she was able to tense her arms and pushed her fingers shakily towards the blade.

A hand reached down past her and snatched it up.

Moments later, she heard Will scream.

CHAPTER SIXTY

Will knew she'd cut the Achilles tendon at the back of his foot. She was making sure he wouldn't get up again. The pain of the incision burnt through him.

Carla remained on her side, feeling her body comply with her demands. She turned to where Will lay. Poppy was crawling up his body with the knife. Carla had no weapon.

Will stared up at the ceiling of the summer house. Multicoloured sunlight coruscated through Libby's mobiles. At least they knew she was safe.

Poppy's blood-smeared face filled his field of vision. She examined his eyes and then looked at his mouth. Her curdled breath filled his nostrils. His teeth were the only weapons he had left. Could he move his neck to meet her?

"Libby's going to live my life now, the life of your real daughter. She'll carry on the family alone," she said, as if it were a consolation.

He felt her lips lightly kiss his and tasted warm, salty blood and sickly sweet cherry.

Then he heard an almost indiscernible crack. A moment later, Poppy lifted her head slightly. He felt warmth inside his collar. She tensed and moved away from Will, standing and looking down at him.

He registered Carla was stood behind her, the intensity of her horror directed at Poppy's neck. Poppy had one broken half of a CD planted in the side of her throat. The shard glinted rainbows as she put her fingers delicately to it. Blood cascaded down the front of her violet dress.

Carla watched the torrent pump through the laceration in time with Poppy's heartbeat. The sharp plastic had cut into the fine spray of freckles there and the torn flap of skin billowed as her severed artery drained her blood onto the floor of the summer house.

She moved stiffly forward, crimson splashing about her bare feet as she walked through it and headed into the garden.

Carla followed and watched from the doorway as Poppy stumbled purposefully towards the pond.

Poppy felt her strength leave her with each step, but she wanted to reach the water. She didn't want to collapse here.

She looked down at the grass. It reminded her of the wedding of her childhood fantasy – red petals scattered at her feet.

She wanted to be face down in the dark pond and have it close over her.

The prongs of wire had engraved Tam's body to the top of his waist with deep scratches. He was halfway through, but his hips were stuck on their sharp edges. He howled as he pulled himself forward, thrashing his tied feet to absorb the pain. Skinny Man didn't hear.

He felt the coils slip from his ankles, but the agony at his sides overwhelmed the victory. Tam shifted himself back slightly and knew from the cold burn that he was bleeding badly. He rested for a few moments, listening to his own dry panting.

Above him he heard the metal shutter being raised and an engine's revs amplified by the enclosed loading bay. The other man had come back.

Tam wriggled desperately against the wire again, its points

sliding back into the wounds already there. He gritted his teeth as hard as he could against the pain as he dragged himself further on.

He heard the shutter slam again.

Tears poured down his face as he frantically crawled and inched while the metal raked through him. His body slid free of the cage. Tam kicked away his bonds and clambered shakily to his feet.

The room wavered as he held his bound hands in front of him. With his numb and prickling legs he pounded a trench through the chickens to the steps, zigzagging past Skinny Man. His face wasn't in shadows, but black with dried blood.

He paused at the bottom and listened, swallowing back his fear in one big mouthful. No more sounds of activity. He put his foot onto the bottom step, but heard the door above open. Tam scuttled back. It was pointless hiding behind the stack of cages. When they realised he'd escaped he'd be trapped inside the chicken house.

Tam knew he had to get up the steps as soon as the man descended. He took a few paces back, squeezing himself against the dank concrete wall and listening to the man trotting down. The light sneaking in from above illuminated his shaved head as he reached the bottom.

Tam thought the man's single eyebrow made it look as if he had two moustaches growing on his face. He watched him stride to the hanging light switch. As soon as he turned it on he would have to run. He edged to the bottom step again and turned just as the bulbs lit up the empty cage. Tam pelted upwards and heard the man's yell as he reached the top.

Once he was through the door, he considered running for the shutter that had just been secured. From where he stood on the gantry, he could see a white poultry van parked next to the lorry and couldn't tell if the exit had been padlocked at the bottom again.

Tam decided to hide instead. He raced for the cold room but, as he grasped the long screw handle and heaved it, he paused at the icy threshold of darkness then ran back to the security cabin. He climbed into one of the lower lockers and pulled the door shut behind him.

The sound of his breath filled the locker. He crushed his lips tightly together and breathed the smell of stale sweat through his nose. Tam held his breath as soon as he heard the door at the top of the stairs open and the man's deliberate footsteps move along the gantry. They stopped as he paused at the security cabin. Tam was prepared to suffocate in the locker rather than release the sob he'd lodged inside himself.

The man's footfalls eventually continued away. Tam silently exhaled then cautiously slipped back out of the locker and peered out. He was just in time to see the man open the cold room door he'd left ajar. He was brandishing a long black stick. As he stepped up and tentatively inside, Tam tore along the gantry and slammed it shut behind him.

Tam stood back and listened to the man's thumping fists and yells. He knew there was no way the man could escape and so Tam stayed there for several satisfying minutes, until he realised the ache about his face was a smile.

He left the gantry, jumping down into the loading bay and limping for the shutter. There was no padlock securing it. His hands were still tied. Exhausted, he leaned his shoulder against the metal and slid his fingertips underneath the gap. As he exerted himself, again every cut on his body felt as if they split wide. He jammed his hands further into the slit. It trembled as he tried to yank the edge up. The shutter remained stuck.

He didn't want to understand why these things had happened to him, he was just a child who wanted his mother and father. Tam felt so weak. He had to get home, but another heave felt like it would finish him.

Tam would know the truth when he was bigger and stronger,

not now. When he was a grown-up he would understand everything. He screamed as every cell of him screamed with the effort. The shutter lifted a foot and Tam rolled through the narrow gap before it could close again.

The nighttime version of his world was waiting on the other side.

Will looked up at the summer house ceiling. He could feel warmth around his ankle; still taste Poppy's blood inside his mouth and caking in the folds of his neck. After calling the police and ambulance Carla had told him she was getting the first aid kit. He'd listened to the slapping of her feet as she'd run back to the house.

By the time she returned, the sensations and raw pain were returning. She spoke to him and he could see the side of her face swelling up where Poppy had struck her. Her fingers gently dressed the burning at the end of his leg. Then she turned him carefully on his side and he felt the chain release and the circulation trickling back into his hands. He rolled onto his back again and she clasped his hands to his chest.

Nineteen years as man and wife,
And still so many years ahead,

He shifted his head back so he could see the pond. Poppy's dead body was huddled about four feet from the water's edge.

He thought about the last time he and Carla had sat in the spot and how he'd talked about Libby's pregnancy and consequences.

Carla's hand clasped his so tightly that it hurt.

CHAPTER SIXTY-ONE

As he made the two-hour trip to Pinellas County in silence, Pope considered avenues that were no longer open to him.

That morning another politician had been implicated in the ongoing revelations about the Lupus Rooms and the high-profile clientele it had serviced. After Wesley Strick and Jacob Franks's involvement had been corroborated using the hundreds of discs that had been found in Franks' apartment, the police had set about identifying the other luminaries that had been recorded in the act.

It was a slow media trickle of names and two months later it didn't show any sign of letting up. Minor Hollywood actors, musicians and politicians were falling over each other to voluntarily answer questions about their membership and the American public were waiting eagerly in front of the news for every new development.

Amberson, Monro, Dr Ren and Eva Lockwood were part of a story being rapidly overshadowed by a bigger exposé on sexual slavery. Poppy's abuse and revenge killings became the catalyst for yet another microscope to be positioned over the moral bankruptcy of the wealthy and famous.

The Frosts hadn't responded to any of the media that had camped out at the gates of their home and Pope certainly hadn't tried to speak to Mrs Frost since his last conversation with her in Chicago. He'd been anticipating contact from Ingram's lawyers and knew it still wasn't too late to get the call.

Pope had left Weaver in the UK, scurrying to get some interest in a kidnap that was the dead branch of a story that now had deeper roots in US soil.

Pope hadn't been back to Channel 55. The trip had reinforced his suspicion that he'd spent most of his life in the wrong place. Where to go from here? Certainly not back to the apartment with Lenora.

When they got to Calvary Catholic Cemetery, Pope got out and opened the door for Patrice. She'd said little, but at least she'd agreed to accompany him. Although Pope wanted to, he resisted offering her his arm. They strolled beside each other at a respectfully slow pace into the grounds.

Pope wished he shared his ex-wife's desire to acknowledge each of the significant dates their son wasn't present for, but he could never make his mind up whether it was apposite or plain morbid. It was a paradox he'd never come to terms with – feeling a duty to commemorate yet not wanting the pain of remembering.

Sean had gone under anaesthetic for some routine dental treatment when he was seven years old and hadn't woken up.

He often wondered about Sean's wishes, if he'd gained the age he was supposed to be now. Would he really want to see his parents punishing themselves at his graveside fourteen years later? He thought probably not, but Pope knew this was all about Patrice. When you lose your child there was no step-by-step program. It was something no parent should have to endure. It had given Pope an understanding of other people's losses all the years he'd been a crime reporter as he'd stood at the perimeter of their lives.

He watched Patrice lay the flowers and having a conversation with the gravestone she didn't want him to hear.

••••

Carla opened her eyes. As her mind clutched at the frayed ends of a dream, she was sure it hadn't been about Poppy. She was still stalking them at night, but the occasions when they awoke believing themselves to be back in the summer house were becoming less frequent now.

She turned to Will and found him sitting up reading his Kindle. She touched his arm and he looked down at her and smiled tightly. The black Taser burns were still visible on his bare chest.

She'd just begun to acknowledge that much of what they'd experienced was beyond her control. This meant she was at least trying to deal with its aftermath and not punishing herself for failing to insure against it. Randomness. Recognising it didn't make whatever the future held for them any easier to handle. But she knew she had to relinquish a grip she didn't have, to stop feeling she could regulate every event. This time Carla had saved the people she loved.

Her parents... Jessie – fate wasn't obligated to favour her. It was good to acknowledge the miracles of the present. The Frost family had survived.

She clenched her hand under the blanket and felt the long scar prickle in her right palm. The jagged plastic of her Walker Brothers CD had cut a permanent reminder of how she'd taken a life, a life that had never stood a chance. That was the one thing Jessie and Poppy had in common. It was difficult to accept that someone who'd been a part of Will had been brought into the world before Libby came into their lives, had been living and breathing while they'd still been anticipating parenthood.

But it had been Poppy or her family, and Carla had no compunction about what she'd done. One thought still gnawed at her, though, something she'd never utter to Will. No matter how irrational she knew it was, Carla couldn't shake the notion that it was his longing for their second daughter that had brought Poppy's destructiveness to their doorstep.

Will moved suddenly away from her, as if the thought's existence had repelled him. He got out of bed and tugged on his dressing gown. "Coffee?"

Carla nodded and extended her arm to him. He leaned in and kissed her. She closed her eyes again, knowing exactly where he was going.

Will limped along the landing. He still had at least another six months before he knew if his tendon graft would allow him to walk properly again. But if he hadn't had the emergency surgery for his ruptured appendix that afternoon, he wouldn't have got as far as the foot cast. A part of him he'd been unaware of had been waiting for its chance to poison him.

He still hadn't stopped relating his past to Poppy's, wondering what he'd been doing when she was suffering at the hands of the men she'd punished. But he recognised that speculating about how events could have played out only sabotaged the present. Eva had kept him oblivious to his daughter's existence her entire life. He couldn't have prevented what she became and what Poppy had done to redress the injustice made him feel utterly removed from her.

He opened the door to Libby's room. It still smelt slightly of paint from the redecoration. Libby was on her back; propped up by pillows, snoring gently. She was exhausted. The last three months had been ferocious on her. Her nightdress hung away from her shoulder and he could see the edge of the bite mark there.

Her belly was so distended, and the baby wasn't even due until early January. His child was going to be a mother. They knew it would be a girl. Whether he was ready for that or not it was time to put aside who she'd been and be happy for who she was about to become. He was just grateful her innocence hadn't been excised as quickly as Poppy's. He hobbled to the bed and put the back of his hand against her cheek. It felt cool and she whipped her face away from him and frowned in her sleep. This was his reality. There'd been enough ghosts, real and imagined.

Libby was going to need all the love and support he and Carla could give her. Their lives were about to change again and he wouldn't miss a moment of that.

A new year and a new life. They all knew how precious that was.

He remembered what Poppy had said about Libby having to carry on the family alone. Had she really been spared to endure the loss of the people she loved, to be robbed of what Poppy had never had?

The Thai authorities had located the place where Libby and Luke had been held after an anonymous tip-off. They'd received a call from a child a day after Libby had been released. Figuring it to be a hoax they hadn't followed up until some hours later.

When they'd entered the chicken factory they'd found a man dead. He was the caretaker of the premises and he'd had his skull fractured by a blunt weapon. They'd discovered the cage Libby had been held in and, as well as the caretaker's, they'd located hairs and traces of DNA belonging to Libby and Luke and another unidentified person who couldn't be eliminated via comparisons to the employees of the factory. They'd been laid off for a month pending hygiene checks that were due to commence a week later. Although the presence of livestock had made the process of analysing the area doubly difficult, the forensics team confirmed that the loading bay and lower quarters of the factory had been wiped clean of fingerprints.

Will's recent paranoia returned. He tried to visualise the last photograph of Luke. His body had never been found. The image had been removed from the website. Who had constructed it?

At Luke's memorial, Will had been reminded of something that, until then, had seemed irrelevant. Luke had been adopted as Libby had. It was probably why they'd connected. He was twenty-one. What had Poppy said about Eva having a fertile womb for a junkie?

It was ludicrous. He was still torturing himself with the guilt of who Poppy was and what she'd done.

Libby had been taken from her hotel room in Penang, remembered waking up with a swab over her face and nothing more. She hadn't seen Luke all the time she'd been imprisoned and had spent most of her time in the cage with a hood over her face.

The photos of Easton Grey, knowing exactly where the holiday destination was, how could the kidnappers have known? But then, everyone had been under observation.

What about the first image of Luke tied to Libby's back? Could it have been set up while she'd been drugged?

Will tried to reconstruct the image of Luke's death, the one that no longer existed. And who had removed the photo of Will at university with Eva Lockwood that had been framed and planted in her home?

Had the summer house been chosen because Libby's child had been conceived there? Poppy had assembled her family photographs on its wall. Luke was in the very first one with Libby.

He placed his hand gently on Luke's child. If he had been involved in the kidnap he'd have to have been insane to play with the life of his daughter. Or perhaps in the process of inveigling himself into Libby's world the baby had been as much an unwanted consequence as Poppy.

Less than an hour later the telephone rang in his office. Will was waiting for it. He quickly shut the door and picked up.

Even though he was waiting for a call, he anticipated the sound of poultry every time he answered.

"Hello?" His blood froze as the receiver settled against his ear. There were no screeching birds.

"Mr Frost?" It was Boland, the private investigator he'd hired.

"So?" Will didn't want any small talk.

Boland sensed this. "I have the information you wanted."

DAN O'SHEA

Introducing Detective John Lynch

PENANCE

One dark secret is
about to rip a
whole city apart...

"A non-stop adrenaline rush,
beginning, middle and end...
a bona fide blockbuster."

OWEN LAUKKANEN, author of

The Professionals

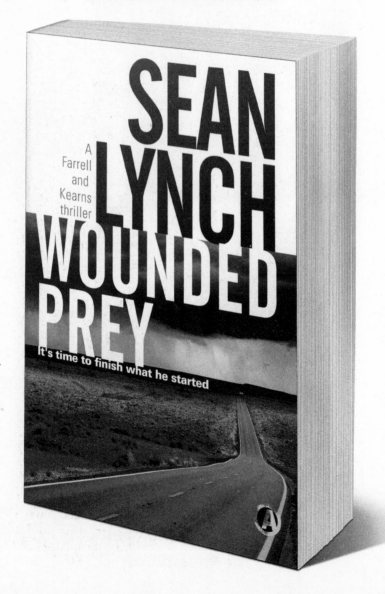

It's where *Apocalypse Now* meets *The Beach*

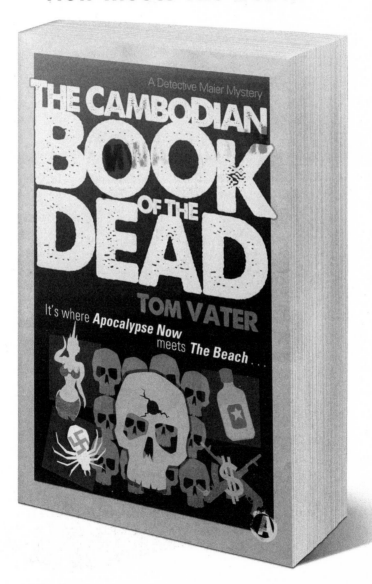

WITHDRAWN

exhibitabooks.com